The Bones of Plenty

The Bones of Plenty

Lois Phillips Hudson

MINNESOTA HISTORICAL SOCIETY PRESS

Borealis Books are high-quality paperback reprints of books chosen by the Minnesota Historical Society Press for their importance as enduring historical sources and their value as enjoyable accounts of life in the Upper Midwest.

∞ The paper used in this publication meets the minimum requirements of the American National Standard for Information Sciences—Permanence for Printed Library Materials, ANSI Z39.48-1984.

Minnesota Historical Society Press
345 Kellogg Boulevard W.
St. Paul
Minnesota 55102-1906

www.mnhs.org/mhspress

First published 1962 by Little, Brown and Company
Reprint edition 1984 by the Minnesota Historical Society Press
10 9 8 7 6 5

Manufactured in the United States of America
International Standard Book Number 0-87351-175-1

Library of Congress Cataloging-in-Publication Data

Hudson, Lois Phillips, 1927–
The bones of plenty.
Reprint. Originally published: Boston: Little, Brown, 1962.
I. Title
PS3558.U3B6 1984 813′.54 84-14701

FOR

MY GRANDFATHER

the last man of his line to live and die on his own land — a man without successors, of a generation without successors.

Preface

IN HIS INTRODUCTION to *Facing West: The Metaphysics of Indian-Hating and Empire-Building* (1980), Richard Drinnon remarks, "The record of history is nearly barren of authentically novel responses to novel circumstances." If I can be forgiven for beginning this preface to a new edition of *The Bones of Plenty* with a pun, I will say that the tragic fact he states so succinctly does, indeed, constitute a major impetus for the writing of many novels, including this one. No matter how many absurd repetitions of human folly and political cynicism I have been obliged to observe, I still cannot bring myself to shrug my shoulders and say, "The more things change, the more they are the same." George Steiner recently wrote, "It is one of the responsibilities of the novel to chronicle small desolations. These are sold short in that harsh artifice of selective recall we set down as history."

This novel tells a story that had to be told, and I was the only one who could tell it. (These, I believe, are the only two reasons a serious writer writes.) This book tells of the "small desolations" which the history of the Great Depression records only as statistics. President Roosevelt's New Deal was far from being an "authentically novel response" to the crisis in which millions of men, women, and children suffered desolations that profoundly scarred their lives, if, indeed those lives were not utterly ruined. Perhaps a truly novel response fifty years ago might have prevented the current repetition of so many of the events I describe in this book. Again we have desperate pleas for moratoriums on farm loans and mortgages, we have farmers organizing to stop sheriffs' auctions, and we have thousands of farmers going bankrupt, despite all the government subsidies which, in a very *un*-novel way, usually seem to help most the rich and powerful. As I write, an eighteen-year-old Minnesota farmer's son has just been convicted of shooting and killing two bank officials who were seeking to sell the family farm, which they had already repossessed. Bruce Rubenstein, writing about the case in the Twin Cities' *City Pages* (May 2, 1984), describes for us how things have not changed—except to get worse:

> If ever an isolated event [a small desolation] served to illuminate a much larger situation, then this was it. In 1977 suicides in rural Minnesota hit an all time high—227—and they've stayed high since. . . . In 1982 a record number of farms, over 5000, were put up for sale in Minnesota. . . . Twenty-five percent of U.S. farms market over 80 percent of all agricultural products sold. The last 65 years have seen the relentless replacement of the family farm by the huge, technologized farm. . . . In 1920 there were five million farms in the United States. Today, with roughly the same acreage under cultivation, there are less than two million farms. . . . The local lender, . . . the unwitting tool of Wall Street, . . . has always made a handy target for the farmers' frustrations. . . . The situation of the small dairy farmer like James Jenkins provides striking evidence that American agriculture is a rigged game.

A critic has said of Maupassant that he wrote out of anger at the difference between the way things are and the way they ought to be. I hope no reader will be able to read this book without feeling some of that anger, and without feeling led to ponder the tendency, apparently so deep in most of us, to try to fix a problem by doing more of what got us into the difficulty in the first place, as Drinnon painfully observes. The ultimate illustration of this tendency—our attempt to solve our nuclear weapons dilemma by building more and more nuclear weapons—must not blind us to the many other examples of that unimaginative conservatism to which the writers of novels so frequently try to draw our attention.

Today we see one frightening example in these very fields which, fifty years ago, seemed about to blow away in clouds falling into the Atlantic, clouds so heavy with precious topsoil that New York City needed street lights at noon. We are now caught in a vicious circle in the production of our daily bread (and all our other food) which begins in these fields and embraces not only their problems but many others as well, in such areas as transportation and marketing. The genesis of this circle is, in large part, an economic system that seems no closer to addressing the necessities of saving our planet and equitably distributing its fruits than that system was fifty years ago. As the economic system dictates that farms must become larger and larger, worked by larger and more costly machinery, we begin to see the breakdown of the soil itself. In many of our richest areas, the soil has become ever more compacted under so much weight, so that the machines we used to work the land fifteen or twenty years ago can no longer plow deeply enough. A novel response is surely needed at this juncture, but so far ours seems to consist of making even huger models of the same machines.

Then we compound the problem by allowing much of our most fertile land to be covered by the endless junk of a consumption-mad society. Shopping malls, warehouses, parking lots, and physical fitness centers cover the wonderfully productive bottom lands of the valley near Seattle to which my family moved when I was ten. I grew up there, staying quite physically fit, along with a goodly number of other farming folks, weeding and thinning carrots, cabbage, lettuce, and radishes, and picking raspberries, strawberries, blackberries, cherries, beans, and peas. Our valley, and the other valleys around us, which now are nearly all filled with the same concrete redundancies, once supplied Seattle with luscious, nutritious, *fresh* produce which now comes from California in ever heavier, more numerous, more dangerous trucks polluting the air with the smog from wastefully burned non-renewable fossil fuels. Unless we depart drastically from our present trends, most experts warn us, more than half the cost of the food the average city consumer buys will soon go for transportation alone. The smaller farmer who cannot afford, as the vast farming corporations can, to engage in the transportation business as well as the food-growing business, finds herself/himself in an increasingly hopeless competitive position. Meanwhile, the multifaceted "vertical" corporation cares little whether its major profits come from producing food or simply carting it over highways obligingly subsidized by all of us captives of the supermarket, who can either buy the plastic tomatoes bred to withstand these long hauls or go without. I submit that the time is ripe for a novel examining all the *human* problems involved in getting an edible tomato from the field to the table of an urban apartment dweller. And I cannot believe that such a subject is not "large" enough for a "major" book. All that is necessary is the imagination of the right author and an intelligent reception by what the late Vardis Fisher called "the Eastern literary establishment."

Twenty-two years ago this book was launched into a social and literary climate of apathy and nihilism. In 1960 Mary McCarthy delivered a lecture in a number of European cities asking, "Is it still possible to write novels?" She replied to herself, "The answer, it seems to me, is certainly not yes and perhaps, tentatively, no." Two years later, with this novel scarcely off the press, I was being asked to participate in panel after panel which discussed the dismal question "*Is* the novel dead?" Part of the problem was that for three decades the critics had been praising—and sometimes writing—the books that seemed increasingly irrelevant to many readers of novels. Harvard professor Warner Berthoff summed up the situation in a *Yale Review* essay (Winter, 1979) entitled "A Literature without Qualities: American Writing Since 1945." He wondered who could find that literature significant, "apart from a bureaucratized elite holding on for dear life to illusions of cultural primacy and the prerogatives and satisfactions of commodity-market 'excellence'." In his 1950 Nobel Prize acceptance speech William Faulkner had described the problem somewhat more poetically: "The young man or woman writing today. . . .writes not of love but of lust, of defeats in which nobody loses anything of value, of victories without hope and, worst of all, without pity or compassion. His griefs grieve on no universal bones, leaving no scars. He writes not of the heart but of the glands."

We had departed drastically from the views generally held by western culture since Aristotle first enunciated them—namely, that writers have an obligation to examine genuinely significant aspects of the human condition, and society has an obligation to listen to those writers for the sake of its own health. But in the last few years such questioning as Berthoff's has signalled a greening of the literary world. In 1977 came John Gardner's *On Moral Fiction*. In July 1983 Winona State University in Minnesota sponsored a writer's conference which set itself to study, for two weeks, "The Writer's Moral Responsibility." Today we don't seem nearly so far away as we were twenty years ago from that day in 1863 when President Lincoln looked down at the tiny woman standing before him and said to Harriet Beecher Stowe, "So you're the little lady who made this big war!"

I am not alone in feeling that stories about such fundamentals as the food we eat and the way it is produced may once again command serious attention. William Kittredge and Steven M. Krauzer, introducing a special issue of *TriQuarterly* dedicated to "Writers of the New West" (Spring, 1980), conclude their essay:

> Well, the other day some wiseass asked us to name a great writer who dealt with agriculture. How about Tolstoy? Sure, this fellow said, but that was a long time ago and in another country. This made us so impatient we had to shoot him down.

Perhaps we have good reasons to hope that many readers are waiting for books that explore the way we *feel* about the earth. Today, many of the people who cultivate and harvest our wheat never even look at the fields they work. Instead, they steer their gigantic tractors and combines by viewing those fields on closed-circuit television screens mounted in their cabs. Do they, *can* they feel the same way Rose and Will and Rachel and George and Lucy felt? *Can* we, with impunity, turn our eyes away from the earth and stare instead day after day into a cathode ray tube?

This seems a good time for *The Bones of Plenty* to come forth in a new edition, and I am grateful to Jean A. Brookins, head of the Minnesota Historical Society Press, and to Ann Regan, editor of the Borealis series, for this second launching. Faulkner ended his Nobel speech with these words: "The poet's voice need not merely be the record of man, it can be one of the props, the pillars to help him endure and prevail." I am glad this book once more has a chance to contribute its record, its props and pillars to our current struggle to endure.

Lois Phillips Hudson

I

Unemployed purchasing power means unemployed labor and unemployed labor means human want in the midst of plenty. This is the most challenging paradox of modern times.

HENRY A. WALLACE
Secretary of Agriculture
1934

Friday, February 17, 1933

For nine years George Custer had picked rocks out of the three hundred and twenty acres he rented from James T. Vick, but still the wheat fields were not clear enough to suit him. Nothing made him madder than to hook into a big rock with a freshly sharpened plowshare or mower sickle. This late in the winter he had finished all the odd jobs that he saved for cold weather, and on a morning like this, with no special chores at hand, he hitched the team to the stoneboat and hauled rocks down the hill to the pile he was accumulating at the edge of the south grove. Every rock he took out of the best soil in the world made that soil even better. If it weren't for drought and rust, this half section would be producing sixteen bushels to the acre. He was only a year older than the century, but he could remember when North Dakota soil yielded twenty or more.

An early thaw the first of the week had finished most of the snow, but a hard freeze last night had turned the earth back into iron. He had to use a crowbar to get the big ones loose. With rocks, a man couldn't win for losing. During the times of the year when the ground wasn't frozen, he was too busy doing other things with it to be taking rocks out of it.

He intended to make something with the rocks — a cool little well house, maybe, or a creamery. A man could build almost anything with rocks if he had the time. George had always wanted a house of stone. He wouldn't build it, though, till he could buy the farm from Vick. He had already sunk so much cash and labor in this place that if Vick ever tried to push him off without making a decent settlement with him, he would be obliged to take a few thousand dollars out of the old man's hide.

Crossing the field toward the small gray building that Vick called a house, he could see how it would look if it was his own house of stone, with the smoke from the two stoves drifting up from the broad stone chimney, and the white of fresh paint gleaming from the deep-set window casings.

He halted the team in front of the house and went in. "Man! It's colder than a banker's eye out there," he told his wife. He scooped half a dipperful from the pail of drinking water and poured it into a cup. "That ground is so hard you couldn't drive a spike into it with a sledge hammer. One of these days we're gonna have enough rocks to build a house with, though. Warm in winter, cool in summer. How'd you like that?"

"I'd like it if we could just get the money to make a down payment on this place," said Rachel.

"Well so would I! But just because we haven't is no reason why we shouldn't think ahead a little, is it?"

He shut the door harder than he really meant to and stomped back to the team. They were matched sorrels, a gelding and a mare, both young horses. The mare would drop her first foal in another three months, and he was working her this morning instead of one of his other two geldings because the weather had kept her from getting sufficient exercise lately. In spite of the outrageous fee, George had bred her to Otto Wilkes's champion Percheron stallion, because with a dam like Kate it was silly not to use the best sire around. Besides, he wanted a colt that would grow to be considerably bigger than Kate, but still be possesed of her intelligence and fine disposition.

Between the horses he could glimpse the distant rock pile, and his eyes focused themselves on the spot, seeing how solid and eternal a stone house would look there, set beneath the thin black crisscrossing limbs of the grove. He was barely conscious of the four peaked ears dutifully bobbing up and down in the vague foreground of his sight, and at first it seemed, when two of the ears precipitately disappeared, that he had only got a flutter in his left eye.

Then he was running, yelling.

"*King!* Kate! Whoa! *Whoa!* King you bastard, *King!*"

A shrieking mindless thousand pounds of horseflesh, his calm and sensible mare, wallowed in its harness, half buried in the earth.

Dragged down by the strap hooking them together, King pulled back into his collar and reared his front legs as high as he could lift them. Every time his great shoes came down, they struck away clods of frozen earth and the hole widened.

George unsnapped two hooks and the freed horse leapt away before there was time to turn loose the reins.

And here was the mare at his feet, rolling white-ringed eyes, bubbling foam through her gaping pink lips. If she didn't already have a broken leg, she would in the next few minutes — if she didn't die of fright first.

He squatted at the edge of the hole. The thawing and freezing of the last few days had buckled the top crust of earth covering an old, poorly filled well. His trips with the stoneboat over that spot had further weakened the ground. He could not even guess how deep the well was, but he knew there could be other gaps in the shaft. Another six-foot drop of the ground beneath her and Kate would be beyond all help.

She was head down, lying on her side, craning her neck up against the wall of the shaft, with her hindquarters twisted and jammed up above the rest of her body in such a way that none of her terrible struggles could possibly bring her to her feet.

"What on *earth!* What on *earth* happened?"

Rachel was running to him, with the fool dog bouncing and barking beside her.

"Why it's an old well, of course!" he shouted. "Now go fetch King while I get some planks."

George dragged some timbers up from the granary and slid them into the hole behind the mare. He hooked her traces and King's into a heavy ring.

"Now lead him straight back," he told Rachel, "and when I tell you, hit him a good one on the rump so's he'll start out fast."

"How can I hit him on the rump if I'm up in front leading him?" Rachel said.

"Oh, Rachel! For God's sake, haven't you got any imagination at all?"

Rachel hauled on King's bridle. The horse made her pull his head and stretch out his neck as far as it would go before he moved his feet. He laid his ears back and bugged out his eyes, trying to look around his blinders and see what George had hitched him up to.

When the slack was out of the traces, George yelled, "Get up, King! Back, Kate, back!"

The mare wrenched and hurled herself dangerously and uselessly. The traces pulled from the wrong angle. Then the ring broke and leather snakes whipped back around King's legs.

"*Hold* him!" George cried. "For the love of Mike, what did you let him go for? My God!"

He sprinted after the horse. King did not stop till he reached the barnyard fence. George grabbed his bridle and ran up the hill with the gelding snorting and side-stepping behind him.

"Now *hold* him here!" He thrust the bit into Rachel's hands. She bent a cold fist around the cold steel at the horse's jaw. The gelding tossed his head roughly, yanking her arm up as far as she could reach. She had always been afraid of him.

"Oh, he's just *bluffing* you!" George said. "He knows he can get away with it, and he'll try it again. Now hang on to him!"

George ran to the porch and returned with a clanking pile of chain. He reached down into the hole and raised up Kate's thick black tail. He tied the tail to the chain with a knot that took the whole length of the tail.

"Oh, George!" Rachel was appalled. "That will *kill* her!"

"Oh pshaw!" he yelled. "Women!"

George snapped the gelding's traces into the chain. "Now make him *pull!*" he ordered. "*Wallop* him one!"

"Get up!" Rachel cried.

George let himself down into the hole, squatted with his legs braced wide apart, cupped his hand around the curve of the mare's thigh, and shoved from his shoulder. Coupled with King's pulling, the shove steered her leg on to the planks.

"Dammit!" he shouted. "*Smack* him one! Keep him going!"

Kate was lifted and righted enough to get her front legs under her. Then her hind feet were digging and sliding on the boards.

King leaned into his collar. George vaulted out of the well, grabbed the chain, and set himself as anchor man at the edge of the hole.

Between heaves he shouted, "Back up, Kate! Whoa back! *That's* a girl!"

In a monstrous, sickening, leg-breaking scramble, the mare wrestled herself up out of the hole, nearly trampling George and causing King to plunge ahead in an access of released power. Rachel lost her hold on him again and stood, numb and shaking, waiting for George to tell her what to do.

But his concern now was for the mare. "Whoa back, Kate," he said. "Back. *That's* a girl. *Back* now, Kate." His voice was low and gentle, and his hands held her bridle lightly and stroked her wet neck with compassion.

The horse trembled but she stood still, with her weight squarely on all four legs. It was hard to believe he had been so lucky. She might go lame, but no bones were fractured. Now if she just wouldn't cast the foal.

"There, now, Kate," he said. "There, now, old girl. That wasn't so bad after all, was it? Not so bad as you and a lot of other people *thought* it was going to be, was it? You never even felt it, did you? You're just lucky it was me that was around, you know that? Yes, sir, Kate. You're just a lucky old nag, here. You're going to be just as good as new once I turn loose your tail."

He went back and disentangled the chain. Swatches of long black hairs were strung through the links. He pulled out a handful of hairs and held them up to Kate's nose.

"See that?" he said to the horse, but loud enough for Rachel to hear. "Now, then, that wasn't much of your tail to lose, was it? Some people around here thought I was going to pull the whole thing right off." He rubbed her ears and ran his hands over her legs. "You're not going to go and get a gimpy leg on me now, are you, Kate?"

Rachel said, "Do you need me for anything else?"

"No, you might as well go on back in. I guess I'll throw this load of rocks into this damned hole here, after I unhitch." He led the horses down to the barn.

She walked back to the house. The baby was fussing in the other room, but Rachel did not go in to her. She sat down on the kitchen stool and leaned her elbows on her thighs so she could hold up her head with her hands. She closed her eyes, and when she opened them again the odd dots kept on falling through the blankness for a moment and then her vision returned. She got up and washed her hands in water she dipped from the bucket on the washstand into the mottled blue graniteware basin. She dried them on a terrycloth towel as thin and bare and flat as flour sacking.

What if they had lost Kate? She didn't see how they could ever have bought another. Without a four-horse team George would never get the wheat in. She couldn't stop thinking about how bad it could have been.

George had apparently recovered by the time he came in for another drink of water. "You know," he said, "a lot of men that don't treat their horses right never could have done that. Their horses wouldn't have trusted them enough. I know some men that would have lost that horse. They would've just had to shoot her, probably, if they couldn't get her out before she broke a leg. You've got to know how to handle a horse, and you've got to really like them."

He rested his hands on his hips, straightened his shoulders back, and took a great breath that swelled out his chest. "Well," he said, "I reckon I better get out there and fix up that hole some son-of-a-gun left for me." He gave her another moment to tell him what an astounding rescue he had made and to admit that hooking on to Kate's tail was the only scheme that would have worked in time.

"Thank God you got her out," Rachel said.

He dumped the last of his water into the wash basin and walked out. He began rolling the rocks into the well. He figured Kate had probably tromped it down pretty well, but a load of rocks was a good bet to cause it to collapse as much more as it was going to. He'd just have to leave it that way till the ground thawed out. Then he'd be able to tamp it down some more and fill it in properly. When he'd emptied the stoneboat he went down to check on Kate.

He was prepared to find that she was going to cast the foal, but even though he was prepared, it made him sick. After the first eight months had gone so well — to have her lose it with only three more months to go. It was queer how an animal as big and powerful as a horse was so hard to breed and so liable to abort at almost any time.

"Oh, Kate," he said softly. "Now what do you want to go and do *this* for?"

Any mare he'd ever known wanted privacy at a time like this, so he went back to the cows' end of the barn and sat on a milkstool. He thought of the stud fee he'd paid that deadbeat Otto, and felt sicker.

He sat down on a milk stool and rolled a cigarette. The match glimmered brightly in the gloom of the barn, and he watched it till the flame reached his fingers. Damn the son-of-a-bitch that would leave a hole like that. Didn't a man have enough trouble from enemies he already knew about without being dealt a blow like this from some idiot whose name he would never even know?

He remembered how a schoolmate of his had fallen down an old well like this one. It was spring and the ground was wet. The well was so old that all the curbing had rotted away and the sides kept collapsing on the boy. They had got him out alive, but he grew up peculiar.

He could tell from the way Kate was stamping around that the foal wasn't born yet. He wished she'd hurry up about it if she was going to do it. He wanted to get back to work. After this morning's catastrophes, he felt more desperately far behind than ever. This last year he had got so far behind that he sometimes caught himself saying, "What's the use?"

George Armstrong Custer saying, "What's the use?"

He thought, as he so often did, of how things had changed so much faster than anybody had ever supposed they would. George had been born a mere twenty-three years after his namesake rode a high-stepping sorrel horse into ambush at the Little Big Horn. His grandfather had come from Illinois to homestead in the Dakota Territory just two years after General Custer was killed. The old man loved to tell about how he had been to Bismarck when it was nothing but a ferry landing on the Missouri River and a place for the soldiers from Fort Abraham Lincoln to get booze and women. And two years after the Boy General was dead, he was still, after booze and women, the main topic of conversation. Fort Abraham Lincoln — four miles from Bismarck — the westernmost fort in the north of the continent. And out of it had ridden the troops behind the fearless redheaded cavalryman — so nearly immortal while he was alive, so obviously mortal when they found his white, naked body lying along with all the others on the hillside.

George's old granddaddy would not believe his eyes if he could see Bismarck now. Here the twenty-story white tower of the capitol rose up from the prairie — there a silver bridge spanned the Missouri, and beyond, Highway 10, the Red Trail, proceeded in a humdrum concrete strip through the country of Sitting Bull and on to the Pacific Ocean. Yet George himself had been born on the western frontier, and his grandfather had seen fit to bestow on him the name of a frontier hero. When he was a lad of six or seven, herding cows in the unfenced pastures, he would kick over a buffalo skull every time he went after a stray calf or ran a badger down a hill-side. Some of the skulls even had patches of hide on them.

It was all over in Kate's stall. He stood up and buttoned his sheep-skin coat. He drew on his heavy leather gloves and pulled the flaps of his hunting cap down over his ears. He was a big man, nearly six feet three, and almost two hundred pounds. He could still spring up from a milk stool as light as a cat on his feet, but the job ahead of him at the moment did not cause him to move in such a manner.

He pushed the wheelbarrow down the aisle, hoping the fetus wouldn't be too hard to look at. It was a light little thing, seemingly perfect. The afterbirth was normal. Kate was feverish, but that was to be expected. He made sure the blanket he'd put on her was se-curely fastened. After he got the foal out of her stall, he'd bring her some water.

He loaded it in the wheelbarrow and pushed it out of the barn. He'd wait till it dried off and then drag it out where the coyotes would take care of it. He might be able to shoot a couple when they came to the carcass and earn himself some bounty money.

He felt like going after bigger game than coyotes. He felt like shooting the bastard who'd left that hole. He felt like shooting the storekeeper whose lousy cash gobbled up land that other people had tamed for him. A man born on the frontier, dammit, had a right to own enough land to build himself a house on.

He looked across the pasture hills to the heavy noon sky. He wondered if it would be snowing by the time he would have to drive into town to get Lucy from school. When *he* was seven years old, nobody had toted *him* back and forth from school, but things were different nowadays. He couldn't think when it was that he had last come across a buffalo skull.

❦ ❦ ❦

Will Shepard braced himself against the eccentricities of the springs under the truck seat while he coasted over the thumping timbers that were laid between the railroad tracks as a concession to whatever traffic found itself at cross purposes with the Northern Pacific's main line.

He glanced out to his right to see if old Millard Adams was watching for a wave from him, but he saw no one at all in the depot—just the boards of the building and the platform. Those of the building had once been painted and those of the platform had not, but for a long time they had all been the same color. Only the letters at either end of the building had been retouched. They said EUREKA.

Most of the town was either to Will's right or straight ahead of him to the north. The tracks to his left stretched west, accompanied only by telegraph wires except for the faraway shapes of Clarence Egger's farmyard.

In front of Will, at the corner across the street from the depot, was Herman Schlaht's store, and on up the street were Gebhardt's pool hall, the bank, and the café. It was the bank that Will was heading for first. He let the truck roll along past it, applying a minimum of pressure on the brake pedal so as to spare himself the awful squalling of the worn steel shoes slipping against the drums. He must get the truck down to Ray Vance for a new set of brakes before the busy season started. He turned the wheel so the tires rubbed into the low bank of snow piled along the wooden sidewalk, and the truck stopped. He opened the door and jumped out; he was in a hurry to get rid of the tobacco plug in his mouth because he hadn't been able to spit since he crossed the tracks.

He sent it plopping into the snowbank, where it added its sprawling brown stain to the other offenses committed against that mound since the last snow. It was forty years since he had begun to chew to prove, when he was sixteen years old, that he was as tough as any other man in any threshing crew in the world. By the time he didn't need the proof any more, he was stuck with the habit.

Except for that pile accumulated from the clearings of the road and the sidewalk, most of the snow had been taken away by the wind. The wind robbed them of the water in the snow. After fighting through ten-foot drifts for six months, they were likely to be told by the official measurers that a hard winter had left them perhaps three inches of water in the ground. So far this winter there had been half of three inches, but the heaviest snows of the season might still be on the way. He looked up at the early afternoon sky, thick and gray with the moisture that didn't come down. It just stayed there, apparently frozen solid for the whole ninety-three million miles between him and the sun.

He stamped down the sidewalk, trying to pound some blood back into his feet. He had got chilled in the three-mile drive to town, for the holes around the pedals in the floor of the truck aimed a frigid wind at his feet and legs.

He was not a tall man, but neither was he quite so short as his stocky body or the comparison of it with the generally taller bodies of his neighbors made him appear. His face was milder than it used to be, his middle was rounder, and his head was nearly bald. The years of his astonishing strength were gone. Nevertheless, there was no one in town who did not know that once when Will Shepard had wanted to get a Ford engine block from Leroy Kellogg's to Ray Vance's garage across the street, he had simply lifted the engine on his back and carried it over and set it down in a spot that was convenient for Ray.

Now, at fifty-six, he still worked right along with the young men he hired on his farm, but without competing — only with gratitude that he was given the strength to continue bearing the great burdens he allotted to himself. Work had rewarded him. In this desperate time he owned free and clear a full section of land as rich as any that existed anywhere on earth, plus buildings, machinery, and stock. He had, in addition, a sizable savings account and a few collapsed securities which had a fair chance to recover, providing, of course, that the nation itself survived. He had been just the right age to ride the country's good years and the best twenty years of all time for wheat — the first two decades of the century. He had been too old to go to war sixteen years ago, but young enough to manage five hundred acres of wheat land yielding thirteen bushels or more to the acre, at prices up to two dollars and seventy cents a bushel. His wheat checks had mounted well into five figures for several years, and the net returns had made the farm his. He himself had made no war sacrifices, and he felt indebted to those who had. His business now was with a man who had gone to war.

Harry Goodman was the man. He had started up the bank in Eureka soon after the war and he was nearly forty now. The twenty flabby pounds Harry had put on since he came to Eureka had transformed him from a thin young man to a fat older man, for his frame was much too short and slight to make any sort of graceful adjustment to so much added weight. For a while Harry had displayed an enlarged, cloudy, full-length photograph of himself in his overseas uniform. "Here I am," the picture seemed to say, "a doughboy just like the boys who boarded the train right here in Eureka. Here are my lumpy puttees over my polished boots, my creaseless pants, and my soup-dish helmet. And here, hanging from my arm, my goggle-eyed mask, to preserve me from the Kaiser's mustard gas."

But after a few years Harry had taken down the picture, perhaps because of the increasing discrepancy between the length of the webbed belt in the picture and the length of the belt he now required, perhaps because no one in Eureka had appeared to see the connection between him and the hometown doughboys, perhaps because he had wished to hang his Notary Public sign over that spot on the wall.

Will had been glad to have a banker come and open up shop in Eureka, even if the fellow was a Jew, even if a few country banks had already failed. Jamestown was nearly thirty miles away, and it was inconvenient to go there every time he needed the services of a bank. He had immediately transferred a small part of his Jamestown savings to Harry's bank and opened a checking account. Over the years his confidence in Harry had grown; and gradually he had increased the amount he kept in Harry's bank until, for the last several years, Harry had had almost all of it.

To some of the tall, belligerent Gentiles who came to his window, or inside to his office, Harry was belligerent in return. To a few he was ingratiating. To all he was adamant. Thus he had hung on, year after year through the twenties, while seven thousand other banks failed, and through the last three years after the crash when another seven thousand closed their doors.

Will did not doubt that Harry was in good shape, but he did like to drop in to the bank fairly often. He had a feeling that he would know if the moment came when he ought to make a withdrawal. He had seen no reason to join those depositors who had withdrawn everything and presumably buried it. Credit was already hard enough to get — mortgages hard enough to extend. Quite obviously the whole country would cease to function if people withdrew their support from all the institutions that kept it going. That truth seemed so obvious, in fact, and Harry's service to the community seemed so necessary, that Will felt impatient with those who had been so quick to panic.

On Tuesday, though, the state of Michigan had been treated to Governor Comstock's Valentine, and that had made Will a tiny bit nervous. Michigan's governor was not the first governor to close all the banks in his state, but Michigan seemed closer to North Dakota than any of the other states.

Will walked up the three wooden steps and opened the door of Harry's bank. Harry came to the window.

"Hello . . . *hello,* Mr. Shepard! I'm . . . so glad you came by today."

"Hello, Harry." Will was embarrassed. He was afraid Harry knew why he came so often for such petty business. "I'm just going to get a little cash. Ten dollars will do it." He began to write out the check.

"Mr. Shepard — wait a minute. Just let me check your balance here. Just a minute."

"My balance?"

"Mr. Shepard, you and I have been friends a long time, right? Ten years, right? You've been a good friend of mine . . . here. Here it is. It's all up to date. Two thousand, eight hundred and sixty-seven. That's your balance — checking and savings. Make it out for that!"

Will couldn't understand it. He'd been Harry's friend; now Harry wanted him to withdraw his entire account. Was Harry so deeply offended just because of these frequent small checks? Will was horrified to think that his petty fears had so injured a man for whom he felt nothing but respect and sympathy.

Harry began counting out bills from his drawer and Will opened his mouth to beg Harry's pardon. But he closed it, in shock, as he would recoil from the lung-searing breath of a blizzard wind. The window with the terrible face in it was the window that had opened at last between him and the storm burying the world. There was nothing at all to say.

Harry scuttled to the vault and came back with more bills. "I'll make it all twenties and fifties," he said. He jammed his finger into a rubber tip and began sliding off the fifties into a pile on Will's side of the window.

The bills slapped down so fast that Will could not begin to say "a half of a hundred dollars" to himself as each one dropped. He lost count after the first three or four and just watched.

"Hurry up!" Harry said, and Will finally understood what he ought to be doing. It wasn't counting. He peered back over his shoulder into the empty street and began rolling up the bills and tucking them into his inside pockets. He finished writing the check for whatever records Harry meant to leave just as Harry finished counting out the last full hundred. Then Harry threw out three twenties, paused an instant, and tossed out another twenty instead of hunting up the seven.

"It doesn't make any difference!" he cried, waving his hands in the air. "What is it all now? Paper! Just paper!" Shocked as he was, Will was shocked anew at hearing a banker say what he himself had always thought about money.

He stowed away the last of the bills and pushed the check across to Harry. He laid down the bank's pen and awkwardly took the short white hand trembling and reaching for his beneath the barred window. Already the guilt of his special treatment was between him and the little man.

"You're a good friend," Harry insisted again.

Will had to get out before he was seen. "So long," he said. He knew he ought to say something else, and before he could stop it, a bit of parting advice he frequently gave to Harry slipped out. It was like a nightmare in which he heard himself speaking obscenities and then more obscenities every time he tried to apologize for himself—all the while comprehending what he was doing, but never able to react in time.

"Don't take any wooden nickels," were the words that leapt out of his mouth.

He touched the bill of his cap in a last helpless salute and furtively closed the door of Harry's bank. The frozen boards of the sidewalk creaked and snapped; they rumbled beneath him, sent alarms ahead of him, and echoed behind him. It was all he could do to keep from looking back or at least stopping suddenly to trick the man following him into taking two more thundering steps than he took himself. And all the while he knew the street was as empty as it was when he walked out of the bank. It seemed impossible that the rolls of stiff new bills did not show right through his sheepskin coat or that it was not written on his face that Harry was going to close the Eureka Bank that Friday afternoon. It had been about fifty years since Will had been a party to any sort of conspiracy. Harry was closing the bank, but Harry was going to keep a few "friends" from suffering. It was no more real than a boyhood game.

After all, Harry had hung on for so long. It was true that the real crisis had finally come. Hoover was waiting out the last weeks of his term like a man tied across the railroad tracks in front of an express train.

Still, he couldn't understand why Harry Goodman had managed all this time and then failed. If he had been speculating with the deposits, he ought to have gone down long before this. His extreme conservatism had made the farmers who needed loans hate him bitterly, but it should have brought him through, too. Will remembered the last statement of assets he had read, and if it was correct, Harry was stable enough. Harry had a total of seventy-five thousand dollars or so in cash deposits, and his loans seemed to be in about the right percentage. But perhaps even Harry had not been conservative enough to protect himself against the terrible deflation of property values. Men had mortgaged their farms in order to speculate in meaningless paper stocks, and when their property declined by more than half, many of the mortgages were only meaningless paper, with figures written on them that represented more than the farms could be sold for. It was all paper — just paper.

Will became aware that he was shaking his head — he felt his day-old beard scratching against his high coat collar. People he would pass in the street would wonder if he had gotten his, and he would wonder if they had gotten theirs, and he would never again be free of the knowledge that he possessed, mostly by sheer chance, a little bit of the money that belonged to at least half of his friends and neighbors. Will wondered how bad the failure was — would the depositors get back fifty cents on a dollar? Forty? Two bits? A dime?

What ought he to do with the money? The only thing he could think of was to bury it. Why put it in another bank? He'd already used up more luck than he could expect to see in the rest of his life. He decided to buy a metal box to bury it in. When he came to a notch knocked through the bank of frozen snow, he stepped down off the sidewalk and crossed the street to Zack Hoefener's hardware store.

He thought, as he opened the door, that Zack would be sure to ask him what the box was for, but the thought came too late. He entered just as Zack came in through the rear door. Zack had been burning packing paper in the dented oil drum he used for an incinerator. His face, a complex map of abused capillaries, was purple with cold, and he smelled of smoke and whiskey. Where did he get it all the time, Will wondered. Drunk or sober he was ornery, but he owned the only hardware store within twenty miles.

Will said, "Hello, Zack," and Zack replied with a bob of his head that sent a quiver through the massive goiter hanging from his neck.

Zack made fists of his smudged hands and leaned on his knuckles on the counter. He always made his customers ask for what they wanted; *he* never asked *them*. He wasn't any god-damn waiter, he often said to himself.

"Have you got some kind of a good strong metal securities box — about like so?" Will measured with his hands.

"Need it to keep all those gold-mine stocks in? Save 'em for your grandchildren?" Zack demanded.

"Well," Will said, "I'll grant you I haven't clipped any coupons for a while. But there's no use starting any fires with them yet. Never can tell. Roosevelt just might get some things to moving again."

Zack hunched his shoulders, sending another spasm through his goiter.

"Roosevelt won't be alive ten days after he's in office," he said, "even if he lives long enough to be sworn in at all. Somebody else with better aim will get him."

"Oh, you know that fellow that tried to shoot him was as crazy as a June bug."

"Who cares how crazy he was! A bullet is a bullet, no matter who shoots it. You wait and see. He'll never make it." Zack bulged his eyes at Will. Then he turned and stalked to the back of the store.

He plucked a small black box from a shelf, hooked two broad fingers under its dusty nickel handle, and dangled it toward Will. "Big enough?" he asked.

"It's fine," Will said. He reached cautiously into a pocket, trying to remember where he had put the twenties. He didn't want to give Zack a fifty. It was quick thinking for Harry not to have given him anything bigger than fifties, but even fifties were mighty rare birds. He fell behind Zack while they walked to the front of the store and managed to get a look at the bill he had pulled out. It was a twenty.

"By God, you could buy me *out* with that!" Zack expostulated when he saw the money.

"Well, I've finally got to break it," Will said.

"I won't hardly have no change left," Zack complained. "This here is the third big bill I've broke today. If I can't get to the bank I won't have no change for tomorrow. . . . That's one-eighty-five out of twenty — for God's sake." He scraped the coins out of the little metal compartments and slid bills out from under their wire holders.

Will wondered if any of the other big bills had appeared for the same reason his had, and if so, who Harry's other lucky friends were.

"See you later, Zack," Will said. He drew on his gloves and tucked the box under his arm. Zack nodded his head once and then fell to stroking his goiter, thoughtfully, as though he could not quite believe that it was there.

Will bought the groceries on the list Rose had given him. They came to $5.87. That plus the cashbox came to $7.72. Subtract that from $2880 and it left $2872.28 — more money than he had had in the bank in the first place, thanks to Harry's haste and ruin. He said goodby to Herman and hurried around the corner and back up the street toward his truck. He passed Gebhardt's Pool Hall with the hotel rooms up above, where the Gebhardts lived. It was the only two-story building on the block, and it made the bank look very small and fragile down below it. The whole bank probably had no more floor space than Will's parlor, though it had never occurred to him before to think of it that way.

He slid his hand under his coat to pat the springy round rolls in the pockets of his shirts and overalls. When the money had been in that little building it had seemed like so much more. Before it became paper in his pockets it had been a varying number on the statements sent out from that building; then it had seemed like an entity that could be expected to exercise some care in its own behalf — not a helpless abstraction, totally dependent on the conventions and caprices of men.

Will looked down as he passed the bank and did not look up again till he was aware of the darkness of his figure mirrored in the window of Gus and Ruby's Café-Restaurant. The sky was a little grayer with the advance of the afternoon. It was possible to believe that the sun had gone another ninety-three million miles away. It was possible to believe almost anything.

He climbed into the truck and started around the block to head for home. But more commanding than the few simple lines he had to look at in order to drive was the persistent image of his last view of Harry's bank. There was the partition across the center of what was really only a single room. On the customers' side of the partition were the greasy floorboards, a shelf suspended from the wall, and a hatrack. The shelf held pen, ink, deposit slips, and blank checks. Over it hung the calendar for 1933 with only the January sheet torn from it. The calendar bore the picture of a tall, narrow building more than half a continent away. The building was the headquarters for a life insurance company. Around its top radiated the beams of a halo that culminated in the legend THE LIGHT THAT NEVER FAILS.

But humble as it was, the bank had been a three-dimensional reality, and it had imparted the illusion of reality to the abstraction it housed. Now there was nothing more to the abstraction than the thin paper in Will's pockets. If the boom had been all on paper, why couldn't the collapse be all on paper too? That was what he hadn't been able to understand for years.

He had never had so much cash in his possession before, and it seemed as though it would hardly make any difference at all if two or three fifties fluttered out of his pockets and whirled away through the holes around the pedals.

Halfway home he began to feel a cold ache in his fingertips and he realized he was squeezing the wheel as if it was the only thing left on earth to hang on to. It had been a frightful week. First there was Governor Comstock's Valentine; on the very next day the President-elect — the country's last hope — had nearly been killed by the six bullets fired at him by a crazy man; and two days later Harry Goodman closed the Eureka Bank.

He drove up his graveled approach and past the house to the shed. He patted two or three of his pockets once more, gathered his purchases in his arms, and walked toward the lamplit kitchen to tell Rose that the final disaster had come to Eureka, too.

⁂

There was less than an hour to go for Harry after Will left. He finished doing what he could with the books. It was just a safe minimum of juggling that he did. After all, any man had a right to the means for a fresh start for himself and his family. A couple of thousand one way or another could not do nearly as much for his depositors as it could do for him.

He doubted that any of them had given him any credit at all for keeping the bank going after the crash, or even for saving some individual necks, too, when the crash came. In all the years he had been here, he and his family could count on their fingers the number of times they had been invited out for Sunday dinner. But if a man wanted to get into banking this was the only kind of place he could do it — if he was a Jew. Back East they would laugh if a Jew even applied for a teller's job. They would tell him to go open a hock shop. He sometimes wondered if the people here in this godforsaken town thought he had come here because he couldn't think of better places to live.

Well, almost all of them had done their bit to finish him, and now they would suffer as much as he would. If they were going to run him out, he could take a little along and still be fairer to them than they had been to him. They had tried to borrow money against damaged crops, rotting barns, starving cattle, and worthless machinery. They came into his bank smelling of manure and they spat all over the outside of his cuspidor.

The final respite from his doubting twinges had come when he figured out how to fix up Will and some other decent ones. He felt cleared and justified — and exhilarated. It was the only time in his life he had ever possessed real power, and it didn't matter that his power came from his ruin. The important thing was that he could reward and he could punish.

The fourth time he hauled his watch from its pocket under his belly he saw that at last it was time to close. He pulled down the wooden window and locked it from the inside. Then he slammed the door of the vault and turned the knob on the dial. He adjusted his silk scarf around his neck and he was putting on his overcoat when he heard the door slam.

"I'm all closed up!" he yelled through the partition.

"I gotta have change for tomorrow," Zack Hoefener yelled back. "You and your damn soft banker's hours. Open up!" He rapped pointlessly against the bars of the closed window.

Harry unlocked the window and slid it up, pushing almost as high as his short arm could reach. "What do you need, Zack?"

Zack was looking at his hat and scarf. "Leaving a little early, ain't you?" Hoefener, of course, had never trusted him. He had been one of the first to draw out nearly all of a big savings account when things began to look bad.

"I'm catching a cold," Harry said. "Never have gotten used to these Dakota winters."

Zack looked at him again, in that way he had, as though he had a right to stare. He thrust his three crisp twenties at Harry. "All this in pennies and silver," he said.

"Fine," Harry replied.

Zack slammed the door the way he always did, and Harry remembered the way he had slammed it after the argument they had had over his big withdrawal.

"I have to have thirty days' notice for a withdrawal like that," Harry had protested.

"You and how many *other* men are gonna tell me that?" Hoefener had asked. He had been a little drunker than usual. Harry had given him the money, and after that Harry had had to listen to him brag about what a foolproof and ingenious hiding place he had hit upon. He bragged about it to nearly everybody who came into his store. And then they came out of the store, headed straight across the road to the bank, and made their withdrawals.

Harry buttoned his overcoat and locked his door. Zack was just entering his store. Harry got one more look at the man's monstrous profile before he turned and headed up the sidewalk, his rubbers thumping on the boards and his satchel swinging heavily from his shaking arm.

❦ ❦ ❦

"What's that?" Rose said to Will when he set the cashbox on the table with the groceries.

She had put the lamp on the table to work by, and the light of it made deep shadows in the sockets of her eyes. She was nearly as tall as he was, but thin from the erosions of her austerity, which sought to conquer all hungers. There was little gray in her brown hair, though it was dull with years, and wind-worn like the boards of a house. She wore it in a bun that was thick not from the profusion of the hair but from the length of it. She swept it back so tightly that it seemed to pull at the fine skin of her temples, drawing out the length of her hazel eyes and smoothing the elegant eminences of her cheekbones. Had she known that her stern and simple hair fashion was the best possible one for her face, she might have changed it, for she had devoted much of her life to the mortification of the flesh and to plucking out the eye that might offend.

After she had spoken she waited, her mouth having returned to the position of a mouth which tried never to make frivolous movements. Her jaws were square without being heavy or hard. Their squareness was perfect for the rest of her face, but the perfection made the face seem unapproachable.

It was the kind of face that in her extreme youth had either frightened off a man or challenged him. Most men had been frightened; Will had first been challenged and then he had recognized that she was beautiful. He kept his eyes on her face while he reached under his coat and brought out a roll of fifties.

"Will, what have you done?" she gasped.

He had always had a tendency to grin, nervously and broadly and uncontrollably, when he really wanted to fight or roar with misery. He could feel his lips twitching as he said, "Harry has closed the bank. All washed up."

"Oh, Will! What will we do?"

"I've got it all." He began pulling the rolls out of his pockets.

The money fell on the steel table-top with little rustling sounds, as of birds alighting and settling upon their evening roosts.

"How will we keep it all?" she asked, when the last roll had fallen. "What shall we do with it?"

His proposal sounded even more outrageous than he had expected it to. "I know it sounds silly, but I suppose we ought to bury it, like everybody else. I suppose it'll be good as long as there's anything left of the country."

Her quick agreement surprised him. "Yes," she said positively. "It mustn't be in the house. . . . Oh, Will, thank God you got it. How did you know? How did you get it?"

He shrugged his shoulders; he hadn't yet taken off his coat and it was getting heavy. He was beginning to *feel* heavy, too — to sag after the shock. "I *didn't* know," he said. "Harry just gave it to me. We didn't talk about what happened. I don't know why it happened."

When they looked at the money again it seemed like less than it had when it was flowing from his pockets. By now Will was getting used to the way the same amount of money could expand and shrink by turns. It lay in loose curls between the slab of bacon tied in brown paper and the twenty-pound sack of sugar slumping in portly wrinkles of lettered cloth.

Neither of them had any impulse to count the bills. They unrolled them and flattened them into the box. Then they closed the lid and flipped the catch in front and tried it in different places in the house. Finally they decided to keep it under the bed for the night.

They sat down to their supper, repeating the Lord's Prayer together as they did three times each day. Then they thought of George and Rachel.

"Will, do the children have anything in the bank?" Rose asked anxiously.

"I've been wondering," Will said. "I don't see how it could be much. I wish they would let us make it up to them, whatever it is."

"George would *die* first!"

"I know."

"Will, if you rushed back into town now do you suppose you could catch Harry and ask him just for George's deposits?"

"Oh, no. Harry's a good many miles away from here by now—that's a cinch. And nobody knows which direction, either."

He leaned back in his chair and stared across his plate at the blackness on the other side of the dining room windows. A long crack split one of the windows diagonally from top to bottom. He could not see the crack because of the darkness, but he could see the button in the middle of it, tied through to the button on the other side to steady the fracture and make the window less likely to shatter. Lightning had done it. He had been in the room when the bolt stabbed through the window—hissing, crackling, booming, ripping out his eardrums and blowing the house to smithereens. Still—even as it trundled away—it possessed him; with its own detonations it commanded and contained the detonations of his heart; within the grinding concussions of its bowels it whirled the bursting organs of his own digestion. Finally it mocked him. It tumbled his splitting, craven head back into the room and declined to execute the claim it had established. Then he found, first, that he was alive, next, that the house had not exploded—it was not even on fire—and last, that his eardrums were in their accustomed place, aching.

Why it had let him go he could not guess. While it possessed him he had thought how coincidental and how appropriate. His oldest brother had died by lightning.

Will never fixed the window, though he was not sure why. Perhaps it was for a bond with his brother. Perhaps it was superstition—so long as the window remained cracked, all other bolts would pass by. Perhaps it was merely to remind him of how capriciously death frolicked in a man's house.

It wasn't that he was afraid to die but that he hoped passionately, perhaps ungratefully or even irreverently, to live long enough to be assured that things were going to get better. He had fathered two children and worked inhumanly hard to give them what he had never had himself. But neither of them, at the moment, was in anything like the circumstances he had envisioned for them.

"Why did Rachel marry George?" he said to Rose.

"George was a very handsome man when she married him," said Rose.

"Would a girl with a mind like Rachel's really marry a man for his looks?" Will demanded.

"I don't know," she said. "Who knows why anybody marries anybody?"

"But why in thunderation didn't she marry that boy in college?" he asked.

"Maybe she was too young. Maybe it was a mistake to send her when she was only sixteen. Maybe if she'd been older . . ."

"But Rose, there was *nothing here* for her! What else could we have *done?* Kept her on the farm driving a tractor till she was eighteen — till she forgot half of what she'd learned? Once you start an education you've got to keep on with it, that's all."

Rose was silent. She was right, he thought. Nobody knew why anybody married anybody.

After a while he couldn't help himself any longer and he had to say it:

"I wonder where Stuart is."

"We'll probably hear when he gets short on money again." Rose pushed away and began to clear the table. Stuart had been gone nearly two years and she still refused to talk about him.

The next morning Will went out early, before the eastern rim of his gray fields had yet rounded toward the sun, and buried his box of money.

He walked through the orchard from the gate — six trees up, two over — and he chopped with his pick on the downhill side of a dead crab-apple tree. As the daylight grew he looked nervously up and down the road. He felt like a criminal or a fool, or both.

He winced a little when he heard the first chunk of frozen earth thud against the box. He filled the hole, brushed the bit of snow back over his digging, and tramped it around a little. He had chosen that particular tree because he knew it was dead. Last summer's drought and this winter's sudden plunging freezes had finished it off. He was almost as tall as the tree. He had to admit that it had not done so well as he had promised Rose that it would do, and it certainly was not so hardy as the catalog had told *him* it would be.

Saturday, February 18

OTTO WILKES trotted his showy team of matched dappled-gray Percherons across the railroad tracks, nearly catapulting his two youngest and lightest boys off the back end of the wagon. A gelding and a stallion the horses were, and they weighed a ton apiece. He had hated to geld the one, but the other, being three years older, was already mature and a proven sire, so he had had no choice. Otto didn't want to try to manage a team of two Percheron stallions.

He pulled up before the dusty window that read "HOEFENER'S EUREKA HARDWARE, Agent for John Deere Tractors & Equipment."

"All right boys," he said. "You can come in with me."

He lifted the smallest of the four, who was scarcely able to walk yet, and they all lined up behind him and followed him into the store.

Zack saw them as they pulled up, and he shoved his dark brown bottle under the cash register. He didn't know who made him sicker — Otto with his brassy, pickthank ways, or Otto's numberless, shivering, dirty-nosed children breathing loudly through their mouths.

Otto bought a box of rivets for some harness repair he was doing and some other harness fittings. The whole purchase came to just under a dollar, but Otto wrote out a check for five.

"I'm not no bank!" Zack objected when he saw the check. "Why don't you ever come in town on a weekday and get your cash over at the bank? Is this thing gonna bounce on me? I'm a pretty mean man when I get a rubber check."

"Oh come on, Zack. I got to have a little cash. We're all out of coal and you *know* I can't get *coal* without cash."

Zack cashed it, mostly to get the pestilential brood out of his store. He just couldn't stand to have that grimy bunch of kids fingering everything in sight.

Monday, February 20

Even though Harry never opened up until ten in the morning, Zack spent almost the entire hour after he opened his own place peering through the backward lettering on his window at the bank across the street. If Otto's check was no good, he would drive out there that very night and either take it out of the oily bum's hide or attach his team, which was the only thing he had worth attaching.

At eleven o'clock Zack hung a sign on his door, "Gone to lunch," and went over to the bank.

It had been such a slow morning that Zack was sure he hadn't missed seeing Harry come, but still he could not believe it when he found the door locked. Harry had had colds before, but he had always sent his wife down to keep the bank open. Zack went down to Herman Schlaht's store.

"Where's Harry?" he demanded.

"How should *I* know?" Herman retorted. "Maybe he ain't gonna run a bank no more. *You* ain't worried are you? *You* got *yours*."

"I just thought somebody might've been in that knew what happened to him," Zack said angrily. "By God, I'll just go on up there myself, right now."

He stamped out of the store and headed around the corner and up the street. He glared at the empty window of the bank and turned and spat at its steps. The sidewalk ended at the end of the block. Then he walked on the edge of the road, past houses that had once been yellow or white or brown. All of them had columned front porches, gables jutting from their high roofs, and privies set squarely in line with their back doors. But they were not really so much alike as they looked. It was just that the same thing had happened to them all. They were like a double row of unfortunate sisters, who for different reasons all remained gray-haired spinsters, staring at each other wonderingly across the frozen street.

In the yard of one house a swing hanging from the branches of a great bare tree played by itself in the wind. In another yard a privy door flapped and banged, and in still another, several paths from convenient approaches crossed to one of the town pumps.

There was only one house beyond the Goodmans' to the north, but it was far out in a field and not on the street. That was where the Finleys lived, and Zack saw, as he approached Harry's house, that Mrs. Finley had already got a big Monday morning wash out, to freeze stiff in the wind. He didn't see how that Finley outfit stayed alive in that big old leaking house. Harry, being the money-grubber that he was, actually demanded rent for the place. Harry owned it the way he owned all the other places, because of a no-good mortgage.

Harry's own house was set in a yard so full of trees that, living or dead, bare or leafed, they nearly hid it from people passing by. Zack's knock, muted by his glove, drew no response. He took off the glove and rapped again with the sharpness of his cold knuckles. He twisted the door knob, but it would not turn. Then he kicked the door.

He tramped down the path to the garage. The doors were locked, but he found a window draped with spider webs and dotted with the dry husks of insects. He could see that the car was not there. He heaved himself up the steps of the back porch, and yanked at the screen door, which opened so cordially that he nearly lost his balance. But the porcelain knob on the back door was as resistant as the brass knob on the front door.

He shouted into the house and pounded on a window. He stood for a moment, his glove cupped around his goiter, while he thought. Then he lunged around the house and up the steps of Harry's neighbor.

Old Mrs. Webber came to the door. She shivered in her long black woolen dress and clutched her shawl around her age-deformed shoulders. "Come in, come in," she said in a high voice that scratched something in her throat. Zack's glove went back to his goiter.

"It's so cold. Come in, so I can shut the door. Martin's in bed today. His laig and his hip is hurting him. What did you want?"

"Where's the Goodmans?" Zack shouted. "When did they go away? Have they cleared out for good?"

"I never see nobody in the wintertime," Mrs. Webber mourned, and her voice scratched on something a notch or two higher. "Just the boy that brings me the groceries and goes down to the pump and fetches me my water. And that old man with the big blue lip that brings the coal." Mrs. Webber no longer remembered names.

"Them Goodmans haven't never been neighborly to us," she went on, and her voice went back down and scratched in the first notch. Listening to it was like watching an old cow bend her head to the side and rake her neck up and down against a knot on a fence post. "Martin says that's the way them Jews are. When they first come here I went over and called on the missus and took her an angel food cake—*angel food*—with *twelve* egg whites. They's a lot of people in this town said I used to make the best angel food cake in the county. But that was before my wrists got too sore to beat it right any more."

"But what about the Goodmans!" Zack cried.

"Why, do you know what she brought back in the dish I took her that cake in? Six rotten little fish! Martin said that would learn me to give something free for nothing to a Jew. We give them fish to the dog."

"Did you see them go away?"

"Are they gone away?" Mrs. Webber asked.

"They're *gone* all right! Their *car's* gone."

"Well, I swan," said Mrs. Webber. "Never even said goodby. Just like a Jew."

Zack ran all the way back to Herman's store, clumping ponderously down the middle of the road, keeping his arms crossed to steady all the burning, jumping things inside his chest.

"He's gone all right," he cried to Herman. "Cleared right out. *I said* he would, didn't I?"

Johnny Koslov, the youngest of the Koslov brothers, loitered in the rear of the store, hopelessly eyeing a horse blanket that he coveted for the bed of himself and his Hilda. He came forward to the counter and demanded, "Who iss gone? Who iss it?"

"The *banker's* gone—*that's* who!" Zack roared. "The little Jew banker. Just like *I* said he would!"

"Oh my!" said Johnny. Johnny had never had any money in the bank and he had not heard about the panic, but he could react to sounds in voices and looks on faces. "Oh my!" he said again.

Zack paid no more attention to him. He despised all Russians. "You find me a Roosian with any brains," he would say, "and I'll prove to you he's probably got German blood in him. And they'll stand around in your place and spit their filthy-dirty Roosian peanuts anywhere they feel like it — just like they act at home!"

Herman didn't care about the sunflower seed husks. When he got around to it, he swept them out the front door onto the sidewalk, where they eventually sifted away between the boards. It didn't bother him when the Russians gathered around his stove, chattering in their foolish language and blowing the salty slivers from their muscular lips. As long as the Russians spent money, Herman didn't care how many Russian peanut shells they spat.

Herman had dust from a sack of chicken mash in his apron, and he beat at it, raising a yellow cloud that settled over the hairs on his hands. He dangled one of the hands in a small vat of dill pickles and brought up half a pickle which he put in his mouth. "You reckon he's gone for good?"

"Well, now then, just what do *you* think?" Zack sneered.

"Why, he might just be taking one of them bank holidays," Herman said. "He maybe will come back when the new President comes in."

Herman had learned how to handle Zack Hoefener in twenty years of running a store in the same town with him. "You make me sick," Zack said. "We should go after him with a rope. We should have a good old-fashioned necktie party."

"You cannot hang a businessman for losing all his money," Herman observed. "Or for taking a holiday, either." He was not exerting himself to be fair to Harry but only to infuriate Zack, who flung open the door and charged through it, nearly ramming into the customer on Herman's steps.

"What ails *him?*" George Custer said, holding the door open and leaning out to watch Hoefener's departure.

Herman crunched the last of the pickle into his mouth and said to George, "He just found out about the bank."

"*What* bank?"

"*Harry's* bank. He closed it up."

"What do you mean!"

"He went away. Nobody knows where."

George took a long breath. "The dirty little Jew," he said. "The stinking tight little Jew. Who in hell did he lend the money to? The stingy scoundrel must've lost it himself! The dirty little swindler!"

George paced to the stove in three enormous strides, and had no more than stuck his cold hands over its searing top than he whirled and paced back again.

The Adam's apple in George's neck sawed up and down. "Maybe he's just took a holiday," Herman suggested.

"A *holiday!*" George shouted. "A *holiday!* Yeah, out to California, maybe, where it's nice and warm — and far away! Well, he damn well better stay wherever he's at. It'll be plenty warm around *here* for him, you bet!"

"If he took money that is not his the police will catch him, won't they?" Herman said.

"*Sheriff Richard M. Press!*" George scoffed. "He's just after the little guy that can't hire himself a shyster lawyer. Oh, the God-damned little chiseler! He'll go scot-free!"

Herman shrugged. He himself stood to lose nothing. His only capital was the inventory on his shelves; his reserve was his own corpulence — a product of the tempting shelves and a margin that could well last him for many days should the shelves go empty.

He was curious to know how much George would lose, for it was obvious that he was going to lose something, but Herman would never ask a question like that to a man like Custer. George's great frame alone was formidable, but the frame housed a violence of soul vastly more formidable than that of flesh. No room into which George stepped was free from tension until he left it again.

"Maybe Harry will come back after Roosevelt gets in," Herman said.

"*Roosevelt!*" George pronounced the "Roo" as in kangaroo. "He's nothing but another rich man. *He* don't care if a few million of us lose our shirts. What's *he* care about a little dinky one-horse bank way out here? There ain't a thing he could do anyhow."

He turned away and stared toward the back of the store, with his jaw as hard as ever, but with his eyes drifting out of focus in a peculiar way — almost like a fellow Herman had known who had a case of the falling sickness. It was queer how mean George looked that way. He wasn't looking at anything at all, and yet he seemed ready to kill anything he might see.

Finally he said, "Better get this stuff for the old lady, I reckon."

He bought a hundred-pound sack of flour and some little things for which he paid in exact change and bills so limp they felt more like silk than paper. Herman wondered how long those bills had ridden around in Custer's hip pocket before he had to use them. And he wished he knew how much George had lost in Harry's bank.

❦ ❦ ❦

George couldn't even look up at the house of his wife's father as he passed below it on the road. He wondered how much the old man was going to lose. He wanted to go up and tell Will about the bank, but he was so angry he couldn't trust himself. Why had he listened to the sanctimonious ass telling him all about how safe that God-damned bank was? Now the money he'd been saving for seed was gone, and he was sure it was gone for good. Yet he could hardly believe his luck could be so bad. He had thought losing the foal was enough bad luck to last for the next year at least.

He drove the last half mile to his own mailbox and turned into the frozen ruts that led through his fields to the farmyard. The land sloped away from the county road so that he could survey nearly all of the half section as he coasted down the quarter-mile incline to the house. On either side of him were his two biggest fields—eighty acres apiece—which he planted in wheat. These two fields stretched the entire width of the property, and their eastern edges cut the farm in half. The north and south windbreaks of well-grown willows, cottonwoods, and box elders defined the limits of the yard. The groves stopped the wind enough so that the snow was encouraged to settle between them, and thus the Custers paid for their bit of shelter from one element by spending the winter half-buried in another element.

Below the house the long swell dropped more precipitously to a trough of the lowest ground on the farm, and then rose again to form the eastern, rougher part of the property—humped, notched by ravines, and quite rocky. Here George had plotted out his pastures and the fields where he grew corn and a hay crop of sweet clover or alfalfa.

Set just above the final drop of the western swell, the house appeared to command the hill and the buildings at the foot of it. But the appearance was deceptive, for those who lived in the house were really commanded by the hill. Nearly everything went down the hill empty and came up the hill full. Water buckets, milk pails, egg baskets, and wheelbarrows went lightly down to the well or the barn or the chicken house or the compost pile and came wearily back up to the wash boiler, the cream separator, the cooler, or the garden behind the house. Once each morning and evening the milk pails went down full — after the cream was separated and the skim milk went back to the barn to feed the calves and pigs.

The house had begun as one big room with an east and a west window and a chimney on the north. Then smaller rooms had been leaned against the north and south sides of the first one, each with a window to the west. The kitchen stove, the shelf for the water bucket and wash basin, a cupboard, a cooler, and a small work table nearly filled the room on the north. The baby's crib and Lucy's cot and a large storage closet filled the room on the south. It was such a simple little house that George felt as though he confronted the inside as well as the outside every time he came down toward it from the western fields and saw the three windows looking up at him — one from each of the three rooms.

In the main room, which they called the dining room, was an expandable round table on which the family ate all its meals, wrote letters, bathed the baby, did homework, cut out paper dolls, butchered, sewed, or spread out catalogs for ordering garden seeds, repair parts, shoes, and clothes. There were four straight chairs around the table, and a high chair. There was a heavy rocking chair covered in black leather, scraped full of furry brown scratches and showing brown rings on the seat made by the springs pressing up through the stuffing. There was an expensive upright piano, a bookcase too small for the books in it, and a clothes rack beside the round heating stove, nearly always hung with diapers and baby blankets. In an alcove curtained off from the rest of the room was the double bed for himself and Rachel.

As George neared the house he looked out once more across the fields. He loved and hated them for the same reason: They represented the hope of independence that grew drier and dustier every year. It was bad enough not to own the land he worked, but it was intolerable to pay rent on that land to a city man — a city man who knew enough about buttons and thread and cheap toys from Japan to make money running a store full of junk, and who thought, since he had made the money to buy land which had sold for taxes, that he also knew how to make money with that land. No matter how much surplus wheat was left over from last year or what plagues of drought, disease, and grasshoppers were predicted, he stipulated that George must plant half the acreage in wheat, of which he took a full third of the proceeds — not of the gross, but the net, after threshing, transporting, and all other costs except a percentage of the seed price were borne by George. If George chose not to plant half the land in wheat, he had to make up in cash for what Mr. James T. Vick figured would have been his share.

George had counted on getting a small loan from Harry for this season. Prices the last September had been the lowest in history, and he had got twenty-six cents a bushel from the elevator, minus the penalty for smut. Out of that he had had to pay threshers. Nevertheless, he had managed to keep nearly two hundred dollars in the bank, and another hundred would have seen him through in fairly good shape. But now he would have to go to the office of that city man in Jamestown, pushing his way between the gaudy counters of junk and squeezing through a doorway half blocked by more cartons of junk, and feeling his ignominious way up the few dark stairs leading to the office of Mr. James T. Vick. It was a low, cluttered little balcony where Mr. Vick sat at his desk, which overflowed with the business of a half dozen enterprises, looking out over the store from time to time to see that no hands went from alluring counter to threadbare pocket. His change-girl and bookkeeper sat at a desk nearly touching his, loading coins into the spherical bottoms of the money carriers, screwing them into the heads mounted on the wires, and yanking the handles to send them back to the clerks waiting below. George would have to sit in the presence of that girl while the frenetic carriers hissed back and forth, clanging into the steel rings that snapped shut around them. They arrived with the solid assurance of money come home — money rushing, rushing to come home. And while the girl doled out coins and smoothed bills and stored them away, George would have to beg for cash so he could get in the spring crop. And he would put up, as the only security he had, his muscles and his hope.

He was home — with his good news. He stopped the car near the house, threw the tanned hide from one of his own steers over the heated radiator, and then wedged a rock beneath each of the front wheels. He ought not to have been able to see more than the windows and the roof of the car. It should have been buried in three feet of snow while he drove a sleigh over the white depths that would leave a little water in the ground and at least protect the fields from blowing. He thought of the snows when he was a boy — twenty-foot drifts in some places, packed dirt-hard. He even had a photograph of himself on his pony atop a drift so high that his head was higher than a telegraph pole. And in the spring the snow went back up into the sky and fell again in rain, and the wheat sent long threads of roots down to the water, and in the fall one bushel of Number One wheat would buy a pair of overalls. A farmer got a fair shake then, and a man who was willing to work hard and who used his brains could manage to buy the land he worked and build a fine big house for his family, like Will, or like his own father, whose farm had been clear till he mortgaged it again in order to speculate. But then Hoover had come along as Food Administrator during the war and pegged the price of wheat at $2.18 a bushel while he let the overall manufacturers hike their prices till they were getting $6.50 for a pair of cockeyed denim pants. Ah, yes! The Great Humanitarian, putting a ceiling on wheat because of the hungry people in the world. But just who cared what it cost the man who grew the wheat to put a pair of overalls over his naked rump? Who cared? That was what George wanted to know.

He scooped up the hundred-pound sack of flour as though he would let the Great Humanitarian have the whole hundred pounds right in his crabbed little face. All a man had to do was buy a sack of flour to see who kept right on making money — who shed none of the sweat and made all the money. Since 1929, in less than four years, wheat prices had fallen over sixty per cent. But retail flour had dropped only forty per cent and bread had dropped less than twenty-five per cent. The more middlemen there were to get their sticky mitts on the wheat he raised, the less of a drop in price there was; yet *he* was the only fellow who had to sweat. Every single time he bought a sack of flour he thought about what Adolph Beahr took at the elevator, then what the railroad took to carry the wheat to the mills in Bismarck or Grand Forks and then to bring the flour back to Herman Schlaht, and finally what Herman took for *his* share.

When George bought back his own wheat, sold from the harvest fields at a price that scarcely more than paid the threshers and the rent to James T. Vick, he bought it back at a price that made him wonder how much longer his family could even eat bread — yes, how much longer a wheat farmer could eat bread.

And now another city man — a dirty little Jew — undoubtedly had run off with the money George had hoarded all winter for putting in the new crop and buying staples until the next harvest. If he could have got that Jew banker's neck between his hands at that moment before he had to go into his dark little house to break the news to Rachel, he could have throttled him. He could have watched without remorse while the face turned black above the white grip of his bare hands, and the legs kicked and dug at the frozen ground and then grew limp. And then, when he saw it was done, he could have unwrapped his fingers from the wrung neck, dropped the body, and left it behind him while he walked toward his house and wiped his hands free of corruption on his overpriced "Oshkosh B'Gosh" overalls.

Still trembling with his vision, he stamped his boots on the porch to signal Rachel to open the door.

"What happened?" she gasped, when she saw his face.

"That dirty little Jew has closed the bank." He pulverized the words with his teeth, letting them drop down to her like chaff dropped by a whirlwind.

Like chaff they blew about her and suffocated her. It took her a moment to put them together. "Oh, he *couldn't* have closed it permanently. He *couldn't* have. It must just be that he was getting too much of a run and he wanted to stop it. They don't close just because there's no money left; they close to protect the rest of us."

He looked down at her, the sack of flour still squeezed in his arms. "You and your father!" he shouted. "Preaching, preaching! Always preaching! Leave the money in there! If everybody would just leave it in there. Then the banks could loosen up and help out the little fellow again. Oh yes! Just have faith! Support the filthy banks and they'll be able to help the little guy."

His tone shifted from fire to ice. "Every one of those damned ignorant Roosians got their money out, if they ever had any in there in the first place. And so did the Germans. Zack Hoefener and Herman and Beahr — *they* won't lose anything! You can bet on that. But it was up to *us* — up to the people that built the country to keep it going. You and your old man! Preaching. Going to church. By God, *anybody* knows you can't trust a Jew. That's what I told you all along!"

Rachel turned back to her bread, hoping he would stop before he woke up the baby. She rarely defended herself or her family when he was like this. She wanted her silence to make him feel that he had won, but instead it defeated him. It left him alone, with his anger gone, to hear again the things he had said, without so much as one culpable word of hers to recall and cling to in his search for justification. He had to bear the guilty aftermath of his rages all by himself. Still he couldn't stop.

"Well, your old man will get just what he asked for now! He'll lose a hell of a lot more than *we* will. I'll just bet he won't drop his damned holy *tithe* in that collection plate *next* Sunday!"

The table and floor creaked with the rhythmic strong pressure Rachel applied to the bread as she turned and folded it on the board, hauling up the dough and bending it back into itself with a little thump and a whisper of the flour on the wood.

He carried the sack past her and set it on the floor by the lard can they used for a flour bin. It stood beneath the window that looked out on the fields that made the wheat. The frost from the night before had melted and moistened the windowsill, making it smell of old wood and the dust from fields. Some of the wetness darkened the streaked pea-green calcimine on the wall below the window.

He took a penknife out of his pocket and cut the linked red and white strings hanging from the top edge of the sack. He lifted the sack and dumped it carefully into the empty can. He pinched the bottom corners of the bag and shook it to spill the last ounce out of the sides of it, and then he replaced the lid of the can and folded up the sack and laid it on top of the lid. The flour-dulled picture of the girl on the sack looked up at him.

"Dakota Maid," her grayish-black braids hanging stiffly to her breasts, held out to him a great basket heaped with golden sheaves of wheat. Her too-dainty moccasins were planted much too close together to balance the weight she carried, and her dusty brown face was stretched in a wide Anglo-Saxon smile. The outline of the same improbable Indian maid showed ever so faintly through the faded dye of the curtains at the window.

George straightened up and looked at Rachel. She did not look at him. She held up one end of the dough until it thinned itself out, sliced off a length with the butcherknife, kneaded it into shape, and laid it in the first of the five waiting pans. She filled the other four pans and punched down the dough.

He couldn't believe it. Surely it must matter to her that they had lost two hundred dollars. Surely she was not going to let him bear the loss alone. Surely she would say something that would commit herself to him. She would express her fear over what would become of them, thus admitting that now they had no choice but to survive together or fail together — admitting that she could not get along without him. She would begin to cry, because of the world's enormous treachery; he needed to see her cry because he needed to cry himself. And her crying would also be an admission of her weakness and a sign that he would have to be strong for both of them — and he needed the sign in order to be strong enough. Or possibly she would burst into the kind of fury he longed for — the fury that would justify his own fury, and bring them once more together in furious righteousness. What was a wife for? Even if she would simply strike back at him with all the fury she must feel about everything (For she *must* feel it? She must!), as he had only now struck at her — even then it would be a kind of commitment. What was a wife for, if she let a man bear a thing like this alone?

But though she worked beside him as hard as *he* worked, all day, every day, and submitted to him silently in the night, she was no longer committed to him. Sometimes he knew why little things went wrong; sometimes he didn't. He hadn't the least notion of why the whole thing had gone wrong. If a piece of machinery misbehaved, he watched and listened and tinkered till he found the cause of the trouble, and then he set about fixing it calmly and competently. He was contemptuous of the sort of man who kicked an ailing machine. A machine had no will to defy the man. Why should the man feel emotions about the machine? But it was things like this that made him want to kick something — things like these grievances of hers that went round and round till they lost their beginnings — these grievances that were more important to her than the ruin of them both. An overpowering heat flooded down his legs, as though he was wetting himself in a nightmare. He knew that if he kicked the streaked green wall under the window, he could put his foot right through it.

He hadn't intended to do it, but once he had the door open, he was afraid he might rip it out of the kitchen — to make her look up from the everlasting little chores that she found so convenient to pile up between them — nevertheless, he had specifically told himself that he would *not* do it; but when the door was in his hands he did slam it with all his strength. Once again she had won.

Rachel had no idea that she had won. Cathy began to fuss almost as soon as the noise ended. She was that kind of baby. Lucy had been that way too. Some babies, when they first woke, would lie and look up at the ceiling with their wide eyes that seemed never to have been asleep, and they would speak softly to themselves with their tiny soft mouths for a long time before they decided they were hungry. But not *her* babies. They were like George. The minute they woke they wanted up, whether they were hungry or not. They couldn't wait for anything. They couldn't even wait to be born; both of them came nearly two weeks early.

Now Cathy was hungry and Rachel would have to feed her very soon. She considered the bone-colored dough. The loaves needed to rise before going into the oven; on the other hand, she was afraid they might rise too much before she had finished with the baby. If she forgot them for too long, the bread would bake out too airy and dry, with a bubbly crust. If she punched them down again right now, they might not rise enough, and then the bread would be heavy and doughy. George had a fit over faulty bread. At every meal while a bad batch lasted, he would wonder aloud how it was that his mother had always been able to bake perfect bread.

Once she had thought that doing her best to please him would be a joy to her, as it had always been one of her greatest joys to please her father. But now, even if he complimented her, she could not help thinking of the crushing ratio between complaints and compliments. Why, then, did it matter whether a batch of bread ever pleased him again or not?

She came upon the question the way she occasionally came upon a serpent as she was starting the garden in the cold spring. The snake, barely sentient after sleeping so long in the frozen ground, would finally become aware of her and uncoil like a rubber band snapping beneath her hand. And even while she was trying to calm the ridiculous physical reaction she always had when this happened, she was saying to herself, "But I was *looking* at it all the time! I *saw* it right *there*, all the while it was so still!"

So it was with the question. Now that she had seen it, she knew how long it had been there, and she knew that, unlike the snake, it would never go away and let her calm herself again. She would live always with this astonished burning in her chest. The baby's crying, she thought, the bank, the baby, *your father!* always preaching! I don't care, I won't ever care again.

The baby was hungry. She must feed her. But she didn't want to be crying while she fed her. That wasn't good for a baby, to be held and fed while the mother was upset. The bank, the bank, the bank, and why should *it* matter any more either? It was not going to matter any more. Neither were his shouts.

She remembered how he had been that first year when he was courting her — in his way. His father's farm adjoined the schoolyard and that was why they had met at all. It was a glorious Indian summer day. She had wanted to eat her lunch outside with the children, but she had to write a geography lesson on the blackboard.

The sounds of calamity sent her rushing to the door. Except for the big boys, the children were flying toward her in terror. Behind them, on the safe side of the Custer fence, stood the big boys, yelling with laughter. A huge Holstein bull fanatically assaulted the other side of the fence. They bellowed and raged at him; they flapped their arms and danced back and forth. One boy took off his shirt and waved it, leaping about in his underwear.

"Boys!" she cried. "Boys!"

She ran out to them, conscious even at such a moment of how short she was beside them, and said all the wrong things.

"Put your shirt on! Get away from that *fence!* What did you *do* to him? He could have killed all of you!" They laughed like demons. They showed off for her.

Then the bull, butting at the fence post, hooked a horn under the bottom wire, raised his head, and pulled the post out of the ground.

She didn't need to tell them to run. They were all far ahead of her, stringing across the schoolyard and pounding up the steps. She had a memory of the giant bull face, twice the size of a cow's, of the great wall of bone that was his forehead and of the two shining black globes in it, rolling, seeking — glittering as they came to focus on her, seeing her as she would look under his hoofs after the fence came down. She remembered the black leather nose, no more bothered by the ring in it than a boot is bothered by a bootlace. She remembered the blunt profile, descended of Ice Age bison and Grecian bulls — the head, created like those others, to be nothing more than a senseless battering-ram proceeding from an enormous, obscenely male neck.

She remembered, too, how the last boy had slammed the door of the schoolhouse in her face and she had thought, he's locked me out, and even in her fear, as she ran up the steps, she was furious at this trick to compound her humiliation. Were they going to make her beg to be let in, with a three-thousand-pound bull behind her? But the door was not locked; the boy had only slammed it out of his own fear. Much later, after they were all safe again, she felt hurt that they would not have thought of her at all. Males, she said to herself when the hurt came.

The bull, in his epitome of male savagery, charged to the steps and stopped. Now there was nothing for him to attack with his aroused maleness. He seemed to know that he was ludicrous and to be further enraged. He shook his head at the bottom step, but there was nothing soft and alive to gore. He bellowed steadily. When he saw the children moving at the window he rammed his skull into the wall below.

The bristling flame of a red-haired human head appeared in the window then — the head of a man whose profile pushed out and down from his red pelt with an impatient force of elongated brutish angles. The mouth was long-lipped and excessively arched, and the jaw, instead of ending properly in a civilized chin, jutted out and down as though it never intended to stop. Altogether it was the face of a cave man.

But then when she looked down to see all of him at once, she discovered that the jawline was remarkably straight and that it led back up to an ear that was large but refined. Nor was the skull that of a flat-headed cave man, for it was high and curved behind, and it balanced the jutting jaw on the slender prideful neck. The neck was set on wide shoulders, the shoulders on a potent torso. The torso supported mighty limbs. Then she saw that the face was not that of a male human throwback, but of a young man so overpowering that before she could stop it, the thought quickened and created itself: He looks exactly the way a man ought to look.

He moved carefully but fearlessly, scolding the bull in curiously soothing tones. Either the bull was very much afraid of the man, or else he was no longer so enraged as he pretended he was, and glad to be persuaded to stop smashing his head into the school building. With not more than a minute of quick footwork on the part of the man and half-hearted dodging on the part of the bull, the capture was done. The man had his lead stick hooked in the ring and the bull followed, rocking his massive shoulders and haunches in a gait calculated to crowd the man. But the man had a great stride to match the bull's, and he kept the leather nostrils stretched into such painful ovals that the bull could not side-step to dislodge the hook. The man never looked behind him. He marched away over the flattened fence, with his straight back no more than four feet in front of the glittering eyes and the cruel secret brain.

The more logical it was to stop trembling, the more difficult it seemed to stop. The big boys took up the siege where the bull had left off. Even after she finally got them to sit down and ostensibly to work, the atmosphere in the one big room, grown stuffy and confining with the warm day, was that of a becalmed ship alive with the vibrations of mutiny. If she asked a question, she was more likely to get an uncontrolled burst of laughter than an answer. She knew they couldn't be blamed for thinking it was funny to see a teacher run away from a bull — even if it was for her life. What she blamed them for was starting the whole thing — wandering far into a pasture where they had no business and getting an animal worked up like that.

When the man came back to fix the fence, she was grateful and yet angry. Why did he keep such an animal in such a flimsy fence? She could not stop being aware of him out there, digging, pounding, nailing, with the sun glinting on his red-gold arms. Once when she looked out the window, her heart beating with the remnant of her fright and with her exasperation over the laughing savagery of the disobedient males ranged in front of her, she saw the man resting, leaning his arm across the new post, gazing at the schoolhouse, and then laughing until he finally had to blow his nose. He must be crazy, she thought.

After school he came in. She saw his inches of crinkly red hair rub the top of the door. He introduced himself politely enough, but then he said in a severe deep voice, "Now then, Miss Shepard, that was our prize bull out yonder in the breeding pasture." He did not apologize by his tone or his expression for speaking the words "bull" and "breeding" to a young woman. "In the future we'll have to ask you to enjoin your pupils from trespassing on our property. After all, it is a schoolteacher's duty to be responsible . . ." A belly laugh that rolled from him as though he were a Barnum and Bailey bass drum put an end to the speech he had been working on all afternoon.

He saw me run, she thought, and hated him.

He was often near the school when it let out, and particularly, it seemed, when she needed him. Once her little Ford got snowed in during the day and he pushed her out of the bank. But just as she could feel the wheels getting traction again, the car started to make a dreadful, sharp, rapid thumping. She stopped and let the engine idle. The trouble didn't seem to be there. Cautiously she let the car move and again the thumping resounded. It was in the back and she got out to see if it was the bumper. But nothing seemed amiss, and she thanked George again for his help, while he stood inclining his head to her with a respectful hand on the bill of his cap. She climbed back into the car and started it once more. This time the banging shook the whole automobile.

She leaned out and called, "Do you suppose it's the transmission?"

"Could be. Sounds like she's all froze up somewheres, don't she?" he said. (She had noticed that he talked much less grammatically when he wasn't making a speech he had prepared just for her. She found the contrast amusing and foolishly flattering.)

She couldn't remember any more how many times she started the car and stopped it again in annoyed confusion before his wild laughter gave him away. He was so good with machinery that he knew just how his hands beating on a rear fender ought to sound. After they were married, she had seen him run stooping behind a car as visitors started to leave their yard, playing the awful tattoo, and she knew, by the way their faces looked, how she must have looked herself. His jokes almost always made her feel stupid, and therefore irritated with him, and yet, as the year went on, she was ever more restless on the weekends she spent at home. Sunday afternoons were endless, even though she could play the piano she missed so much all week. Finally she began to be irritated with him because her Sunday afternoons were so dull and empty.

All the while she kept wondering how she was supposed to feel, and how she *did* feel, and what the truth was about various sorts of physical mysteries. There was the way her body vacillated between an energy so great that she had no peace and could not even digest her food and a lassitude so profound that she had no will and did not care at all what happened to her. And there were more subtle and complicated physical mysteries which caused a recurrence of the shocked feelings she had had about her father when she first knew some things had to be true, as they were true of all men.

Now all she knew was that the feelings of that year, whatever they were, whatever love was, had resulted in a wedding as soon as school ended. All she knew now was that there had been a roomful of bad boys, Sunday afternoons when she was nearly paralyzed by her need for some unknown thing, a snowbank, a snowbank — the bank, the bank, the bank. This must have been a love story and now this must be the end of it. She knew more than she thought she knew. She knew, after all, what love was and how it ended.

The baby was screaming in hunger and outrage. Rachel wondered if some accident had happened while she stood in the kitchen staring at five pans of bread dough through tears that would not stop. Did the baby have a pin scratching her stomach or stuck in her throat? She was afraid even to go and look at the baby.

A few nights before, she had gone to cover Lucy and seen what she could not put out of her mind. The child labored with a heavy cold, and her body was twisted, her head straining back at a broken angle from her neck, while she fought her loud unconscious battle for air. Her braids had come undone and her long hair streamed across her face, covering it in the darkness as hair covered the faces of dead children flopping in their mothers' arms or gaping in the gutters of Spanish streets. The picture was sometimes static, sometimes moving. Sometimes Rachel saw how it happened to one after another in the procession of mothers carrying dead children. One had looked out her window just as the bomb fell or the grenades exploded or the men, appearing from nowhere, opened fire in the street. This mother would have seen the child fall but she would not have been able to reach it in time. Nevertheless, when she got to its side, she would know how it had been — how her little girl of six had borne alone this agony still on her face, had wondered why her mother didn't come to explain what was happening to her and to save her from it — for here, on the child's face, was the terror and grief of dying all by herself.

The next mother did not know; she was searching, but of course this tiny body here was not what she had set out to find, not what she would allow herself to find. The hair tangled over the face hid the features, but this was her shoe, her dress, her jacket. But this was not her hand, no, this was not her face. Another little girl had died here when the men threw the things in the street. But here, under the blood, this was her dimple. (Lucy had dimples, round and sudden now, like pin pricks, but when she grew up they would be deep short lines at the corners of her mouth, like George's. But no, she would not grow up, for here, under her hair, was the place the blood had come from.)

This, *this* was the way love stories ended. Husbands killed each other in the streets and wives went out and picked up their babies. Banks failed, nations died, babies starved — this was a fine world, wasn't it, that men had built to live their love stories in?

Her own baby was screaming. The procession of mothers sank into the weary blackness beneath her mind and the blackness snapped back a maddening primitive retort. Life goes on, it said. Why? she retaliated. Why? — the silly question prompted by the awkward assertions one's foolish instincts were always making.

George for instance, like all males, had absolutely no reasons except those of his instincts for anything he did. That was why it didn't occur to him not to go on, even now, when they were so obviously ruined.

She had not stopped shaking but she had stopped crying, so she wiped the flour from her hands and went in to pick up her baby.

Saturday, March 4

THE DRIFTS of the blizzard around the steps of the Eureka Bank were all undisturbed, so that it could as well have been tenantless for two years as two weeks. But not even having every other bank in the nation for company could make it look less lonely.

The President had closed them all. Harry Goodman's Eureka Bank—assets $78,000, liabilities undetermined—was no more tightly closed than the biggest, oldest bank in New York. On that day the Eureka Bank was no more of a failure than any of the others with their good and bad mortgages and other kinds of good and bad paper.

The President's inaugural address came over Herman's radio in the forenoon, and the store was filled with men who had come to hear it. Some of the men had radios at home, but they came to Herman's store anyway, so as to have company while they listened. Even George was there, standing far back against the shelves, not joining the men around the stove or the ones who leaned on the counter, hovering over the radio, so possessed by the voice in it that they forgot themselves and let their hopefulness and their anxiety show in their faces. George, standing apart from them all, ground his teeth and wondered how they could be so taken in. He didn't like the phony accent and he didn't like the highfalutin language and it was just too much when the President said, "The only thing we have to fear is fear itself." By God, what rich man was going to accuse him of being afraid and get away with it, anyhow? He hardly heard any of the rest of the speech, he was so angry at being called afraid.

When the speech was over and the first murmurs began, he said loudly, "I'd like to get that hothouse pansy out on a farm for just one hour. I'd like to watch him pitch bundles into a thrashing machine when it's around a hundred and ten in the shade — or wrastle a bull calf that's taken a notion he just don't want to grow up to be a steer!"

Zack Hoefener began to laugh, holding his goiter with his hand, as though he must not lose track of the upsetting vibrations of his laughter and his heart beating there. Otto Wilkes laughed too, and so did Wally Esskew and Lester Zimmerman. Even the Koslovs began to laugh, though George doubted that any of them could understand what was funny about giving a man with that accent the chore of emasculating a calf.

Clarence Egger, whose arm had been gobbled up by a threshing machine, waited for them all to stop. "Don't you sheep brains know that the guy can't even walk? He had infantile paralysis, for Christ's sake!"

George was not going to be made a fool of by Clarence Egger. "Well, he got a great big infantile silver spoon, too, didn't he?"

"I'll take walking any day," Clarence said. He was the only man in the room who dared, because his right arm was gone, to stand up to George. At times when he was drunk enough, Zack would do it, but nobody else ever did.

Nevertheless, George felt that they were displeased with him for making them laugh at a crippled man. God-damn them — they were so dumb and ignorant — always confusing the issue. The issue was that a rich man was telling them all not to worry even if they had just lost their last red cent to a little Jew banker. A rich man who couldn't possibly imagine what it was like to work sixteen hours a day for six months of the year and to sit in a dark house smothering in snow for the other six months, wondering where the money for coal was going to come from. *That* was the man who was telling them not to worry, and *that* man's coddled, polished ignorance was the issue — not whether or not the man could walk.

George considered himself a well-spoken man, but he had no words to substitute for the obscenities he wanted to say to these silly bleating sheep. Clarence Egger calling *him* a sheep brain. He put his hands on his hips and lifted his shoulders as though he would sashay into a wrathful jig and he roared the chorus of a bitter song —

Oh, Lady, would you be kind enough to give me a bite to eat —
A piece of bread and butter and a ten-foot slice of meat?
A cake, a pie, a pudding, to tickle my appetite —

Let them *see*, if they could, that this was *their* song unless things were radically changed. He shoved his way past them as he sang, and stamped out the door. He went on singing as he took the blankets off the horses and climbed on to the seat in the wagon box —

Come all ye jolly jokers, and listen while I hum.
A story I'll relate to you of the Great American Bum.
From North to East, from South to West,
Like a swarm of bees they come.
They wear a shirt that's dirty
And full of fleas and crumbs.
I've met with all the toughest cops — as tough as they can be.
And I've been in every calaboose in this land of liberty.

Sunday, March 12

BY THE TIME the President got around to making a speech on the radio about the banks, a good many of them had already reopened. He called his talk a "fireside chat," and the image was not reassuring to George. "Chat" was an effete word, used either by women putting on airs or by wealthy people of either sex who had the time to waste in small talk while they sat around in parlors that bulged with bay windows hung in velvet and lace. A fireplace was an expensive luxury which added to the cost of heating a house by inviting down the chimney every prowling wind. The fireplace that came to George's mind was accoutered with hundreds of dollars' worth of brass, polished by some ill-paid servant. And over the mantel was an oil portrait of the Wall Street grandfather who made the fortune by speculating in Western land or by other questionable means.

"It is safer to keep your money in the reopened bank than under the mattress," the President said.

"*What* money?" George cried to Rachel. "Another rich man in the White House. Oh, how they love to tell us how they know all about being poor. '*You* ah fahmahs. *I* am a fahmah, too!' Oh, yes, *he's* a farmer too! What a nice little farmhouse he has there at Hyde Park!"

George sat at his own fireside, a bearable distance from the plump round stove that blistered the air in a six-foot radius, and helplessly cursed Harry Goodman while the President urged the people to bring their money back to the banks. But George predicted that putting the bankers back in control of the country might not go so smoothly as the President thought it would, and sure enough, there was quite a piece in the paper just a few days later. He read it aloud to Rachel after supper, yelling out into the kitchen over the noise she made doing the dishes.

"Look here what happened down in Oklahoma," he said. "I *told* you there was going to be bloodshed. Unless I miss my guess this is just the beginning. Fellow here—a state bank examiner—W. C. Ernest, his name was, was looking over the Citizens' State Bank. Paper says he telephoned the State Bank Commissioner to come and take over the bank. Then it says, 'As Mr. Ernest replaced the receiver of the instrument and turned to speak to the bank president, he was shot in the head and died instantly.' Well, I tell you, it'll get so the government don't dare send *out* anybody on jobs like that any more. Or anyhow they won't be able to find anybody that'll *go!* You know how that fellow from Bismarck roared in and out of here when he came to clean out Harry's bank. *He* knew his life wasn't worth a plugged nickel around here! Who cares? Might as well hang as starve. You wait. It can't help but start pretty soon."

Most of the time Rachel believed he was only relieving his feelings by talking this way. But once in a while he worried her. "Who do you think is going to start it?" she called in.

"How should *I* know?" he said irritably. "Who *ever* knows who starts a revolution? It just starts, that's all. Maybe the coal miners. Maybe the veterans . . . Hah! How do you like this? Right on the same page with this other story. President said he got ten thousand telegrams 'applauding his bank policy.' Well, that's a little late for

W. C. Ernest, isn't it? I wonder if Roosevelt has heard about *him* yet."

Thursday, March 23

THE NEWLY ELECTED German parliament organized, held its first meeting, handed all its power over to the newly elected Chancellor for four years, and dissolved itself again. Almost everywhere new officials were taking over, they were doing drastic things. Wild Bill Langer, the new governor of North Dakota, proclaimed a moratorium on payments of farm mortgages and decreed that there must be no more forced sales of premises or personal property used for agriculture.

George thought about that decree while he rode behind his team, round and round an eighty-acre field, turning two furrows at a time. The governor swore he would call out the state militia to restrain the county sheriffs from carrying out sales. They were already having battles over the Minnesota governor's proclamation to the same effect. George wondered if Langer would really follow through on what he'd said. Above all, he wondered if what Langer had said would carry any weight with Vick. According to Wild Bill Langer, Mr. James T. Vick would not be able to attach George Custer's stock and equipment in order to collect rent. George did not propose to try to beat Vick out of his rent, but on the other hand, if Vick did not loan him the money to get in the crop, Vick would have everything to lose and nothing to gain, the way George saw it. After all, there were always just two ways for Vick ever to get his rent — out of a crop or out of George's own possessions. Now there was supposedly only one — out of a crop. The more George thought about it, the more reasonable it was to expect that Vick would let him have the money.

Every day he plowed and figured. With his four-horse team and a two-bottom plow he could turn over four acres in a twelve-hour day. He could get by without plowing the other wheat field because he had plowed it last spring and it was loose enough just to disk and drag and seed. Even so, he had oats and corn and barley and hay to get in. He might have to get Ralph Sundquist over for a week or so with his team, and he would have to pay Ralph in cash because he didn't have either goods or labor to trade for Ralph's work.

On the last day of March the weather was unseasonably warm. This early in the year they were already falling behind their normal seasonal total of moisture. If it was going to be another drought year, he should get the crops in as soon as it was humanly possible in order to take advantage of what little moisture the winter had left behind. He decided he could no longer put off going to bargain with James T. Vick.

❦ ❦ ❦

Will had been watching and hoping to catch George driving by alone in the car. He was just coming from the barn when he spotted the old Ford below on the road and he jogged down his driveway and flagged George to a stop. George did not turn off the engine; he couldn't bear to be interrupted in a project — especially one that was so unpleasant to think about. Will found it even harder than usual to talk to him.

"Have you got a minute, George?" he asked.

"Just about that," George said.

"Rachel's mother and I — that is — I don't know whether you lost money in the bank or not," Will began, "but if you did, we'd like to let you have whatever you lost for as long as you need it. We've always kept an account in Jimtown. That is, I wish you'd ask us if you need help this spring, regardless . . . we . . . Rachel — might not need to know." He saw that George was already angry and he wondered miserably what he had done wrong, besides telling a lie about a sizable Jamestown account.

His first four words had been wrong. George took them as an affront to him as a son-in-law. Why hadn't Will said, "Rose and I"? Why "Rachel's mother and I," as though Rachel still belonged in her father's tall house on the hill, not in his own?

"We'll get the crops in, I reckon," George said. "Much obliged." He shifted into gear and pretended not to hear Will shouting, "Well, now, you know where to come if you change your mind!"

Will walked back up the hill. His legs seemed uncommonly

heavy. They made his toes come scudging into the ground at each step just an instant before he expected them to. He glanced up at the orchard, at the dead crab-apple tree over the box of money. He wondered if it was the pain in his belly that made his legs so heavy.

The thirty miles to Jamestown were gone before George had even begun to exhaust the choice words he might have said to Will or that he would like to say to James T. Vick. He had, in fact, spent the entire time assembling choice words, so that he found himself parking the car down the street from Vick's store without any clear idea of what he was actually going to say.

He made his way past the disgusting counters, wondering if Vick was watching him from the balcony. He flinched as one of the little change carriers whizzed over his head, so close that he could feel its breeze parting his hair. A damned store for women.

He stood in the door of Vick's office, holding his light summer cap in one hand, shaking Vick's hand with the other.

"How's the farm, Custer?" Vick shouted above the noise of the little cash carriers coming home.

"Still there, Mr. Vick," George said.

He decided to make an oblique approach. He began while Vick cleared papers off a chair for him. "They say it's going to be a bad grasshopper year, and the drought's going to be bad, too, maybe. I think I ought to put in more hay this year — hay and pasture. No rust and smut to worry about; not so much pest damage; drought don't hurt it so much; good for the land. If the hay don't bring any price, maybe I could feed a couple-three more cows through the winter. Cream prices are going up a little."

"Oh, no, Custer!" Vick burst in. "This is just the year for wheat. Government says the drought'll have the prices way up — better than they've been for years. No, this is the year to plant wheat and get whatever we can."

George had learned that an argument inevitably and quickly led to the same conclusion. Vick always confronted George with the same simple alternatives — George could obey or lose his lease. If George lost his lease, he would also lose all the improvements he had made. George knew that if Vick even got around to offering him those alternatives today, he would hit him. He started over. "I want to plant a new kind of seed this year. The money for it was in the bank. I never saved back any seed last fall. If I don't put in a crop, I guess you don't get any rent, do you? That is, if Langer sticks to his guns." His hand was being forced too early in the game. With Vick he always found himself having to bet his chips before the draw.

Vick tilted back his swivel chair and smiled. He had big, oddly flat lips. When he stretched them to smile, George thought of the ragged strip of dull red rubber tied to a boy's slingshot.

"Always burning your bridges, aren't you, Custer? That's no way to do business. Why didn't you save some seed?"

"It's *useless* to keep on planting Marquis year after year! The rust takes more of it every year. I figured last fall I might as well make the switch to Ceres this spring or — or just get out! The rust don't bother Ceres and the smut *couldn't* be any worse than it is in the Marquis, and the Ceres is supposed to take the drought better. I *didn't* burn my bridges! I saved every dime I could toward this seed."

"Did you actually have enough in the bank to see you through?"

God, how he hated the impertinent way the man had of pinning him down! Landlords! Vick was so lucky that nobody had killed him yet.

"I figured on a very small loan." George never could lie.

"Well," Vick said. He let his chair fall forward and bounce him out toward the file where he kept his claims on the sweat of men. "I think we can arrange for the seed."

He pulled out George's papers. He figured on scratch paper for a moment and then laid the paper on the edge of his desk, inclining a shoulder toward George to indicate that he should move his chair closer. George did not move his chair, but he leaned forward. Vick pointed with his pencil to his scattered bits of arithmetic, as though George would have trouble following him. George gritted his teeth.

"Here's the way the deal works," Vick said, in a tone he might have used in explaining the store's policies to a new clerk. "Another sixty acres in wheat — that will still leave you a hundred for pasture and corn and hay."

"How do *you* know how much hay and pasture I'll need?" George cried. "It depends on how *dry* it is, for Christ's sake! It depends on how soon I have to start feeding hay when the pastures give out!"

"Get rid of some stock."

"I *told* you, the cream is what's keeping us going! And I've got to have *horses*, for Pete's sake. You want me to hitch my *wife* to the plow, maybe, like them Roosians used to do?"

"The *hell* with cream," Vick said. "You and I don't have any agreement about cream. I don't care how much cream you sell. It's wheat I care about. That's the deal. Take it or leave it."

George's heart shook his great chest under the denim jacket he had worn as an insult to Vick. He was very hot. His hands were slippery on the varnished arms of his chair. His hands were hungry, pleading to wrap themselves around a neck. He stood up.

"I can get along without your money, Mr. Vick," he said. "I'll put the crops in the way the lease stands now. A hundred and sixty acres of wheat. A third of the net to you. Good morning."

He strode from the office and before he had taken three steps he knew he had got out just in time. A minute longer and he might have killed him.

On the way home he thought about Will's offer. He would have to take him up on it now, or else get out. He would have to go to the one man he had vowed never to go to. And even after he had borrowed from his wife's father, he still had to put up with the same galling agreement with Vick. Before, he had been running to stand still; now he was going in debt to stand still. Now he would be entirely dependent on what the Ceres and the fall prices did. If they let him down he would be hopelessly ensnared by two old men — James T. Vick and Will Shepard. It wasn't right that the accident of birth should place one generation in a position of such power over another — just because they had been around to get when the getting was good. Will had cashed in on every good year since the beginning of the century. He had bought a section of choice land that had increased in value more than three hundred per cent in a decade, so that the original mortgage, which had once been so huge, had decreased to an almost insignificant percentage of the value of the farm. And then Will had paid off that mortgage with war-inflated dollars and with wheat prices five times what they had been when he bought the farm and a dozen times what they were again now, a dozen years later.

And where had *he*, George Armstrong Custer, been during those good years? Working for nothing on his father's farm, that's where. A boy in his late teens, already stronger than most men, doing more work than most men, thirsting to go to war, kept home by his father to raise the wheat that would win the war. Oh, yes, win the war, and make so much money for his father that the old man had felt rich enough to speculate with it and finally lose his shirt. He managed to lose it even before the crash, and then he managed to die from drinking a little too much Indiana Red Eye and leave a farm, mortgaged in inflated dollars, to the boys who had earned him the money that had made him feel so rich.

Then a very young schoolteacher had come to take the one-room school where he had gone himself. She had not the vaguest notion of how to make the big boys behave, and he had been amused by her helplessness. In fact, he had been infatuated by it. He had wanted to protect her, even though he had enjoyed teasing her himself.

He had married her, and moved off his father's farm, leaving the financial wreck to his brothers. The next thing he knew, he was leasing a half section conveniently adjacent to the farm of his father-in-law. That was his life in a nutshell, he thought.

Yet all it took to succeed, if a man had been born at the right time, was a good piece of property, the strength to farm it profitably, and the sense to hang on to it, to get it free and clear, and to keep it that way. Then a man could get through the drought years; he could farm the way he wanted to. What did a man's good farming sense count for if a city man made all the rules? But his father-in-law and his own father had been born at the right time. His own father had been a fool. His father-in-law had been a hard-working, conservative farmer. It was all that simple. And now Will Shepard was in a position to make loans to his son-in-law even when millions of solid citizens all over the country were finding themselves entirely wiped out.

When George got home it was nearly two in the afternoon. Rachel had just finished draining some soured curds from their thin pale yellow water.

"You haven't eaten yet, have you?" she asked. "I'll have this Dutch cheese ready in a minute. I can fry you some bread if you want it. I'm ready to bake this batch and the last of the old loaf is pretty dry."

He looked at her standing before her cupboard, adding another dollop of cream, getting a clean teaspoon, tasting the cheese, sprinkling on a bit more salt, mashing it into the cheese. Her short, durable figure, built like her father's, was clothed in a cotton print dress and an apron she had made herself. Her arms, bare below the short sleeves, were still tan from last summer. She never burned. He, on the other hand, never seemed to stop burning. And every winter he became white and vulnerable again. She did not look at him, pretending that the cottage cheese took all her attention. She was letting him choose exactly what and when to tell her, and her delicacy defeated him. It neutralized him, just as Vick had succeeded in neutralizing him. There was never anything to strike at.

He sat alone at the round table, looking down the hill toward the barn and chewing the food she put before him. The day was shot as far as accomplishing anything in the field went. He might as well let the horses rest for the afternoon. They needed it. If he hustled he could clean the barn in the time left before evening chores.

He mopped his plate with the last piece of bread until it was polished free of cheese and potatoes. He changed into his old overalls, put his rubber boots back on, pulled his cap hard on his head, and paused, with his cotton work glove on the doorknob. He opened his mouth again, but when he spoke it was only to bring up a small question concerning their daily existence.

"You can go over to fetch Lucy from school, can't you?" he asked. "This job'll take me right up to milking time."

Why don't you ask me now, he thought. Why don't you say, "Well, how did it go? What luck did you have?"

Her failure to ask was another indication that she no longer cared what became of their future together. Her lack of curiosity was another sign of her lack of commitment to him. She did not ever ask to know what he was thinking.

"All right," she said. "I need a few things at the store anyway, so I might as well go after her."

He tipped her chin roughly in his glove and made her look at him. "I sure picked a swell time to get born, didn't I? Twenty-five years sooner and I'd have cleaned up on wheat. Twenty-five years later and I'd have been chauffeured back and forth from school like Little Lord Fauntleroy."

He banged the door against the weatherstripping and walked down to the barn. He did the cows' stalls first because they were the most offensive to him. He never liked to put off a distasteful job, because he could not stop thinking about it till it was done. He didn't mind the droppings in the horse stalls, for unless the smell became too concentrated, it was actually pleasant to him — rather like a faintly decaying hayfield, much distilled.

As he squeezed the handle of the shovel and lifted the mushy loads out of the cows' trench he said over and over to himself, "That liver-lipped swindler will *never* know how close he came today. He'll *never* know."

How could an ignorant dime-store owner be expected to know anything about a new kind of wheat, anyhow? He was too busy buying celluloid dolls from Japan for a penny each and selling them for a dime. And then the Japs were using every American dollar they could get their hands on to buy guns to kill the Chinese. If nobody else on earth made a thing George needed, he would get along without it rather than buy anything that said "Made in Japan." But a man who made his money selling celluloid dolls and supported Japanese aggressors who were slaughtering Chinese farmers and their families — *that* man was going to twit *him* about burning his bridges when he decided he had to change the seed he was planting.

Nobody in the vicinity was planting it yet, but they all would. He knew they would just as soon as they all saw how well the Ceres was going to do for him. It took a little guts to be first to try something, that was all.

For a long time Marquis had been the favorite of hard red spring wheat growers, but stem rust did more damage every year, as the rust spores became ensconced in a wider and wider area, and new varieties, traveling north on the rigs and clothing of the threshing crews, mixed with the old spores and grew strong through hybridization.

Rust and smut were the two ravaging diseases. Smutty wheat brought less from the millers because cleaning it was an expensive proposition, but at least there was some wheat to cut with the binder; smutty wheat wasn't collapsed on the ground in red-brown broken stalks devoid of kernels. Seed wheat could be treated for smut, but nothing could stop rust except the kind of state-wide effort to wipe out its winter host — the barberry bushes — that the government would not make. So Ceres was George's last hope. It was rust resistant and more drought resistant than Marquis. It had been developed at the North Dakota Experimental Station just a couple of years ago, and it ought to be right for North Dakota if any wheat was any more.

No brand of wheat was immune to wheat midges, sawflies, pink maggots, cutworms, leaf hoppers, plant lice, billbugs, army worms, black chaff, Hessian fly, chinch bugs, true wireworms, false wireworms, strawworms, jointworms, white grubs, or grain moths. And if the grasshoppers were bad enough they could strip the fields, as they had done a couple of times within his father's memory, and the brand of wheat would not make any difference at all to them, either. Moreover, Ceres and Marquis were equally vulnerable to dust storms and wind. Hail, or even a hard rain, would dislodge the hardening kernels during their maturing weeks, and the kind of seed he had planted wouldn't make any difference at all.

But after the way his Marquis had surrendered to rust last summer, George had made up his mind never to plant it again. He had simply sold every bushel he harvested and decided that one way or another he would find the money for the new seed when the spring came. Now spring had come, and he was left with exactly one place to get the money. He squeezed hard on the shovel handle again. The man he had sworn never to go to for help — the man he had cut off this very morning.

He pushed the wheelbarrow down the aisle and laid a row of planks from the barn door to the manure pile across the slushy barnyard. That morning the ground had been hard with thickly frosted ridges outlining the hoof prints in the mud of yesterday's thawing, and water had been frozen in the deeper tracks. Tomorrow morning it would be the same. Spring came reluctantly to this northern place, but it was here, nevertheless.

Ceres, goddess of growing things, was the name that had been in his mind all winter long. No more Marquis, that debilitated aristocrat which bled so easily that he could lose up to fifty per cent of his crop in a bad rust year. Ceres, after all, was of the family of aristocrats also, as far as wheat went. Hard spring wheat was bread wheat — the best in the world. All the soft wheats and the winter wheats grown farther south and west were used for inferior products — restaurant pies and crackers and abominable new kinds of cereals to be eaten cold. Durum wheat was used for macaroni and spaghetti and other foreign things. But the bakers had to have hard spring wheat for bread, even when they mixed it with winter wheat. When there was an American surplus of the softer wheats, they still would have to import Canadian spring wheat in the years when North Dakota did not produce enough. It took an austere climate to create that kind of wheat — wheat that grew hard and full of protein under the withering semidesert sky. It was the kind of durable, determined grain that could survive and flourish on the smallest possible margin — very much like the men who grew it. Like George's ancestors, who had fought for and built the state that men like James T. Vick were now taking away from them. Half the farmers in the state were tenants now, like George.

Nevertheless, George was still proud to have been born in a state that created distinction from hardship. It pleased his Scottish blood. If ever there was a one-crop state, it was the one he lived in.

The trouble was that a state with such extreme dedication to one crop — bread — was so helpless when something went askew with the market for bread. When the world was lean with war and could buy bread, North Dakota fattened; when the world was lean with peace and could not buy bread, North Dakota starved — through drought and bumper crops. A North Dakota farmer ought to be able to lay up enough cash and own enough livestock so that he didn't have to plant wheat at all in such a bad year as this one promised to be. But half the farmers in the state had to do what a city man told them to do. The economy needed radical changes that were long overdue. The absentee landlords must be stripped of the absolute power they had over their tenants, the railroads and elevators must be forced to abandon their monopolies, and the Wall Street and Chicago speculators must be outlawed. Until these changes were made, George Armstrong Custer must go on obediently plowing up a hundred and sixty acres of dry blowing land and trying to get a wheat crop out of it.

That night he sat down after supper with his books and figured out how much money he would have to borrow. He needed a little over two hundred bushels of seed, for he always planted the optimum amount — roughly a bushel and a half to the acre. It would be around a hundred and fifty dollars for seed alone. Considering all the other things he would need cash for, including the biggest expense — paying the threshers — he didn't see how he could possibly get by on less than three hundred dollars cash between now and September.

He must not count on more than forty dollars from cream between now and then, for the prices always dropped in the summer when the market was glutted from all the freshening cows. His five-year record book showed that the year before the Wall Street crash a decent cow, producing around a hundred and fifty pounds of butterfat a year, had brought in sixty-nine dollars cash just for her cream, not counting the skim that had gone to pigs, calves, and chickens. But last year, just four years later, a herd of six cows had netted him less than a hundred and fifty. Last year, of course, had been the worst year in history, but even so, when he put the two sets of figures together, they were hard to take.

"Rachel!" he called out to the kitchen. "Do you realize that a man could make as much money with *two* cows in 1928 as he can make with *six* now? It just works out almost to the last penny. A man sweats just as hard and grows just as much feed and cleans out just as much manure and he makes a third as much money. It just don't figure, does it?"

"Nothing makes sense," she said.

"What did you say?"

"*Nothing* makes sense!"

It bothered him to have her agree with him. "Yes it *does* make sense! It's just the same old story. Just the rich getting richer and the poor getting poorer. Just Jay Gould and J. P. Morgan and Jim Hill and all the rest of them getting crookeder and richer every day. Why, these senators are *proving* it on them every day — what they all did on the stock market, and the way they got their monopolies on the railroads! *They're* the only ones to blame for the crash — all those birds on Wall Street. *They're* the fellows we have to thank for getting twenty-six cents a bushel last fall. But you don't see any of those big guys losing their shirts, do you? No. Only the little guy."

But even with the farmer's market ruined, cream prices were a little better this spring because of the drought. George thought he was safe in counting on forty dollars cash from cream between now and when the wheat checks came in. He would ask Will for two hundred and fifty dollars. Four years ago that much money would not have looked like the fortune of half a lifetime.

He wouldn't have been quite so reluctant to borrow if he could have done it a little later in the season — June or July, with a stand of growing wheat as security. But this way he was borrowing against ground that still froze every night — ground that wasn't even his — ground that he was utterly committed to, though it was in no way committed to him. His operating margin had narrowed into a wedge that was threatening to pinch him to death. Everything and everybody had a hold on him, and *he* had a hold on nothing. So long as rich men wrote the laws, what could a little man do?

Wednesday, April 12

George awoke in the prairie dawn at four in the morning, too hot under the quilts that had been just right when he went to bed, knowing what that hot feeling meant — that the south wind of spring had come and that today was the day he would finally have to borrow money from his father-in-law.

Money became more confusing every day. There were forty bills in Congress calling for some kind of inflation. There was an embargo on shipments of gold from American shores. But rich American citizens who knew the revolution was imminent had already sent so much gold to Switzerland in the last three years that the Swiss, feverishly building vaults, had stopped paying interest on the gold and started charging storage costs.

Some people, convinced by William Jennings Bryan and his Cross of Gold, predicted that leaving the gold standard would be the salvation of the country. Other people, usually rich Easterners, predicted that leaving the gold standard would lead to the violent end of Western civilization — as they put it. George, being a follower of the silver-tongued Nebraskan, believed that his silver standard was already half a century overdue. But whether Roosevelt followed the lead of Bryan or not, there was one thing about money that George was dead sure of when he woke up that morning. Today was the day he had to go to his father-in-law and ask him for two hundred and fifty dollars.

All the while he milked he became more and more furious with his wife's preaching father — hypocritical old man! He must have kept *plenty* of it in Jamestown all the time or he wouldn't have it to spare now. No wonder the old man didn't want inflation — not with the amount of cold cash *he* had stashed away. When he got back up to the house and found that Rachel had not quite got the separator together, he erupted.

"For Pete's sake! *I* go down and pitch hay to six cows and milk every last one of them by myself and *you* can't even get the damned separator together!"

"Maybe that's because *you* forgot to run the rinse water through it last night, and when I started to put it together this morning, it was so sour I had to wash every single disk!"

She clamped the two spouts over the thirty-two disks, banged the last fitting on top of them, snatched up a large aluminum float, and let it drop into place with a clang that stung his ears.

"Rachel!" he shouted. "What on earth *ails* you!"

He began turning the handle with a retaliatory spleen. A bell on the handle rang with every revolution until the speed was up. "*Ting! Ting! Ting!*" it went, as the thirty-two disks spun faster and faster, building up the force that would separate the milk, particle by particle. When the bell stopped ringing he turned the valve and let the milk flow from the bowl on to the float. The whining groan of the heavy parts whirling in the machine was the only sound in the kitchen.

After he had run all the milk through, he poured the warm cream into one of the cans on the porch and wrote out two tags on the kitchen table.

"I'm going over town to take in the cream and I'll take Lucy," he said. "Is there anything you need?"

"Why do *you* have to take it? Isn't Otto going to pick it up today?"

"I want to go in and weigh it myself on old man Adams's scales," George said. He was being half honest. He *did* want to check on the weights he'd been getting from the creamery in Jamestown. But mostly this was the best excuse he could think of for getting over to see Will during the daytime when he could try to catch him alone outside. "Besides," he added, "I don't trust Wilkes as far as I could throw his Percheron by the tail. If he thought he could get away with it, I wouldn't put it past him to bring along an empty can of his own and just fill it up with a few dips out of all the other cans he hauls."

"Oh, George," Rachel said. "You *mustn't* talk that way about a *neighbor!*" She glanced at Lucy, waiting behind George with her lunch pail. Lucy looked back with that assured gaze that said as clearly as a seven-year-old could, "Do you think *I* don't know all about the Wilkeses?"

"Phooey!" George said. He couldn't stand her sob-sister delicacy — just like her old man's. "*You* know the scoundrel as well as *I* do!" He started out the door. "Is there anything you need? You never answered my question."

"No . . . not really. But if you have time I wish you'd stop by the folks' and pick up that old brooder Dad said we could have. You're going to have to fix it before we can use it and you might as well get it so you can work on it this Sunday."

George was simultaneously grateful and annoyed at being handed such a good excuse for stopping to see Will. He was angry because he had to have feelings of gratitude or relief at all, and because now it would look to Will as though he had thought up the brooder himself as a way of reopening the conversation he had so rudely closed. But still, if he should get caught with Rose and be unable to find Will, it would be handy to have a ready-made bit of business with *her*.

"I reckon I can manage that," he said.

In the car he said to Lucy, "Days are long again, and three miles is no distance. You ought to be walking home from now on. When

I was a boy, I used to walk almost four miles to school every day, whether the days were long or short, till they built that new school next to our place. When I was your age I could have walked home from town in less than an hour."

"So can I!" Lucy cried. "I'll do it tonight! I can walk just as fast as a boy!"

It tickled him to be able to get her goat so easily, but he was irritated, too, because she had no business using that tone of voice to him.

"*Just* watch yourself," he said coldly.

She bent her head so he couldn't see her face and outlined with her finger the reflections in her lunch pail. Her cheeks were scarlet. She had a Custer temper all right.

"You can walk tonight," he told her when he stopped the car at the schoolyard gate.

She jumped out and ran with a straight, easy stride toward the building. She had the best body and the strongest run of any child he could see in the yard. What a waste it was that she hadn't been born a boy!

He drove back over the tracks from the depot with the two weight tags for a net total of seventy-six pounds of cream, dated and signed by Millard Adams, stuck in the big pocket of his overalls. There just might be some fireworks now, if the creamery check didn't square with this weight. And if the creamery *did* agree, there might still be some fireworks. He just might have to ask Otto, how come? Prices were low enough to make him pretty mean about being cheated by a deadbeat who already overcharged him for hauling. And when George Custer felt mean enough . . .

Rose heard the car when he was halfway up the drive, and stepped out of the house with a welcoming smile that flickered from happiness to civility when she saw that nobody was with him. She didn't expect to see him during plowing season at this time of day, though Rachel often came with the baby on her way back from taking Lucy to school and stopped for a few minutes.

"Rachel said you folks had a brooder you wasn't planning to use this spring," George said.

"Oh, I'm so glad you decided you could use it," Rose said. It seemed to George that she always said the wrong thing. He always saw through it when she tried to be polite to him. "I'll just run down and see if it's in the cellar," she went on. "I think that's where I had Will put it."

She was forever rushing off to frenzied activity when George appeared. It didn't hurt his feelings any, but it made him nervous. Sometimes it left him standing idle and intensely conscious of his two hundred pounds of unemployed muscle while he had to watch a thin old woman do something she refused to let *him* do. It was a way she had, he felt, of putting him in his place. Now she proposed to wrestle an unwieldy five-foot disk of galvanized tin up a dark steep set of stairs while he stood uselessly at the top.

She was already down there rummaging about below him.

"Let *me* carry it up, Rose, for Pete's sake!"

"Oh, I'll just see if it's *down* here," she fussed back up at him.

He stood looking through the kitchen window to try to catch a glimpse of Will. Finally she came back up to report that the brooder was not in the cellar.

George had one more chance to find Will alone, if only she would let him go now by himself. He would pack up the whole family and head West before he would let Rose hear him ask Will for money.

"I'll call him," she said. "He's out in the sheep shed, I think."

She pushed up the window and yelled, "Will? Will?" The way she would start on a high note and then let the one syllable of the name slide down her throat, straining and gargling to get volume from an "l," was enough to make a man come running to see what awful thing had happened. George was certainly glad that Rachel didn't call *him* that way. Not that he would have stood for it.

"Why, *I'll* go find him, Rose," George cried.

He started for the shed, hurrying to head Will off. Sheep were one of the things he and Will disagreed about. George wouldn't have a sheep on his place. He simply couldn't stand the beasts, and besides, they ruined good pasture land. Will was putting salve on the ewes' teats so they wouldn't crack and chap in the freezing nights. He, too, was a little surprised to see George at that time of day. He pulled a blue bandanna out of his hip pocket and wiped his hands on it. "How's it going, George?"

"Pretty fair," George said. "Rachel thought I might as well pick up that brooder you folks don't need. Rose can't seem to find it." He thought Will looked relieved. Was that because Will had had second thoughts about the loan?

"Oh, I meant to tell her," he said. "I left it out in the granary. Let's go get it."

Even after the sliding door had stopped its grumbling and echoing, they could still hear the scraping flight of rodents. "*Damn* the vermin!" Will said. He had to be really exasperated to swear, and he was. He had stored as much wheat as the granary would hold rather than sell at last fall's prices. But the rats and mice and insects had seemed to converge on him from the whole country. Their multiplying and marauding had gone on despite his traps and poisons, and the price rise he had been waiting for was still so slight that it would hardly finance the war he had been carrying on, let alone make up for the wheat he had lost.

Will had read the Bible through more times than he had counted — the first time before he was twelve, the age of Jesus in the temple at Jerusalem. And one of the verses he had memorized from early childhood was the one that whispered above the scuttling of the mice each time he opened the granary door, as though the grain spoke from the heavy cold bins: *Lay not up for yourselves treasures upon earth, where moth and rust doth corrupt, and where thieves break through and steal. . . . Take no thought for the morrow. . . . Consider the lilies of the field. . . .* Wasn't a man supposed to look out for his family the best way he could? It was certainly hard to know.

They walked into the room where he kept the sacks of feed and chicken mash, and he pulled the brooder away from the wall.

"Some of the braces have to be fixed," he said. "You'll have to find some kind of top for the water jar and clean up the burner a little. It's really in perfectly good shape, but we just can't use it this year. We got too many chicks last spring. A big flock don't hardly pay its way now, anyhow."

George could see that it wasn't going to occur to Will to bring up the subject. "Well, now then," he stalled. "I reckon it won't take too much to get her in shape." It was now or never.

"I figured I could make a deal with Vick for the seed wheat and the thrashers," he said, "but the damn fool won't let me put in any feed and hay if he lends it to me. I had — most of it in the bank."

"How much do you need?" Will asked.

"Two hundred and fifty would do it, I guess."

"Are you sure that's enough? I can spare you three hundred without hurting myself at all." Will felt that he hadn't said that the way he wanted to. It sounded as though he was rubbing it in.

"Two hundred and fifty will be a great plenty, and I'll be much obliged," George said icily. He'd taken it the wrong way, of course. "I'll pay you the same interest Goodman would have charged me — the dirty little kike."

Will wished he could defend Harry, but he didn't dare.

"I'll get it here the first of the week and we'll write up a little note," Will said.

George picked up the brooder and Will followed with the glass accessories. They were loading the brooder in with the two empty cream cans when Rose came out with a pan of hot cinnamon rolls covered with a dish towel. She put the rolls in the front seat and George climbed in beside them. "Much obliged, folks," he said.

They watched him go. "I can't see why George is so set on Ceres," Will said. "I bet I'll beat him with Marquis this year, just the way I beat his Marquis last year. Seems like there's a couple new hybrids every year, but they never do anything except right in the spot where a bunch of Fargo professors are coddling them along in a little kitchen garden. Look at what happened to Clarence Egger when he planted Hope. That just about ruined his hopes for good — that's what *Hope* did. Ceres probably won't work out a bit better, either, but then, you can't make a young man see things like that."

❧ ❧ ❧

George was irritated by the banging of the brooder against the cream cans, but he was even more irritated by the spicy smell of the hot bread. He was sure that Rose was always sending food to his house because she felt his family might not be properly fed.

He walked back into his house carrying a new burden now — no longer of anticipation but of fulfillment. The burden of humbling himself was past, but the burden of debt was just begun. For him the debt was by far the easier burden of the two. Still, if he didn't get a harvest, there was absolutely no place left to turn. He had already gone to the man he had managed to avoid going to ever since he had married that man's daughter.

"I got the brooder," he said to Rachel. And then, as gratuitously as usual, it seemed to her, he added, "I'll bet your dad has lost a hundred bushels of wheat this winter. That granary is a regular breeding ground for pests. I *told* him he should have gone ahead and got rid of some of that wheat. I've never known the time that that man has listened to reason."

He stopped to hear what was coming over the radio. Then he guffawed bitterly. "Well, *somebody's* happy *somewhere* today! Beer and wine *over* the counter! Roosevelt better look out. All the bootleggers'll be voting Republican next time. Yes, sir! Roosevelt — the friend of the forgotten man! No more Goat Whiskey and Indiana Red Eye. What in the world will the politicians and cops do for graft money now? Why, even your little brother can go on a legal bender today — that is, if he's in one of the right spots. Where was he, did you say, when he sent the last letter?"

"Arizona. On a ranch."

"Well! He's in business then. Did you hear it? Arizona was all ready for Roosevelt. Stuart can go on a nice safe drunk, without losing his eyesight or paralyzing his hands and feet. And he won't have to guzzle any more canned heat nor antifreeze."

"Oh, George, why do you hate everybody in my family so much!"

"Because they're hypocrites! Lucky hypocrites that just happened to get born at the right time. They got in when the getting was good and now they try to tell *me* it wasn't luck — it was their hard work and their God-damned religion!"

❦ ❦ ❦

In a few more weeks Lucy would be promoted to the third grade, beginning the next fall. And still she would be in the same room where she had been this year and last year, and probably have the same old teacher. There would not be a single new thing to look forward to except the miseries of multiplication. She had finished the third-grade reader before she was out of the first grade.

If there had been anybody at home to play with, Lucy would have preferred never to go to school, but Cathy was too little to be much fun. At school she sat at her desk and dug her toes into her shoes all day long, waiting for the big clock over the door to release her. After she had had a pair of shoes for two or three months, the innersoles were worked up into ridges between her toes and the ball of her foot.

By this time of the year the humps were as big as they could get and she could feel the shapes of all her toes in them. She had torn away all the lining from the uppers by scraping at them with her toenails, and large holes were wearing up through the soles, layer by layer, to meet the holes she made with her toes. It was because she skipped so much, her mother said, that she was so hard on shoes, and Lucy tried to remember not to skip, especially in gravel.

Now, with the winter wind suddenly gone and the heated gravel making the bottoms of her feet warm, she felt a hateful itchiness under her skin when she thought of being trapped in the second-grade row, between the first- and third-grade rows, for this whole first day of spring. All day long she had not got over being mad at her father, either, and she had hunched over her papers so Douglas Sinclair couldn't copy from her. If boys were so much smarter than girls, why did any boy she had ever sat behind always want to copy her papers? If only she dared ask her father *that* question! And she could chin herself more times than Douglas could, or than either of the other two boys in her grade. She *had* told her father *that*, and he had said that was because the boys lived in town and weren't like the farm boys he had in mind. But he would see, now, how much faster she could walk home than Douglas Sinclair ever could.

Right here, however, she had to walk slowly and make as little noise as she could, for fear of Mr. Greeder's mean bull, and she put her hot coat back on because she was wearing a red blouse.

It was not polite to say the word bull, or even to think it. In fact, it was practically a sin. Lucy had begun to wonder, lately, how a person was supposed to keep impolite or even terrible words out of her head. She even knew two words that were so bad people only wrote them in different places and never said them, but still the words said themselves in her head; they were very simple words and she knew how they would sound, even though she didn't know what they meant or why they were terrible.

She couldn't see the *cow*, she said loudly in her head, but still she did not dare to unbutton her coat. Two things were sure to make a *cow* sense your presence, no matter how far away from the road he was. The two things were running or showing something red. It was just the same thing as having a dog smell you if you were afraid.

Finally she reached the foot of the long hill with her family's mailbox at the top of it, but just as she was starting up, she heard the horses and the creaky buggy behind her. She knew who it was, without looking, by the buggy and the voices. The buggy was so old that there were no more like it in the world. Its black leather top flapped and tilted over a trio of struts coming up on either side of the seat. Behind the double triangles made by the struts sat the stiff black figures, strangely flat and hazy, as though they were hiding in a very old photograph from which they would jump out and come alive at any instant.

At once the sounds of being under water began inside Lucy's head, and that showed she was afraid, even when she had made up her mind that she wasn't. It's only Gid and Gad, she said. Sissy! *Sissy!* SISSY!

But they looked exactly like every picture of a witch she had ever seen. One appeared to be skinny and the other fat, but all the skin and shape of a woman that ever showed on them was their faces. From their chins down they were heaps of black tassels of shawls and cloaks and heavy black cloth of sleeves and swooping skirts. The buggy drew closer and the sounds of being under water became loud and continuous in her ears.

They're not witches. They're just old maids. That's all that ails them, Daddy said. But they're mean. Horses don't pick up their feet that way, so high and fast, as if the ground was afire under them, if they haven't been trained with chains looped around their legs above their fetlocks. And it's even against the law to bob their tails like that. Daddy said so. It's too cruel to cut off a horse's tail. But they just have horses like that because their family used to be rich and rich people always used to have them. That's what he said. Gid and Gad were too good for the men around here, they thought, and now they're nothing but old maids. Old maids are nothing but grown-up women who don't get married. Not witches.

Anyway, why would real witches need real horses? But perhaps the horses were not real either. A clock could chime or a magic bugle could blow and the horses could turn back into something else.

"Let us give you a ride!"

She had been going to jump into the ditch and run for it if they came after her, but her legs just stood there.

"Put your foot on the step there. There's lots of room."

She could feel the way the bones under the black cloth were swaying and pressing together in order to fold her in. At the level of her eyes a pointed shoe stuck out from under the cloth. A line of black fasteners ran down the side of its wrinkled instep. It was impossible to imagine a foot inside the shoe.

"I just go up there," she whispered, waving her hand at the tiny mailbox so far away.

"But that's the hardest part of the walk. Hop in here, and we'll take you up. Do you climb inside, now, and see if the oven is warm yet."

"Oh, *please* let me go!"

The witch shut her mouth and her lips disappeared as if she had eaten them. She slashed the horses with her long black whip and the team went into a gallop from a standing start.

Lucy was afraid to move till they were halfway up the hill, still at a gallop. Then she began to run. She didn't stop until she had turned into the driveway. By then the need of her lungs for air and the underwater sounds in her head were as bad as they were the time last summer when she jumped off the dock into the James River before she knew how to swim. A laughing high-school girl whom she still hated had reached into the water, finally, and pulled her out by the straps across her back. At first she had been thankful, but then she had become embarrassed as she stood there coughing and coughing and coughing, surrounded by laughing people. Sometimes at night, and often when she had done something silly, she would think about that laughing girl who saved her life and grit her teeth trying to stop the embarrassment from burning her face and prickling her eyes with terrible dumbbell sissy tears.

She was beginning to feel it now. Her mother had told her always to be polite to Gid and Gad and not hurt their feelings, because they were sad not to have any little children, and not ever, ever to say they were old maids when they could hear her. Polite, polite. Bull, *bull, bull!* Old maid, *old maid!* "Oh, *please* let me go! Oh, *please* let me go!"

The mimicking noise in her head could just as well have been Douglas Sinclair running after her, mimicking that unbelievable scream. It went on and on, no matter how many impolite words she shouted back at it.

And still, with all the noise in her head, she thought of how horrible it would be to be an old maid. And then came the thought that even made her stop running. Could she ever marry Douglas Sinclair in order to keep from being an old maid? There was only the one hope left — the miracle she prayed for every night — that God would turn her into a boy so she wouldn't have to be an old maid, or marry a man either.

"Hello!" her mother said. "You're home so soon. Did somebody give you a ride?"

"Just ran," Lucy said. . . .

❧ ❧ ❧

It was getting cool in the shadow of the house, but it was warm in the pasture. Lucy slipped under the gate by the barn, straightened up, patted the two little celluloid ducks in her overall pocket to make sure they hadn't spilled out, and started for the far corner of the farm, running again.

Long before she rounded the hill that stood between her and the slough, she heard the innumerable, unceasing calls of the new flock of blackbirds that had come there to nest. She stopped to listen and watch for a minute. There was at least one bird on every cattail or bit of brush still standing after the winter storms. It was hard to see how a bird hung on to a straight-up-and-down stem that swung under it like that.

She followed one of the rivulets that fed the slough. Its source was a shady ravine where the snow and frost tarried the longest. The rivulet was deep and swift for a long way up the ravine. She took the ducks out of her pocket and launched them tenderly into the water. One of them was brown and the other was gray-blue. She had had them for three years now, and she saved them just for April.

The miniature river wound about hummocks sloped as subtly as the mile-round hills rising behind her. The hummocks were beginning to be green, and the washed black mud of the stream bottom was embroidered with sparkling circlets of unfolding leaves. Here and there the water gushed between dark rocks and the ducks leapt and twirled in the rapids. She made bridges of straw for them to swim beneath because she had always wanted to swim under a bridge herself. She rescued them from eddies and spoke to them about the adventure they were having and warned them about the huge and dangerous ocean they were sailing toward. If only she could be as small as the ducks and live in this enormous kingdom of brilliant water and unexplored forests. That would be a hundred times better even than being turned into a boy.

Each winter as the time for thawing drew near, she began to be afraid that the kingdom of the ravine must really have been a dream. Then she would look at the ducks waiting in their proper spot on the kitchen windowsill, so small against the great swirling feathers of frost on the glass behind them. She would know that in the interlude between the glacial winter wasteland and the flaming summer wasteland, those very ducks had swum down an emerald river in a fairy country that was wet and green, like the places she had read about.

When they reached the ocean, she left them in a safe cove and searched for a rock with which to make a great wave. In just a little while there would be no place to splash a rock for another whole year. The entreaties of the blackbirds rang wildly around her. What did they say to each other that excited them so much? It was awful to have to be a human being and never know what all the animals said and never get to live in a cave or a nest or a tunnel or the waving grasses in the slough.

A flight of small gray birds swept over the water, so close they nearly touched their own shadows. They could have been leaves blowing across ice. How glorious to fly like that and see your own luminous image like an arrow flashing beneath you.

Beyond the slough in the burgeoning pasture lay the blue pools of sky. How lovely to be a baby frog trying out first one pool and then another. Sometimes a cloud briefly dipped a white edge in a blue mirror. Sometimes a big cloud would blot out a mirror. Then suddenly Gid and Gad wheeled their black chariot between the earth and the sun, waving their black sleeves and spreading their barren skirts to eclipse the warm light, transforming the blue glass into a cold murky lake and causing the baby frog to kick out desperately with his long webbed feet and hide in the mud.

Sometimes even the whole pasture would go dark, and then the sun would streak through in some far spot and ignite the ground; she would see the spot burn with an unearthly yellow-green fire. Then the clouds would move again and the darkness and the fire would both be gone.

The sun told her that there was time for only one more voyage down the ravine. She must not be late with the cows. Cows could be very stubborn in new grass, especially this time of year when they were not in a hurry to be milked. Most of them were half dry because they would soon be getting new calves.

At last she put the two ducks back in her pocket, wrapped in her handkerchief to get dry and warm. The clouds had multiplied and massed in the sky and the shadows of them raced over her and turned the air frosty around her. She began to notice how icy the soaked wrists of her sweater felt and how wet the knees and seat of her overalls had gotten.

She ran up the hill that bordered the west end of the slough, hoping to find the cows before dusk overtook her. They were there, lined up against the fence and reaching through it, though there was not a whit more grass on the other side. Cows were never happy, once they came to a fence.

"Hie on there!" she yelled. "Cuh boss, cuh boss! Hie on there!" They swung their heads on their flat supple necks and looked at her, but they did not move. She picked up a small stone and shied it off the flank of the nearest one. They started off then, but they stopped to chew at every likely tuft they passed.

She studied the western horizon, feeling so much smaller now that the sun had gone from the pasture. The clouds banked above the hills had turned in a few minutes from white to deep blue. The sun was behind them, lighting their upper edges with a cold pale gold. Her father could always tell when it was going to rain by looking at the clouds. She wanted to be able to tell, too, so that some day he would *have* to say that she was just as smart as a boy.

He was waiting for her at the barn, smoking a cigarette and leaning against the edges of the open double doors.

"Right on time," he said approvingly. He seldom sounded that way, and she was encouraged to try again to please him.

"It looks like it might rain tomorrow, doesn't it?" she said, looking once more toward the west before they followed the cows into the barn.

"Could be," he agreed, in a half-listening tone. "Could be," he said again, for the rhythm of it.

She could tell he had forgotten she was there. She went up the hill to the house.

"How on *earth* did you get so wet?" her mother said. "You just got over one cold, and now you'll probably get another. Hang your sweater by the stove and change into your other overalls. And you better take off your shoes and put on your slippers. Then hurry and set the table."

It was impossible for Rachel not to worry over how thin Lucy was when she saw how purple the cold made her. Her little body seemed so breakable, with such long bony legs and such sharply pointed wrists and ankles. But whenever Rachel mentioned getting Lucy's tonsils out so she could gain weight, George would say, "Oh, pshaw! You ought to have seen *me* at that age! She's *fat* compared to what I was!"

"Why do Gid and Gad always wear such long black dresses?" Lucy asked.

Where did *that* question come from? Rachel looked out the west window of the kitchen at the gold-and-blue clouds. "Why, maybe because they're poor now, like all the rest of us. Maybe they don't have any other clothes."

She turned from the window to confront the deep inscrutable blue of the clouds in Lucy's eyes. They looked at her just the same way George's did when she didn't manage to say exactly the right thing to *him*. And sometimes those eyes, only seven years old, could look just as implacable as George's, and sometimes as shocking and furious.

Lucy took the ducks out of her pocket and arranged them on the windowsill. When she looked up again, the blue of her eyes was the happy artless blue of the clean melted-snow pools in a greening pasture.

Monday, April 17

THE WHEELER inflation amendment to President Roosevelt's farm relief bill was defeated in the Senate, thus leaving the value of the money under Will's dead crab-apple tree still in doubt. Most of the big banks in the country were open again, and whole cities, so Will read in the papers, were going on spending sprees. However, there were no spending sprees in Eureka, North Dakota, nor in a thousand or so other places a great deal like it. The Treasury Department closed permanently the banks in those places. Most of them were very like Harry's bank — little square wooden buildings set between other square wooden buildings on graveled prairie streets: little concentrations of desolation in the midst of millions of acres of desolation — emptiness distilled from emptiness. The desert sky and the blowing acres were omnipotent — immune to accusation. But the empty little banks with the boarded-over windows were there to point at, to explain all the other emptinesses, to be responsible for what had gone wrong with the world. The Treasury Department was so busy reopening the banks in big cities and restoring confidence to the country that none of the government auditors had got around to making final disbursements to Harry's depositors yet, but the depositors all knew what to expect, and it didn't matter that the auditors took their time about coming out to the country.

Will went out to dig up his money and take it back to the Guardian Trust Company in Jamestown. With the snow gone and the ground loosened up, he came upon the box after only a few spadefuls. It startled him; he had had the feeling that it was deeper than that. He held it in his hands and thought how he had no more right than any other man to be holding a box with his life savings in it.

He heard another whisper, like the one he always heard in the granary. *The rust of your gold and silver shall be a witness against you, and shall eat your flesh as it were fire. Ye have heaped treasure together for the last days.* And the one he must have had for a Sunday school memory verse before he was four years old — the one as short and unequivocal as a bullet — *For where your treasure is, there will your heart be also.*

Could his heart really be in this rusted box? Would he break the rusted lock to find the money gone and a jeering comic valentine — his heart — in its place? No, here was the paper money, not so crisp as it had been, but not rusted either — the treasure he had heaped together for the last days.

He took it into the house and stuck three hundred dollars in a vase far back on the top shelf behind the good dishes. He hoped he'd have a chance to slip it to George soon. He didn't like having that much money around loose. He changed into his suit and went out to the kitchen to say goodby to Rose.

He thought of something at the door. "Maybe we oughtn't to let Rachel know about this — let George tell her. And I let him think *you* weren't in on it either."

"I don't *expect* to talk to him about it! And I won't to Rachel either. She's got *enough* worries. I don't care *where* George tells her he got the money."

"Well, so long then," Will said. He didn't feel a hundred per cent safe about putting his money back into a bank. He wanted to stay in the kitchen with Rose and not go to Jamestown at all.

He tossed up the box, twirling it end over end, so high that it nearly touched the ceiling. "Come on. Get your hat and go to Jimtown with me."

"Will, have you gone out of your head?"

He would not have known, from the way he felt, that spring had come.

❧ ❧ ❧

That spring came like a wandering, useless uncle of the family, welcomed only by the dogs and children who could not see that it was a shabby deceiver. In the prairies from Texas to Saskatchewan its carousing roiled the dust of nine years of drought. Dust thickened over the new leaves before they were fairly uncurled, and dust now, instead of frozen miles of water, choked the space between the earth and the sun, causing that northward-moving star to swell and bleed in prophetic tides across the evening sky.

But the birds still flocked to the north in their sudden vast numbers, and the children played in the mud, and the seeds knew that it was springtime.

Rachel was in the dining room, delicately sprinkling the thread-thin seedlings of tomato plants, when she heard the babble of red-winged blackbirds arriving in the north grove. She went out to the porch to watch them come. The bare tree limbs were clotted black with them, and the whole sky seemed hardly able to contain their singing. She thought how harmonious they were — how the staccato flash of red on their obsidian wings was so like the staccato music they wrenched from their tireless throats.

They would wait only a little while in the grove before they followed the other blackbirds to the slough and began building their nests in the reeds. They would eat insects until the wheat began to head. Then they would eat wheat.

She never ceased to wonder at the incredible powers of birds for adaptation. These had flown perhaps a thousand miles from the South to raise their families in the northern prairie. Some people thought migrations were a habit left over from the Ice Age, but nobody really knew why birds migrated. Why didn't they just stay in the South all the time? Perhaps it was their migrations that kept them hardy and pliable and able to survive drastic changes in the world. Perhaps *people* ought to migrate too, and never strive to put down roots at all. It often seemed to her that the desire of human beings to own land was the cause of all their troubles. Their desire kept them enslaved, from one generation to the next. Yet how would a human being know who he was, without roots?

❦ ❦ ❦

George was getting the plowing done at an encouraging pace. The weather had been so favorable that he was actually doing as much work as he had planned to do, and that happened rarely. There was no land like this North Dakota prairie anywhere else in the world, he thought. But it was no good if it never got water, or if it was all allowed to blow away.

A man who wanted to farm that land had to do what the land

did. He had to explode with the spring explosion, and work as close to all the hours of the day as he could, just as the thawing winds and the germinating seeds worked all the hours of the day. And in the fall he ought to leave the ground strictly alone, the way the buffalo and Indians left the dying grass to hold the sleeping soil in the clasp of an ancient root system while the winds blew through the fall and winter and spring. But in the last few years George had seen more than one summer-fallowed field where the wind had completely leveled six-inch furrows. That was six inches of topsoil gone in one winter. It took a hundred years to make an inch of topsoil.

But the people who tried to farm too much land plowed up as much stubble as they could find in the fall, so they could have that much more time in the spring for disking, harrowing, and drilling. Will was one who did that. He had begun farming in the days when there were sizable stretches of unbroken prairie to help stop the dust, and like all other old men he figured that what had always worked should go on working.

George looked ahead and behind at the two incisive black lines he drew through the stubble — at the latitudes and longitudes he created. Among all the lines in the world that crossed and crossed and went to unknown points, only his own were significant as he rode the steel seat mounted over the two fourteen-inch plowshares, while the sixteen obedient hoofs plodded ahead of him, day after day.

When the flock of blackbirds passed between him and the clouds, he did look up for an instant. It wouldn't be long before they would be back to feed on the grain. Just one of the plagues visited upon the helpless earth by the busy sky. He looked back down between his legs at the plow blades just in time to see a fair-sized snake slither away behind him. Too bad a wheel or a blade hadn't got it. That snake would eat a hundred toads that would otherwise eat a hundred thousand insects. There were precious few creatures of a field that were on the side of the farmer, that was a cinch.

Halfway up the south side of the field he heard the clear brave call of a meadowlark. That was one of the few creatures on his side. Meadowlarks ate no grain at all — only insects by the millions — especially grasshoppers. The hoppers loved drought; they throve on it as the wheat perished from it. The USDA was putting out a lot of publicity about how bad the grasshoppers were going to be this year, trying to get the farmers to put out poisoned bait. But the farmers who had to borrow money for seed had none to spare for bait. In spot-checked areas around the Dakotas the USDA found 10,000 grasshopper eggs per square foot of sod. Four different varieties of them would begin to hatch in another week or so. Last year they had even stripped the leaves from the trees in some places, and left cornfields as bare as fallow prairie.

Yes, so far as George was concerned, there was no sound in the world like the call of a meadowlark — his friend that preyed upon his enemies. He heard it call again, beginning on a high G natural and dropping about a third to an E, then back to G, then down five notes to a C, then back to E and G, with a final trill all the way down to C.

He had an acute ear for music. When he was young, the boys had got together a little band for dancing, and he had played the clarinet. He had fingered out the meadowlark's call one day, and had been surprised to find how high it was. That call was one of the earliest sounds in his memory. When he was five or six years old, herding cattle far from the house, that call in the early morning had made the long day ahead seem less lonely.

As he passed a bunch of dead Russian thistles caught in the fence, he glimpsed the brightness of the lark's yellow breast. No doubt it was making a nest there. When it sat on the nest to hatch its eggs, the yellow breast would not show; only the brown back, striped and speckled with black, would be visible, so that from above the bird would look like the shadows of the thistles on the ground. But that clever coloring hardly helped it or its eggs or its babies so far as rats, weasels, barncats, coyotes, and egg-sucking dogs were concerned. Well, he hoped that particular one would manage to raise a hungry brood or two, to discourage the grasshoppers a little. He'd remember where it was and leave those thistles when he got around to burning.

A little way past the lark, the fence was sagging from its load of thistles and the dust they had stopped. He'd have to replace a post there if he didn't clear it out pretty soon. When he was growing up, the days of the real Western tumbleweed were still not over. It grew six or seven feet tall on a tough stem that broke away from the ground in the fall after a few frosty nights. It would roll on the round crown of its branches until the wind flipped it up and it landed on its stem. Then it would bounce into the air like a clown on a circus net. Tumbleweeds had no stickers, and if they were young enough and the cattle were hungry enough, the stock on the range would eat them.

But Russian thistles were a different story. They were shaped less like the tall cowboys who made the songs about tumbleweeds and more like the squat round immigrants who had stupidly transplanted them from the Old World. Russian thistles grew long hard barbs, and when they broke loose and started to roll, a man had to dodge or get nettled right through his overalls.

After the lark stopped singing, George heard few sounds save those made by the horses and the machinery. But the silence was filled with the mute strugglings of a multitudinous embryonic hostility — in the wombs of rodents, the egg sacs of birds, and the laid and unlaid eggs of insects. Even the seemingly impeccable air was at this instant drifting over his field the spores of ruinous diseases. . . .

Oh, it ain't gonna rain no more, no more;
It ain't gonna rain no more —
How in the heck can I wash my neck,
If it ain't gonna rain no more?

He sang loudly to the horses, to cheer them along and to do something about the silence.

"Hey, George!"

He almost jumped off the plow seat. Trust his wife's father to sneak up on a man from behind like that in the middle of an empty field.

Will held out an envelope. "I wrote this up for four per cent," he said. "Keep it for as long as you need it."

"Four per cent is not what I'd pay anywhere else, and you know it," George said. "I'll pay you eight."

"Whatever you say. But don't let it be on your mind, George. See you later."

"You bet," George shouted after him. "Much obliged."

I'll pay him *ten* per cent, he thought. "Don't let it be on your mind." Oh, no, of course not! Don't let a loan from your pious father-in-law be on your mind, especially when it's more money than you cleared on your whole damn wheat crop last year, especially when you had to borrow it because of the dirty Jew who was going scot-free at this exact instant while you were riding around a field making two furrows at a time with a four-horse team that ought to be replaced by a tractor which ate only when it worked.

No, don't let it be on your mind. I'll pay him *twelve* per cent, he said to himself, and he began to see how the wheat would grow around him—the good Ceres that would not rust, that would harvest maybe twenty bushels to the acre if the whole world didn't burn up before the summer was over.

Then the wheat was pouring out of the threshing machine, making a golden-brown mountain in the truck. He was driving it to the elevator where Adolph Beahr was unusually respectful. "By God, George! You was on the right track, after all!"

The price would be up because of the drought. Down South, the papers said, more than a third of the winter wheat acreage had already been abandoned. When the wheat checks were all in, his neighbors came to buy from him the seed they were now deriding him about, for the Marquis had barely been worth harvesting because of rust. And when George repaid the loan, at a higher interest than he would have paid Harry, he would offer to sell Will some Ceres seed at a much lower price than it was worth. He would show him that the *young* men were still able to hold their own when it came to passing out big favors.

❦ ❦ ❦

After he dropped Lucy at school the next morning, George went around to the elevator to order the seed. Adolph wasn't even there yet. The elevators and the railroads — even after thirty, forty, fifty years of battles — they still ran the farmer. They could even afford to keep bankers' hours. He didn't want to wait around. He'd come back in the afternoon to hand his borrowed money to this leisurely middleman. Then he could give Lucy a lift too.

Middlemen got sixty per cent of the consumer's food dollar. City people didn't know that. They blamed the high food prices on the farmer. Why didn't the newspaper editors and the trade union rabble-rousers take the trouble to come out and see just how rich the farmer was? The government had given the railroads so much land on either side of their rights-of-way that the grain elevators and flour mills had to be built on railroad property. Very simple to see what kind of schemes and monopolies this situation led to.

There were always ways to get around antitrust laws if you were big enough. But when the farmers got together and tried to build their own cooperative elevators — ah, that was a different story. The Supreme Court ruled that the farmers' cooperatives were an illegal "combination in restraint of trade."

As far as George was concerned, most farm organizations were not allowed to be anything more than vehicles to carry the ballyhoo of the big farmers to ignorant city people. The Farmers' Union appeared to be on the side of the little fellow, but what did it ever accomplish?

Last summer, for example, the Union organized the first of the big farm strikes that still went on here and there. But what happened? Half of the delegates to the Farm Holiday Convention could not get to Des Moines because so many banks were already on "holiday" that the farmers couldn't scare up cash for railroad fares. And what did those farmer delegates actually do about the crooks who were sitting on their money? Why, they wrote a catchy little song about it.

Let's call a "Farmers' Holiday" —
A Holiday let's hold.
We'll eat our wheat and ham and eggs,
And let them eat their gold.

Phooey! Then these earnest delegates went on to figure out that with taxes, mortgage payments, and costs of nonfarm products at the level they were, a little man farming a cash crop of a quarter section of wheat, like George, could not continue to exist unless he got ninety-two cents a bushel for it. But even while the strike was on, farmers like George were getting twenty-six cents, and none of the road blockades, the slogans and songs, the fights, the picketing, the storming of jails and capitol buildings moved the prices one iota. No, it was going to take a much bigger, sterner outfit than the

Farmers' Union, with its fine songs and statistics, to fight the fat middlemen.

In North Dakota, where the Farmers' Union was strong, some state and national congressmen met in Bismarck and put out a grandiose statement urging the farmers to organize and barricade themselves on their farms and refuse to submit to foreclosures. The farmers were advised "to pay no existing debts, except for taxes and the necessities of life," unless satisfactory reductions were made to bring farm prices on a par with other prices. George remembered that one part of the statement exactly, because he had been so incensed at those inane exceptions. Why agree to pay taxes to a government that did nothing for him? Why exempt the "necessities of life"? What else did a farmer ever buy? Nobody had gone far enough yet to get George really interested. He had seen too many schemes for wild political action in the twenties and too many farmers' cooperatives fall apart. It was going to take bloodshed to change things for the farmer.

He stopped at the mailbox and took out the *Jamestown Sun*. FARMERS ATTACK DISTRICT JUDGE was the headline. More of the same B.S. He could have written it himself. So they all signed a useless little petition to a judge who was paid by rich men for his favors. So what! In Le Mars, Iowa, the story said, a hundred farmers had tried to make a district judge promise to sign no more farm mortgage foreclosures. Yeah! You bet!

But wait a minute — when the judge said no, the farmers dragged him off his bench, socked him good, blindfolded him, hauled him in the back of a truck to a lonely spot in the road, put a rope around his neck, choked him till they nearly scared him to death, smeared his face with axle grease, and left him without any pants. A district judge without any pants.

He laughed all the way down to the house and he was still laughing while he harnessed the team and hitched up to the plow. Now that was the kind of action those boys would understand — just what he'd been advocating right along.

That Le Mars must be quite a town. He recalled reading a couple of months before how the farmers had almost hung an agent of the New York Life Insurance Company there. The agent came out from New York to foreclose on a mortgage of $30,000 and submitted the highest sale bid himself. It was the highest bid, but it was only $20,000. That was the legalized tyranny the insurance companies enjoyed these days. They took away a man's whole farm and the farmer *still* owed them ten thousand dollars.

There must be two or three real men down at Le Mars. That was all it would take in any one place. And then when the good men got together, the revolt would begin. Not a man now old enough to run a farm could forget how a dozen years ago the insurance companies had been *begging* the farmers to borrow money from them. The moneylenders all wanted to get in on the skyrocketing land values. And now that land values had collapsed along with the farmers' markets, the moneylenders would get their money back any way they could. Every man for himself and the devil take the hindmost. Well, that policy could work both ways, as they would find out one of these days.

The day was coming when neither the rich men in the government nor the rich men in business would dare to send their lackeys to squeeze money out of the West and take it back to Wall Street.

Around and around rode George Armstrong Custer, drawing his two furrows behind him, and the vision grew and took the shapes and sounds of life. First he would get an eviction notice from the city man. James T. Vick would be coming with the sheriff, despite the threats and proclamations of Wild Bill Langer to call out the state militia against the county sheriffs. But George would not need any militia. No man in the county was a better shot. He and his family would be fortified in his own haymow. It would be a cinch compared to fighting Indians. *Indians* would burn him out up there, but not Vick. Before George fixed the old wreck, it could hardly have been called a barn. Vick wanted that barn now. He wanted to repossess the barn with all the lumber and work that George had put into it. Vick would not burn it to get him. Very comfortable up in that mow — plenty of food and water, blankets to spread over the hay. Plenty of rifle shells. Hardly any challenge at all, for a man whose ancestors had fought their way across nearly two thousand miles of frontiers.

When Vick arrived, riding in the official car between Sheriff Richard Press and a deputy, the yard would look deserted. Vick would have a moment of feeling foolish, having brought the Law thirty miles to a place already deserted. Then the dust would explode about a foot away from Vick's polished city shoes. It made George smile to hear the way the yellow storekeeper would scream and to see how he would dive back into the sheriff's car. The sheriff would have to put on a show, and he would discharge his pistol in the direction of the barn. Another dust explosion would occur a few inches away from the sheriff's boot.

The sheriff would have everything to lose and hardly anything to gain, except a campaign contribution and a little graft. He would also retreat to the official car. The deputy would never have got out from behind the wheel at all. They would confer for a moment. A bullet would ring a terrifying alarm on the front bumper. In the midst of that echo, the starter would whinny for a moment and then the engine would turn over. But before the deputy could get the car into gear, the three quaking men in the front seat would feel a front tire burst beneath them. They would turn in a wide giddy circle, thumping along on the raw rim, and waver back up the rutted lane like the scared rabbits they were. George and his family would climb down from the haymow, then, having spent exactly four bullets to defend their rights.

No, it wasn't that George Custer was not ready to fight. It was just that he hadn't seen any fight worth getting into yet. The *Farm Holiday News* could go right on "declaring war on the International Bankers and lesser money barons," and never make the monopolists and the speculators bat an eyelash. It was going to take blood; they would faint dead away at the sight of a little plutocratic blood on the ground. One thing those potbellied bankers never seemed to realize was that there were a lot of men like George A. Custer who had a hell of a lot of time to think about things while they rode a plow around and around a field.

❦ ❦ ❦

Lucy sat in the front seat of the old Ford, parked in the afternoon shadow of the elevator, while her father ordered his seed wheat. She had begun to understand that people had complex feelings about the elevator, and her own feelings about it were also mixed. She couldn't help being excited by it because so many things happened there. On the other hand, she knew that her father did not like

Adolph Beahr, and she had her own reasons for being uncomfortable around him.

She did not at all mind being left in the car while her father went up to talk to him. Often while she sat and waited, a freight train of a hundred cars or more would go by, creaking as though its weight would tip it from its wheels, slowing for the station and then lumbering on to the east or west.

But as big as the trains were, the elevator made them look very small, with its plain lines rising so much higher than any other building she had ever seen. When she went inside with her father, she was stirred by the smells and sounds of it, and the height of its ceilings, and the stairs going up and up and up, as in a great castle. At harvest time the great iron doors were pushed back and she got to ride the truck inside, couched on fragrant, dusty wheat.

Once they weighed her along with the wheat, and then Mr. Beahr, laughing as grownups did, swung her down and took her over to a set of scales at the side, where he weighed out sacks. She could still remember how his fingers had been around her bare ribs. He had kept one hard hand far down on her stomach while he fiddled with the scales till they balanced at fifty-one pounds.

She had been wearing only the boxer shorts that her mother made for her, and he had reached down and hooked his finger under the elastic at the back of her waist, pulled it out and let it snap against her skin. Then he had laughed again until his laughter came back from the faraway ceilings, and he said loudly, "We'll have to take off a little for the shorts here." What he said echoed too, and it came back sounding like "We'll have to take off the little shorts here."

Her father had been terribly mad at Mr. Beahr, though he did not show it at all right then. That night she had heard him telling her mother about it.

"That hoary old buzzard," he said. "One of these days I'm going to smash him on top of his fat head so hard he'll have *three* tongues in his shoes. I just wish he'd lay his dirty paws on *me* sometime!"

Whenever she thought about Mr. Beahr weighing her, she was a little relieved just to be waiting in the car. This time it took her father so long that she was rewarded by the passing of a train. She saw the semaphore to the east uncannily raise its arm long before she could even hear the train. Her grandfather had told her that meant for the engineer to go straight on through. Then when the train was in sight, the flat round bell at the road crossing began to clang desperately back and forth. That red bell made her feel that even while it was warning her away, it was calling her, too. It gave her the same feeling she had when she climbed so high in a tree that she knew it would kill her to fall to the ground. Then part of her was afraid of falling, but another part of her kept calling, "Jump! *Jump!* Try it! Jump!"

Then while the bell clanged, the engine rushed through so fast that she barely saw the big glove of the engineer waving out his window at her before the cars with faces at the windows began to stream by. She had to look hard in order to count the cars, watch for the mail sack to be snatched from its post, and wave back at all the waving people. She usually didn't like waving at people because it made her feel silly and strange, but she liked waving at people in trains because they went away so fast.

She was deeply pleased to have seen the whole thing, starting with the semaphore arm and ending with the brakeman saluting her from the open platform of the last car. It was so necessary to get through things from start to finish. One of the reasons she was in such a hurry to grow up was that people interrupted her whenever they felt like it, and didn't care whether something got finished or not. When she was grown-up herself they couldn't do that any more. She was glad it was taking her father so long up there in the office.

Her father did not like the railroad at all. He was always saying that the Northern Pacific owned the state of North Dakota. But she herself liked absolutely everything about a train. She liked to keep track of the different pictures painted on the box cars and notice interesting things about the long numbers on them — like a one-three-five-seven or a three-three-three-nine or a two-two-four-eight. If she watched hard enough, she got a wonderful blurred feeling as though she was moving with the train.

Some trains would be made of almost every kind of car, and then she wouldn't bother with the numbers. She would just watch the red-brown flanks of the steers through the slats of the cattle cars and smell the sweet raw lumber on the flatcars and admire the enormous cylinders of the tank cars.

And always at the beginning and end of every train were the

trainmen who gave her a long, deliberate, majestic wave, as though she was somebody very important.

⁂

Adolph was charging him too much, George knew, but not as much too much as he had feared. He could make it, all right, with what he had borrowed and what the cream would bring. As they finished up their deal, Adolph said, "Looks pretty bad down South, don't it? Should help us all a little up *here,* anyhow."

"I reckon the biggest hog has finally got what he had coming to him," George said.

Adolph was a blindly devout Republican, almost as bad as Zack Hoefener, and George took a great pleasure in twitting him with quotations from the Hoover administration. Hoover's Farm Board chairman had gone to Kansas last fall to plead with the winter wheat men to cut back their acreage, and he had become so infuriated with the responses he got that he told a large farm audience in Wichita, "The biggest hog will always lie in the trough. Kansas is now in the trough."

Even Northern wheat farmers were aghast at such a statement from a government man who was supposed to be on the farmer's side. And to add insult to injury, that Farm Board chairman was also the president of the International Harvester Company and he had made his millions by selling machinery to wheat farmers. And the kind of machinery he manufactured was one of the major reasons why there was now the kind of wheat surplus that had caused him to make his remarks about Kansas. The Farm Board chairman's cloudy view of the wheat farmer's world seemed surpassed only by his enormous ingratitude to that world for making him a millionaire. Newspaper editors were still lambasting him, even now that a new administration had come to power.

Adolph had got what he'd laid himself open to, and he knew it. "Well, good luck with the seed," he said.

"You bet. Prosperity's just around the corner," said George.

For *me,* he added to himself as he walked out of Adolph's office. The way things were now, it was dog eat dog when you farmed wheat, and one man's catastrophe was another man's salvation. That was why he had to risk everything this year to switch his seed. It would be different if he could farm his own way, but so long as Vick could tell him how much wheat to plant, he had to do his best to profit by what had happened to the Kansas winter wheat men. Let the trough go dry and the hog starve for a while.

He almost ran down the short flight of wooden steps, worn and scooped in their centers by the boots of farmers who kept Adolph well-to-do, whether they succeeded or failed. Adolph could always wait for the good years, his comfortable operating margin stored away in the great chambers above him, while he gazed out over the town backed up against the railroad tracks. He could always wait till some farmer had to have cash and then he could buy wheat at any price he named. In this late afternoon he could see the shadow of his building stretch nearly across the town.

George pulled open the door and climbed in under the wheel next to Lucy. "What's the matter, pickle-puss?" he said. He had found out she hated that nickname, so he teased her with it—to get her so the town kids wouldn't bother her so much, he said.

"Nothing is the matter," she said.

He grabbed her thigh and rolled the muscles of her leg between his great fingers, exclaiming in a scolding voice, "Why Lucy, what's the matter with you? Have you gone clean out of your head? What ails you, anyway, Lucy? What makes you carry on like this? What're you laughing so much for, if something's bothering you? Can't you make up your mind whether to laugh or cry? Just like a woman!"

She was giggling hysterically and screaming at him to stop, wanting the awful tickling to stop, but wishing he would go on noticing her — and he must have, because when they went to the store, he did not give her a penny, but a whole nickel.

Sunday, April 30

THE NEXT DAY was May Day. Next to Christmas and the Fourth of July, it was the biggest holiday of the year. Lucy lay in bed, but she could not sleep. It was eight o'clock but the sun had set only an hour ago and the long twilight was still there, behind the thin shade. Tomorrow was May Day. Tomorrow was May Day. Her father was reading a long piece in the paper, interspersing the reading with comments and raising his voice so that her mother could hear him above the noise of the dishes in the kitchen.

"This is just what I told you would happen, Rachel," he was saying loudly. "I told you it couldn't help but happen. It says here that yesterday Henry Morgenthau liquidated the last million bushels of September wheat owned by the government. Sold it in the Chicago pit. Says that from May of 1930 to this last March the Farm Board bought nine million bushels of wheat through Hoover's Grain Stabilization Corporation, and now that they've sold the last of it they figure the government lost over a hundred and sixty million dollars. It took them just three years to lose a hundred and sixty million dollars. Oh, they'll admit now that it was a crackpot idea. Any little farmer like me could've told those fatheads exactly what would happen — just in case they didn't know just as well as *I* did!

"Pay prices way above the world market and what do you get? A lot of men that never farmed before jumping in and plowing up virgin soil so's they can get their hands on those government *loans*. But you notice a little guy like me can't even get a *sniff* at those loans to help out the *farmer*, can he? The *rich* man that never did a day's work in his life — *he* can get paid by the government for a bunch of wheat stored in his own granaries that he's never even *seen!* He gets a *loan* on it! A loan he never has to pay back. But they fix it so a little guy like me can *never* get one of those loans. A man has to have *this* qualification and *that* qualification, and be the head jackass of some damned *lodge!*"

He was quiet for a minute and then he yelled, "You know what Morgenthau sold that last million bushels for? *Sixty-nine* cents! *I* got *twenty-six* last fall from Adolph — the same time the government was buying that wheat from the rich men. If the government is losing millions of dollars selling twenty-six-cent wheat for sixty-nine cents, then who in hell is getting their fat hands on all that dough? It don't make sense no matter how you look at it, does it? It just *has* to be as crooked as a bear's hind leg. Who is it, anyhow, getting all that taxpayers' money?

"Rachel, can you hear me?" he called. "Just who do you think is getting that forty-three cents, anyhow? Who? The government sells at a *loss* for nearly *three* times what *I* could get last fall. *Think* of it!"

"I *am* thinking of it," she said. "But I don't understand it any more than *you* do! The whole world is just crazy, that's all!"

Lucy got scared when she heard her mother say things like that. What happened, anyway, when the whole world was crazy?

"Oh, no, it isn't!" her father cried. "*Some* of us are not crazy, and we know *exactly* where all those government *losses* went to. I can walk right down the street tomorrow and point to the pockets our tax money has gone into."

Lucy could see how they would walk down the wooden sidewalks in Eureka, looking for bulges in pockets, and listening for jingling sounds.

"The elevators owned by the big men got the best rates in history for wheat storage! That's *one* set of pockets. And the rich *farmers* got such generous *loans* — and I reckon the railroads got even better pay than *I* have to pay them. I tell you, the whole thing is rotten! It stinks to high heaven! How can you fight a thing like this, anyhow?"

"I don't think you *can*," her mother said.

"Oh, *yes* I can! You just wait till enough little guys like me figure out just how bad they've been skinned. *We'll* fight it all right."

It was quiet for a while, and Lucy could begin to hear the sounds of the late spring twilight. Then her father gave a mad laugh. " 'Stabilization,' they called it. 'Grain stabilization!' My, aren't the prices going to be *stable* now, with the government unloading an accumulation like that just a few months before we try to sell a crop this fall! It's just as bad as the damn Roosians unloading all their wheat all over the world for three years now. Stabbed in the back by your own government! And you have to pay for the knife yourself! How much longer do they think they can *do* this to us? I tell you, there's going to be *blood*."

Blood! She never could understand what he meant when he said there was going to be blood. Sometimes when they thought she was asleep they talked about getting her tonsils out or taking her to the dentist. Sometimes it was about this terrible thing that was going to happen to the world. It always seemed to have something to do with blood.

Finally she was too sleepy to keep up with what they were saying. Tomorrow was May Day. Tomorrow she would win a race and get a quarter for a prize. The sounds of the frogs singing in the slough came clear and liquid above the dry rattle of the *Jamestown Sun.*

Monday, May 1

THERE WERE ENOUGH races and other strenuous contests to last the whole day, for people who lived by muscular toil knew no other way to play. There were long races and dashes for all age groups, beginning with the five-year-olds, and specialty races such as the sack race and the three-legged hop. There were broad jumping and high jumping, throwing, horseshoe-pitching, and weight-lifting. And there were such unclassifiable events as the hog-calling competition and the rolling-pin-throwing contest, where two prizes were given — one to the woman who threw the farthest and one to the husband who ran the fastest. There was a conscientious dance done by the primary pupils, and afterwards their crepe paper streamers danced around the Maypole alone in the wind.

The celebration was always held in the same public field — a two-acre rectangle bordering the railroad tracks. It was pleasantly green at that time of year and it was big enough to hold several times as many people as there were in the town and all the farmers the town existed to serve.

All the dogs in town were there, stopping races and knocking over children. Horses munched in their feed bags, stamping and switching their tails as the newly hatched swarms of gnats and horseflies hurried to the feast.

Young men jostled and insulted each other as they stood in the sidelines panting and sweating from one event and getting wind back for the next one. Women pushed together the folding tables from the church, the town hall, and the school. Then they spread them with the tablecloths they had brought from home, making each long table a mosaic of checks, flowers, colors, and whites. Finally they superimposed another mosaic on the first, made of the individual intricacies of pies, cakes, salads, sandwiches, pans of meat loaf and pots of beans. Old men leaned their blue or white elbows on the tables, waiting near dishes they were especially interested in.

The May Day field itself was made of all the common ingredients of festivals kept by the anonymous servants of life. It was a canvas for the portrait of hope in equinoxes and solstices that had for centuries made tolerable the lot of those whose lives were, in fact, not tolerable. The feast and the faces might have been painted by Brueghel, and so might the dogs and horses and grass and sky—extreme, wantonly brilliant, blown by the wind, and embraced by the young, tender fire of a returning sun.

When Lucy thought about the many spectacles in this cornucopia of spring, she saw herself speeding across the finish line first, and then she saw Fred Wertzler, the postmaster, reaching down and leaving a big heavy quarter in her hand. Last, but not least, was the picture of herself showing the quarter to all the town kids who had raced against her.

To George, May Day was the one day of the year when, for many years, he had been bested by no man in half a dozen contests. He was no good at the dash, but once he got his great strength in motion, nobody could beat him running a long race. The momentum he created at the beginning seemed to move his iron legs around the rest of the course without any more impetus from him, and his deep chest never ached for air. His keen eyes, his powerful, long-fingered hands won him more laurels. Nobody else could throw so hard or so accurately; nobody else could squeeze a raw potato into sheer pulp that dripped through his fingers. It all came from working hard when he was very young. He would stand and watch now, and compare the softness of the twenty-year-olds to the way he had been himself. If he were not afraid of embarrassing this new generation of pantywaists, he would get out there and make them eat his dust—show them what a tough old man like himself could do.

Still, he liked to watch them trying—he liked to get to the field in plenty of time for the first event. Above all he hoped that Lucy would follow in his footsteps—it was hard for a man like him not to have a boy, but Lucy could beat the boys at most things anyhow. She had been so shy last year. Another year of school ought to have made her more confident and competitive—like him. He had watched her shinnying up her swing rope, chinning herself on the bar he had put up for her between two trees, running easily, as he did himself, across half a mile of pasture. Like him, if she got up enough momentum she could jump a remarkable distance; he had seen her go over a seven-foot puddle with inches to spare. Like him she was physically fearless. She would tease her mother from some precarious place high in a tree, hanging by one hand. If she were only a boy, what a magnificent athlete he could make of her.

The sun was up before five o'clock and so were the Custers. They hurried through the chores so they could get to town and let Lucy deliver a May basket to her teacher. Rachel had gone through school and college with Alice Liljeqvist, and she could not understand why Lucy hated her so. When her own life seemed barren, Rachel sometimes thought of Alice living in that big house with her aging mother, teaching the children of all her friends.

Lucy understood perfectly well why her mother was always having her take little presents to Miss Liljeqvist at Christmas and Easter and other holidays, and she knew those presents did no good at all. She delivered them, but they never made Miss Liljeqvist like her any better.

Her mother sat in the car while she ran up the front steps, hung the basket on the doorknob, knocked, and fled to the back of the house till she heard somebody answer the front door and go back inside again. She waited and heard nothing and decided it would be safe to go back to the car. But all of a sudden she heard Miss Liljeqvist sneaking up behind her, and before she could get away Miss Liljeqvist grabbed her and kissed her, because that was the penalty for being caught giving a May basket. She could hardly believe it.

"She *kissed* me!" Lucy cried when she got back to the car.

"Why, now, you see?" her mother said positively. "I've *always* tried to tell you how much she likes you. Are you going to like *her* now?"

Lucy hung her head far out of the window and made the kind of noises she would have made if she were violently carsick.

Rachel changed the subject. "Do you remember your piece for this morning?"

Lucy scraped out some last retching sounds.

“All right, now. That’s enough of *that!* You’ll have your tonsils all sore again.”

“Good! Then I won’t be able to say that dumb thing at all!” She did seem slightly hoarse. She was always doing odd things with her voice, mimicking frogs and birds and animals. Rachel couldn’t remember that she herself had ever been like that. Lucy was so much like George. Every day Rachel worried a little more about what would ever become of a girl who was like George. . . .

❦ ❦ ❦

May Day always began formally with a program at the school. Each of the thirty-odd pupils in the first six grades was given a piece to recite. When her name was called, Lucy stood up and said, “Buttercups and daisies oh the pretty flowers coming ere the springtime to tell of sunny hours while the trees are leafless while the fields are bare buttercups and daisies spring up here and there.”

Rachel couldn’t help being irritated. Lucy had managed a civil amount of expression when she’d gone through it last night. Watching her stand there with her eyes on the floor and listening to her babbling monotone, who would believe that she even had the wit to do an imitation of a frog — or of a person stricken with nausea?

❦ ❦ ❦

All day long, no matter which way Lucy looked, she saw Miss Liljeqvist. It seemed to her that she spent the whole day hiding, instead of seeing the things she had come to see, and she was standing behind a wagon when they called for the six-to-eight-year-old race. She had to run so far and so fast to get to the starting line that she was too tired to do her best. There were only seven entrants with the whole width of the course to run in, and she realized, at the last minute, that she had run in a long diagonal. She came in third and won an ice cream cone.

Her father yelled at her from the sidelines. “What in the Sam Hill did you think you were doing out there? Don’t you know a straight line is the shortest distance between two points?”

“What?” Lucy said.

“Why didn’t you run in a straight line? A *straight line?*”

“I don’t know,” she said. “Can I go get my ice cream cone now?”

"Go ahead! Go ahead!" He turned to the man standing next to him and said for her to hear as she walked away, "Ain't that just like a woman?"

She *hated* to be called a woman! Whenever her father said the word, it always seemed to come at the end of that expression. She began running as fast as she could.

"Look at her go *now!*" he shouted. "*Women!*"

She ran the width of the field, across the tracks, and all the way up the street till she got to the Café-Restaurant. She stopped and looked in through the window. The ticket in her hand was a small slip of ordinary yellow construction paper with typing on it. The typing read "Good for ONE 5¢ ice cream cone at Gus and Ruby's Café-Restaurant." It didn't look very valuable. It was just the same kind of paper she sometimes got in school. It was hard to see how it could really take the place of a nickel. Why hadn't they just given her a nickel? A nickel with a good stout buffalo and a smooth-faced Indian on it. A nickel that would not have wilted and blurred from the moisture in her hand. The more worn the paper looked, the less confidence she had in it. It would be so terribly embarrassing to order the ice cream cone and then have the paper refused. Everybody in the Café-Restaurant would laugh. She decided she would show the ticket first, just to be on the safe side.

There were three big boys sitting at the far end of the counter. One of them went to high school. He was Douglas Sinclair's big brother. They were all kidding with Annie Finley. She had quit high school to go to work for Gus and Ruby, which was not a good thing to do. Now she wore a lot of lipstick, which was an even worse thing to do. She had a huge amount of fuzzy reddish hair which was curled with a curling iron. She had a long, dirty butcher's apron gathered around her waist in such a way that she looked very billowy on top, and she was wearing a sleeveless light pink dress. In the darkness of the café, the combination of dress and apron gave Lucy a first upsetting impression that the only clothing on Annie's breasts and upper parts was the apron bib. Lucy was sure that such a laughing big girl with red grease shining on her lips would never take a yellow ticket in place of a nickel.

One of the boys stood up from his stool on the platform, leaned over the counter, and reached a long arm clear across the dishpan in which Annie was washing some glasses. He pinched her arm, high up among the freckles.

She gave the kind of stupid shriek Lucy often heard high school girls make when they were around boys. He laughed. "Now you've got another one! Wh-where do you *get* all them little s-s-spots, anyhow?" he said.

"None of your business!" she told him.

He leaned forward again. "Be careful!" Annie said. "You're going to knock over the ketchup. You almost did before. And you almost hit the soda water, too."

That seemed to give him an idea. He grabbed the big knob and yanked it back. A narrow white stream went hissing into the dishpan. Annie pulled her rag out of a glass and flung it in the boy's face with a wet splat that sounded exactly like the sound of a cow enriching the pasture.

He wiped the water from his lips with the back of his hand. The hand was big-boned and rolling with tendons, like a man's.

"S-say, Kewpie-Doll, I ought to *f-f-fix* you for that!" he stammered.

"You fix *me* and I'll fix *you* again, Mister Smarty!" Annie said.

"Are you going to the d-dance over to the Town Hall tonight?" he wanted to know.

"None of your business!" she said again.

The boy looked down toward the door, as though he was going to do something he knew he shouldn't do, and wanted to make sure nobody was coming in. Lucy could tell he was surprised to see her.

"Hey, you got a *c-customer* down there," he shouted. Lucy hated him. How he would laugh if it turned out that her ticket was no good.

Annie came down and looked over the counter. She had round starey blue eyes, and Lucy saw, up close, that she appeared to have put some brown stuff on her eyelashes.

"This isn't like a nickel for an ice cream cone, is it?" Lucy asked. She was so sure of the answer that she was already sliding off her stool.

"Lord, yes!" Annie said. "This here must be the fortieth one today!" She took the ticket. "What flavor?"

Lucy had been thinking so hard about the ticket that she had not thought about the flavor. That was a very hard decision. It always took her a long time. But here was the girl, standing with a scoop in one hand and an empty cone in the other. Lucy wanted to go to the ice cream end of the counter and look down into the little wells filled with such wonderful cold colors, and watch the frost misting on the underside of the thick steel lids, but she did not want to go near that boy. It was almost impossible to make up her mind so far away from the ice cream.

"I'll tell you what, I'll give you a little bit of all three, shall I?" Annie asked.

That was almost too good to be true. "Okay," Lucy said.

"I'll tell the boss," the worst boy said.

"Mind your own business," Annie replied.

Lucy noticed the way the boys looked at her as she walked away from them. They certainly acted as though they liked having her talk back the way she did. Lucy couldn't understand it. She couldn't imagine a male liking to have a female sass him.

Annie held out the cone in a freckled hand. Lucy still felt as though it must be a gift, since she had not paid any money. If the boss came back he would probably not let her have it. She took the cone and got out as fast as she could. Once in Jamestown she had had an ice cream sandwich, but that was the only other time she had ever had all three flavors at once. That Annie was certainly confusing. She was obviously not a nice girl, but who else would ever dish up a three-flavored ice cream cone?

Lucy remembered, as she walked back to the field, licking first one flavor, then another, how people had talked last spring when the Finleys came. At first everyone had thought they were gypsies. They talked with an odd Southern accent and they were living out of an old truck they parked along the railroad right-of-way. At first people weren't going to let them get water from the town pumps, thinking that would make them move on in a hurry, but then Mr. Finley had gone and stood with the other men who lined up in front of the Town Hall, waiting to get hired. Then people knew the Finleys were not gypsies, because gypsies never worked — just passed through in their wagons or old trucks, camped for a little while, stole anything they could, and disappeared again.

But Lucy also had bad feelings about the whiskery men who were *not* gypsies and proved it by standing in the Town Hall line — leaning back and bracing a heel against the dry boards, hooking their thumbs in their pockets, and staring off across the street. She didn't like to walk past them. Once, when she was only four or five, she had asked a man, "What are you standing there for?" When he hadn't answered, she had asked again. She had been with her grandfather, and he had grabbed her hand and tried to pull her on past the man. She had pulled back and asked the question once more, loudly.

The man's face got red. "I'm waiting to get hired," he said in a funny voice.

"You must *never* ask those men why they're standing there!" her grandfather said when they got back to the truck. "That's an *awful* thing to do! You made that poor man *so* embarrassed, and you embarrassed *me* too! You should have come right along when I took your hand." Her grandfather stayed mad all the way home, and it was the only time in her life that he had ever been angry with her — absolutely the only time — and that was why she had bad feelings whenever she thought about any man standing in front of the Town Hall.

And another thing about the Finleys — they had come to town only a few days after a terrible thing had happened that everybody was talking about all the time. People had been looking everywhere for a little boy that had been stolen from his house and they had finally found him, but he was dead. She had heard her mother and her grandmother and her great-aunt talking about it and about all the kidnappings that were happening everywhere. Her aunt had told, two or three times, about how she had heard that they found human skin under the little boy's fingernails. That showed how hard he had fought and fought while he was being killed. He scratched so hard that the skin of the man who killed him was still stuck in his fingernails.

Everybody knew that gypsies were kidnappers. They would steal any child for a little bit of money. And Lucy had never quite got over thinking of the Finleys as gypsies, because of the way they had camped out until they moved into that big falling-down house. They were shiftless, at the very least. They admitted they were on their way to Canada when their truck gave out in Eureka. That was what came of living on a big highway, Lucy's great-aunt said. You never knew *who* was coming through your town. Look at all the bums and tramps they had to worry about! It seemed like every day, through the warm months, there would be one at the back door of her house for a handout. That was partly because there was a town pump in her yard where they came for a drink, and partly because she had one of the nicest houses in town and they thought she was made of money.

Lucy spotted her mother and father standing with the crowd listening to the hog-callers. "Sooo—eeee! Sooo——eeee! Hog! Hog! Hog!" Oscar Johnson began his call with drawn-out syllables, and then finished with three short ones, imitating the quick snorting grunts of hogs shoving each other back and forth along the trough. Lester Zimmerman was next, and he went "*Ho!* Pig pig pig! *Ho* PIG!"

"Look what Annie Finley gave me!" Lucy said, pulling at her mother's arm.

"Why, wasn't that *nice!*" her mother said.

"But *you* said she wasn't a nice girl," Lucy said.

"Sshh! You mustn't say that. I never said that. I just said it wasn't nice to wear so much make-up. I don't want *you* to do that, *ever*."

Lucy had her face stupidly buried in her ice cream cone when Miss Liljeqvist came sneaking up behind her for the second time that day, and before she knew it she was trapped in the circle of six legs belonging to her mother and her father and her teacher, who went on and on smiling and talking above her, dropping down little sayings to her that she was supposed to think were funny, pretending that Miss Liljeqvist had never kept her in at recess, never made her stand in the cloakroom, never given her a D in Deportment, never made her copy over perfectly good papers because they weren't neat, never punished her for wiggling a loose tooth with her tongue and making Douglas Sinclair laugh, never written her name on the board for whispering, even when she wasn't, or never made everybody laugh at her by telling her that she had the messiest desk in the room. Oh, no! None of those things had ever happened, had they? It made Lucy sick, the way grownups always pretended around Miss Liljeqvist.

Four more weeks of school after May Day and another whole year in the third grade. Lucy sometimes even used up a good wish on a first star in order to wish that somebody would marry Miss Liljeqvist, but she couldn't imagine who ever would. Some day Miss Liljeqvist would be just like Gid and Gad — only worse.

Sunday, May 14

It was a day that would have been too hot except that Lucy still remembered winter so well that no day could be too hot. Besides, the day was the color of spring, not summer. Nothing was brown yet.

They were driving to her grandfather's house from church and she was watching the wheat grow. The fields that were newly seeded would look black, but if you stared at them without blinking, sometimes they would turn suddenly from black to green. Then you would know that you had seen the wheat grow. You had seen the little green blades from millions and millions of wheat grains all come cutting through the black ground at the same time. It might happen that after you blinked the field would seem black again, but if you squeezed your eyes and stared a minute, you would see that the green was there after all, and the millions of tiny wheat sprouts were growing away.

They were going to have dinner with her grandmother, and the table was set with the beautiful pure white Bavarian china that was kept for Sunday. The kitchen was hot because of the oven, but the dining room was cool and dark, shadowed by the half-drawn blinds. The cherry desk in the corner was closed to cover the pigeon holes full of papers, and the only light spot besides the table itself was the white cloth across the high sideboard. On the cloth stood a big clock in a case made like a building, with pillars holding up a peaked roof and brass lions' heads looking out — far out, to the North Pole and to Africa.

Lucy liked to go in and stand in the readied room while everybody else was still in the kitchen. The damask cloth hanging halfway to the floor, the massive white dinner plates, the slim gravy boat, the cut-glass relish dish full of precisely arranged dills, bread-and-butter pickles, and spiced beets, the platter waiting for fried chicken —

these all had a Sunday cleanness, and a reassuring plenitude after a long starving morning in church.

Her mother was feeding Cathy and her father was talking the way he always did. One realized, when one was far enough away so that his voice didn't sound quite so loud, that he said some things that were funny.

"Those Hindus," he said. "A whole country full of grown men wearing diapers. That's just what they are. There's a hundred or a thousand or *ten* thousand of them to every British soldier in the country. Who *knows* how many? If they can't get rid of the British by fighting, what kind of yellow-bellies are they? The Ma*hat*ma and his *hunger* strikes! *We* got rid of the British when we felt like it, didn't we? Phooey!"

"Well, what do you think of Roosevelt's new inflation bill?" her grandfather said.

"What's the matter with *that* idea?" her father said. "*Nine billion* dollars the farmers owe in this country—in deflated money. If you don't want the banks and insurance companies to take over every last farm in the country, what else are you going to do, besides inflate the money again?"

"Well, anyway," her grandfather said in that voice he used when he was trying to make her father stop shouting, "this parity idea of his is a good one. Getting the farmer back to where he was with the city man before the war."

"Pshaw!" her father shouted louder than ever. "What does it mean, anyhow? Just words! It won't have the least little effect on the mess in this country. You wait. It'll be so bad over here, it'll make Spain look like a Sunday school picnic!"

"Who are you going to be fighting, George?" her grandfather asked.

"It's ready," said her grandmother.

They came in and sat down around the table. They all bowed their heads and shut their eyes, except for her father. Her mother and her grandmother and grandfather said the Lord's Prayer together. . . .

⁂

Will had a stabbing pain in his abdomen; nevertheless, his mind was fixed on Lucy. He watched her now, staring out past him without seeing him — her eyes fixed on the button in the window as though she were willing herself out of the room — willing herself free and alone in the fields wherever the button floated ahead of her. She was doing something with her eyes, narrowing them and then letting them go out of focus to make the button move one way and then another. He could remember when Stuart had done such tricks with his eyes. Although Lucy had an undeniably strong resemblance to George, Will could see so much of his own line in her too. Her mouth was like Rachel's and her lips were chapped, the way Rachel's always used to be. She bit them unconsciously, as she stared out the window. Rachel had done that, too. And Will saw that she seemed to be doomed to wandering the prairie alone during her childhood, like Rachel, with a baby sister too much younger to be company for her — if anybody would ever be company for her. And the world she must enter, if she was ever to be less lonely, was moving always farther away from her.

Will could not see how George and Rachel would ever manage to put her through college, and yet college would be the only door that would ever open to the world she ought to be in. He believed she had the intellect to win a scholarship some day, but by the time that day came, the stubborn, defiant streak she had inherited from George might well have so alienated her teachers that her record would in no way reflect her true capabilities. He knew — now that it was too late for the knowledge to do any good — that something like that had happened to Stuart. He would hate to have Lucy's chance at college depend on her winning of a scholarship, and so he had drawn up a tentative will that would see both her and Cathy through. But he had never gone ahead and had the will made legal because things had been so uncertain the last few years. He had to think of his children before he thought of his grandchildren, and he had to think of his wife before he thought of his children. He wanted to leave Rose a little more than just his life insurance, and Rachel and Stuart might need the money long before it was time for Lucy to go to college. And there was the possibility of other grandchildren — either Rachel's or Stuart's children. He wanted to be fair to them all.

"Who wants to come and help feed the lambs?" he said.

"*Me!*" Lucy cried. That was another thing he remembered — how

Stuart had once been able to come back into a room instantaneously when there was something he wanted to come back for.

They filled three baby bottles with morning's milk and Will slipped the black nipples over them. When the lambs were smaller, he had warmed the milk, but that wasn't necessary any more.

One of the lambs was an orphan and the other two were twins their mothers wouldn't own. Sometimes a ewe did that — just bunted away one of the twins when feeding time came around. In the natural state, that lamb would simply starve to death. Will could never understand such an apparent distortion of the maternal instinct. What other instinct was stronger? He'd always wondered the same thing about those human twins born to Isaac, that other keeper of flocks. Why had the mother loved Jacob and not Esau? In the case of the ewe who pushed away one twin, did she choose between them for such obscure and female reasons as caused Rebekah to choose between Jacob and Esau? Or was there some practical instinct working — did the ewe know that she had only enough milk to raise one lamb, and did her instinct force her to push away the weaker one, even while her mother's heart bled that the world must be so?

When he thought of Jacob and Esau, Will thought of Rachel and Stuart. It was impossible to believe that he had not loved them equally. Surely, surely, he had loved them equally. Why then, had one of them run away, bitterly renouncing his birthright? Esau had at least cried out to his blind father. (*Hast thou but one blessing, my father? bless me, even me also, O my father!*) But never once had Stuart spoken of the things that troubled him. He had simply run away, leaving his father to wonder, for two tortured years, what terrible blindness of his own had driven his son away from him.

They stopped a little way from the sheep shed and the lambs came running, crying in their high baby voices. Will held a bottle in each hand and stuck them through the fence.

He let Lucy have the third bottle. "Now hang on with both hands," he told her. "When he gets ahold of that, he'll really wrastle it!"

The bottle throbbed in her hands from the pulsations of his hungry little tongue. His small black jaws never let go, no matter how fast the milk came. She could see it welling and bubbling at the corners of his mouth, but never a drop rolled out on his chin. It wasn't that way with Cathy at all. She could swallow only so fast, and after that the milk poured down her neck. But the lamb had no trouble at all. He could waggle his little black tail, and do a dance with his twinkling black legs, and butt his head up and down, as though he was nursing his mother, and pull at the bottle — all at the same time. He finished the bottle before Cathy would really have got started, and then he pulled harder than ever.

"Take it away, now," her grandfather said. "He'll chew up the nipple."

Lucy put her fingers next to the little black muzzle and pulled out the nipple. The lamb bleated for more.

"What a little pig you are!" he laughed. "Look how full he is." The lamb's stomach was bulgėd out under its thin baby wool.

"*All* babies are little pigs, aren't they?" Lucy said.

"They sure are," he agreed. "They'd never grow up if they weren't."

The smell of the milk had seemed like the soul of the gentle, fertile day itself. Now that the milk was gone, it was as if they still smelled it in the soft south breeze — a wind so soft that it scarcely seemed to be there, but still it was — as elusive but as alive as the pushing wheat in the fields. Lucy said hopefully, "Have you got time to tell me a story?"

She was as hungry as the lambs. He felt it. He wondered how it was that he knew so many things about her, and how it was that sometimes a child could be closer to the parents of its parents than to its own parents. His own grandfather had been full of Indian stories and Civil War stories, and Will now had his grandfather's medal, hung on a red-and-blue ribbon, packed away in the trunk along with the other Civil War things. That seemed so long ago. Yet his own father was already twelve years old when the war ended, and his own father remembered when Lincoln was shot.

But Lucy was not interested in war stories, nor in Indian battles, though she liked stories about Indians in the forests or on the prairies, so long as there were animals in the stories too. She could not tell him what she expected from his stories, but he had begun to understand that she looked to him to build a plausible passageway between the two disparate and distant places in which she lived.

The two far-apart places were irreconcilable. The first was the world of the little dark house set between its two narrow groves in the prairie. The other was the world in her head that changed and expanded as she grew, and slipped ever farther away from the first. Many years ago, when Rachel was only a year or so older than Lucy, he and Rose had bought the books that now made Lucy's second world. The set was called *The Young Folks' Treasury*, and it ran to twelve thick volumes bound in red, generously adorned with heavy shiny color pages full of beasts, giants, fairies, princesses, and heroes of legends.

After several years of being read to by her mother, Lucy was now working her own way through them. She was presently in the stage where the enchanted world was intertwined with the religious one. She believed that if she only wished hard enough for something, and worked hard enough to deserve it, she would surely get it. She wanted stories from him that proved she was right. She was getting harder and harder to tell stories to.

"Have you got time?" she begged. "It's *Sunday*."

He teased her while he tested such ideas as he could snatch away from the pain that was as determined to destroy his brain as he was determined that it would not. "You won't let me tell about fairies or princesses. It has to be so it really could happen. But when I tell you about something that really could happen, then you're sad."

"Only that one time!" she protested. She looked up at him, pleading for the bridge that could never be built from the real world to the good world.

He leaned back against the fence and hooked a heel over the bottom board. A lamb tried out the black rubber, but found it was not the proper shape. The pain shot through his abdomen again. He loosened his belt another notch but it didn't seem to help.

"Shall I tell about a lamb?" he asked.

"*Yes!*" she whooped. He didn't know anybody who could say *yes* the way Lucy could. The one sudden syllable was like the whole world crying *Joy!*

"Well," he began, "there was a little girl who had a pet lamb. What shall we call the girl?"

"Sally," Lucy said at once. She was always full of names.

"Sally had wished for a baby lamb for a long time," Will said.

"Every night she wished on the first star for a lamb. She wasn't like a little girl I know who wishes every night for a dapple-gray pony like her cousin's. She just wished for a little baby lamb.

"One night when she went to fetch the cows for her father, she heard a little weak ba-a-a, ba-a-a. She couldn't imagine where it was coming from because her father didn't have any sheep. That was why she had never had a baby lamb of her own. She looked all around, but she didn't see the lamb."

He had to repeat himself while he thought. Usually he had only to choose between alternatives that waited in his mind, but not today.

"The sound seemed to be coming from a little bit above her in the gulch. She looked up, but she still couldn't see anything. She climbed up the side of the ravine a little ways and she saw a dark spot in the side of it. It was a tiny little cave! She was so surprised! She had never seen that cave there before. And then she saw that there really was a lamb lying in the cave, but it was a black lamb—all black, not just feet and muzzle and tail. That was why she couldn't see it in the cave.

"She wondered how the little lamb had ever got there. When it saw her it tried to stand up, but it had a sore foot, and it stumbled and fell back down again. She picked it up and it didn't even try to wiggle out of her arms. It wasn't afraid of her at all. It knew she wanted to help it."

"Was it very heavy for her?" Lucy asked.

"Yes, it was. It was all she could do to carry it, because she was not a very big girl. I doubt if she was as strong as you are, either. But she carried it all the way to where the cows were grazing and then home. When her father saw her bringing in the lamb, he was very surprised. But he said that if she would take care of it she could keep it. He even built a little house for it, inside a little fence. He looked at its foot and said it had been cut on the barbed wire but it would get better. So Sally fed the little black lamb and soon it was well, and it could run and jump like any lamb. In fact, it got so it could jump over its little fence, and then it would run away. Sally thought it looked so funny jumping over its fence that she would laugh and chase after it, and she begged her father not to make the fence higher.

"So, one day the lamb ran very far away, and this time Sally looked and looked, and couldn't find him. He was a real black sheep, that little lamb. He was really a bad little egg." He repeated again, waiting for some more story to come. Where did the lamb run to? Where? Where?

"Sally looked all day long. She didn't notice the sky getting darker and darker and darker, until it was almost as black as her little lamb. Her mother had told her always to run right home when the sky got black like that, and to watch for a tornado. Her mother had told her that if she ever saw a tornado coming along, she should not even try to get home, but lie down in the lowest spot she could find and hang on to something. If she was out in the stubble, she should just hang on to that. But Sally had forgotten that, because she was so worried about her lamb.

"So she kept on wandering around and calling for her lamb while the clouds got bigger and blacker. Suddenly she felt the tornado come and grab her right up, and the next thing *she* knew, she was blowing around and around with all the other things it had picked up, but she couldn't see any of them because it was *so* black.

"Now, you know, I've seen a tornado do awful queer things. You just can't believe it till you see it. Once right down here in Jimtown a tornado took a roof off one house and set it down again, just right! on another house. Down South, where they have a lot more tornadoes than we do here, the wind does a lot of crazy things. You know, just last week they had some storms down there that killed a lot of people, they were so bad. And yet the wind lifted up one man right out of his house and carried him prit-near two blocks away and set him down again, just as pretty as you please. Didn't hurt him a bit. And I've seen, myself, back in Indiana, a straw that went through an oak door two inches thick. It never even bent or broke on account of hitting the door so fast and so hard. Just went *clean* through it — just like that!"

"What happened to Sally?" Lucy said.

"Well, sir, just the same thing that happened to that fellow down in Kansas. That tornado picked her up and whirled her around and around and set her back down again, about a mile away, just as easy as pie.

"And guess who had been there with her, twirling around in the big black tornado all the time, so coal-black she never saw him at all?"

"The lamb!" Lucy cried.

"Right!" Will said triumphantly. He had feared she wouldn't accept the idea. He knew he just wasn't up to snuff. "And the tornado set *him* down, too, just as nice as could be. And she ran over to him and she saw that he had got himself all tangled up in something up there in the tornado. And I bet you can't guess what it was!" He thought desperately.

"Well, it was a — a — a . . ." Now was the time to try some magic, but it would have to be probable magic. "It was a golden bridle — just right for a pony. She untangled his little woolly black legs from it. It was gold, all right. It glittered and glittered. It was heavy, too. But she ran all the way home with it. The little lamb ran right behind her. *He* had learned *his* lesson, you just bet. *He* wasn't going to run away any more!

"And when she showed the bridle to her father, he got a wonderful idea. He said, 'Say, Sally, I bet we could find some rich person who would buy this bridle. Then I bet there would be enough to buy you a pony, with a regular saddle and bridle. What do you say? Should we put an ad in the paper?' And sure enough, some rich man came and bought the bridle, and Sally's father took her to the horse auction and they came home with the prettiest little dapple-gray pony you ever saw. So then Sally had *both* a lamb and a pony, and it was all because of her bad little lamb that she got a pony!"

He felt deeply relieved at the smile she gave him. She had not been disappointed. Her smile, when she was really happy, was like her *yes*. There was no other smile like it.

"Let's go get the checkers and have a game out here in the sunshine, shall we?" he asked. It wasn't polite to leave the others for so long, but he just felt too blamed bad to get back into an argument.

"*I* tell you what." He had an even better idea. "I'll just be out here looking after the ewes while you take the bottles back in and fetch the board and checkers."

"Okay!" she said. She was running before she finished the word. He stood watching her and thinking again how easy it was for a child to change worlds. Very soon she would reach the age where she would be trying to make the leap between her worlds all by herself, just as she already didn't need to hold his hand any more when they walked in town, though she always did.

He thought about how small her hand still was, and how sharp her little knuckles felt when he pressed his thumb over them. She had not stopped fighting against her solitude; that was why she still wanted to take his hand when they walked in town.

He wondered when she would surrender to solitude, as Rachel and Stuart had, so that it would become necessary to her. For many years he had wondered if everybody's soul had to be defined by solitude after a certain stage of maturity, or if it was only prairie people who almost always grew that way.

Saturday, May 27

It was summer and school had been let out the day before. George was seeding the last of the Ceres. A good part of it in his first field was up already. It looked as though it was going to make a fine stand. Still, he didn't trust Adolph as far as he could throw a steer by the tail. He knew Adolph would get away with anything he thought he could. He could only hope that the seed had been properly treated for smut. It was too late now to do anything about it if it hadn't. He had paid for treated wheat, but there would be no way to come back on Adolph if it became clear that he had lied, except to take it out of his hide. There were so many crooks a man could never get at.

That big crook J. P. Morgan, for example. The Democratic Senate Committee had been investigating him this whole week, and proving what any sensible man had known for a long time — that if a crook was only a big enough crook, he could get away with anything. Even Calvin Coolidge had been in on Morgan's stock market manipulations — just two or three months before the crash back in 1929. Ah, but Morgan could dole out a little money here and there, and people thought he was a wonderful philanthropist — "a builder."

Nevertheless, George knew that things were going to change. He liked to remember what Lincoln had said about how nobody could fool all of the people all of the time. The time was coming — the time when the majority of the people would no longer be fooled. The time was nearly here when there would be enough men like himself to make a stand. Then all of those Wall Street jackals could damn well run to their hypocritical churches and sit and quake in their plush high-priced pews. The little men would be waiting for them outside.

And when the little men were finished, there would be a new economic system. Countless paper transactions could no longer transform this wheat he seeded here in this solid earth to paper wealth that enabled speculators from New York and Chicago to possess even the government without shedding a drop of sweat.

A flock of crows scratched busily at a safe distance behind him. *These* were the robbers he could shoot. The idea of having seed wheat go straight from the drill box into a crow's gizzard was almost more than he could tolerate. He stopped the team and took his shotgun from a set of hooks he had screwed into the drill. He blasted both barrels into the crows and a screaming "Caw! Caw! *Caw!*" mocked him from behind. He whirled around with the gun and saw Lester Zimmerman sitting on his wagon box, laughing.

"You're a lucky bastard! If I'd had a shell left in here you'd be full of shot right now!" George roared.

"Caw! Caw!" Lester answered.

George went over to the road and leaned on the wagon. He pushed his hat back on his wet forehead. "In fact, Lester, you use up more luck every week than I've ever had in my whole life. That old barn of yours gets a worse lean to it every day. If I was to walk in that thing it'd fall down on me before I so much as picked up a milk stool. But I'll tell you *one* thing — if I was you and I was in there milking, I'd never aim a sneeze at that south side. Now, for a small fee, I'd jack that thing up for you." He bowed. "You see before you an expert with a building jack."

"To hell with you!" Lester said. "You'll never catch *me* fixing up *my* place for no landlord! And if he goes ahead and kicks me offa there, I'll fix it so's that old barn will fall right on his bald pate. That reminds me — how come you got all that hair everywhere but on the top of your head? If a redheaded man gets bald, is he *still* mean?"

"Just twice as mean," George assured him. "By the time I lose the last hair up here, there isn't one of you boys that'll dare look cross-eyed at me."

Lester started up his team. "I'm gonna butcher that old Jersey bull this fall. He ain't worth feeding through the winter. You wanta buy a little piece of hide to cover your scalp? It'll just match. And one of you's about as ornery as the other."

"I got a *brain* that keeps my scalp warm!" George shouted after him.

George went back to the field that seemed no more and no less empty than before. The sounds of his neighbor moving away down the road were lost in the sounds that accompanied him around the field — the scraping and creaking of machinery, the monotonous thudding of the sixteen thick hoofs, and the calls of birds and insects. There were so many sounds more indigenous to the prairie than the sound of human speech. By the time he had made one round of the field he no longer heard any echoes of his conversation at all, and he began to sing to himself and the horses.

They were the songs he had heard his own father sing in the field — about the bulldog on the bank and the bullfrog in the pond, the mockingbird, the Red River Valley, and the goose that died with a toothache in her head. He often sang a song about the railroads:

Oh I like Jim Hill, he's a good friend of mine,
And that's why I'm hiking down Jim Hill's main line.
Hallelujah, I'm a bum, hallelujah, bum again . . .

He liked all the songs of American soldiers too, and he would march along to "Yankee Doodle" or "Dixie" or "The Girl I Left Behind Me," hearing in his head the quick piercing notes of the fife playing above the drums and horns in a parade — martially gay and painful. "How I loved that gal, that pretty little gal — The girl I left be-ee-*hind* me!"

That was the song played by the band of the Seventh Cavalry as Colonel Custer rode out of Fort Abraham Lincoln, heading for the draw above the Little Big Horn River. Custer's widow had died just a few days ago. She was ninety-one years old, and she had been a widow for fifty-seven years. The *Sun* had carried a long piece about her and the fort and the massacre, and how the steamboat *Far West* had come out of the Yellowstone country and down the Missouri to bring the news to Libby Custer and the other wives waiting at the fort. George had always been proud to be named after the Boy General, and he always paid particular attention to anything he came across in his reading that had to do with him.

Like his namesake, George was a gambler. Nobody could farm that country without being a gambler. One good year, with enough moisture, plus high prices in the fall — that was all it took to make up for six or seven years of failure. There were smart gamblers and stupid gamblers, but every North Dakota farmer was a gambler, and even the smartest one reached a point, every season, where all he could do was stand and watch what happened to his crop like a man watching the spinning of a gambling wheel constructed in Hell. When several good years came along in a row, he cashed in on his lucky streak and put his winnings back into the game, like any other sporting adventurer, by investing in new buildings, new machinery, more stock, more land.

But when the good years came even farther apart than the seven promised in the Bible, perhaps he failed utterly. Then he watched the last days of the earth, while plague after plague was unloosed upon him, with the hailstones as heavy as cannon balls, and the great star falling on the fountains of waters and scorching his unrepentant head, and the grasshoppers as big as horses, with breastplates of iron. Then he stood in the midst of the ruin, smelling the smoke from the bottomless pit, hearing the echoes of the last thunder and the final trumpet blasts, and he did not repent of the work of his hands. He was proud of having played out the game, even though his name be blotted out of the book of life. He was brokenhearted and wounded with the kind of permanent wounds that only the proud sustain, but still he was proud. If he had it to do all over again, he would choose to gamble again.

❦ ❦ ❦

Lucy sat on the rough, hot boards of the porch. She was all ready to go to town, having sponged off her chest and legs and put on a clean pair of shorts. She was waiting for her mother to finish putting the bread to rise so they could leave. The sun flashed from a rust-free spot on the Ford and in line with that flash was another flash, fifty yards away at the edge of the grove.

She took a languid step from the porch, wondering if she had time for an investigation before the car left for town. She fixed her eyes on the flash and she saw it move as sun reflections never did. She walked quickly but quietly toward it. She stopped when she saw what it was — a straying young jack rabbit, running in short crouching steps, snuffing at the unfamiliar ground.

She wetted a finger and held it up — a trick she had read in one of her mother's Ernest Thompson Seton books. Good — the rabbit was upwind from her. She was sure she could catch it, for it was hardly more than a baby. It kept its long, kangaroo-like hind legs in tight circles against its flanks, the way rabbits were always drawn in books. She wondered if it was hurt, and thought of how she would love it and pet it and feed it and make it well again.

At last she was so close that her shadow, short as it was in the late-morning sun, passed blackly over the baby's haunches and turned the circles of brindled fur into miniatures of the galvanic hind legs on a full-grown jack rabbit. It leapt away in short, strong jumps, but it went in a fatal direction. She forced it away from the shelter of the grove, making it dart back and forth in front of her, expending valuable energy, before it struck off across the yard, heading for the wheat fields.

If God had just reached down and suspended the rabbit's motion for only an instant, she could have caught it easily, for she was always so close that she needed just an extra moment to bend forward, stretch her arm to the ground, and scoop it up. Instead, they went all the way across the yard with neither gaining on the other. As they veered past the house she used the last breath she could spare to shout at the open kitchen window, "I'm catching a rabbit! Don't go without me!"

Her legs began to ache and something hot swelled and swelled inside her head. But the little rabbit, too, was exhausted and frantic. He no longer tried for distance, but only for deception. He would dart to one side and freeze next to an extra-large clod or a rock, and then, when he saw her stumbling shadow, spring off to find another bit of hopeless shelter.

She fell, finally, and if he had been wise enough to hop away immediately, he could have got the head start he needed. Instead, he remained in his last hiding place, shrunk into the smallest possible ball of grayish, white-tipped hairs, and she closed her hand over his back just as he started to jump away.

He uttered a frightful sound halfway between a squeal and a whistle. The claws of his little hind foot dug into her wrist and scraped down her arm. When the foot came to her elbow, it pushed against her upper arm and catapulted him into the air.

She stood watching him go, scarcely noticing that the blood was beginning to fill the long white scratches, wondering why it was that wild things were so afraid of people. Why didn't he know — why wasn't there some way to tell him that she wished only to take care of him and keep him for her own? It was always the same. She had caught wild things before. Once she had followed a little white-breasted nuthatch all over the grove for half the morning. She managed to touch its wings once or twice, but it always flew away to the bottom of another tree and started working its way up the trunk, pecking at the bark with its tiny beak. Perhaps at last it got used to her, for it ignored her an extra split second and she captured it. But when it was in her hands, fluttering its wings and scrabbling its many wire-sharp toes against her palms, she let it go because of her own fright.

It was even worse the time she tried to lift a woodpecker baby out of its mysterious hiding place. She waited till she saw the adult flicker fly out of the hollow tree, and then she stuck her hand inside the hole to feel in the nest. Her defenseless arm was horrifyingly attacked by a beak that drilled holes in wood, and when she finally got her hand out of the hole, another grown bird shot straight into her face. After she got over being scared, she did remember something about the secret house in the hollow tree — it was so hot in there, from the bodies of the birds. And there was still the smell of warm feathers and down-covered babies clinging to her own skin.

It was always the same. She could catch almost anything she went after, if she only tried enough times, but once she caught it she could never hang on to it.

She sat down on the ground and watched the blood still oozing in the scratches. A person would never think a baby rabbit could have such strong legs or such long toenails. Why hadn't she hung on to him? She could have tamed him — she *knew* she could have.

For two years she had been trying to catch a rabbit, and now that she had finally caught one, what had she done? Let him go again!

⁂

Rachel was in a hurry to leave for town and get back in time to bake the bread. When she looked out the window, the two running specks were so far away that she thought Lucy must have decided she would rather chase the rabbit than go to town. She took off her apron, changed the baby, and put her into the car.

On the way to town she began to wonder if Lucy had caught the rabbit and what in the world they would do with it if she had. Lucy would never be persuaded to let it go and George would never consent to feeding and keeping an animal that was one of his worst enemies.

It seemed to her that the smallest events had a ridiculous way of juxtaposing themselves with other small events so that the confluence of trivialities became suddenly a bitter maelstrom involving them all. She was always caught in the center, trying to steer each disputant out again, still clinging to whatever splinter of righteousness he had ridden into the maelstrom in the first place. If George did allow Lucy to keep the rabbit till it was full-grown, he would surely never hear of letting it go again to reproduce itself. He would shoot it, as he shot scores of rabbits every winter, for the skins and for dog meat.

The rabbit would not be so attractive to Lucy after it was grown-up, but she would certainly never be able to resign herself to having it killed. George and Lucy would both be right and they would both look to her to uphold their respective cases. She did not at all enjoy being an arbitrator. It was not a job she had ever been cut out to do, but she was continually caught in the battles of these two who would never have been brought together if it were not for her. The battles were always part of her responsibility. She hoped the rabbit would escape, but she ached for Lucy's disappointment.

If only she had got the bread set ten minutes earlier, they would have been gone by the time the rabbit wandered into the yard. Sometimes her life seemed ruled by such meaningless little accidents of time and place. How difficult it was to see what rational purpose such a situation as this could serve in a rational existence. Yet one must believe that either everything or nothing had a rational purpose.

In the store she seated the baby on the counter and shuffled through her purse for her list. The list was not to keep her from forgetting something, but to keep her from buying anything that was not essential. Herman went off to collect the things on it while she stayed with Cathy.

Propped on one of the dusty shelves behind the counter, looking even grindier than the shelf it sat upon, was a stuffed pink rabbit that had sat there since long before Easter. It was lined up with the other punchboard prizes, and she had scarcely noticed it before.

When Herman came back to dump a sack of sugar against the front of the counter, she said casually, "Which of these boards do you punch for that rabbit up there?"

"Why it's right here, Mrs. Custer," he said. "People just seemed to quit punching on it. But you can see for yourself how good the chances are. Why there ain't more than fifty-sixty punches left on it. Look here! There's only five of 'em in this here section. Punch out all five and you get . . ." He rummaged around till he found a greasy sheet of cardboard.

"The last punch in each section wins a pound of Kissinger's Candy Easter Eggs. . . . I reckon them Easter eggs are melted all together, but I could throw in a Hershey bar if you was to punch out the five."

"Oh, *no!* I just meant I wondered which board the *rabbit* was *on*, that's all. I couldn't be buying candy like that."

"Oh, well," said Herman. He went back to get the Bull Durham and the canned pears. Rachel picked up the sheet with the prize numbers listed on it and studied it.

"Cuddly Easter Bunny," it read. "#8510."

She picked up the board with the little punching key dangling from its string. *Something* would guide her fingers and make her put that key in the right hole. For once an accident of time would be good — it would be time for the pink rabbit to be won.

She pushed the key into a tiny tinfoil seal and drove it firmly through the board. The curled-up paper with its fateful number dropped on the counter. She picked it up. #5305. She had not had the slightest idea that she would lose. In fact, it hadn't seemed like gambling at all when she was pushing the key through the board — because she had believed, in that instant, that she was pushing out the rabbit's number. She had thrown away a whole nickel. How often, this summer, would she have to tell Lucy there was no nickel for an ice cream cone? She couldn't believe she had done it.

Herman came back with the last of the groceries and added them all up. "Four dollars and thirty-seven cents," he said. "Say, Mrs. Custer, I could maybe sell you that rabbit cheap. It ain't very new-lookin' any more. Then I could put the money you give me on another prize when somebody punched out that rabbit."

She knew she must be blushing. "Oh, that's all right, Mr. Schlaht. I was just looking at it. . . . Oh, and add a nickel to that bill, will you? I just took a punch for fun."

He stared at her. "Well, where's the punch? You might've won something even better than the rabbit."

"Oh, no!" she cried. "It was just for *fun!*"

She couldn't bear to face him any longer. She started toward the door.

"But you never —"

"I'll run ahead and open the car door for you, so you can bring out the sugar," she said.

She followed him back into the store, swept the sack of groceries off the counter, and fled.

Herman had found the number she punched and unrolled it. "Hey!" he called. "Hey, you won a prize! Your number's here in this here red prize section!"

He held up the tiny bit of paper, thinking she could not hear him.

"Hey, you won a free punch!" He stood in the door yelling at her, shaping his lips to help her make out what he was saying.

She shook her head at him and drove off.

When she got home, George was down at the house waiting to help her unload and to be fed his dinner. He took the can of pears out of the sack. It was one of the few things that bore a trademark, because most of the staples came from Herman's bulk bins and sacks. He looked at the label.

"What did you buy these pears for?" he demanded.

"Why? I just thought it would be nice to have a can of fruit on hand. I'm all out of my own, till the fruit comes in again.

"Oh, now, Rachel, you *know* that's *not* what I mean! You *know* it's not the pears; it's the *principle* of the thing. Why did you buy *this* brand?"

"Why, I never even saw it," she said. "Herman reached it down for me and I . . ."

"Herman!" George exclaimed. "Boy, how dumb can he get! What's he doing, carrying this big store stuff anyhow? He's just cutting his own throat, that's all. These chain stores would be happy if they could put every little fellow in the country out of business. They own *millions* of acres right now. They crowd out the little guys and then they let the little guys come back and work for *them* — for whatever *they* want to *pay*, that is. It's just a slow way to starve, that's all. That's what the Finleys were doing before they decided to try and get to Canada — picking tomatoes down in Indiana on a big company farm."

"Did Lucy catch the rabbit?" Rachel asked.

"Yeah, she caught it all right. You'll probably have a *fit* when you see how it scratched her — *you'll* have her *dead* from lockjaw or gangrene."

"What happened!"

"*Nothing!*" he retorted. "She caught him and he kicked her and she let him go, that's all. It's a good thing for her, too. I can just *see* myself growing feed for a damned *rabbit!*"

"Where *is* she?" Rachel said.

"Oh, she'll be along. She's still out roaming around and pouting over it. Boy, when I was that age I sure wasn't out using up good energy on such foolishness, I can tell you *that!* My old man would have had me out with the hoe, planting potatoes! It's getting drier by the day. Quicker I get everything in, the better chance it has."

"Will you call her to dinner?" Rachel asked.

George walked around the house to the west side and beamed his voice toward the fields. Rachel thought perhaps it had been a good accident after all when she didn't win the rabbit. How in the world would George have taken to *that?*

Lucy was furious at missing a trip to town, and she would not talk when she came in.

"Lower lip's a *mile* long," George observed acidly.

"Why, *honey*, you should have put something *on* that right away!" Rachel said. "Come over here to the window and let me look at it in the light. Does it hurt a lot?"

Lucy stared away without speaking.

"You *answer* your mother when she asks you a question or you'll eat your meals *standing up* for a week!" George shouted.

"No," Lucy said defiantly.

"As soon as I slice the potatoes to fry, I'll fix it," Rachel said.

Lucy did enjoy the big bandage. It made her feel that perhaps, after all, she had fought a good fight. After dinner she poked about in the cupboard to see what was new from her mother's shopping. She could always hope that there would be a tiny white sack there with a little candy in it.

"Why didn't you bring me some candy, for leaving me at home?" she said.

"Oh, honey, I *forgot!* I was thinking of so many things!" (The nickel — the whole nickel she had wasted!)

Rachel fixed her one of her candy substitutes — dry uncooked oatmeal mixed with several teaspoons of sugar in a tin measuring cup — Lucy always insisted on the tin cup. She went out and sat on the porch to eat it, staring off at the edge of the woods where she had first seen the rabbit — brooding.

Each vertebra, it seemed to Rachel, was painfully sharp along the round of Lucy's drooping back. How could there be any resistance in such a spare body? What if she *should* get an infection? She would be gone, before they had time to get her to a doctor. Why was her cheek so flushed and why was she so listless? She might very well be coming down with blood poisoning. Stuart had had it once, when he was about fourteen. *That* had been just a scratch, too. He didn't even know how he got it. He had almost died, and he was a husky boy then, not tall yet, the way he got later, but with a bit of early adolescent fat still on him — much, much more to spare than Lucy had. His whole arm had become horribly red and swollen, and red lines ran down it and up his shoulder. They had saved him, but just barely. He kept a fever for over a week.

She went out on the porch. "Let me feel your forehead," she said. Lucy lifted her face. She seemed hot, Rachel thought. "Now let's look at your arm." It seemed very red.

George came down for the new package of Bull Durham which

he had forgotten. "I'm worried about Lucy's arm," Rachel told him.

"Oh, pshaw! You just *look* for trouble, don't you?" he said.

"No, I don't! I wouldn't *have* to look for it if *you* would look a little more! You should have put something on that as soon as it happened!"

"*I* didn't even *know* when it happened," he protested.

"Well, and just *why* didn't you? Because you've *trained* her never to say when she's hurt. You've *shamed* her into not talking about how bad she may feel. You tell her to be like an Indian — no matter if she's *dying!* Well, she's *not* an Indian. Maybe Indians *didn't* care if their children died from blood poisoning, but *I* do!"

"Now, then, just what are you trying to say, Rachel? You know I care what happens to her just as much as you do! It's just that I can't stand a sissy, and I'm not going to let you turn her into one!"

"It's not sissy to complain when you have something wrong with you and you need help! If Stuart hadn't let Dad know when his arm first started to hurt, he'd be dead by now. Just don't forget what happened to Danny McNelis! All because his father had *beaten* it into him never to talk about how he felt!"

It was no use arguing with her, once she brought up Danny McNelis. George put down the dipper he had been drinking out of. "All right, pack her up and drive her thirty miles to Jimtown and use all that gas and pay some damn doctor two dollars to pour some iodine on her and send you home!"

Listening from the porch, Lucy did feel a little sick thinking about what happened to Danny McNelis last year. When he came to school that morning, he had not looked well. Even Miss Liljeqvist had noticed it and asked him if he wanted to go home. He said no, he felt fine. All day long he got whiter and whiter. In the afternoon he fainted and fell out of his desk. His father came then and took him to Jamestown. That night Danny died from appendicitis. And Danny's father, though he felt so awful, still was very proud of the way Danny had acted. Lucy often heard him talking over at the store. "Never a single word did he say! Can you beat that?" Danny's father would ask.

But Lucy's mother had told her afterwards that if Danny's father had not been so set on making a little boy act like a tough grown man, Danny might still be alive. It certainly made more sense to *say* when you had a bad stomachache, and never mind if your father called you a sissy or not. Fathers were not always right, were they?

❧ ❧ ❧

It was going to be another hot summer, Rose thought. Here it was still May, and only midmorning, and the sun beating on the tarred roof of the chicken house had already made the air impossible. She would have begun the cleaning much earlier if she had known the day would turn this way. The stench was so strong it hurt her nose. She leaned against the door frame, still sticky with the creosote they had sprayed to get rid of the mites. The fumes of it grew more intense in the heat, like the chicken manure, but a hot breeze brought unpolluted air to her.

What *ails* me, anyway? There's *nothing* wrong with you! What ails you for *thinking* something's wrong? You haven't changed a bit since you were ten years old. You've had fifty-four years to learn how to clean a chicken house without dirtying your mind as much as your rubbers, and still you can't do it. Just think of what you've been thinking in there. How much you hate chickens. How much you hate to wash eggs. How much you hate to butcher chickens and smell the filthy brown of their warm intestines in your hand. How you wouldn't care a bit if the chicken thieves took every last hen in this place the next time they come. How you could watch the whole flock get coccidiosis and die slowly and miserably and never feel a qualm of sympathy. Yes, how you could watch them all, and God knows, *nothing* can look as sick and pitiful as a chicken.

Your own father, Rose Stuart, would have punished you with his buggy whip for saying such thoughts aloud. Is it any better, now that you're fifty-four years old, to say them to yourself? Now that there is no one to punish you but God? Should you not be thankful, every minute of your life, that you have not had to live the life of your mother and to bear eleven children in a sod hut to a man who would not control either his wicked temper or his evil desires? And should a woman who has been married for thirty-six years, Rose Shepard, be still remembering a dead father's cruelty — and, far worse, should she be remembering him as if she had not forgiven him long ago? Should there be any hatred in a Christian woman who has had fifty-four years to learn to follow Christ?

You may well ask, Rose Stuart, what ails you when you let your mind be filled all morning with complaints and vicious thoughts. You should thank God for every egg you wash and every chicken you eat. People are starving to death everywhere in the world. You should be on your *knees* before God right here in this stinking manure, thanking Him that you do not have to steal the chickens you eat.

Oh, God forgive me, God forgive me. I don't hate him any more. No, and I don't hate the chickens. Don't let the things come into my head. How do they come there when I have continually commanded them to stay away, when I have prayed for strength to fight them away? It's the smell; the smell becomes my brain. Now here I am, already pitying myself again, excusing myself, and yet a whole lifetime was given to me so that I could learn gratitude. Forgive me, forgive me.

My back is worse than usual today. That must be what ails me. What was he thinking of, my father David Stuart, when he set me to drawing buckets of water from the deep well, hand over hand, before I was eight years old? Didn't he know it would bend me so I would never be straight again? He didn't care, that was all. Stop, stop, stop! I've had good health all my life. My back is my only cross and I have always been able to work. What if I had been asked to bear tuberculosis or paralysis or the loss of a limb or insanity? Can I not ever, ever learn to be grateful? I have had enough air. The more I breathe, the more my mind disobeys.

She set to work again, loosening the droppings with her hoe and scraping them into shovel-sized piles. When she had to stop to breathe again, she shoveled a load into the wheelbarrow and took it to the compost pile in the orchard.

They had so carefully cultivated and protected that little orchard. Will had dug a fence deep into the ground to keep out the gophers and other burrowers that would have chewed the roots of the baby trees. They had done everything they could to nurture and guard it; yet a predestined force had prevailed over it—the same force that had overtaken Stuart, when he had gone on a lark with some other boys and they got hold of some bootleg liquor. There was only one way to explain the force. There was only one reason why there should be a difference between what people knew was right and what people did. There was a force far stronger than mortals which intervened between them and their consciences, and that force was Satan.

The burning hellish years had come. Never before had the world been so evil. The thousand-year reign of the Beast had begun, and the mark of the Beast was on all who bought and sold, as it said in the Bible — for if the mark of the Beast had not been on men during these last years when governors and judges and senators had been the open and avowed friends of the bootleggers — even pallbearers, yes pallbearers, for bootleggers who had been shot by other bootleggers — if the protecting mark of the Beast was not on those men, then why had the world not risen up and overwhelmed them?

This drought that slowly stifled the orchard — it was only one of the many symptoms that the Thousand Years had begun. Everywhere among the great and powerful of the earth there was fornication, idolatry, drunkenness, and blasphemy. And her own son had run away into that doomed world — for two years he had been there — dragged there by those whose greed drove them to damn the souls of boys.

She hurried back to the chicken house to finish the cleaning and scatter new straw before she should have to go in to begin Will's dinner. A hen clucked at her from a nest. It was a warning all too easy to interpret this time of the year. The hen would have to be captured and put in a breaking-up coop before it managed to sneak off and make a nest in the weeds where coyotes would get the eggs.

She leaned her hoe against the wall and walked slowly around the roosting poles. The hen became louder and more quarrelsome. She wished she had her heavy leather gloves. It bothered her to be pecked by a chicken. She shot her hand beneath the warm feathers to grasp for the horny legs. Instead of pecking and standing its ground as she expected it to do, the hen half jumped, half flew at her face, with a startling rush of feathers and venomous exclamations. In her surprise, she missed her chance and the chicken squawked past her and thudded on the floor.

Rose got to the door first and slammed it shut. The hen retreated under the roosting bars and fluffed the feathers on her neck and spread her wings. She stalked about under the poles, uttering low wrathful sounds, and glaring from her red-rimmed, unblinking eyes.

Rose pushed at her with the hoe. The hen shouted savagely from a wide-open beak and zig-zagged under the poles, always out of reach.

Finally Rose stooped quickly, doubled herself under the poles, grabbed a leg, and straightened up too soon, knocking her head against the befouled roost. Dizzy from her sudden move and the blow on the back of her head, she staggered to the door, dangling the screeching chicken from her hand. The hen battled with her wings till Rose flung her through the door of the first empty coop. One more hen that would have to be fed and watered separately for a week or more while she sat on the slats until the air circulating under her superheated breast cooled her nesting ardor. There was no use taking a setting hen out of the breaking-up coop until she had stopped clucking for a couple of days. So long as she clucked, her feeble mind was on nothing but hatching eggs.

Rose went back to her scraping, still dizzy and still determined to be done with this job before she went in to clean herself up and peel the potatoes.

❧ ❧ ❧

Will wanted to finish drilling his flax field before he went in for dinner, but he stopped the Fordson for a minute anyway, and climbed down from it to lean against the drill box and rest.

Even standing on the ground he still felt the vibrations of the tractor, like a sailor without his land legs. The engine missed badly. He'd have to have it gone over as soon as he could spare it for a day or two. Maybe George could find the time to fix it. It would be a way to put a little cash into George's two big proud fists. He unscrewed the top of the tank behind the seat and poured gas into it from the five-gallon can stored on the tractor platform. The engine continued to sputter and he thought he better get going again before it stalled and died on him. He didn't want to have to crank it.

He did finish the field, pushing himself and the Fordson hard, and then he rode the tractor in and left it standing in the shade of the barn. Thirty feet above him, the galvanized blades of the windmill spun a blurred aureole from the beams of the sun.

Everything was in a straight line — the sun with its invisible ring of blazing million-mile petals, the tin flower of the windmill blooming with hot light, the point of the well pipe four hundred feet below the revolving blades, and the middle of the earth. He and his windmill were suspended between two fires — the fire ninety-three million miles away in frigid space and the fire at the core of the planet.

The water came up warm from the well, because it tapped a warm spring in the earth. Rose had never been satisfied with the well. It looked to her as though the men who drilled it had simply been trying to get as much money as they could. They had gone through vein after vein of refreshing, cool water, charging more for each foot they drilled, until they struck this warm, salty, heavy stuff under the layers of rock and clay and sand and gravel. But the suppy was inexhaustible. As the drought got worse and worse, Will was more and more thankful that those well-drillers had tried to skin him. It just went to show how often a bad turn really worked out for the best.

Before he had got used to the sharpness of the water, it had only made him the more thirsty when he drank it, but he had learned to like it and so had his family. They had a big cement cistern under the house from which they could pump fresh cold water into the kitchen all year round if only they got enough snow and rain during the wet months. The gutters along the roof caught the water and piped it down through a charcoal filter into the cistern. Then they pumped it back again through a brick filter. But in the years when the cistern went dry during the summer, they all drank the salty water brought up by the windmill, just as the stock did.

The water was flowing now out of the long, moss-lined cattle trough down the hill to the sheep trough, and then out of the sheep trough into the pasture. He hardly ever shut off the windmill, because he had never had the slightest indication that there was any end to the water supply. Still, with both tanks full and the water evaporating so quickly — there was no use tempting fate. He walked under the tower and pulled on the wire leading to the blades. The flower folded shut, the companionable nagging sounds of the rubbing parts ceased, the long rudder behind the blades creaked and drifted in the wind. For a while the salty river where the well pipe drank was free to flow wherever it would — there below the layers and layers of earth.

He walked away from the flashing iron skeleton of the tower and looked up its narrowing height and the ladder that went to the top of it. He shook his head, remembering the day he had had to go all the way up to fetch Lucy back down from that ladder when she was only four. Stuart had pulled the same stunt, too, when he was about the same age.

Stuart was dark now, but he'd been almost as light-haired as Lucy. The two heads had looked very like each other up there — tiny bright flowers a few feet beneath the great spinning flower. And when he climbed up to them, the two expressions had been the same — absorbed, purposeful, astonishingly innocent. The heads that had looked so tiny, so many miles away, looked so big when he got to the top of the ladder with them. Their chests, their stomachs, their narrow little seats were all smaller around than their heads. How did the baby bodies balance the heavy heads? How did the two-inch fingers grip so confidently the wide flat ladder rungs?

Both of them were wounded and bitterly indignant. Neither of them felt the slightest need to be rescued. They had simply wanted to go as high as they could go and see as much as they could see, and it happened that they were not through exploring when he came after them. He grinned and shook his head again.

Rose was pumping up the kerosene stove for a last jet of heat when she heard Will speak to the gold-and-white collie in the shed. He sloshed water from the basin over his arms and face and then he called in to her.

"You know, Rose, every time I read in the paper about how they're shipping water all over the country on freight trains just to keep the stock alive, I'm mighty thankful for that salty well out there."

"I suppose we ought to be," she said. She was not in the mood for conversation. She was exhausted and she felt like a ninny for having got such a knot on her head because of a stubborn old hen. She had a headache now, but she refused to take an aspirin for an ailment that she had stupidly brought upon herself.

Even his first washing out in the shed had taken enough dust off Will's face to show the whiteness of it, but Rose did not let on that she noticed it. She never gave in to illness herself and she never encouraged anybody else to. There had been only one time in her life when she had almost given in. That was several years ago, when she got pneumonia. Will had brought the doctor, but it was not because of the doctor that she had lived. It just hadn't been her time to go, that was all. Her mother and her grandmother had died of pneumonia. Weak lungs ran in the family, and her own bout with pneumonia had just been the first sign that she was going to go the same way the rest had.

"Rose, do you suppose George would have a fit if we gave Lucy a pony for her birthday this summer?"

"Why, Will, I'm *sure* he'd never let her have it. He's even mad every time I give Rachel some old thing to make Lucy a coat or a jumper out of. I declare, what *ever* made you even *think* of such a thing?"

Will leaned against the wall, still rubbing his hands and forearms with the towel. "Well, maybe it hurts his pride to think that he can't buy new clothes for Lucy. Maybe he'd look at a pony in a different light."

"*Everything* hurts his pride," Rose said. "No, I'm *sure* he wouldn't hear of it. It would just make trouble."

"I wish there was some way for her to have a pony," Will said wistfully. "Wouldn't it be fun to watch her come galloping over to visit us? She's such a wild little cuss. I bet she'd get a horse all lathered up just bringing in the cows."

Will ought not to encourage Lucy's turbulent behavior. It seemed to Rose as though she herself was the only one in the family who cared whether or not Lucy grew up to be a lady. Even now it was a fight to get her to wear a dress or to keep her legs together when she *was* wearing one. Rachel was working too hard to think about what Lucy's behavior might turn her into, and George and Will both did their best to make a tomboy out of her. It was awful. What would become of the child? After all, she *was* a girl. Every day she walked more like George, with long, unfeminine strides. "Whistling girls and crowing hens always come to some bad ends," Rose often told her.

Lucy would either sulk at this or laugh impertinently and whistle loudly. The child was a caution.

"Maybe it's just as well if she *doesn't* have a pony," Rose said. "She'd probably just kill herself on it."

"Oh, no," he argued. "She's really a pretty sensible little girl, I think. She'd handle a horse all right."

"Well, George would never hear of it and you know it. Come and eat."

❧ ❧ ❧

It was one of those smoldering spring days that just kept getting hotter and hotter — a foretaste, Rachel feared, of another scorching summer. In the middle of the afternoon she sent some water to the field with Lucy.

George saw the nimbus of her light hair, brilliant against the black earth, as she came over the rise of the hill toward him. There she was again, with nothing better to do than run over the fields. Why hadn't she been a boy?

He had not been too disappointed when she was first born, because he realized that one girl was an asset in a farm family; otherwise the mother had a hard time keeping up with the housework and the other babies as they came along. But no other babies had come for six years, and finally, after long months of hope, there was Cathy.

And the older Lucy got, the more it seemed to him that she should have been a boy. She was running so easily now that he could see she had no notion that she was coming up a hill. She brought him a quart of water in a gallon lard pail. A tin cup rolled and thumped around the bottom of the pail.

"You should have carried the cup in your other hand," he told her. "This way we have to reach our dirty hands down through the drinking water to get it."

He noticed the way something set in her face and it angered him. A man couldn't even make a contribution to the practical education of his child any more without having the child act abused. He handed back the drinking cup. She set off for the house again, picking up momentum as she began to go with the hill. When she was twenty or thirty feet away, he called over his shoulder, "Much obliged." He couldn't tell whether she heard him or not.

She put the pail in the kitchen and then she went and sat in her swing. She pulled the bandage aside to peek at the end of the longest scratch the rabbit had made. Then she stood up in the swing and began to pump. She wedged her feet against the ropes and shoved mightily. Higher and higher she went, until the long swing ropes stretched out almost parallel to the ground and she stiffened her body to keep from flying out at the forward end of the arc. Then the ropes would snap with a dangerous jolt and she would begin the descent and the backward curve that pulled on her back and legs and made her feel as though her stomach was dropping away behind her. At the other end of the arc she would be suspended for an instant, nearly horizontal, unable to breathe, looking down, like a bird, with just time to wonder before she started down again, if this was the moment she finally was going to fall.

There was a tantalizing branch at the end of the arc. She could almost touch it with the swing board, but not quite. Every day she tried it. Every day, when she had pumped up till the ropes went lax and free for that moment when she knew she might flip clear back over the branch from which the swing hung, she would begin to chant, "Please . . ." on the way up, "God . . ." on the way back, "make me . . ." on the way up again, "a boy," on the way back. There had to be the awful jerky moments at either end of the arc before she could begin the prayer. One had to be very brave to bear the sight of those ropes buckling and rippling with indecision. Every day she proved to God that she was worthy of being changed into a boy.

Saturday, June 17

WILL SAT reading the *Jamestown Sun* in the scuffed brown leather chair he had sat in almost every night for as long as they had lived in the tall yellow house. Rose filled half the living room with a quilting frame. The quilt was a generous double-bed size — five large white squares across and eight down, separated by wide bands of pale green. First she had quilted it all, in two-inch squares standing on their corners like diamonds, then she began stitching in the sunbonnet children. They were pleasingly conventionalized, with long flaring dresses cut from various scraps of print and huge sunbonnets of different solid colors. Even while she worked, Rose thought of how near the end of the world might be, and she wondered why it mattered to her to leave a thing like this behind her. This quilt, when it was finished, would be washed to brighten it after the long hours under her working hands, and then packed away in a trunk. When Lucy was married it would be given to her, and then, when her first daughter was married, to that daughter.

"Well, they're still after J. P. Morgan," Will said. "Seems they uncovered another railroad he got control of by shady means. That's what I try to tell George. A man's sins will be found out sooner or later. I've always believed in the justice of this world. Here . . . here's another piece here. Did you read this piece about Henry Wallace's speech, Rose?"

"No," she said. "I want to finish this square tonight. I probably won't get to the paper at all. Why don't you go ahead and read it to me?"

"Well, there's just a little bit here, but here's what he said, and he said it to a bunch of bigwigs, too. Just goes to show you that selfish men don't always run the government in this country. Here . . . he says, 'How much more socially intelligent it would be to redistribute purchasing power in such a way as to put it effectively to work. Unemployed purchasing power means unemployed labor and unemployed labor means human want in the midst of plenty.' There, now, isn't that just what ails us in a nutshell? That's mighty well put. Whatever you say about Roosevelt, this is quite a change from Hoover."

Rose nodded grimly. "I suppose they'll start finding out things about *Hoover*, now," she said. "Just the way they have about Coolidge."

"Oh, I think Hoover's probably an honest man," Will said. "Just scared to do anything for fear of getting on the wrong side of his

Wall Street friends. I don't know that there's anything a Republican could have done. The country was just going crazy, that's all.

"Say, I was just going to tell you how I got hold of some shearers today, and here I see the Happy Farmer wrote his poem about that. Says, 'Along about wool-clipping time, I'm jealous of the sheep, Who skip away and leave their clothes, Behind them in a heap.' He makes it sound awfully easy. Sometimes I wonder if he ever lived on a farm, you know that? But other times he hits it right on the nose. Well, anyhow, I was going to tell you, I talked to a gang of fellows today over at Larsen's, and they said they can come day after tomorrow. There's four of them, and they look pretty fast. They think they can do the flock in a day and a half, so that will be just a few meals for you to cook. They figure on finishing Larsen's tomorrow, and he had nearly six hundred. I didn't get much of a chance to talk to Larsen about them, but I gathered he was satisfied."

"They're all alike," Rose said.

"Well, I can tell you one thing, they were making *him* hump. He ought to have hired himself one more man — two helpers aren't enough, with four shearers. I'll get Ralph and George, I guess. I imagine George won't have quite so much to say this year about what a mistake it was for me to feed the flock all winter.

"Why, just think! Last summer we got seven cents a pound — that was hardly fifty cents a fleece — minus ten or fifteen to get it sheared. But the way the prices have been going up, by golly, it wouldn't surprise me if we'd get around two dollars this summer. I bet it'll be two bits a pound by the time they get around to paying us for what we ship. And Hoover's been blaming the low prices on the wool-growers. Too much wool, he said, that's why there's no market. But Roosevelt comes along and gets things to rolling again, and all of a sudden it looks like there *is* a market after all!"

And it wasn't taking another war to move prices either, the way a lot of people said it would. In fact, there was good news of peace in the paper. Italy, Britain, France, and Germany had just signed a Four-Power Peace Pact at Rome. It was a treaty to last ten years and then be renewed.

"I think maybe the world is starting to get some sense, Rose.

It looks like maybe people are finally going to spend money on something besides war. What do *you* think?"

"I think," she said, "that we're living in the Thousand Years of the Beast, right now."

He tried to josh her out of it, or think of something else to talk about whenever she said that. "Oh, Rose! Well, then, if you think that, let's take a vacation! We've never had one in our lives! Let's *go* somewhere this winter. When the boom was on, everybody else took their big wheat checks and went off to Florida or some place. But we just stayed right here in the cold and snow. It's cheap down there now — two or three dollars a day would get us a luxury room and meals. Come on, it's *our* turn now."

"Oh, Will, you don't know what you're saying! Ever since Harry closed the bank you've had one crazy idea after another! I couldn't enjoy myself for one minute spending money we ought to leave the children." Rose thought and then added, "George won't take it now, but I don't imagine he'll be quite so proud after we're gone and can't see the good it's doing them."

"Oh, Rose, he's not that way! He doesn't want to *spite* us. He's just an extra proud young man, that's all — but I wish he wasn't so blamed stubborn."

He gazed at her quilt a minute. "You wait and see. George won't let me pay him what I pay the shearers. 'They're skilled men,' he'll say. 'A skilled man is worth twice as much as a helper.' And then he'll work harder than any other man here, all day long."

He searched for his glasses and then, remembering that he hadn't been out of his chair, felt on the top of his head and flipped them back down to his nose. "I haven't had such itchy feet for forty years," he said. "I'd sure like to get a look at that Chicago fair.

"Says here, 'The most spectacular event in the opening of the Century of Progress Exposition was the turning on of the thousands of lights in the Hall of Science. By some highly scientific process, which has to do with a photoelectric cell, the light which left Arcturus, a fixed star of the first magnitude, was caught at four observatories in the nation and beamed to throw the master switch at the fair when Postmaster General James A. Farley pressed a button. The light which threw the switch had been traveling through space for forty years to reach the planet Earth.' Isn't that remarkable, Rose? Think of it! Think of the things man has discovered just since the turn of the century. It hardly seems possible. By golly, I sure would like to go to that fair."

"I suppose Mr. Farley thinks God made all the firmament so that *he* could push a button that was connected to a star some way."

"No, no, *that's* not the idea! The *light* was *there!* It was there all the time! And men just now figured out how they could use it."

"Of *course* the light was there all the time. And now man thinks he can step up to the throne of God because of some puny trick. I tell you, the days are at hand. We will *all* see how puny we are."

It depressed him when she was like this, and he felt as though he ought to do something about the terrible way she felt. He knew it was Stuart that made her feel this way. But he just felt too tired tonight. He shuffled his feet back into his slippers and wandered out the kitchen door. The full moon hurtled across the sky, riding over a wind-scattered flock of softly gleaming translucent clouds. The moon looked the way it looked through the wide-open door of a breezy boxcar when he rode it across the Kansas plains forty years ago.

He wondered where Stuart was tonight.

❦ ❦ ❦

Shearing day dawned hot and muggy. The wind that Will had hoped would bring a bit of cooler weather from the northwest had died down during the night, and there were no clouds at all. He and Rose got up extra early, but it was already hot enough to make them sweat as they did the morning's milking, and by the time George and the family arrived, Will had a bandanna tied around his forehead under his hat to keep the sweat out of his eyes. He was nervous with excitement. It was worth shearing this year. He wanted to get at it. Besides, any kind of harvest excited him. That was why he had come back from roving to be a farmer.

"What's the matter with that Sundquist boy, anyway!" he wondered. "I *told* him to get here so we could get set up before the shearers come! Well, George, I guess you and I can wrastle the dip tank."

The women lingered in the yard for one last bit of air before they began cooking. Finally Ralph Sundquist showed up, riding bareback on one of his father's workhorses.

"The old man promised me the truck today," he said, "but she wouldn't start, no matter what I done to her. Like to've cranked my arm off." He massaged the large muscle of his upper right arm.

"You can just turn your mare loose down below there," Will said. "We'll be fixing up the tank."

As they headed for the windmill George said, "You'd think the old man would have sense enough to do something about that mare's withers, wouldn't you?" Will nodded, half sick. One thing he and George agreed on. They couldn't bear to see an animal mistreated. The mass of weeping sores on Ralph's old mare revolted them both. It was really inexcusable to let a horse's shoulders get in that shape. Sundquist was just too tight to buy a decently padded collar for the poor beast. If it had been George's horse, he would have bought the collar even if he had had to sacrifice something he badly needed for his own health or comfort. Think of that mare pulling a load against a pair of shoulders like that.

"Maybe they're easing off on her," Will said, wanting to believe what he was saying. "Maybe that's why Ralph rode her today."

They still had not finished pumping the dip tank full and getting the chemicals into it when the shearers arrived in a rattling pickup. The truck came up the driveway so fast that the dust it raised still hovered over the whole length of the lane by the time the truck had stopped. Will nailed the driver as he jumped out of the cab.

"You come up here like that again and you're fresh out of a job," he said. He thought he smelled beer. Perhaps Gebhardt was already selling it in his little back room, even though it wasn't legal for two more weeks.

"Okay, okay," the driver said.

The other three men had already unhooked the single chain on the tailgate and begun to unload their equipment. They were as rough-looking as the driver. Will had noticed before how a crew of roving workers always looked ornerier and more suspicious the minute they came on his own place than they had looked when he observed them on somebody else's place. Itinerant workers were a different lot nowadays. Forty years ago, when he had been a temporary hobo, the crews were full of boys like himself, out to see a bit of the world on a harmless lark before settling down. But the men who had been coming through for the last two decades tended more and more to be like these ruffians — beaten men, looking forward to nothing.

What would they do with the sheep, he wondered. Two full days of pay from Larsen was enough to get them all three sheets to the wind. It was a cinch he wouldn't pay them anything till they were through. With the price of wool up as it was, he wanted a good close job. He could lose as much on every fleece as it cost him to get it clipped if they didn't take it off properly. He wished he hadn't contracted to pay them by the hour; it might have been better to pay by the fleece so he could dock them on any sheep that wasn't properly sheared.

Each of the four men set himself up in a separate stall with his equipment. The double doors at either end of the barn were wide open, but the building was airless; it was going to be mighty hot labor. Will hoped they would sweat out their beer in a hurry.

Ralph and George, with the collie circling the bleating sheep, drove a dozen head down through the yard from the shed and into a couple of stalls where Ralph stayed to be supply man for the shearers. Will herded each newly sheared sheep up the incline leading to the platform above the tank and shoved it off into the amber water, which reeked with creosote and tobacco and other poisons meant to kill various pests — the worst being ticks and scab mites.

George grabbed the terrified, sputtering animal by the folds of its neck, forcing it to swim the length of the tank, and then pulled and pushed it up to the platform at the other end. From there the sheep usually needed no more encouragement to run down the ramp and into the lane, bellowing and dripping and shaking from its cold bath and its drastic haircut. A newly shorn ewe, George thought, could look about as ridiculous as any critter in the world. Her neck was so surprisingly thin and long, and with the thick wool gone from her face, her forehead was low and bony.

As the oldest of the three men, Will ought to have assigned himself the least taxing job of keeping the shearers supplied with sheep and tying up the fleeces, but he wanted to be where he was in order to keep an eye on the kind of job the shearers were doing. He checked the closeness of every clip, running his fingers over the lightly fuzzed wrinkles of shorn skin as he guided each sheep up to the tank. He also made sure that any gouge got well dosed with a virulent solution of iodine. He had discovered a long time ago that the best way to run a farm was for its owner to be everywhere at once.

The first time he looked up at the sun to estimate the hour, he wondered how he would last till dinner. He had known the time in his life when he could work steadily and never even think to look up until the sun was standing so straight and hot over his shoulders that he knew it was noon. But now he felt the shocks of the struggling sheep tear at his middle, and when the first ewe with a couple of clipped teats came through, he burst into fury. He examined her quickly. She was still nursing. A lamb was in for a kick or two. He swabbed her with iodine and pressed a palmful of salve against her to ease the smart of her bath. Then he stormed back to the shearer from whose hands he had received her a moment before.

He had to shout above the uproar of the engine turning the long flexible shafts and the clippers buzzing at the ends of the shafts and the sheep bleating beneath the clippers. "Now if another ewe comes through with her tits cut like that, I'll dock you an hour's pay! Either that or I'll take it out of your hide. I'm paying you by the hour just so you'll take your time and do a good close job without nicking these animals. You talked me out of paying you by the fleece, and now, by God, I expect you to do first-class work! Now go and take five minutes off and have a smoke and don't send me any more sheep like that!"

The shearer, a bristly-faced young man wearing shamelessly taut Western-style jeans over his solid thighs, flopped his new sheep on its side and attacked it with the clippers. When he finished the sheep, he gave her a shove with his foot, not looking at Will, rolled himself a cigarette, and strolled out toward the fence where Lucy sat watching the dipping.

"Jesus, what a dirty business this is," he remarked to her. Lucy did not know what to say to any stranger, least of all one who would swear for no good reason right in front of a child. She had been told to smile at people who talked to her, so she parted her lips to show the two top teeth that were still so big for her mouth and closed them again. She was conscious of the way her upper lip felt over the teeth, and she drew it down and hooked the teeth inside of it.

After she smiled she looked away from the shearer down at the damp trails scuffled into the hard ground by the horrified sheep.

"No critter on earth as dumb as a sheep," he said. "Look at that old grammaw jumping around like a spring lamb."

"It probably feels good to get all her wool off on a hot day," Lucy said.

"Well, if she knows it's gonna feel so good, why don't she just set still then, when a fella's trying to shear it off her? Tell me that? If a sheep ain't the dumbest animal in the world, why don't they learn, after while, that getting clipped off makes 'em feel good?" He blew a smoke ring that collapsed before he had time to show it to Lucy.

"Well, I don't know," she said, "But I'd like to have a lamb and feed it with a bottle every day."

A thought came to him — a very funny thing that he had learned recently. "You know what happens to this here wool now?"

"Sure," she said. "Grandpa and Daddy and Ralph put all the tied-up fleeces into the wool sacks and tramp it down to get three hundred pounds in each one and then Grandpa takes them to town. Then after while he gets the money. He told me he was going to get a whole lot this year, too."

"Ya, but what happens after that?" he persisted.

"They make sweaters and coats," she said dubiously. It was hard to imagine how this manure-matted, bug-infested stuff could be transformed into the red and blue sweaters she saw at Christmastime in the Penney's store.

"Ya, but *before* that," he went on, satisfied that she didn't know, "they wash it, see? You know what happens when you wash a frying pan or something, that has a lotta grease in it? You know how the grease all floats up to the top?"

"Yes," she said, frowning distractedly at the pastures shimmering with heat. It was far from noon but she was feeling hungry.

He was irritated. She was pushing him out of her mind. "Well," he said roughly, "they wash this here filthy-dirty wool just like a frying pan, see? And then ya know what they do with that dirty old grease all fulla manure? They make stuff for women to put on their *face* out of it! All kinds of cream. They put something in it to make it nice and white and some stinky *per*fume so the women don't ever know how it used to smell, and all them women never know what they're smearing all over their faces!" He laughed in coarse triumph. She was looking at him *now*, all right. "Your *own* ma uses it, I bet!"

"She does not!" Lucy cried. "She doesn't *ever* put *anything* on her face, because we don't believe in it, that's why." She stopped. If her father ever heard her contradict any grown-up person he might whip her, but she said it anyway. "Anyhow, I bet they don't *either* do that." She looked at him to see if he would tell on her.

"Oh, yes they do!" he said. "Maybe *your* ma don't, on account of she knows where it comes from, but them city women all do." He added in a high sissy voice, mimicking a woman talking on the radio, "Lady Esther's Cole Cream. At your favorite drugstore cosmetics counter." He flipped his cigarette butt into the wet path made by the sheep. "*You'll* smear it all over *your* face, too, in a couple more years!"

"I will not!" she yelled so loudly that her father heard her above the noise of the sheep and shot her an ominous look, the way he did when there was company and she said something wrong. The shearer laughed lewdly. He was looking at a picture he had evoked for himself of a city girl wearing plenty of paint, like a girl in a movie, saucily angry with a man the moment before she succumbed in his arms.

He leered up into the little girl's face. Then he flexed his spine against the fence rails, snapping his body forward and into a reluctant shamble back to the job.

Lucy sat glowering after him. There was always some new reason why it was an intolerable joke to be female. But she intended to find out if that was true about cold cream — not that she had ever thought of using it. . . .

In the house Rose and Rachel worked making ready the first of the season's harvest feasts. Itinerant workers expected a well-stocked table; it was the women's job to try to make up for the murderous pace their husbands set in the shearing stalls and the threshing fields.

The workers often tried to get the women to feel competitive about cooking. At noon they might say, "My that was good lemon pie, Mrs. Shepard. I reckon lemon pie is my favorite dessert next to chocolate cake with white frosting on it. Over at Mrs. Larsen's last night we *did* have a good dark cake."

That night there would have to be a devil's food cake — three layers of it, topped by a thick gleaming crust of seven-minute frosting.

Most of the afternoon Lucy licked pans and dishes, ran errands, and herded Cathy about the house to keep her from being too much in the way.

"I'll be glad when she decides to walk and gets up out of the dirt a little," her grandmother said as she carried an enormous kettle of boiled potatoes away from the stove to drain them into another big kettle on the tin table. For supper she was going to make potato salad, because the weather was so hot.

When she had finished pouring off the water, she looked down at the baby, scooting about in a grindy pair of diapers. "I sweep it out and the wind blows it back in faster than I can sweep it out," she said. "*My* mother walked when she was only eight months old, and she had eleven babies and of the eight of them that lived, there wasn't one that didn't walk before it was a year old. It ran in our family to walk early. When you think of all the petticoats we wore, I wonder how we did it."

Both her grandparents liked to tell Lucy how her mother had been so little and walked so early that when she first walked she went right under the tin kitchen table without ever knowing it was there. They would laugh over how mad her baby mother got when she first started bumping her head on the drawer under the table. "You could tell she was just crying because she was mad. She really had a temper when she was little like that, but then she got over it. And talk! How she would chatter on and on. You ought to have heard her talking to her doll. It was just an old corncob doll, not a nice one like yours. Hardly any little girls had real dolls then. They cost so much more money in those days. But you just should've seen your mother put that corncob doll to bed every night, and cover it up just like it was a real baby."

Lucy loved to hear them talk about when her mother was a little girl, though she could not have told why.

Tuesday, July 4

THE MIDSUMMER was no less muddled than the spring. The British restrictions of food imports were beginning to ruin the South American farmers the way the North American farmers had already been ruined. Thousands of sheep were being slaughtered in Chile and left dead on the ranges because the farmers could find no market for mutton. In China the drought was so bad that no grass grew and the trees died. The people of China were eating each other and ants were dining on mutton in the Chilean hills. It did seem as though Secretary Wallace was right when he kept saying that the world's problems were essentially a question of distribution.

On the other hand, Wallace's experiment to redistribute the consumer's dollar so that the American farmer would get more of it and the middleman less did not seem to be working. The price of a loaf of bread in wheat states went from six to eight cents — the thirty-three per cent increase being blamed by the flour millers on the thirty per cent processing tax they were paying. The AAA tax was being passed on to the consumer, exactly the way George had predicted it would. It wasn't costing the middleman a thing. The question of distribution was going to have to be settled by the little men.

This very day he had talked with men at picnic tables who appeared to be wholly of his opinion. Freedom for poor men was no longer a reality, and the celebration of Independence Day was a mockery. The men in the Jamestown park seemed to be as restless, as ready as he was himself. Why sit tamely through this empty ritual of firecrackers when what the country needed was the kind of action that established Independence Day? Why settle any longer for the pops and bangs of a make-believe battle?

Holidays almost always disappointed George, even when they didn't commemorate something that had become a lie. He worked fourteen or sixteen hours a day from the time plowing began until the harvest was in. He worked as long as the daylight would serve him and as long as his horses could last. Why could he not rest one day and enjoy himself? Today's swim in the tepid James River had only enervated him when he had expected to be invigorated. Instead of resting him, a holiday seemed only to break his stride. It was as though he had got himself perfectly paced for a desert marathon that would end in failure and death if he so much as broke his stride a half dozen times. Now he fought for balance in the vast emptiness, while the sky tilted and the world fell away under him. The momentum that got him through the summer was temporarily gone, and he was aware that some day he would be old and this was the way it would feel.

The sun was still high and the main street of Eureka still broiling. Nobody had spoken for the entire thirty miles of the trip back from Jamestown. Lucy was half asleep in the back seat, and Rachel sat in front beside him with Cathy asleep on her lap. For the whole trip she had been as far away as the slowly moving, slowly mutant horizon. The whole space between them and the dry line of sky might as well have been between him and Rachel in the front seat.

He parked the car near Gebhardt's Pool Hall — the only place in town that was open. They were going to get a celebrative pint of ice cream for supper. His throat was so dry he could hardly speak. "What'll you have?" he asked Rachel.

"Oh, it doesn't matter at all to me," she said. "Ask Lucy — or get what you want yourself."

Never would she commit herself to him — not even about the flavor of ice cream. He saw how it was — if he presented her with something she had asked for, then that gave him some claim on her. He didn't give a damn what Lucy wanted. Lucy was a kid — she liked all ice cream. But his wife used his children a dozen times a day to hold him at a distance.

"Well what's the use of getting any at all if you don't care about it?" he asked angrily.

"*I* care! *I* care!" Lucy cried, quickly wide awake.

"All right, what'll it be?" he said.
"Chocolate!" she said.
"Okay with you?" he asked Rachel.
"Fine," Rachel said. "The baby's going to wake up now that we've stopped, and she'll be awful till I can get her fed. Let's just get home as soon as we can."
Who the hell wanted a holiday, anyhow? He wanted a fight. He stalked into Gebhardt's.
Everybody in the pool hall was too happy to want to fight. Legal beer for the first time since North Dakota entered the Union in 1889!
George looked around to see who was there. He might have known Wilkes would be sponging a drink on the Fourth of July. He was surprised, though, to see who was bustling about refilling the glasses. It was Annie Finley. Business was so brisk that it kept her sweating, and she had wiped her face so much that her mascara was all down on her apron. Dark wet half-circles showed under her arms, but as she passed by George the only smell he got was one of cheap perfume. She was obviously making a hit with the customers. Old Gebhardt stood over behind the counter watching her like the lewd old goat he was.
"Hey, neighbor!" Wilkes called. "Custer! Come on over and have a drink! Oh, my, doesn't it make you sick to think of them making this stuff for thirteen years and then taking all the alcohol out again! *Near beer* for thirteen years! I tell you one thing, boys, I bet there was plenty of sampling that went on at them breweries before they took the kick outa their damn near beer! Come on, George! Have a drink! Good stuff, this is. None of that rotgut green beer. *This* ain't out of Benjamin's alley; it's right out of that barrel over there! Come on, George! Three cheers for Roosevelt! And three more for Wild Bill Langer that took the near out of this here beer, by God! And three more for that great man, Richard M. Press, the finest sheriff this county ever had!" He waved at the big placard Press had put in Gebhardt's window. The placard announced that Otto Wilkes's real property and chattels would be auctioned on Saturday, July 15, to repay a long delinquent mortgage.
"No thanks, Otto. The old lady's out in the car and she'd make me walk home if I come out of here smelling like you. Now if

you was to offer me some of that dandelion wine Lester made that time, I might not be able to turn you down."

Lester howled. "Oh that was plenty skookum! Tastiest, smoothest stuff you ever drank, if I do say so. A man could drain down a glassful and think it didn't have no more bite than a glass of milk, but wait till he stood up — if he could!"

Rachel sat in the car wondering what was keeping George. The baby's cheeks were deeply flushed and her hair was wet enough to wring out. She stirred, woke, and struggled to stand up. She began at once to make the complaining noises that preceded an earsplitting demand for food.

Despite Cathy's grumblings, Rachel was aware of the paralytic silence around her. There were no trains, no cars, no horses, no one passing on the sidewalk. Except for an occasional loud laugh coming from Gebhardt's down the street, the whole planet could have been a tomb. There *was* one other sound — the sound of an empty schoolyard on a twilit afternoon. It was the sound of the wind banging the hooks on a flag rope against a hollow flagpole somewhere behind her. It was not the sort of sound one associated with the flag on the Fourth of July. Where was George?

Finally he emerged from the pool hall, calling something gay over his shoulder. He came grinning back to the car.

"I bet he's cleared a thousand dollars in that place since Saturday noon! And guess who quit at Gus and Ruby's to cash in on the beer?"

Rachel didn't really care. "Who?" she said.

"That Finley girl. She's doing all right, too, I can tell you! She had an apron pocket about ready to bust with dimes. Pretty little thing, isn't she?"

"Oh, George! What's *pretty* about her? It's all make-up!"

"Well — I can see why the boys at Gebhardt's think she is." He knew he never should have said it.

"They're probably all so drunk they wouldn't know Annie from her mother," Rachel said. "Langer! Oh, I just hope the people of this state let him know what they think of him for this! Haven't we had enough trouble here without making it legal!"

"Well, now, Rachel, that's just *why* we've had so much trouble, for Pete's sake! Why, before Prohibition, the Minneapolis bootleggers made *huge* fortunes bringing booze across the line. Why, every other store on Hennepin Avenue sold wine and liquor. And there was never a time when a man couldn't walk down any street in Jimtown and hold out his hand behind him, like so, and say 'blind pig' out of the side of his mouth, and have somebody take the money out of the hand and put a jug of beer in it. The only difference between having Prohibition and *not* having it was that the bootleg stuff *before* Prohibition probably wouldn't kill you — that's all.

"But this stuff since nineteen-twenty — why, everybody and his brother have been cooking up mash from *something* — prunes, potato peelings, garbage — anything that would cook. Get her up around a hundred and eighty degrees so's you get most of the alcohol up into the condensing pipes and not too much water and sour mash taste. Then you take the alcohol out of the pipes. For God's sake, that's all you have to *do* to make alcohol! But if you wanted to do it by the book, you could always write the U. S. Department of Agriculture. They had a good set of free instructions they'd be glad to send you, no questions asked.

"Hell, if a man wants to drink himself to death, he'll find the stuff to do it with. Of course, if he gets a little Jamaica Jake or Old Horsey or the like, he can save himself money. It won't take too much of that. I hear they've been making a lot of the stuff out of rotten cactus down there where Stuart is. Why don't you ask *him* whether it's a good idea to go ahead and make hooch legal?"

Rachel looked out her window without answering. George knew he'd gone too far and he wasn't even sorry. He shut up, though, and started whistling "Turkey in the Straw."

Presently he said, "This sure isn't like the July Fourths *I* remember. We used to have a great big family reunion. Twenty-thirty-forty people — maybe more. Big baseball game, just in the family, after we ate our dinner. Did I ever tell you about the time Uncle Lon got a frog up his pants leg? I can see that just as clear as if it happened today! Uncle Lon was just sitting there stuffing himself and all of a sudden he started in yelling and jumping around, kicking the dishes and sandwiches every which way, shaking his leg in the air like he'd gone loco. I tell you, I never saw anything so funny in my whole life. There was Uncle Lon — he had a long white beard, did I ever tell you? And he was a schoolteacher, too — and mighty proud of his dignity.

"Well, I guess he stuck his leg so far in the air that the frog just couldn't fall out. All I know is — I was just a little fellow then, about Lucy's age — it seemed to me he must've jumped around like that for at least ten minutes before that frog let loose of his leg and fell out. Smack in the middle of the chokecherry jelly! You couldn't believe it! You never saw such a sight as that scared frog in that gooey jelly.

"But at that, he wasn't half as scared as Uncle Lon. When he finally got rid of that animal, Uncle Lon sat down and never said a word for about ten more minutes. He just kept pulling his pants leg up and sort of rubbing his leg there where the frog had been hanging on to him — he had the hairiest legs of any man I ever saw. It was no wonder that frog couldn't get loose. But you know, you never could kid him about that frog? Never! But I'll never forget that beard waving in the air — came clean down to his chest — took him years to grow that thing."

Lucy was laughing. She had heard the story before, but it always made her laugh, partly because her father always sounded so gay when he told it. She wished too that families were big, the way they used to be, and that somebody would get a frog up his pants leg. That would be even better than going home to eat chocolate ice cream.

Friday, July 14

ALTHOUGH HE didn't feel up to it, Will had the meeting about Otto's auction at his house. Most of the men who came were members of the Farmers' Union, and Will had been a supporter of the union too long to back out now. After all, this was exactly the action the union advocated, and even the governor himself told them to do it.

If they let the sheriff get away with this sale, it just might be the beginning of the end for a lot of hard-working farmers in the county. All over the nation a thousand more farmers lost their farms every day. The year was half over, and in a hundred and eighty days of 1933, nearly two hundred thousand farmers had been dispossessed by banks and insurance companies.

The men at the meeting talked a good deal about the banks. What they were planning to do did not seem like much of a crime compared to what Harry Goodman did, that was a cinch. They were getting checks from the auditors of Harry's bank now — for ten cents on the dollar. There were rumors that Harry was all set up in business far away. The Jew receivers had seen to it that their brother was taken care of. You couldn't fight them, the way they stuck together. Not unless you got together among yourselves, too, and showed the sheriff that the farms around here were not going to be handed over to the city speculators for a song. If the law was going to let Harry Goodman go scot-free, then the law just better keep away from the farmers, because the law was good for nothing at all except to help the rich get richer at the poor man's expense.

It was still fairly light when George came home from the meeting. He took his rifle out on the porch to clean it. This was what he'd been waiting for. That damned Press thought he was pulling a fast one — starting off with a deadbeat like Wilkes. But Sheriff Richard M. Press would learn a thing or two tomorrow. He might even learn that farmers could shoot rings around his pantywaist deputies with their silly Sunday afternoon target practice. Let those deputies go practice on white jack rabbits running against the glare of a snowfield before they tangled with the men who would be at Otto Wilkes's place tomorrow.

Inside the house Rachel finished the dishes and put the yeast to set in the potato water for the Saturday's bread baking. She could smell the fine oil on the rag George attached to the end of the long wire. She saw the way his great shoulders hunched over the rifle and the way his arm bent and straightened as he swabbed the inside of the blue-black barrel, and she saw the brass jackets of the shells he had taken out of the rifle lying behind him on the gray porch boards.

Finally he finished with his gentle twistings of the rag inside the barrel, and he held up the business end of the gun to sight down it into the light showing through from the unlocked breech. Then he wiped the outside of the barrel with the same rag, loaded the shells, snapped the bolt closed, swung the butt against his shoulder, drew a lightning bead on a small tin patch on the barn, and sent a bullet through it.

He twisted around and stared in at her through the screen. "What's the matter with *you?*" he said. "I can always patch the patch, can't I? I've always wondered if I could hit that little bit of tin from here. And I did it in bad light, too. Did you hear him ring!"

"Are you going to take that gun tomorrow?"

"Sure," he said. "Might have to get me a crow or a buzzard with it. Lots of mean critters around. A man can't tell when he'll be able to pick up a little bounty."

"Oh, George, please don't take it," she begged. What had got into him? He was hot-tempered, yes — but his violence had never before been calculated like this.

"You don't understand," he said. "The farmer has to make his own law now. That's all we're aiming to do — show the sheriff that those crooked Jews in Jimtown are not going to take over this whole damn county. We can't wait any more for the government to stick up for us. If the government was going to stick up for us, Harry Goodman would be in jail now — isn't that so? We *built* this country. We fought for it before and now we have to fight again. You just can't seem to understand that, can you?"

Saturday, July 15

It was a beautiful morning for mowing hay, lying in a hammock, weeding the garden, having a picnic (watermelons were ripe), or experimenting with anarchy.

George stood in the open screen door. "Looks like it's going to be another scorcher," he said. "I'll take the car if you're not going to need it."

"I don't need it," Rachel said.

He put the gun in the back seat and laid an old blanket over it. This was not the first time he had headed for Otto's place to help him out of some kind of mess. He could never say no to Otto, maybe because he despised him so much. Otto owed him seed corn, a post-hole digger, God knew how many pounds of assorted nails, a couple of butchering days, and weeks of transporting Lucy to and from school to repay him for the transporting he did of Otto's brood. Oh, the sheriff thought he was pretty safe, all right, picking on Otto. What the sheriff didn't know was that hayseeds weren't as dumb as they might look. They understood the principles the sheriff operated on just as well as if they'd been all dandied up in tailor-made suits of clothes.

Although George was Otto's closest neighbor, he was far from being the first man to arrive. He was surprised to see so many there already, because he was an hour early himself; he'd been too nervous to stay around home any longer. He wondered just what they would all do when the chips were down. After all the big talk last night, were they going to back out at the last minute? It might take only one weak man with one honest bid to upset the applecart. He had the feeling that they were all watching each other. Well, they could watch *him* all they wanted to, by God. Nobody had to worry about G. A. Custer turning yellow.

He looked around for Otto and saw him hovering on the edge of a conversation. They were all going to be tough on Otto today. They were going to let him know that the meeting and the things they were going to do didn't change a thing — that he was nothing but a loudmouth deadbeat and they were here mainly on account of their *own* skins, not *his*.

Somebody tapped his elbow and he whirled around to find Otto's half-witted nine-year-old behind him.

"What do you want, Irene? *This* is no time for a little girl like you to be pestering around! You get along into the house, now."

"I just wondered if you brought Lucy to play with me," Irene said.

"I just *told* you this isn't a place for little girls to be fiddling around. You get along, now!"

She turned and headed for the house, but she stopped on the steps of the porch to look back to the road. The sheriff's big car pointed its nose into the driveway, but the men were making no move to clear the way for him.

Treat us like mules and we'll *act* like mules — so far so good, George thought. The sheriff leaned steadily on his horn and the men began to inch aside. But he didn't follow behind their slow withdrawal. He waited till the driveway was entirely clear and then he roared up it at thirty miles an hour and braked with the bumper of the car almost touching the steps. A brand-new Oldsmobile followed the sheriff like a scared kid hanging on his mother's skirts.

Nothing made a farmer any madder than having a city man drive down his private road like it was Highway Number 10. If a city man killed one of the chickens he sent squawking into the dirt, he would try to jew the farmer down to a few cents less than the market price and then go home and complain to his wife about how a hayseed had held him up. George remembered how a lightning-rod salesman had driven into his yard that way and broken a rooster's leg. Then the fellow had had the gall to ask George why he didn't keep his turkeys and chickens penned up.

"Well, now then, I reckon they don't clutter up the yard as bad as birds like you! Those droppings help out the grass a little. What do you do with your *own* manure, besides come highballing in here and try to sell it to me?" George had asked him.

The salesman argued that George could eat "that old hen," as he called it, and George had delivered the worst insult he could think of on the spur of the moment. "That's no *hen!* That's a *rooster!* How come a queer bird like you don't know a *cock* when you see one?"

Now if the fellow *hadn't* been a pansy, he certainly would have crawled out of his car then, and let a man get a fair swing at him. But the city men never did get out of their cars.

George knew that every man there had had experience with smart-alecks driving into the yard and nearly clipping a dog or a kid, and even more experience with crazy hunters trespassing on his property and leaving a gate open, or worse — just *making* a gate with a pair of wire-cutters so he had to chase his stock all over the county by the time he discovered the break in the fence. George had a notion that the sheriff's dust-raising entrance might do just the opposite of what he intended it to do. No doubt he was trying to show off his authority to a bunch of hicks, but George didn't think anybody was going to look at it that way. No, they were all just going to remember the times when some other city man had done the same thing.

The representative of the law opened the driver's door and pushed a putteed leg out into the dust settling over the fenders and running boards.

The leg was followed by the rest of Sheriff Richard M. Press, who was nearly as fat as George had expected him to be. His heavy leather Sam Browne belt seemed much more necessary to support his belly than to help hold up the pistol that rode on his left thigh.

Both his deputies were on the thin side. Apparently the sheriff himself got all the graft; the deputies must not have anything on him yet. One deputy climbed out of the other side of the driver's seat and let the second out of the back. The second deputy was obviously low man on the totem pole; he had to sit in back behind the wire, where there were no inside handles on the doors. George wondered if anybody he knew would be riding in that back seat on the way back to Jamestown.

The second deputy had been riding with the sheriff's auction block and he lugged it up toward the porch where Irene was still standing, her mouth even farther open than usual. He trod on the prongs of a kitchen fork left on a step by one of the little boys, and when the handle of it flipped up at his leg, he jumped as though it was a rattlesnake, fell against the elegant splintered balustrade, and went through the weak step with his boot heel. Irene began to laugh wildly, clasping her hands over her shiny lips while she staggered back and forth on the porch.

Somebody yelled, "Make him pay for that step, Otto! Don't let him get away with that! Call the sheriff, Otto!"

George wished he had thought of that crack himself. It sounded like it came from Lester Zimmerman.

The representative of the Big Man in Jamestown climbed out of his Oldsmobile with a whole briefcase full of authority under his arm. George could see him wince when the dust squished up over his pointed, two-toned shoes, perforated in a dandy style. He was wearing a silk suit and a panama hat with a silk polka-dot band around it.

George noticed that both he and the sheriff mounted the steps very respectfully. The sheriff's star was dwarfed by the size of his chest. He'd probably taken half his hush-money in moonshine for the last thirteen years. He'd probably drunk enough of it to kill a man who wasn't too mean to die.

The second deputy set up the auction block while the first one hovered near the man in the silk suit, like the rich man's stooge that he was. All four of them stood in a line on Otto Wilkes's rotting porch — soldiers of the old order on a rampart of Victorian gingerbread. Behind them, Irene giggled in her corner. The silk suit man scowled and spoke from the side of his mouth to the deputy. The deputy stared at Irene and whispered to the sheriff. The sheriff jiggled his shoulders and grinned. Nobody approached Irene.

Big and fat as he was, the sheriff had a high tenor voice that rose to an almost effeminate pitch when he strained to be heard above the crowd. It was a crime for a man like that to try to run an auction. Take off the bastard's uniform and what would you have? A pot-bellied, bowlegged dude that pretty near any man there could lick in a fair fight. His .45 pistol was nothing but a joke in open country where a man could be picked off from a mile away. A gun like that belonged in the movies. It was not guns that made a man like George respect the law — or cease to respect it.

"All right!" His voice cracked. "You men out there! Let's have it quiet, so we can have a fair and square sale here!" The men quieted at once, as if by a signal decided on beforehand among themselves — a signal that had nothing to do with the sheriff's order. He seemed taken aback by such prompt obedience, as though he hadn't quite got ready his next sentence when he was confronted by the silence he had commanded for himself. He took a paper from the hands of the man in the silk suit, listened to a few things the man had to say, and turned back to the auction block. It was clear, all right, who ran the law in Stutsman County — silk-suited money-lenders, that was who.

The sheriff walked back to the front of the porch, looking like the employee he was, and began to read from the paper, which explained that the mortgage-holder, having made due allowances for "conditions," was now forced to sell the mortgaged property in order to fulfill obligations to stockholders in the insurance company. Not that everybody didn't already know what it was going to say.

Still, the words of the paper were almost like the words of the

Bible, and the ideas were those on which the whole American economic and political system had been built. Anybody would have to admit that hardly a man there could ever hope to own land without the institution of mortgages. George could feel the faltering of the crowd, and he could tell the sheriff felt it, too. Were all those men at the meeting last night going to turn out to be nothing but sheep now, after all?

It wasn't hard to see how a man like the sheriff got ahead. In times like these there was practically unlimited money behind a man who could run a county. George wondered how far the sheriff was prepared to go today to show the Big Man how well he could run his county.

The sheriff announced that the first offering on the auction block would be Otto's Percherons. He was a shrewd one, all right. He obviously figured that some weak lover of horseflesh was going to break down and bid on that team. The Percherons, like Otto's house, were his last legacy from the bonanza-farm days. Old Man Wilkes had owned close to a hundred champion Percherons, and he never sent an eight-horse team into his fifty-seven hundred acres that wasn't perfectly matched for color. The ancestors of Otto's team had broken the sod on George's farm.

But the Percheron strain had proved to be more glorious and durable than the Wilkes strain. To George it no longer seemed appropriate for a Wilkes to own such horses. Otto did not deserve them. It was not hard to figure out that that was just what the sheriff hoped they were all thinking. Almost every day a farmer had to try to think one step ahead of what some mean animal was going to do next. It wasn't nearly as much of a challenge to figure out what was in the mind of the sheriff as to figure out what was in the mind of an old cow that had hidden her new calf somewhere in a fifty-acre pasture full of gullies and six-foot weeds.

Little thousand-pound Morgans could supply as much horsepower as a man usually needed now that there was no sod to break, and they ate about half of what a two-thousand-pound Percheron required. Nevertheless, if a man couldn't get rid of feed grain for love nor money, then he might as well feed champion Percherons as Morgans, mightn't he? The sheriff understood that every man there would be asking himself that question.

When the two deputies gingerly descended the steps and headed for the barn, every man knew they would not come back without the horses, because Otto had been complaining ever since the sheriff had come out and laid down the law about what chattels were to be where. But no man was really prepared for what the deputies led out of the gloom beneath the high open doors. Otto must have risen even earlier than any of the rest of them. He had curried the last bit of chaff and manure from the dark-gray fetlocks and polished the last loose hair and speck of dust from the enormous dappled rumps. He had tied their clipped manes into red-ribboned soldiers marching up the mountains of their necks. He had braided their tails with red ribbon, too, but it was the frivolous parade of tiny ribbons arching over the magnificent necks that emphasized, as nothing else could have, the four thousand pounds of horse perfection that were being offered for George and Otto's other neighbors to bid upon.

George's heart leapt as though he had been transported into the show ring of a great fair. Here was a team such as men like him had yearned for all their lives — ever since they had been three-year-old boys at the fairs, standing as close as they dared to the stalls in the Equine Building, breathing in the sweet smell of hay and sweat and *horse.* They had all spent hours looking up at those horses and they each possessed an infallible image of such a horse from every possible angle. They had begun their loving admiration when they were so short that they still stood far beneath the horses' bellies and their eyes were but a few inches above the splendid hocks — marvelous peaks of bone, majestic as the knuckles of God. Every fall at the fair their eyes had been a little higher, and they had committed to unfading memory a little more of a champion's configuration.

George remembered the feeling of stepping worshipfully aside when the owners came to lead the nervous animals from their stalls, and he remembered how it was to follow along and watch what happened in the hot, brilliant ring before the grandstand, where the judges paced back and forth with dazzling white spats over their shoes, swinging their canes, cocking their white straw hats, writing on score cards. Otto's Percherons were the kind of horses that wore the ribbons away from the ring.

The sheriff turned his head from the horses to smile at the silent men. He was a man, George thought, lower than a worm's belly button.

"I reckon you men all know these horses!" the sheriff yelled. "You all know they've won some prizes at the State Fair! A beautifully matched team. Who'll start in at one and a quarter for the team? One and a quarter, one and a quarter!" He was trying to sound like a professional auctioneer, but he wasn't very convincing.

Not that he needed to be convincing. There wasn't a man there who could not have scared up a hundred dollars or so by selling his two best horses. They were shabbily dressed men and they all had to go home to stricken farms after this shindig was over. How could they help lusting after the glory of that team?

"All right, men," the sheriff shouted. "If I don't hear one and a quarter, I'll up it to one and half before I even hear the first bid. Now who'll give me one and a quarter?"

George felt an earthquake unhinging his legs and rattling his head. He lifted his voice over the crowd. "It's an insult to fine horseflesh for us men here not to bid on an offer like that! I'll give you one and a quarter — *one dollar and a quarter*, I bid — one buck and two bits. That team is worth that *any* day!"

The tremors still fluttered in his stomach. Now, surely, somebody would jump in after him and help to break this thing up quickly before the sheriff hypnotized them all.

There was a fair amount of nervous laughter, but nobody said anything. The men were dazed, as though they had wakened from a beautiful dream to find the dream standing in front of them. Nobody could take his eyes off the Percherons.

Both of them were restive under the fearful hands of the city men. They couldn't use their braided-up tails against the flies swarming over them, and the muscles of their thick hides flickered steadily over the ribs and shoulders and down the legs. The deputy holding the gelding apprehensively eyed the dappled skin rolling over the mammoth planes and joints of his horse, but the deputy holding the stallion had much greater worries.

He looked very small and impotently urban. The brim of his hat came below the stallion's nostrils and the broad chest of the animal was like a wall behind him.

The stallion was in a state of monstrous excitement. It was the kind of moment to bring a fleeting wistfulness to the purest of men — the kind of moment that had for centuries inspired cave paintings, tile murals, and ceremonial costumes. It was the kind of moment that the deputy was scarcely qualified to deal with.

The men emerged from their dream to become conscious of a mare standing by Lester Zimmerman's wagon. She was making feverish signals to the stallion and Lester had both hands on her halter. Otto looked over toward Lester and gave him a quick grin.

Lester had prudently unhitched the mare as soon as he arrived, and now he let her go. She sprang away from him to meet her muscular prince.

The stallion plunged and knocked the deputy off balance. The man yanked himself back to his feet by the halter rope and ran with the horse. He bounced behind the driving shoulders like a man tied to a locomotive. The stallion, as unhampered as a locomotive, had forgotten all about the man attached to his halter. The rope burned out of the deputy's grip and he fell aside without even a wound to show for his disgraceful efforts.

The men who had demurred so long in letting the sheriff's car up the drive took no time at all to clear a path from the stallion to the mare.

George wondered at the ignorance of the deputy in trying to manage such a horse with nothing but a halter. Had the fellow thought a halter was a bridle? Didn't city people know that no man could ever trust any stallion? Didn't they know the world was full of stallions so mean they'd as soon as bite your arm off as look at you? Wilkes himself had a goat running around the farm that had climbed into a Percheron stallion's manger for a peaceful summer afternoon's nap. When the horse returned to his stall from the day's work, he went in after the goat and took the tip of its face off in one snap of his jaws. Otto's goat had no nose now, but its nostrils were still there — just holes in its blunted muzzle. It had recovered, but it was a funny sight — and a memorable one.

Didn't city people know that out on the range with nobody to get in their road, the mustang stallions ripped each other to the bone with their big yellow teeth and commonly fought till one was killed? This little city man was probably damned lucky that the mare had been there to distract the stallion before he got other ideas.

The horses thundered away together, the mare's harness jangling and sliding from side to side. It was a cumbersome, workaday wedding garment. Watching them fleeing toward their assignation, Lester remarked to George that it was too bad about the crupper strap, but probably it wouldn't bother a pecker like that too much. Oscar Johnson heard him and passed the remark on to his neighbor.

"Who brung that mare in heat in here?" yelled the sheriff.

But nobody heard him. The jokes and guffaws wended their way through the crowd. The sheriff dropped his hand toward his pistol and then he picked up his auction hammer instead. When the men were ready, they fell back into their complete, unnerving silence. They wouldn't even bother to heckle him — any more than the stallion had bothered to kick the deputy.

"All right," the sheriff said. "We'll put the Percherons up again. Who'll give me a hundred and fifty *dollars?*"

"Who'll fetch the stallion back?" Oscar Johnson roared. "I didn't hardly get a good enough look at him to risk a bid."

"Now you men out there watch your step or I'll run you in for inciting to riot!" the sheriff cried.

"Don't arrest *me,* for Christ's sake!" Oscar yelled back. "Arrest the *horse!*"

"Now, by God, we've had *enough* of this!" The sheriff spoke to the two deputies and both of them took hold of the gelding's halter to lead him back to the barn — a hundred and fifty pounds of man on either side of a ton of horse.

"Those little fellas look as useless as tits on a boar, don't they?" George inquired of Lester.

"If their brains was dynamite it wouldn't blow their nose," Lester agreed.

Some of the men in that crowd had not enjoyed themselves so much since the days when they ganged up to badger a female teacher, feeling the first restless power of their manhood. They hadn't run into this schoolroom kind of authority since their graduation from the eighth grade, and they were beginning to be exhilarated by their return to the game they used to play — the mass defiance of the helpless against the authority standing before them.

Only this time the game was more fun than it had ever been before, because it was so much more serious.

The deputies came back with Otto's other team, contrasting so pitiably with the Percherons that the crowd began to laugh again. These were an ungainly pair of sinister creatures that had recently run half wild on ranges in the far West. When the Depression had got so bad that farmers couldn't afford to buy gas for their tractors, the horse traders out West began corralling bunches of wild mustang mares, running them with domesticated draft stallions — big males to increase the size of the colts — and raking in fancy profits. By the looks of them, these two had been sired by Belgians that were more than twice as big as their untamed mothers.

This team was as badly mismatched as the Percherons were perfectly matched. They were both geldings but one was black, with a complicated brand on his rump that had burned off all the hair on a patch the size of a man's hand. He had probably been stolen once, and therefore branded twice. The other was a sorrel as ewe-necked, paunchy, and buck-kneed as a living horse could be. Neither of them was worth more than twenty-five or thirty dollars, and the buyer would be sure to discover that they had various nasty stable vices which would not show until they were taken home.

After the laughter, though, the crowd was quiet again. George couldn't bear the tension any longer. "I'll start this pair of moth-eaten critters at two bits!" he shouted.

"Thirty cents!" came a voice from behind him.

"Thirty-five!" came another.

"Take it easy, boys," Lester scolded. "You're getting way past me. Thirty-six!"

"Thirty-seven!"

Clarence Egger appeared beside George. "It's as good as a vawdville show," he snickered. "I never really thought it would work. I gotta hand it to you, George."

"Thirty-seven and a half!"

"Thirty-eight!"

"Hell," said George, "if Lester wants them two roarers that bad, let him have 'em. I'm not going any higher."

"Now listen here," shouted the sheriff. "This man standing right here behind me has got a perfectly legal mortgage on this property.

Now let's just cut out this tomfoolery and get down to business. Who'll give me thirty dollars for the team?"

"Which team?"

"I said, cut it out! This sale is going to go on!"

"Forty cents!"

"I'm not having that kind of sale!" the sheriff screamed.

"If you don't aim to have a sale what did you waste our tax money printing up those signs for?" George wanted to know.

The little zephyr of levity had blown itself out. It was as though a wind, lifting up the light silver backs of the willow leaves along a river, had died down and let them drop to show their dark tops again. The crowd showed how quickly it could become another kind of crowd. George's chest grew tight with exultation. This was the way it was going to be when the *big* fight came.

"Yeah, if he don't want to have this sale, maybe there just might be some other way we can get our tax money out of those signs — or at least our money's worth!"

"All right, now," the sheriff said. George thought he sounded desperate. "We'll just forget about horses for a minute and go on to sheep. You all know how wool is going up. Wilkes has fed them sheep for you all winter. Keep 'em this winter and cash in next summer. Now then, I'll start 'em at two dollars a head, in lots of twenty, take 'em as they come, young or old, or any wethers along with the ewes and lambs. Just the fleece off'n each one of 'em this summer brought in two dollars or more. Who'll start, now, at forty dollars for lots of twenty?"

George spoke up again. "Yeah, and once Otto got the wool off, it was a wonder those sheep held together at all. Skinniest sheep I ever saw in my life. Five cents a head."

The sheriff conferred with the man in the silk suit. The man said something to Irene.

"A *telephone!*" she shrieked.

The man turned back to the sheriff, and the two deputies started down the steps. It's over, George thought, but the sheriff pounded again with his hammer and shouted, "Now, then, we'll have a little *re*cess for a while till some real bidders get here. Anybody that wants to bid can stay. Anybody that doesn't might as well go home. It'll be a long hot spell of waiting," he finished solicitously.

"I think we got a few too many slickers around here right now, don't you?" George asked. He moved in front of the deputies just in time to cut them off from the sheriff's car, and leaned innocuously against the door of it. He rested the heel of one large work shoe on the running board and braced an elbow in the open window.

The deputy who had let the stallion escape stepped up to redeem himself.

"Get away from there," he said. "That's county property."

"That means I own a little bit of it then, don't it?" George said. "I reckon, for the time being, till you can get your pettifogging shysters to work on it, I'll just settle for this little piece of running board, here" — he clunked his heel down, sending a shudder through the car — "and this little piece of windowsill."

"This here is county property," the deputy said again. "You get away from there, now, and let me get inside. I got my orders from Sheriff Press, and you know it."

George took his elbow out of the window and swung his foot to the ground and straightened up. He looked around the crowd. Didn't they all know that if Press got some city bidders out here, the jig was up? Nobody made any overt move to back him up; on the other hand, the men had pushed in around him and the deputies, so that there was no chance for the sheriff to worm his way through to them.

A gigantic double-barreled shotgun materialized like a thunderbolt in the fidgety grip of Wallace Esskew. Nobody ever knew what to expect from Wally. He had a funny high laugh that was more scared guinea hen than it was human. He wasn't married — just lived at home with his parents and brothers. More than any man there he could afford to get himself out on a limb.

Wally let out his funny deranged laugh. The deputies jumped when they saw the cannon. "Nothing but rock salt in here," Wallace giggled. "I was just afraid one of these little Wilkes kids might get at it there in the car. I just remembered I had it cocked and ready to go because I was aiming to chase down them chicken thieves the next time they come back to our place." He grinned and respectfully bobbed his head again and again at the deputies, while the gun wavered in his uncoordinated hands. Nobody claimed that

Wally was crazy — just peculiar. Nobody ever knew what was in his head.

No man considered that giving a rock-salt lesson to a chicken thief was really shooting him. The sheriff and the deputies obviously understood that the thought of filling official pants with rock salt would appeal to almost every man in the crowd. The sheriff had come to perpetrate a farce, not to be the hero of one. It might be disastrous to his reputation if he had to drive back to Jamestown with his pants full of rock salt. If all the men there had rock salt in their guns and he fired into the crowd, it would be said that he returned lead for salt. Farmers still had one vote apiece, and they took their votes seriously. And if any rock salt should find its way into that silk suit . . .

It seemed to George that they had him. He probably had a couple of tear-gas bombs in the car; he could use one to show the Big Man that he was doing his best. But that might be the best way to stop a load of rock salt — fired, of course, by a man who was so blinded he couldn't see what he was doing. He could place them all under arrest, but George didn't imagine they would all just climb in their cars and follow obligingly along to the clink. He could start taking their names and addresses, but he would probably have to do that at gunpoint, and it would hardly be sensible for him to encourage any more gun-thinking with the kind of reinforcements he had at the moment. He could come back with a posse, but he might find himself confronting a troop of state militia. Who knew what Wild Bill Langer might do? They were only seventy miles from Bismarck, and Langer had only been governor for a few months — he might still be crazy enough to do what he had said he would do.

In any case, George reasoned triumphantly, if Sheriff Press left and came back, it was certainly more likely that he would find the militia waiting for him than that he would find any of the men facing him now, with the exception of Wilkes, of course.

Like most politicians, the sheriff had got elected because of his big broad smile that forced people to smile back at him. He smiled his way through the tight crowd, and he was still smiling when he looked up at George. The man in the silk suit was so close behind him that he might have been joined to him, like a Siamese twin.

"Stare him down, George," somebody said.

"I never argue with a fellow this big," the sheriff said lightly. "I just ask him if he'll kindly move aside so I can get in my car and go home."

George hesitated and then stepped back. Sheriff Press climbed into his official car and started the engine to show that he meant what he said. The deputies found room to pass through the crowd then, and got into the front seat with him. Everybody forgot about the real villain till it was too late to give him a scare—the man in the silk suit was already sitting behind the wheel of his Oldsmobile. He had his window rolled almost up, and it was a safe bet that he had the door locked.

The sheriff took off his cavalry hat and leaned his head out the window. "I reckon *you'll* have to back out first, Mr. Burr," he called tactfully. Mr. Burr did not need to be coaxed.

Once again the dust took a long time to settle over the crowd but this time the dust proved that little men, not the moneylenders, were in control. The little men had shaken off the county sheriff with as much impunity as that impetuous stallion had rid himself of the useless deputy.

The law was an abstraction, like money, that functioned only so long as the majority partook of it, possessed it, believed in it, and felt committed to it. The law seemed quite as insubstantial now as the numbers they had once believed in—all the numbers that represented what they thought they had safely stored in Harry's bank.

What had happened this morning in Otto Wilkes's squalid yard proved that the system of the whole nation was so rotten it was on the very edge of collapse. It was too late to try to restore the system in pieces, with Roosevelt's bureaus and bureaucrats.

"Well, we did a good morning's work, boys!" George said. "There goes a couple of weasels that found out it's going to take more than a damned piece of paper before they can kick a man off his land."

He wanted to make a speech. He wanted to say, "We are fighting in defense of our homes. Our petitions have been scorned; our entreaties have been disregarded. We entreat no more; we petition no more. We defy them." It had been a long time since William Jennings Bryan said that. He'd been dead for nearly ten years now. George had memorized that speech for his oration when he graduated from the eighth grade. A man never forgot things he memorized when he was young. Kids nowadays didn't do anywhere near enough memorizing. They didn't even have to learn the Declaration of Independence.

"Now that we know how to do it," George said aloud, "we have to stick together and break up the *next* sale, too. We can't let let them get the jump on us again. This revolution is fifty years overdue now."

"By God, that was the funniest thing I ever seen!" Clarence Egger was nearly beside himself, carried away by the morning's entertainments, not by what had been proved and accomplished. Talking about vaudeville shows. Lapping up other men's fights. The bleating little sheep. He kept pounding Wallace Esskew on the back with his one arm. "Old Dick Press really thought you was going to pepper his ass with rock salt!"

Wally's blankness could be comical. "*What* rock salt?" he said.

II

What are the roots that clutch, what branches grow
Out of this stony rubbish? Son of man,
You cannot say, or guess, for you know only
A heap of broken images, where the sun beats,
And the dead tree gives no shelter, the cricket no relief,
And the dry stone no sound of water. Only
There is shadow under this red rock,
(Come in under the shadow of this red rock),
And I will show you something different from either
Your shadow at morning striding behind you
Or your shadow at evening rising to meet you;
I will show you fear in a handful of dust.

T. S. Eliot
The Waste Land
1922

Tuesday, July 18

Every day the temperature climbed a little higher. At four in the morning the house was already hot enough to wake the bluebottle flies and send them buzzing and bumbling over the faces of humans trying to sleep. The pastures were dry and brown.

At dinner George said to Lucy, "I've got a good kid job for you this afternoon. I want you and the dog to take the cows over to Oscar Johnson's land there, across the road, and watch so they don't run away or get out on the road. I saw Oscar over town yesterday, and I promised him I'd fix up his car for him this winter if he'll let us get whatever pasturing we can out of that section of his. He isn't going to use it anyhow. There's a lot on the hillsides there that doesn't get burned too bad in the afternoon. It'll give our pastures a little rest. Maybe if we'd get one rain we'd get some more grass yet. Anyhow, we'll see how it goes for a couple of weeks over there."

"Oh, George," Rachel said. "She's too little to do such a long hard job as that! She's not even eight yet!"

"*I* herded cows when I was *five!* And not just in the afternoons, neither. I got sent out as soon as the morning's milking was done and I got told not to come back till it was time for the evening chores. And I knew what I'd get if I came back too early, too! They gave me a piece of bread and a bottle of water and packed me off! That's the *trouble* with kids nowadays. They're spoiled and lazy and good-for-nothing. I'm not *asking* her to go out all day — just afternoons!

"I saddled my first horse when I was five. By the time I was her age I'd be out in the barn of a morning, harnessing up the team, while my dad finished the milking. I had to stand up on a block of wood to reach over the horse's back, but I harnessed up a *team,* I tell you. I don't expect anything like *that* of a *girl*, but she can certainly herd a few milch cows for a few days. It'll be the best thing in the world for her. Why, I learned how to keep myself from ever being bored — I could watch a bunch of ants working for hours — or a hawk trying to catch a gopher — or — any one of a hundred different things. . . ."

Rachel did not argue. She walked into the kitchen and started the dishes. George sat whittling a match down to a fine enough point so it would get at a spot that a toothpick wouldn't reach. Lucy was numb and still. When her parents quarreled over her this way, she realized that she was the cause of all the trouble in the house. If only she were not here, there would be nothing for them to fight about. And if only she had a dappled-gray pony like her cousin's. She would love to herd cows with a pony like that.

The cows were gathered under the spreading box elder tree, chewing their morning's cuds while they lay in its shade. They kept the ground bare beneath it, and the dust they kicked up heavily coated its leaves. They had come in for water around noon, as they did almost every day now, and they would not head out to the pasture again for an hour or so — and then only out of desperation. George was already supplementing what they foraged for themselves with his precious hay, but he hated to be using it up when there was still a little pasture available anywhere. They never produced as well without green stuff, and since the price of butterfat was staying up so high this summer, he felt it was worth a great deal of effort to get as much cream as possible.

"I'm going up towards the road myself, so I'll help you get them started," George said. "Looks like they're a little low on water. We better give them some first."

He primed the dry leather and began to pump. The cows walked eagerly to the stream of water. What little water they had left was thick with red box-elder bugs and other insects drowned in the feathery slime on the bottom of the tank and when the water was like that they would blow into it, trying to push the bugs aside before they drank. When the tank was half full, the pump began to strain and then came the sound of sand rasping against the leather. The water choked off into spasmodic, discolored, thin spouts. George let go of the pump handle.

"Is it going dry?" Lucy asked anxiously.

"Well, now, that's a silly question!" George said. "Of course not! You can see we got water, can't you?"

"Let's go," he said. When they reached the edge of the wheat, he turned off to go and hoe in the potato patch.

"Just go on up and straight across the road, and let them go anywheres on that unfenced section. All you have to do is keep them off the road and bring them home at chore time."

Lucy went on behind the cows. A leaning barbed-wire fence along the driveway kept them in line and out of the wheat. There was no challenge to the job. Their hoofs were almost silent in the deep dust but the air was full of insect noise — mostly of grasshoppers. Without the indifferent cows ahead of her to deflect them, the grasshoppers that rose in hordes from their feasting in the wheat would be rattling through the air, smacking their hard-shelled bodies against her own nakedness. She would feel the whirring of their long, brittle wings, and some of them would become entangled in her hair or hang on her bare arms and legs and chest, half stunned by the force with which they had struck her, clinging frantically and spitting their filthy brown juice in big drops on her skin.

She would flail her arms at them, and jump up and down, and brush herself all over, and run to get out in the open again. Even in winter when she walked between the fields she remembered how it would be when summer came again. Even in winter she had nightmares in which an endless stream of thick bodies flew at her and pressed their millions of resined feet into the flesh of her neck.

She wondered if there could possibly be as many grasshoppers all through the acres of wheat as there were along the lane. It seemed as though all the grasshoppers for miles around must be concentrated along that one stretch of wheat, just waiting for her to have to pass them every day to fetch the mail or do other errands.

Her mother had explained that they flew up at her because she scared them. Well, then, why didn't the silly things just stay where they were and mind their own business, since she was just as afraid of them as they were of her?

She followed the cows across the county road, and she noticed that their pace quickened as they scented the new pasture. Even here the grass was withered and sparse, but still it was much more appetizing than the worked-over remnant that had been their pasture for the last month. They were no trouble at all to herd, for they set to work hungrily, moving slowly and not spreading away from each other too much.

They no longer grazed the way they had early in spring, flitting from one place to another, unable to settle at one spot because the grass was so new and green everywhere. Now they sank their noses into whatever turf they could find and tugged at the very roots of it till they had cleaned out every blade and leaf.

Still they would not touch the pungent rosinweed. Perversely, its gummy leaves grew lush and healthy beside the dying edible weeds and grass. From the porch in the early morning the smell of the nearest rosinweed patch was fresh and clean, like sagebrush sprinkled with cinnamon. But later in the day the smell altered and intensified; the weed exuded a sour mustiness. Then the strong fragrance that accompanied the glad sounds of birds at their breakfasts and the gentle touch of the only cool moments of the day became instead the reeking adjunct of hot sticky skin and dust that crawled in her scalp. She could see why the cows might try eating rosinweed once and then resolve to starve to death before they would touch it again. She had been so surprised, herself, to find that the same thing that sent the beautiful smell blowing across the porch in the morning could also give off such a rank and nose-burning stench in midafternoon.

"You can start them home when the sun is about there in the sky," her father had said, pointing to a place above the northwestern horizon. "It'll be about six o'clock then."

But the sun seemed to have caught, today, on an invisible snag in the sky. She had read the story of Icarus, and she could imagine, with the sun on her shoulder blades, how it must have felt when the wax began to melt away from the feathers of the boy's wings and the sun just got hotter and hotter. There was no shade except the short shadow at the base of a huge rock that was half the size of their house. The last time she had sat there she had been too near a hill of fierce red ants nearly half an inch long. She had gone home full of bleeding welts. This time she decided she would climb the rock instead, but it blistered her hands even to touch it.

All these rocks had been left here by the glaciers, her mother said. The giant rock hung restlessly on the brow of the hill, brooding over the smaller strays below it. Her mother had told her that the earth had worn away from it — that it never would have just stuck there that way of its own accord.

It was hard to imagine a glacier on this parching hill. The rocks shot flecks of gold and silver into the sun. Lucy searched around for a while, thinking that some time she would surely have to find a gold nugget. Her father had told her that gold nuggets did not look at all like gold; they did not shine that way, and that without knowing what a gold nugget looked like, she could walk past a million dollars' worth of gold and never know it. It was the same with diamonds. The biggest diamond in the world had been mistaken for a clod of earth. But she had a feeling that if she ever got near that much gold or that big a diamond she would surely know, somehow, that it was there. After all, God wouldn't let her get that close when they were so poor and not let her find it, would He?

What was it that her father said he had done when he herded cows — all those things that were so interesting? There were the ants to watch — foot-high cones of deathly dry pulverized earth, blank and smooth on the outside but horribly populous on the inside, with rooms full of tiny eggs and big pupae, and hallways up and down where millions of ants rushed about on mysterious errands. She could see all the ants anybody could ever want to see if she just poked a stick into one of those cones. She could watch them — terrified and angry — scrambling over the ruins of their city, rescuing the long white bundles encasing their next generation. One had to respect the organized speed with which they could disappear when there were so many of them. Still, she did not really like ants well enough to want to watch them all afternoon. What else had her father done? Watched a hawk after a gopher, he said. She searched the sky for a hawk, but it seemed too hot up there even for birds. She couldn't even hear the call of a meadowlark. She couldn't think what else he said he had done. It was easier to imagine that she was in Africa than to try to think of the things her father had done when he was a little boy.

Compared to glaciers, African animals here were perfectly believable. In fact, she needed only to think of them and they populated the rolling hills, hiding behind the rocks, treacherously blending their stripes and spots and tawny skins with the clumps of thistles and weeds that made wavering black shadows in the wind — it *was* really only the wind moving, of course. She sat down on the highest curve of the hill and looked down to where there was a draw which was mostly hidden from her by another ridge above it that ran along the big hill. The draw was a moist, cordial little place in spring, blooming with crocuses, and later with buttercups. It was the kind of place she would have picked to live in herself if she had been a wild animal. There was a rocky ledge a bit above the bottom of the draw, and once she had found the skull of a rabbit there. A hawk had probably got it, her father told her.

In summer the ledge was sparsely tufted with rough brown grass, and it looked savage and strange, like a ledge pictured in the *National Geographic Book of North American Mammals*. A yellow-eyed cougar waited on the ledge in the picture. He peered down in feline concentration, holding his haunches tightly and leaning on his forelegs, making the muscles of them swell against the white chest that seemed, even in the picture, to breathe with the lion's lungs and to throb with his heart. She wondered if a cougar could have eaten the rabbit that belonged to the skull she found, instead of a hawk.

Or why not a real *African* lion or tiger? She had been to a movie once, in Jamestown, after she had had to go to the dentist there. It was a Tarzan movie, and it had all the animals in it, alive, that she had studied in the pictures in a book on Africa. People should not be so sure that there could be no such animals around here. Circuses and carnivals went through on the highway all the time. They never set up their shows any closer than Jamestown, but thirty miles was no distance for an angry lion to travel. Animals could escape from those flimsy red cages. There was plenty of unfenced room around her for every single animal she had seen in the movie or in the book or ever even imagined.

The most terrible thing in the movie had been the way, time after time, the great mane and wide-open jaws of a white-toothed lion could emerge from the empty grass. The grass in the movie had been very like the grass that grew in this abandoned grazing land. The grass in the floor of the draw was especially tall because the shade of the hill protected it from the drought. Plenty of room for whole prides of lions down there. They would be asleep, for it was too hot to hunt unless they were disturbed, just as a house cat or a dog would sleep in the shade on such a day as this.

At home she had a four-year collection of illustrated Sunday-school papers that she liked to look through on stormy days. The very best picture of them all was the one of David when he was only a shepherd boy, hardly bigger than she was. The picture showed him on a hillside that looked like her own hillsides under a hot blue sky that was like her own sky. His sheep were spilled down the hill around him, like her cows, and a huge lion was jumping over a rock at him.

On the inside of the paper were the Bible verses telling about it. "Thy servant kept his father's sheep, and there came a lion, and a bear, and took a lamb out of the flock." Here the teacher had explained that the lion and the bear did not both come at the same time. "And I went out after him, and smote him, and delivered it out of his mouth: and when he arose against me, I caught him by his beard, and smote him, and slew him." The memory verse that was printed in black type at the end of the lesson read "The Lord hath delivered me out of the paw of the lion, and out of the paw of the bear."

David, of course, was a boy. How much more wonderful if she, a girl, should manage to triumph over such a lion as that one in the picture. She kept an eye on the entrance to the draw, which was in deep shadow now, though the sun was still fairly high. The cows had all disappeared in it, as she had known they would. She had to keep a sharp look around her all the time. Bing was so hot and sleepy he probably wouldn't smell a lion even if it came right up behind them. What good was a dog anyway? No dog could kill a lion, and especially not Bing. He was part Boston bull and part terrier and he wasn't any bigger than Cathy.

Occasionally she would hear a sound and whirl about on her knees, her heart banging, to see what was behind her. Then she would whirl back again to make sure the sound behind her wasn't just a queer echo of a danger in front of her that she had somehow missed seeing.

If she lay on her stomach, so that the next hill rose up against the sky in her line of sight, the sun was low enough. She manuevered stealthily down the hill and over the little ridge, keeping close to the ground. Bing was close behind her. She started running the last lap down to the cows. Bing rushed after her, yipping and begging to play. She whispered frantically to him. "Shut up! Shut up! Be quiet!"

But he was determined to play. He ran at one of the cows and barked straight into her face before she had time to raise her startled head out of the grass. She tossed her stubs of horns at him and he jumped at her face again. Lucy shouted at him to stop. But Bing never minded anybody except her father.

The cows broke into a sham stampede. Bing barked and nipped at their flying heels, and Lucy ran far behind them — the straggler, the helpless one with the delicious human blood, and no one at all behind her to divert the lion for even a moment. The grass shivered and rippled. Shadows leapt from thistles to hollows to rocks.

Bing worried the herd into an honest gallop. They labored up the hill and Lucy began to gain on them, but when they reached the top they shot over the crest and down toward the road, making a beeline for the faraway barn. They tumbled madly into the ditch, clattered across the dusty gravel, tumbled in and out of the next ditch, and bunched up in the driveway.

Shoving and bumping against one another, they snapped one of the posts of the weak fence. Lucy got to the ditch on the far side of the road just in time to see them jumping over the fallen wires and fanning out through the wheat field.

George looked up from his potato row. He dropped his hoe and ran along the edge of the wheat. By the time the first cow reached him, the dog was far behind in the grain, taking extra high leaps into the air to get his bearings. George headed off the cow and turned her toward the barn. The rest slowed down and followed her, leaving their meandering, trampled swaths behind them.

"Bing! Come here!" The dog slunk toward him, showing teeth in a half-grin, half-snarl. George swung his fist down into his ribs, holding him by the scruff of the neck while he beat him.

Lucy had lapsed into an exhausted trot and she stopped far down the road when the dog began to howl.

"Get along here!" It was the same voice that had called the dog. He was waiting for her. When she came to him, he grabbed her arm just below her shoulder. She could feel how his fingers went around and lapped half way around again. All of her arm — bone and flesh from shoulder to elbow — was contained so easily and so tightly in the palm of his hand. When he took hold of her like that, she knew what would have to come next, just the way Bing had known. She felt as though her arm no longer belonged to her. He hurried her along toward the house, shouting down to her, "What in the Sam Hill did you think you were doing?"

"I don't know," she said.

"What do you *mean*, you don't know? Haven't I told you never to run a cow when she's got her bag full of milk? Never run a cow *any time*. It's a wonder they haven't all got their legs broke in the gopher holes. And they've gone and tromped down forty bushels of wheat into the bargain."

He was holding her arm so hard and lifting it up so high that she felt as though her feet did not touch the ground at all. This was the first part of the nightmare — this swift movement toward the beating when she did not tell her feet to take the steps they took, when a force rushed her through the air to the pain that she would finally not be able to bear without screaming, even though the humiliation of screaming was worse than the pain.

She hovered above the porch steps and felt herself flung toward the door.

"Get the razor strop!"

"No! It wasn't my fault!"

"I'll *teach* you to talk back to me!"

The feeling came back into her legs as he tore open the door to get the strop, but before she could take one step the strop was swishing, flaming, cutting. The bare skin of her thighs and back burned away and still the strop rose and fell, still it branded her with its own passionate torment.

At last the sounds she could not stop became the screams that showed she had learned what he wished to teach her. He let go of her arm and kicked her away like a loathsome thing. She ran into the house.

He did not go back through the door. Instead he hung the razor strop on the outside nail where he kept his straw hat. Then he walked down the hill to let the cows back into the worn-out pasture.

He lifted the pump handle and then let it drop. It was too soon to try it again. If it had really gone dry, he didn't want to know it yet.

The beans and peas and the root-cellar vegetables — carrots, beets, turnips, rutabagas, onions, parsnips — were far enough along to produce something without more irrigating and the potatoes would probably make it without much more water, but it would be a hard thing to watch the tomatoes die. Tomatoes took so much water that he had already begun to wonder if they weren't a luxury this summer. But they took the place of fresh fruit through the whole long winter. Rachel always put up quarts and quarts of them.

They were more work than anything else to raise. They had to be started in flats, transplanted, staked, tied, irrigated, and conscientiously weeded. Nine-tenths of the work of growing them had already been done. It would be hard to watch them die now, but if the well acted up any more, he wouldn't dare to water them and they would dry up long before they produced anything. He had to think of the human and animal needs first, and the hottest, driest month was still before him.

❧ ❧ ❧

Rachel came back from a trip to town for canning rubbers and took up where she had left off with her pea canning. She already had one boilerful of jars nearly processed and she wanted to get the next load ready to go before she had to stop to fix supper. The baby played about her feet, chewing on an empty pea pod and always being in the wrong spot when boiling water had to be poured or a few hot peas from the parboiling pan escaped and plopped on the floor. She wore only her diapers and her skin was as red with the heat as if she had been scalded. Up above the stove, Rachel felt as scalded as the peas. It couldn't be quite so bad in the rest of the house. She walked the baby into the dining room, hoping she would decide to stay there.

A little later, when she heard the baby making happy exclamations of discovery, she thought she had better make sure the discovery was not the button drawer in the sewing machine or Lucy's paper dolls. In the bedroom she found Cathy peering under Lucy's cot. That was the place Lucy had hidden ever since the first time, when she was barely three years old.

"Lucy! What happened? What did you do? Come here to me!"

The only sound from under the cot was an indrawn breath, fighting its way into her lungs against the spasms of her chest.

"Lucy! *Please!*"

But this child was already so proud. She would keep her shame under the cot rather than bring it out with her and come for comfort.

Rachel was afraid even to stoop down to her, knowing how that would shame her. She wanted to roll under the cot with her and sob with her and never come out again.

How many times had he done it since that first time? Twenty? A hundred? Five? How was it that she had gone on living with a man who could turn into an insane wild beast? She couldn't believe it.

She could never believe it when the man she had married became a beast. He would not come back to the house until he was in control of himself again. Then he would look like a man, speak like a man. She would pity him as a man. He would be her husband; he would not be a beast. He would explain how he had beaten his child out of his love for it — out of his obligation to rear it properly. What was there to do? End her marriage? Go back to her father and the farm that joined this land? Watch from there while the man she had promised to cherish forever went ahead and killed himself trying to keep possession of the place to which they had both given nearly a decade of their lives?

He had not been this way in those first years. He had truly loved Lucy when she was Cathy's age. While Lucy was still creeping she would scramble to the door when she heard him scraping his boots on the porch. She would make little baby shouts of excitement waiting for the door to open. He would throw her in the air. He would swing her up and down on his foot while she held his fingers in her fists and clamped her strong, tiny legs around his instep. He had been so powerful, the baby so confident. They had reveled in their combination of power and confidence. They had laughed hysterically together, and even then it had been so easy to see how much they were alike. And it had been so charming to see how the giant red-haired father and the elfin platinum-haired baby were so alike, how they both loved what their bodies could do, how they could intoxicate each other with the wildness of their spirits.

When they played that way, she, the mother, the one who had brought the spirits together, had herself felt a wild gaiety that was new and exquisite, as though a great and remarkable thing had come to pass because of her. It had been such an unexpected feeling. Always before, her life had been spent watching on the edge of something and never understanding what it was, but then suddenly, with the bass drum rolling and the miraculous bell pealing, with the laughter of the man and baby all around her in the house, she saw that she had been caught unawares and made a part of the very mechanism of the universe. Paradoxically, she felt that she had already accomplished what she had been put on earth to do, and yet she also knew that her life had only just begun. The hand of God moved her and her own will submitted as it had never done before, and yet she was necessary to the will of God in a way that she had never been before. That was how it was when a woman had her first baby. Every day was filled with unprecedented, humbling, exalting paradoxes.

In those days could the beast have been in the father of the baby? Was the beast in him the day he led the three-thousand-pound bull away from the schoolyard? Did a man have to have a beast in him to deal with such a beast? If the beast had been in him then, why hadn't she seen it in time? If it had not been in him then, where had it come from since, and why had it come? What was there to do? What was there to do?

And now this child was still like him, so much more than he knew. Now she was proud and there was never anything to say that did not make things harder. The worst part of the beating was not over, but only beginning. It was the humiliation that hurt now, and it was the humiliation that would remain. Long after the welts had gone down and the last greenish-yellow mark of an old bruise had disappeared, the humiliation of a child would defile the house. What was there to do?

Her arms, her body, her throat, her face, even her eyes ached with her need to comfort the child who would never be comforted.

She yearned for one thing only — to sit in the corner on the floor of the shadowed bedroom holding the proud doomed little head against her breast till night fell and the merciful angel came for them both. What else was there to do?

❦ ❦ ❦

It was very hot under the bed. Lucy lay looking up at the lines of short springs hooked together and crossing each other to fasten into the little holes along the frame.

She heard her father come in with the milk and run it through the separator. She heard them all sit down to dinner.

"Where's Lucy?" her father said.

"She's not hungry," her mother answered.

"I'm telling you, Rachel, I'm not going to raise a kid that doesn't obey me! Absolute obedience *must* be required of a child! Otherwise, they grow up spoiled rotten. They're no good to *anybody* then. Not even themselves. I don't see why you can't understand that you don't do a kid a *favor* when you *spoil* him."

Lucy did not hear her mother say anything. Only after she had heard them all go to bed did she creep up to lie on top of the mattress that she had contemplated so long from below. She had not answered when her mother called to her again after supper. She was beginning to feel a little hungry, but not hungry enough to give in and ask for food.

That night she dreamed again about the great yellow-eyed lion sleeping in the grass. Then the mischievous, noisy monkeys woke him and he saw her and came bounding after her like a flaming thistle in a black wind, while she ran through fields and jungles in a rampant maze with her feet never quite touching the ground. In the morning it seemed that this hysterical landscape had burned against her eyelids all night long until it was replaced by the burning of the early hot day shining strongly down on her bed — the day that finally brought back memory of the reason why her eyes were so dried and salted.

❦ ❦ ❦

"Lucy isn't going out with the cows again," Rachel said to George, quietly, so Lucy could not hear. She was cutting the bread for breakfast; and she paused, resting the knife on the breadboard, and looked up at him. He forced himself to meet her eyes, to prove that he was right.

Then he turned his back to go out the door and summed up the situation as it looked to him.

"If a man can't count on his own family for help," he said, "I don't see how he can be expected to make a go of it. If he has to fight every fat middleman in the country and then his family too, what in Sam Hill is he going to do? When I was *half* her age, if I'd done a fool thing like that my old man would've beat me with a blacksnake. *Your* father spoiled *you*, and you want *me* to spoil *her*."

"I *love* my father! And just how did *you* feel about *yours*?"

"What has *that* got to do with it?" He grabbed his cap in one hand and the milk pail in the other and headed for the barn. It was nobody's damned business how he felt about his father — *nobody's*.

After breakfast he went out to rake the hay he had mowed a few days before. Hay-raking was about as pleasant as any job he could think of. It was a job that went much faster than most, and gave a man the feeling of having accomplished a great deal in a little while. When he finished a field he liked to look at the long low mounds of half-cured hay, sweetly pungent with the stored work of the resting acres.

But two things spoiled his pleasure in the job today. The hay was so thin this year because of the drought — thinner than he could ever remember it. That was the first thing. The second was that he would have to start using it up almost immediately if he couldn't figure out some way to get the cows to pasture. Now he was committed to paying for grazing land that would go to waste for the lack of a fence or a herder. How maddening could a man's life get, anyway?

He could always just drive the cattle over there and hope they'd stay. They probably would, but he could not be sure; and anyhow, he wasn't the kind to let his stock run loose the way Otto Wilkes did. He could stake out the whole herd, but that would be so much effort for him that it would hardly be worthwhile, considering how rushed he was. The only thing to do was find a herder somewhere or just forget about the pasture. This was what happened when a man's family let him down. Well, he'd let them know he could manage without them. Next time he went to town he'd find himself a boy. All the farm boys would be working for their own fathers, as children ought to do, but he could find a town boy to do it.

There was one big thing to be optimistic about. He still saw little rust damage in the wheat, though the fields of Marquis all around him were in bad shape. It was just a little too early yet to tell about smut. He didn't even have to look at his Ceres to know that it was suffering from bad grasshopper damage. But so was every other field. His competitors had nothing on him there. If the smut didn't get him and the rust got everybody else, then he would be one up, at least, on the others.

The price of cream was another thing to be hopeful about, if he could only keep up the production of his herd. Cream was up ten cents a pound over July of last year. He decided to go to town that very day and see if he could find a boy.

He went to Herman first, to ask him if he knew of anybody and to get a package of Bull Durham. Mrs. Finley and her boy Audley were getting their week's groceries. Now *there* was a likely-looking lad — about ten, George would judge, and certainly in need of the money. It was handy to have his mother there, too. He could ask them right now.

George cleared his throat. "Say, how would you like to make a loan of this boy here?" he said.

Audley looked as startled as she did. "*Loan* him? What for?"

"Simplest job in the world. Herd six cows on a section that isn't fenced alongside of the road."

"Well," she hedged, "he's quite a lot of help to me around the house with the littler ones. I don't know if I could let him go just now."

"I'd fetch him and bring him back and pay him a quarter a day for five days a week. How's that?" George said.

When she got a check at all, Pearl Finley got a relief voucher for four dollars' worth of groceries a week, for herself and the five kids. Another dollar and a quarter was a lot of money.

"Why, I think that's just wonderful," she said. "Audley would *love* to do that, I know."

"I don't like cows much," Audley said.

"Oh, that don't matter," George scoffed. "Who *does?* A fellow doesn't have to *like* them to herd them, does he?"

"Audley would thank you kindly for the job," Mrs. Finley said firmly.

"Would it be all right if he started today?" George said. "I can wait a minute and run you home with your groceries."

George waited by the counter, tapping an aimless rhythm on it. He couldn't get the well out of his mind for a minute. It had filled up just enough in the night so he could water the stock, but they'd have to forget about the tomatoes. What if he had to take time off now to sink another deep well? And what if he couldn't find water at all? What then? Haul it? Where would he haul it from? And how could he spend all day hauling water, even if he did find somebody who would let him have all he needed? Get rid of the cattle? Then no cream checks. What then?

That was why it was worth a lot to him to get the cows to green pasture, or what passed for that. He was going to pay the boy as much, almost, as it would cost to feed hay, but when cows ate grass they didn't need so much water. And for the next six weeks, literally every drop made a difference. He could always buy hay, too, though the price was going up. But water he might not be able to buy. If the railroads had to start hauling it in, he could certainly never pay their prices. Other men in other places were doing that, to preserve herds they had spent a lifetime breeding, but he was in no position to buy water.

He and Audley did not talk on the way home after they had let Mrs. Finley off. George felt too triumphant to mess with kid talk. He hadn't told Rachel what he was going to town for. He jumped out of the car. "Come on in," he said. "I'll get the old lady to fix you a bite to eat and then we'll fetch the cows."

Audley followed him into the kitchen.

"Well, I got me a *boy!*" George said loudly. "You know Audley Finley, don't you? Got me a cow-herder!"

"That's wonderful," Rachel said. She knew George wanted her to be angry, but she wasn't. He never seemed to understand that such things would not anger her.

❦ ❦ ❦

Haying was the first heroic once-and-for-all job of the summer. The wheat had a month to go yet, and the corn had more than two months. Most of the work between planting and threshing was gardening — long days of weeding and fussing with bugs and sprays. A man got to hating every tiniest seedling weed that had used up some drops of precious water — precious enough when the well had given plenty and only the labor of hauling it up the hill to the garden had made it costly. It was nerve-wracking and degrading to have to feel such anxious solicitude for each root, such anger with each pale green cutworm.

It was a relief to get away from that hard, dry ground, to stand upright with head and shoulders against the sky, and pitch clean hay into the loader. Nobody had to worry about weeds in the hay. The cows could eat around the spiky brown thistles in this, their winter pasture, just as they could eat around the fuzzy green thistles in the summer pasture. A man could charge into haying with all the impatience he had accumulated hoeing in a garden all day.

Lucy loved haying because she was in charge of the hayrack and she drove the team. Every once in a while her father would vault into the hayrack and pitch a few huge forkfuls to the front to make room for more hay coming down from the hay loader in the rear, and then he would jump back to the dusty stubble to pitch to the loader again.

Then it was Lucy's job to tramp down the hay he had pitched to her. After five minutes of tramping, her legs began to balk, and after ten minutes her thighs turned to stone and her raw tendons disconnected themselves from her ankles and stopped lifting her feet. After that, with a boy out there across the road herding her father's cows and shaming her, she kept her legs working only by praying all the time that God would not let her be humiliated any more.

She was just turning around the corner of the field and feeling the hot wind shift to her other cheek when she noticed a car stopping at their mailbox. A man got out and read their name. Then he turned down their road, but instead of going on to the house, as they expected him to, he parked as near to them as he could. He climbed through the barbed wire, stretching it badly, and cut through the wheatfield.

"*Look* at that bird!" her father yelled. "All I'd need is fifty or sixty more like him and there wouldn't be any wheat left standing to cut. I thought he was the Watkins man. Don't the Watkins man have a green car like that?"

"Yes, he does," she yelled back.

The man hurried toward them. Once they saw him skitter sideways and take a few running steps while he watched behind him.

"Scared of a garter snake!" George shouted.

"Good morning," the man said. Then they knew for sure he was from the city. Nobody in the country said that, just as nobody in the country would say lunch for dinner or dinner for supper.

George swung his fork down and planted the tines a good two inches in the rock-hard ground, gripping the handle with only one fist. The tines struck into the dust very near the man's shoes. "You know, Mister, nobody ever sold me a thing by trespassing on my property and tromping down my wheat, but bigger men than *you* have got in trouble for provoking me a lot less than you just did. This here is private property, and I reckon you just better take whatever it is you want to sell me and get right back to your car. And you better walk *around* that wheat this time or I'm liable to hit you on top of your head so hard you'll have three tongues in your shoes."

The man seemed surprisingly unworried — insolent, in fact. George wished the fellow would do something that would justify hitting him. "*You* must be George Custer," he said in a peculiar way.

"That's *me*," George said, "and that's George Custer's wheat you just walked through."

"Well, this must be for *you*, then" the man answered, smiling up at him.

He thrust an envelope into George's hands and walked away across the hayfield, almost running.

"Now just a minute!" George yelled after him.

"It's self-explanatory, Mr. Custer!" the man yelled back. "That is, if you can read!"

"Why you little yellow . . ." George took a half step after him and then stopped to look at the letter. It might be a telegram or something.

The return address impressively printed on the outside was

enough. He knew what it was. It was trouble from the office of Sheriff Richard M. Press in the courthouse of Stutsman County. Well, the sheriff had to make it seem as though he was doing his job. Since the law was already working for the really big crooks, it was forced to look hard for some legitimate business.

George watched the little city man backing his car out of the lane. He didn't even have the guts to drive on down and turn around in the yard. They were all yellow when they weren't on their own territory. They had to get him alone, down on their own ground, before they dared to go to work on him. He wondered what would happen if he didn't go. They'd probably come after him with a posse twice the size of the ones that used to go out after Jesse James. That would be gratifying. He'd think about it. After he saw that it was a kind of subpoena, he stuck it in his overall bib pocket and jerked his fork out of the ground. He would have to tell Rachel about it because Lucy would tell. She was looking down at him now from the hayrack.

"Is it a telegram?" she asked. They had got a telegram once when somebody had died. She could barely remember it.

He didn't really read it until that night after supper. Then he showed it to Rachel. It seemed to him that it was oddly worded. He wished to God he had the money for a lawyer or the time to read up on subpoenas himself. He was positive they were pulling a fast one on him. It ordered him to appear the next Monday as a material witness in a sheriff's investigation of conspiracy to obstruct the due processes of the law. All the fancy language was there, but that didn't mean that this was a really legal subpoena.

"What do you think would happen if I didn't go?" he said, feeling her out. Was she willing to back him up now? To go to war?

"Oh, George," she said miserably. "For heaven's sake, do what they say. They'll fine you, probably, and if they have to come after you, they'll fine you even more. And besides, how awful that would be — if they came and took you away in one of those cage cars! Oh, *why* did you do it?"

"Oh now, Rachel! They're not going to do anything like *that!* You're just hysterical. And I did it because once in a while a man has to take a stand and act the way he believes!"

"I don't think you acted out of any belief at all!" she cried out. "You did it because you got mad, that's why!"

"That just shows all you know about it. Women!"

Monday, July 31

George rushed through his chores and breakfast and then changed his clothes. He was supposed to be at the courthouse at ten o'clock, and he wanted to be on time. He didn't want to give them an excuse to add additional penalties to any they might now have in mind. The one thing that terrified him was a fine. He didn't think they'd dare to lock him up; that would arouse the rest of the men too much. But a fine could easily take at least a month's extra checks.

He put on the only suit he had — the one he had bought to get married in. It was still new-looking; it had maybe too many buttons on the sleeves, or maybe not enough — he didn't worry about such things. It fit the way it fitted nine years ago, except that it was a trifle looser here and there. Rachel had starched his collar as stiffly as she could, to make it survive the heat as long as possible, and he wore a smart-looking figured maroon tie to set off the suit.

If only he had a summer hat. He needed it to complement the rest of his outfit. He bent to see the top of his head in the mirror over the washstand. His hair was thinning in an unattractive way, with kinky, sandy wisps straggling over the sunburned skin of his scalp. His neat instincts were bothered by the way his hair was going. He wouldn't have minded being completely bald so much as he minded this. He felt that he had always looked very youthful for his age. It wouldn't matter if he did get bald young. But he needed a hat to make himself look really snappy, and cover up that ragged hairline.

"Well, Mrs. Custer," he said. "You have to admit I make a good-looking jailbird. I'll be the best-dressed con in the hoosegow."

He had a way, it seemed to her, of always refusing to admit that things were as bad as they were. He could conceivably be on his way to signing away every bit of cash they would get from the wheat before it was even harvested. How could he joke?

She had a way, it seemed to him, of deflating every effort he made toward rendering an impossible situation possible. All she needed to do was to look up at him the way she looked now.

He knew he couldn't kiss her goodby. She would turn away. So he turned himself away first.

On the way to Jamestown he decided to buy a hat. He'd get a good one, too, by God — one that went properly with his suit. He'd show them that just because a man wore overalls to get in his hay, he wasn't any hayseed. In another few weeks he'd show everybody, when he harvested the Ceres. The smutty whiffs he got from the wheat didn't mean anything. One smutted head in a square yard of healthy heads could stink up the atmosphere. He wasn't going to worry about it. The well was a more immediate problem.

He paid two and a half for the hat — more than half of a week's cream checks. To hell with it. Maybe the hat would scare them into giving him his legal rights, whatever they were. He walked up the steps to the second floor of the courthouse and presented himself at the sheriff's door at exactly ten o'clock.

A sweating, red-faced woman sat before a typewriter at a desk on the other side of the counter from George. Her breasts appeared to be rolled, like thick wads of heavy cotton batting, and they were haphazardly and precariously straining the thin silk blouse.

George took off his hat.

"What can I do for you?" she said. She acted as though anything she did for him would be a very big favor that would put him forever in her debt. Political job, of course, George thought. She probably had something pretty good on Sheriff Richard M. Press. Otherwise he'd have a *pretty* girl behind that desk.

George pushed the subpoena across the counter. She scudged back her chair and hauled herself out of it. The contrast between the amorphous weight in her pink blouse and the straight narrowness of the skirt encasing her thighs was enough to make a man wonder what she would look like — not that it would be especially desirable. She studied the subpoena — or whatever it was. George could have sworn she knew it was at least questionable, if not downright illegal.

"I see it's for today," she said finally. "Couldn't you serve it yet?" He had a pleased moment, knowing that she did not take him for a criminal, but then he was irritated at having her class him with the little weasel who had served the thing to him.

"No, this is *me,*" he said. "*I'm* George Custer!"

She looked at him with a different expression — the one she used for people she could browbeat with impunity. He looked back, and he thought he could see her deciding not to browbeat *him.*

"Well, I don't know what he aims to do about it," she said. "He ain't in any special place that I know of, so I expect he'll show up around here sooner or later. He usually checks in around lunchtime. You might as well just set and wait for him."

The picture was not developing the way George had expected it to. He looked around for a hatrack, but he saw none, so he sat down on a bench and laid the new summer hat beside him. He read the subpoena once again, and wondered for the hundredth time if he could just walk out of the office and forget the whole thing. He reconstructed the picture the way it should have been. He walked in, looking so dapper and polished that the sheriff didn't recognize him. He handed the subpoena to the sheriff in the envelope so that the sheriff had to take it out himself. The sheriff looked fat and awkward as he fumbled with the envelope. George looked down at him, composed and waiting.

When the sheriff looked back up at him, George would be able to detect his surprise. He would be expecting a chastened farmer in sweaty overalls; instead he would be looking up at a well-dressed, self-possessed man of the world in a new hat. He would realize he didn't dare go very far with this fellow. George would watch that realization dawning on him. Then they would have a little talk, with the sheriff blustering out of the mess he had got himself into, and George would leave, after letting the sheriff know that he had taken up the time of a very busy man.

And when wheat was pushing three dollars a bushel again, and the rain came again, the picture enlarged with the inspiring clarity of a movie closeup. He would have his own lawyer in Jamestown then, and he would simply pick up his telephone and tell his lawyer to fix everything up — the way his enemies did. But of course they never tried to pull anything like this in the first place with a man who could afford a lawyer.

George picked up the front page of the morning's *Jamestown Sun*. It was wilted and used, the way his suit and shirt were beginning to look. In New York State the farmers of four counties were refusing to ship milk into the city at the rates set by the Milk Control Board. They stopped trucks and dumped the milk into ditches, just as the men along Highway Number 20 had done last fall in Iowa. Babies in New York City were dying of malnourishment while the roads leading into the city ran with milk, said the paper. A Pennsylvania coal striker was killed by the state militia. Those poor devils — 27,000 of them out on strike while their families starved. The mine-owners who controlled the militia knew damned well their whole ill-gotten empires would collapse if those miners ever *really* started marching. A five-day heat wave in New York City was blamed for fifty-one deaths. Phooey! In the first place those fifty-one people probably just *starved* to death, and in the second place those pantywaist Easterners didn't have the vaguest idea of what a heat wave was.

Noon came and went. The secretary took a sack lunch from her desk drawer. "He probably won't be back now till after he's ate," she said. "You might as well go on out and get a bite yourself. I'll tell him not to leave till you get back."

"I'll wait," George said.

"Suit yourself." She shrugged her flabby shoulders and the movement wobbled down the front of her blouse. George went back to the paper.

At a quarter of two the sheriff walked briskly through the door. He nodded toward George and said to the secretary, "Any mail worth looking at?"

"Well, just these. But I think they can wait. This man here —"

"I got some phone calls to make," the sheriff said. "I'll get around to him in a while." He disappeared behind the frosted glass in the door of his office.

George sat for another half hour. A man came through the door behind him, chirped, "Hiya, Toots," to the secretary, and walked into the sheriff's office without knocking. Presently Toots's desk buzzed and she said to George, "You can go on in now."

Both men sat waiting for him. "Close the door," the sheriff said, before George had quite managed to get through it. "You wasn't born in a barn, was you?"

George slammed it hard. The sheriff turned to the man sitting with him behind the desk. "I reckon maybe he *was,* at that."

"You *are* Custer, aren't you?" he said. "You ain't dressed quite the way I remember you, but I never forget a face." George felt as though he was in overalls again. "This here's the county prosecuting attorney," he went on, pointing with an elbow at the man beside him.

"Mr. Custer," the lawyer said.

"A pleasure," George said savagely.

"Now then, Mr. Custer," the sheriff began. "We're busy men—the county attorney here and me—"

"I'm a busy man *myself!*"

"Well, fine, then, we'll start right off understanding each other, won't we?"

"You *bet!*" George said.

"The attorney here, and me, have the lawful duty to collect money that rightfully belongs to holders of delinquent mortgages. If a sale of chattel property is the only way to do it, then it's our lawful obligation to hold a sale. When something goes wrong at a sale, we got to have an investigation, see? We got to have *records* to show just how things went. And we got to have witnesses to them records, so's nobody can come around later and say to us, 'No sir, I just don't believe that's the way that happened at all. You must've been in on that swindle yourself, Sheriff Press.' Just suppose, now, that Mr. Burr has sent in his report on the sale—just suppose that a man from the head office out in Hartford was to come out here and put it to me—suppose he was to say to me, 'You're the man this county elected to enforce the law. What have you done about it?' So you see, we try and get these records all fixed up while everything is still fresh in everybody's mind. Do you follow me?"

"*Perfectly!*" George shouted.

"Now, then, Mr. Custer, I'm just trying to do my job here. Just ask yourself where would *you* be without the protection of the law."

"A hell of a lot better off than I *am!*"

"Now then, Mr. Custer — the county attorney and I have simply got a factual statement of the way the Wilkes auction went on, and we simply have to have that statement attested to by a man that was there. The county attorney here can notarize your signature, of course."

George was sure, now, that he was being slickered. "What's the matter with those stool pigeons you *had* there?" he asked. "Can't they write? They need a farmer to come all the way down here to Jimtown and show them how to make an X on a dotted line?"

"Oh, my deputies will sign it, too, don't you worry. But we think, Mr. Custer, that there'd be less chance of argument from *your* side of the fence if one of *you* signed it too. After all, you might want to argue some day that our version of the goings-on was attested to only by stool pigeons, mightn't you?"

"What the hell are you getting at, anyhow! *You* know I'm not going to argue with you about Wilkes's sale, and neither is anybody else. It's all over and done with! Let's cut out this pussyfooting around. You know damn well that moneybags back in Hartford isn't going to know me from Adam, and *I* know my signature on a piece of paper isn't going to get him off your tail if he takes a notion to send you back out to Wilkes to collect his money for him. Now let's quit beating around the bush."

"All right, Mr. Custer! You don't suppose I'm going to go out and conduct another foreclosure sale with rabble-rousers and crazy men there, do you? I don't have to explain to you that it wouldn't be smart for a man with his name signed on a paper like this to show up at any more sales in this county, do I? Now I advise you to sign your name here and stop wasting everybody's time. Go ahead and read it."

George snatched the paper from the desk. He was prepared to see Wilkes's name there, and somehow the sheriff had found out who *he* was, so he expected his own name. But how had Press found out that they met at Will's house the night before the auction? Good God — they had even found out who owned the mare! And who had told him that Wallace Esskew had been the one to haul out a gun at exactly the right moment? Oscar Johnson's name was there — every man who had opened his mouth in the sham bidding was named. Who was the stool pigeon whose name wasn't on the paper? But the shocker was the last brief paragraph. It was written as though he himself had given all the information that preceded it.

It was so far-fetched that he began to laugh.

He stood up. "*I* advise *you*," he said, "to get the Judas that *gave* you this to sign it. Whoever he is, he'd steal the pennies off a dead man's eyes, so you shouldn't have no trouble."

"Oh, there *is* one trouble, Mr. Custer. He's not nearly such a dependable witness as you. If a man like *you* signs his name, it means something, doesn't it, Mr. Custer?"

"You *bet* it does! There's not a man that knows my name that doesn't know it stands for an honest man and a gentleman!"

"Well, now, that's just why that name is worth a lot to *me* — and to *you* too, I imagine. Maybe it's even worth enough to you so if it sets here in my file when I go out to the next foreclosure sale, you just won't be able to find the time to be on hand. What do you think?"

George did not say what he thought. He was so far gone in rage that he was becoming two men — one observing the other — the way he often did in dreams — one wondering what the other might do.

"Well," the sheriff went on. "I was hoping we wouldn't have to show you this other paper here. I was hoping we could just tear it up." He twisted his ugly square head toward the attorney. One man in the dream twisted it the rest of the way around — all the way off.

The attorney hauled another sheet of legal-size paper from his coat pocket.

"Compliments of the county attorney's office," he said, smiling.

One man in the dream read the paper and saw that it was a warrant for his arrest on a charge of inciting to riot, and saw also that it looked very legal, except that nobody had incited a riot. The dream ended with a noise made by both men and then by George himself. "There *wasn't* any God-damn *riot!*"

"Oh?" The county attorney smiled again. "That could be kind of expensive to prove, couldn't it? And if you *did* win your case, you'd still have to sit in jail for a few weeks before you got to court — *unless,* of course, you could lay your hands on a considerable amount of cash bail. Otherwise you might sit right here when you ought to be out threshing, mightn't you?"

"*You* haven't got a *jail* in this town that could *hold* me!"

"Oh, come, Mr. Custer. Take another look at this statement. It's really a perfectly accurate statement, is it not? *We* wouldn't ask you to perjure yourself, now would we? There's no reason for this paper ever to bother you again, if you'll only remember to conduct yourself in a sensible manner henceforth. Don't you agree? Come now. We're all busy men."

There was only one way to spring the trap — for a little guy without any money. So what if he could win a case? He couldn't spare even *this* day away from the farm. Weasels were the cleverest creatures at getting out of traps, and here was the weaseling all written out in front of him, waiting for the signature of the weasel. But somebody before *him* had been the *big* weasel. That was the first traitor — the one to blame. But the *first* traitor was nameless. He was protected by the sheriff. George realized that now he himself would have to have the same protection from the same repugnant source.

"If you get my name on that statement," George said, "What do *I* get?"

"It doesn't seem to me, Mr. Custer, that you are in a position to ask for anything at all," the attorney said. George could see him hesitate. They obviously hadn't expected him to be quite so difficult. He was losing, of course, but not so easily as they had thought he would. "How would you like *this* for a little keepsake?" the lawyer asked, holding the riot arrest warrant at George and looking at the sheriff.

George didn't understand for a moment, and then he saw that, in his own hands, the arrest warrant had considerable power. For one thing, it was certainly not a document he would have legitimate reason to possess. He could bother them with it if they bothered him with his signature on the statement. They still had the upper hand, for they could ruin him with his neighbors if they wanted to, but if he didn't bother them any more, they would not want to waste time bothering him either. This was the law in practical operation. Learn something every day.

George flipped the warrant out of the attorney's hand and stuffed it into his inside coat pocket. He took the pen the sheriff was holding for him and scratched his name across the paper beside the X.

"Very *good,* Mr. Custer," the prosecutor said.

It wasn't till he was going to turn on to the highway and he looked up into the rear view mirror that he realized he had left the new summer hat on the bench in the sheriff's office.

All the way home he could think only far enough to feel his fists beating the body of the stool pigeon — the anonymous first traitor, the betrayer from the ranks of little men who had stood together, for once, against the conspiracies of rich men and government.

As he drove through Eureka, he glimpsed Otto's Percherons trotting down the road to the elevator.

The witness had a reputation for being undependable, the sheriff said. The witness would also be a talkative man, wouldn't he? And a man over whom the sheriff had power — a man who would be eager to make a deal with the sheriff — a man who would gladly exchange a few of his neighbors' names for the promise that his precious pair of Percherons would not be put on the auction block again.

If anybody had tried to tell him early this morning that *he,* George Armstrong Custer, would put his own priceless signature to the statement of a deadbeat cock-sucker, and that he would do this in order to survive for one more year on a rented half-section of dried-up prairie — if anybody had tried to tell him that G. A. Custer would sell his honor and his guts for a chance to harvest a drought-stunted, grasshopper-infested hundred and sixty acres of wheat — well, he probably would have killed the man that had tried to tell him that.

❦ ❦ ❦

Will had mowed his last field of hay and raked it and turned it once when the clouds appeared one day in the clear northwestern sky. The clouds probably did not mean rain, for rarely had summer clouds brought rain in the last nine summers. But while the wheat could still profit from rain, and rain on the garden could save rows of dying plants, rain on nearly cured hay would only damage it, cause extra labor in turning it, and run him short of time for other things he had to get done before the threshing began. He already had all the outside haystacks he had planned on, and this premium hay was slated for the mow.

He walked through the field, studying the sky, feeling the formidable drag of the pain. He didn't know but what he might be too sick to work one of these days. If he lost time with the hay and then had to take a couple of days off in bed, he'd be impossibly far behind. He stuck his fork into a long pile of sweet alfalfa and lifted. The hay was on the green side, no doubt of it. If he put this hay into the mow and turned it into musty compost, he would never forgive himself. But his abdomen felt as though he had used the pitchfork on himself instead of the hay.

Rain, sickness, mold, time — these things all had their laws, some of which he understood and some which he did not. Sometimes the laws worked together usefully, from a man's point of view, and sometimes they did not. Sometimes rain and mold and time made compost just as he wanted them to. Sometimes, if a man had been unlucky or foolish, they made spoiled hay. Decay, sickness, death — sometimes, from a man's point of view, they were good — sometimes bad. A man's life was totally dependent upon the same microscopic events that would eventually destroy his life and return him to dust. Sometimes it appeared that he had more choice, or at least more leeway, in his manipulations of the laws than he had at other times. Sometimes he felt forced to confront the laws with his own needs and risk himself to his own ignorant impertinence.

The hay was green, but he would put it away now. He went to town to get help before the rain came. He bought some chewing tobacco and hired Herman Schlaht's boy Buddy on the spot. Then they got Carl Stensland from the pool hall and rushed back to the hay field.

They set to at a frantic pace. The clouds rolled and blackened, and heat lightning flashed around them in tiers of silent white flames that ignited half the sky. In a few hours the three men had swung the last load on the hay lift in through the high gaping doors of the mow, and stuffed it to the roof with the rich-smelling hay. Despite the drought, the alfalfa had not done too badly. Will was well satisfied to have the top half of his big barn filled with such fine winter pasture, and he was glad he had decided to put it away before rain could wash it out and a second curing would bake more of the nourishment out of it.

The clouds remained all day, but they did not move any nearer and they began to turn lighter again. Perhaps a breeze would spring up in the night and blow the clouds over them and they would wake to the sound of rain. Then he would lie in the darkness rejoicing that rain had come and exulting because for once he had managed to win against the weather.

The next morning the clouds were gone but the sky was less pure than usual. The air was sultry, but there was no rain in it; if they got any precipitation at all, it would be a twenty-minute hailstorm that would beat the wheat down flat and thresh out all the grain and bury it in a slushy white wasteland. In the afternoon the sky began to clear, with the sun growing ever brighter and hotter. The vanished clouds had not been, after all, the overtures of a repentant universe about to send forth the fountains it had so long stopped. Still, there was reason to be grateful; for the murderous balls of ice had been up there and they, like the rain, had gone away again.

After that there were no more clouds. Each day seemed unnatural, endless. When he went out to milk in the evening at six o'clock, with the sun still hours away from setting, the air seemed as hot as it had at noon or at two or four.

Finally one night as he leaned in the doorway of the smothering barn, he confessed to himself that he would have to take it easy the next day unless either the heat or the pain let up a little. The combination was doing him in.

He was so tired that his eyes kept losing their focus on his nine milch cows filing through the door. They kept fading into insubstantial blotches. He was shaken by his pity for the weary blotches. All day long the sun crushed them, withered them. How could they hold back enough water to make their milk? Maybe he ought to skip the milking tonight. Maybe they wouldn't care whether they were milked or not. Maybe this was the day he should have spent resting. Maybe this was the night he wouldn't make it through the chores.

He directed himself into the barn, into the first stall. He slid the wooden stanchion against the neck of the first cow. The block of wood that braced the bar felt abnormally big in his hand. Fingers swollen with the heat, he thought. He went in and out of eight more stalls, pushing the stanchions, letting the wood blocks fall. The blocks made a hollow sound as though they were quite far away — much farther away than the length of his arm. The heat, he thought, the heat deadened the air between his ear and the sound.

He went to Charlotte — black, mean, grouchy Charlotte — and clipped her tail to the wire above the stall. Then he snapped the kickers around her smeared legs. She always dirtied herself worse than any other cow. He looked around for the rag to clean her with, but it seemed to be missing. Rose would bring another.

He began milking the cow by the pasture door of the barn. Rose would come soon and begin at the other end of the line. The first jets of milk broke sharply against the sides of the pail between his knees and made a hissing metallic echo that was too close to his ear. Peculiar, how sounds were all coming from the wrong distances. He settled in to the rhythm of the job, leaning forward on his one-legged stool and resting his forehead against the cow's soft, heated belly. The two thin lines of milk steadily punctured the rising white froth. The sound of the first stream was always pitched higher than the second. Spit-spat, spit-spat, spit-spat, spit-spat, spit — he was sprawling in the straw, the white froth was wetting his legs, the pail was banging the cow's shanks, the cow was trampling him, she was bending his shin the wrong way, she was breaking it, the roof was flying apart and the hurricane was booming in his ears.

He heard Rose's screams contending with the cows and the flames, and then the screams shaped themselves into his name.

"I'm all right!" he shouted. "Go back! Go back! Shut your doors! The draft! Stay out! Go back!" Even while he was shouting, gulping smoke, tearing his throat, he could not hear any of his own words. He was as demented as the screeching cows. He lay in the straw commanding his sanity to come back. No matter what else he did in his life, he could do this. He could be sane now.

The heat pressed down out of the mow, but no flames broke through. There was enough fuel up there so the fire would continue to follow its natural upward direction for a little while. There was time, he thought. The smoke was getting bad, but there would be time.

He wormed his way through the straw beside the cow while

she did her terrible dance — bracing her feet and hauling back till her jawbones locked against the wooden bars, crying out, plunging forward to crash her shoulders into the stanchion as though she pursued the screaming head there on the other side of the bars.

He pulled himself up by the side of the manger, balanced on his good leg, and lifted the wood block. She was gone before he could get back down on his knees to crawl to the next stall. Thank God it was cows, not horses in here. A cow could get herself out of a fire, but a horse couldn't. Thank God it was cows.

He got another bad kick in the next stall and he could not really see the cow escape. His streaming eyes had stopped seeing anything but smoke. He felt his way in and out of two more stalls and knew that four of the nine were liberated. He understood that he ought not to try coping with Charlotte, but before he could get around the years of morning and evening habit, he was hanging on the side of the stall and reaching up for the clip that held her tail. It burnt his fingers, but he squeezed until the tail stripped itself away.

Still there were the kickers to undo. He worked at the clamp on the chain between her knees, telling himself how he would shove with his good foot and fall away from the blows of the unfettered legs. But when he shoved, he did not seem to be altogether sure of which direction to fall in. He seemed, in fact, to fall directly into a hoof and knock out his wind on it. When he finally could breathe again, he discovered that there was no air to breathe anyway; it was amazing that a man could keep on moving after he had stopped breathing air, but he found that he had got himself dragged up to the wood block on her stanchion and black, mean, grouchy Charlotte was free.

He started on his hands and knees to find the next cow, keeping one hand cupped over the edge of the refuse ditch in order to know where he was going. The smoking boards of the haymow floor still intervened between him and the holocaust, but down through the knotholes and crevices rained the live sparks — the meteors spewing from a galactic ambush that had been waiting such a long time for him — billions of years it had waited for this blunder of the stellar system containing him. Now the earth fell into the fire, fell at ten thousand miles a minute into the fire, and the meteors rained into the stalls of his barn — the drops of incandescent rain came now to drown his dry planet with light, to transmute it to an evaporating star and to scatter it in darkened cinders.

He thought of Rose, but he couldn't hold on to the thought long enough to wonder what might have become of her — the thought was only her name, as her screams had been his name. And then he heard only the ancient recapitulation of anguish. In a flight as blazing and lucid as the flights of the meteors raining around him, he understood and entered into the fellowship of despair. . . .

My God, my God, why hast thou forsaken me!

⁂

She found him lying across the ditch near the next cow he had been going to save. Her scorched eyes barely saw, through the yellowish liquid smoke of the burning grass, the way his body joggled over the strawed floor after her as she backed down the aisle toward the door.

Some burning hay dropped down through a feeder hole over a manger and she imagined she heard above all the other sounds the one last sound that came from the head between those stanchion bars.

She dragged his body over the graveled yard toward the house till his weight collapsed her on the ground beside him. She lifted his head and laid it in her lap.

"Will!" she cried. But the only sounds were the wind of the fire, the snapping of beams, the rasping supplications from the smoke-seared throats of the roasting cows. "Will!"

A cough as frightful as the sounds from the barn vibrated his throat. She began to sob. "Oh thank God! Oh thank God!"

She went on repeating it as she plucked at him — unbuttoning his shirt and pulling the underwear back from his chest, as though by exposing the outside of him to the air, she could clear away the smoke from the inside of him. He smelled like a firebrand. He smelled as if he were a living sacrifice tumbled down from a funeral pyre. His clothes were full of brown-ringed holes and there was a red spot on his skin beneath every hole.

A sensation of movement made her lift her eyes from the face on her lap in time to see the great flower of the windmill plummeting into the flames. The few surviving beams of the haymow gave way and the floor of the fire dropped into the main part of the barn, burning away the bars from the throats that screamed no more. Oh, God, God, God, what if he was in there now?

"Oh, thank God!" She began saying it over and over again.

She never heard the Custer car come up the hill behind her, and when she looked up to see them running toward her, she began to cry again. Only a few tears fell — she was too dried out to have any tears left — but the sobs shook her body and the unconscious head on her lap undulated with her motion in a dreadful acquiescence, as though it would never again move of its own accord.

Rachel knelt beside her mother and took her father's head into her own lap. "He's alive," she said. "He's alive. He's alive."

Rose clutched at her daughter's arm, yielding as she had not yielded before in all her life, and fainted, drooping forward while a little humming sigh came out of her white lips. George rubbed her wrists. Then he ran into the house for a cup of water and bathed her face with it.

Miraculously, as though her soul had deserted her unconscious body and gone clear to Hell for him this time, refusing to come back until he came too, dragging him back out of the smoke once more, Rose opened her eyes just as Will opened his. He coughed and began to groan softly from his fiery throat. Rose heard him and raised herself on one elbow. "Oh, thank God!" she cried again. The sound of her voice made him aware of the sounds he was making himself. He realized he was groaning and he stopped at once.

"The stock," he whispered. "Is all the stock out?"

A stampeding litter of shoats came pouring around the side of the granary. Their mother lumbered after them. Her torn snout dripped blood and her face was blood-smeared all around her maniacal little eyes. She had battered through the planks of her pen to get her babies out of the fire.

Rose counted the baby pigs. "They're all there, Will," she said. "They got out — every one."

Will settled more heavily into Rachel's arms. He closed his eyes.

Neighbors began to arrive and Adolph Beahr came with his big truck and some volunteers. The nearest hospital was in Jamestown, and they decided to go and meet the ambulance. They laid Will in the back seat of Clarence Egger's new Chrysler and Rachel sat in the front, helping her mother sit up. As Will felt the car slant down his drive, he thought, It's all downhill now—just one direction now. . . .

⁂

The Eureka volunteer firemen finally ceased their touring inspections and gathered in a watchful, awed knot at the truck. Buddy Schlaht was the most awed of all, for he felt that he bore some responsibility for what had happened.

"I *wondered,* when I seen how green that hay was, if the old man really knew what he was doing," he said for the third time.

"I never seen such a sight in my life," said Ed Greeder. "I was out yonder in my pasture there and all of a sudden I seen that whole roof just blow up. The whole roof afire—all over, all at once. I bet you that thing burnt to the ground in twenty minutes flat. And that was a big barn, too."

Adolph had reason to be an authority on that kind of fire. "Well, this ain't the first time I've gone out to throw water on what's left of one of these things—not by a long shot. Usually happens around this time of day, after the sun has beat down on the roof all day long. They always go the same way, too—all at once. Think how hot that hay has to get to just blow up like that. It stands to reason they're going to go mighty quick.

"I just got a little booklet here the other day from the government," he said. "I always send for them things. The government says last year there was over a million dollars lost from spontaneous combustion just in grain elevators around the country. Lots of people killed, too. Remember that dust explosion back in Chicago just a couple days before Christmas? Blew the whole damn elevator into little pieces—and two poor devils into *littler* pieces. You just can't be too careful when it comes to this kind of stuff. You just can't believe how hot a big mow jammed up with green hay can get. It ferments and then it's just like green beer in a bottle. Put a little heat on it and the bottle blows to pieces. You just can't realize that *anything* can get so hot till you've seen one or two go like this." He waved his hand toward the spotty red lines around the spaces where the barn used to be.

The sky darkened and the long timbers, broken and fallen into chaos, glowed like the framework of an elaborate burned-out set of fireworks. The wind shifted and the odor of the four cows came around with it. The men smoked and chewed their tobacco and did not mention the smell.

❦ ❦ ❦

Rachel had been trying to prepare herself for the way her father's farm would look without its barn, but even from the road none of the other buildings looked right. They were sad, mute orphans, cowering around the spot from which the cords of each proceeded and returned — the sheep shed which sent its population to the barn every year to give up the winter fleeces, the granary which held in its bins the corn and oats that went to the horses, cattle, and pigs, the outbuildings housing the machinery that harvested the hay for the vanished mow. Even the tall yellow building that sheltered the farmer and his family looked as bereft as the others. The most stalwart farmhouse was too frail without a barn looming between it and the outstretched prairie.

For thirty years the structure above that hideous bared space had sheltered animals from week-long blizzards. It had penned in soft-haired calves smelling of the milk they drank. It had provided a high, warm, prickly privacy for the births of generations of barn cats. It had provided eaves over the barnyard to be plastered full of the straw and mud nests of the swallows who swooped through the dusk and helpfully devoured the blood-sucking insects drawn by the animal smells. Now the distraught birds fluttered about the roof of the granary. There were no babies to feed this morning.

The barn was the comfortable meeting place of all the dwellers in its precincts. Even those who properly lived in the other houses were drawn by the barn. The poultry strolled in and out to peck at stray bits of grain and to dust in the straw on blistering days and the dog sought out the coolest stall for a summer nap. If a sheep managed to squeeze under the fence around its shed, it would go to the barn, followed by the rest of the flock, to investigate the interesting sounds and smells there. Children went to the barn to watch a row of tiny pink pigs gluttonously nursing a sow, or they went there to hold a bucket of skim milk for a calf or to seek out the newborn kittens whose eyes were so tightly shut and whose fearful claws, like burrs, sought always to implant themselves in the hay or a sweater or a bare leg.

The menfolk would retire to the barn to perch on the rails of the calf and pig pens whenever womenfolk filled the house. City men, because they had no barns to retreat to, almost always became shockingly coarse on the infrequent occasions when they found themselves in a barn with a farmer. Rachel's father had often remarked on how surprised some salesman's wife would be if she could hear what came from her scissor-bill husband out there. Once in a while even a preacher could come up with something that set an old hobo on his ear.

A farm without a barn was like a body with its digestion stopped and the warm and sensual lower portions of its brain gouged away.

"Oh, how will he stand it!" Rachel moaned. "How will he bear it? How will he bear it!"

"Oh, now Rachel! Don't get hysterical, for Pete's sake! He's got insurance, hasn't he?"

Rachel went into the house with the baby; but George saw Lester Zimmerman's car slowing on the road below, and he waited for him by the porch. Lucy slipped away and went to the place where the barn had been. She had rather expected to see it there this morning. It had *always* been there.

The four cows lay where they had fallen at their stanchions. In a few spots where there had been little flesh between the hide and the bones, the hide had burned completely away, leaving the bones a dark dirty yellow. The legs stuck straight out from the bellies as though the cows were standing on a vertical floor that she could not see. The black gristle of their noses was shrunken, and the thin skin that rippled under their jaws was gone, exposing the appallingly long lines of their yellow jawbones set with the jaundiced teeth that had chewed a cud out in the pasture yesterday morning at this hour. Bone showed all around the great eye sockets, swimming with dark jelly.

She stepped over the shards of two crossed beams and felt the heat from a crumpled black milk pail against her leg. Another bit of metal brushed her and she recognized it as the far, proud weather vane she had so often wished to touch. It was much bigger than she had thought it was.

She began to perceive the enormity of the thing that had happened, and she was afraid they would be angry with her for coming to the barn. They often seemed angry when she understood something that she was not supposed to understand. She ran to hide in the granary before the men coming from the house could find her. She sat inside the door on the powdery, rumpled top of a sack of chicken mash and watched what they did.

Her father drove the tractor down from the shed, towing the stoneboat. The other men cleared away enough of the burned wood so he could maneuver it down the aisle. They looped ropes around the stiff legbones of the first cow and pulled her body toward the stoneboat, resting between spurts of hauling.

"Jesus, I never *seen* an animal burnt up like this," said Mr. Zimmerman. "A haymow fire don't usually take off the skin this way. I seen a bunch of horses once that was in a livery stable, and outside of not having no hair left, they could of been just normal. They looked like they just had their hides scraped off and tanned. But I never seen anything like *this!*"

"The ceiling give way," Mr. Greeder said. "I could tell, even from where I was at. It just dropped right down onto 'em. Probably twenty, thirty tons of hay burnt right on top of 'em. . . . Ready! *Heave! Heave!*"

⁂

When Rose came home from spending the night in the hospital, she refused to go to bed. "I've *been* in bed all *morning!*" she said. "*I'm* not sick! Just leave me be, now. Will wants to see the papers right away."

She sat down at the desk and located a paper that folded and unfolded like an accordion. "I can't believe this is all we had," she said. "There must be a later one than this." She took the papers out of each pigeonhole and finally emptied each drawer. George loitered in the kitchen, wondering if she already knew about the money, and wondering if she would come across the promissory note for his loan, and if she would be surprised. Will must have kept a record of it somewhere.

"Well, I guess this is all. As far as I can see, this may or may not cover it," she said. "I just don't know what I'm going to tell him.

He thinks we got them all out. I just don't see how I'm going to tell him. He would have stayed right there and burned up with them, trying to get them out, and he blames himself for the whole thing. He thinks *I* got them out. He doesn't remember."

"Do we have to tell him?" Rachel asked.

"Now, Rachel, just stop and think a minute!" George said. "Just where is he going to think they are when he gets back?" George was only too well acquainted with where they were. They were in an enormous hole that he and Will Shepard's neighbors had damned near killed themselves to dig so that Will would never come upon their stinking carcasses or their burnt bones as he went about his farm.

"How am I going to tell him?" Rose asked again.

❧ ❧ ❧

Will lay in his room in Trinity Hospital, his cracked shin in a cast, his wried shoulder on a hot pack that aggravated two cinder burns on the skin more than it helped the shoulder muscle, and his smashed thumb wrapped in an oversized bandage. Pills to dull his various miseries were dissolving in his stomach.

"Why did I do it? Why did I do it why did I do it?"

He had said the words to himself so many times that they became as abstract and confusing as the pain in his body. The words ran into each other until they wouldn't go into the rhythm of a sentence any more. All that day he lay adrift in his abstractions, but that night he slept, and when he waked up the next morning his head was clear again.

A doctor came in and poked at him. "Now let's see about your middle, here," he said. "We just want to know that nothing is ruptured down here. We didn't want to pester you with X-rays yesterday, because what you mostly seemed to need was air. You obviously got a kick or two, if we can judge by these." He touched a couple of spots that Will didn't have to see in order to know they were black-and-blue.

"When can I go home?" Will said.

"Mr. Shepard, yesterday you acted like a man with a lot of trouble somewhere. We have to make sure you're all right before we release you. Tomorrow we have to get some pictures."

The doctor probed farther down in his abdomen. Will could not stop an agonized reflex in a couple of places.

"I don't see why it should hurt *here*." He delved into the bad spots again. "No contusions at all, that I can see."

Of course it doesn't show — what's really gone wrong — Will could have told him. You don't know what I know and how could you? You know about *your* microscopic events and I know about *mine*. You can't see what's wrong with me, but I understand it. It's a set of laws working a different way, toward a different end. I thought that if I wasn't going to save my hay it would be because the laws destroyed it with mold, but the laws destroyed it with fire instead. All perfectly legal — however unexpected, however unprepared for.

That morning I put the hay in — then I saw only as far as those clouds — the half-inch of water that might have fallen from them, the hay grown in a few mortal weeks on a tiny piece of a tiny particle in space, the few mortal days of my own that I coveted as though they were mine alone and not a part of all those laws around me. Now I see that rain, that field, those bits of time — I see them from the other side of the clouds. There was that moment in the hot rain when I was so foolish as to believe that God ought to save me from the laws. But now I can see things in a longer light, from the other side of the clouds. Go ahead and take all the pictures you want.

They took the pictures the next morning and in the afternoon the doctor came again. He looked at the purple thumbnail, felt the shoulder, tapped the cast nervously with his pen.

"Mr. Shepard," he said. "I want you to go and see a specialist in Bismarck as soon as you can comfortably travel there." He wrote on a prescription pad and handed it to Will.

"He's as good a man as there is in the state."

"When can I go home?" Will asked.

"Probably day after tomorrow, if the leg seems to be doing all right. Of course you'll have to stay off it for quite a while. But it's not a bad break and you ought to mend nicely."

Will looked at the scrap of paper. There was the name of a drugstore on it, and a telephone number. Under that the doctor's handwriting said, "Oliver Murdoch, M.D. Internist. Bismarck. Mercy Hospital."

He laid it on his bedside table and then he picked it up to throw it away, but instead he stuffed it into his billfold.

⁂

The Eggers came all the way down to get him because their Chrysler was so much smoother-riding than the Custers' old car. Where Clarence had got the money for it, Will couldn't imagine. For a one-armed man Clarence drove with amazing skill.

Will had the whole back seat to himself, and he was comfortable enough, but he couldn't think of anything except how his barnyard was going to look without a barn in it. And he kept trying to remember how he had got all those cows out.

When he and Rose were finally alone, he said, "We got them all out, of course."

He knew, because she wouldn't look at him.

"How many?" he asked.

"Four. Four cows. All the pigs got out."

Four cows tortured to death because *he* had locked them in stanchions under hay *he* had put away knowing that it was too green.

But it had been harder for Rose than for him. He had been lying in a hospital, not having to know, while she had been here alone with the knowledge, with the cleanup, with the night memories and the screams.

"You ought to have told me right away," he said.

"What good would that have done? Do you want to go to sleep now?"

For four days he had been fighting to extricate himself from the clawing images of the fire. Every time he closed his eyes he was like a fly trapped in an infernal kaleidoscope. He was surrounded by the multiplying images of flame and torture and guilt and condemnation that fell together and then fell apart as the garish triangles spun and spun. Even before he knew about the cows, he had wondered when the mirrors would slow in their spinning — when he would be allowed to crawl to their convergence and escape through the long empty eye of forgetfulness. But now he knew that the kaleidoscope would never let him go. No, he did not wish to close his eyes just now.

"No, I think I'll just catch up on the *Sun*, if you saved the back copies."

❦ ❦ ❦

The Custers did their own chores early and came over to help Rose and to have supper with Will. After supper George lingered in the bedroom while the women did the dishes, waiting for Will to mention that the loan would come in handy now, for the doctor and the hospital, not to mention finishing the new barn.

I should simply bring it to him, George thought, but since he had no idea of where he could get what he had spent of it or how he could last through the summer without the rest of it, he continued to talk of nothing and to sit with his kitchen chair tipped back against the dresser, his wrists dangling at his sides, his fists curling and uncurling around the rungs of the chair. He was positive that Will knew what he was waiting for. Why didn't the old man go ahead and spring it?

But Will was thinking of the boy last heard from nearly eight months ago in Arizona. Would he come home in time or not?

Finally George let down the front legs of his chair and stood up. "Well, take 'er easy," he said. He went out to the kitchen to start the family moving toward the car. He couldn't stand it any longer.

After they had gone, Will called out to the kitchen. "Rose, do you think if we could get in touch with Stuart he'd come home?"

"I think he'll come home if and when he feels like it. He'll come home if he runs out of money or if he gets sick. We wouldn't have heard from him the *last* time or the time before *that* if he hadn't needed money to get out of trouble — or to spend on liquor! Where does he always find it? What good are the *laws*, anyway?"

❦ ❦ ❦

George lay awake in the stagnant air of the low little house. A man might as well try to sleep in a fireless cooker as a one-story house after a day of so much sun. The house, like the cooker, absorbed heat all day long and cooked all night.

The old man expects me to bring it to him, George thought, but he's not going to ask me for it. After he practically forced it on me in the first place. What if he needs it to get his wheat threshed? He must have finished off his Jimtown account to bail himself out of the hospital. Now Rachel will have to know. Damn him — if he needs it he ought to ask for it. How am *I* supposed to know what to do? God-damn it, this is what comes of borrowing from a man's in-laws. . . .

A small futile sound escaped from his throat. From the way Rachel moved, he knew she heard it and was not asleep either. He rolled over to her roughly, and roughly took what was his.

Afterwards, like the man in the desert whose last reckless strength has brought him running to an illusion, he was more alone than ever. What the hell had made her change so much, anyway? He'd never forgotten the joke his brother had made when he got married. "You just remember what I say, Georgie-Porgie. Put a bean in a jar for every time during the first year, and then take one out for every time *after* the first year. I'll bet you dollars to doughnuts you'll never get all them beans back out of the jar again."

❦ ❦ ❦

Rachel didn't wake up until just before five, and she hurried to make a fire in the kitchen range. "Monarch" was stamped in the nickel-plated frame around each of the warming-oven doors at her eye level. She wondered idly, as she had a thousand times, what could possibly be royal about the black monster that dominated her life. She doubted that the manufacturer had meant quite the quality of dominance she had in mind. She lifted out the two lids, each as big around as the bottom of her gallon teakettle. Lately in the mornings her wrists had been so weak and achy that she had to use both hands on the lifter. By the time she went out to get the first bucket of water she was usually all right, but still it made her desperate to wake in the morning and not have her joints work properly. The only hope left was in the strength of their limbs. The strength of the land was wasting away, and they had to make up for that depletion with their own strength.

She went out to the porch to get the boiler and she saw how the weeds that had managed to survive in the afternoon shade of the house seemed to be wilting already in the morning sun. It was going to be a bad day to wash, but there were no clean diapers left for the baby.

She was just ready to start down the hill for water when George came into the kitchen.

"I'll fetch you a couple of pails full," he said. "Just as soon as I tie up my shoes here." He guarded the well now, even from her. He was like a dragon brooding over a magic fountain. If he was attentive enough, the temperamental fairy in the fountain would feel propitiated; she would not give the order that dried up the fountain.

He came back up with the two buckets and dumped them in the boiler for her. Then he brought two more, but he dumped only one into the boiler.

"Can you get along on that?" he said.

While he was milking she started wringing out the diapers she had had soaking in the wash tub on the porch. She unfolded them and dropped them into the boiler, poking them down into the warming water and stirring the soap around to try to get a little suds. Then she dipped the mop pail full of the soiled water in the tub and carried it out to the garden where she poured it gently around several hills in a row of beans. It was not good to do any watering now, early in the morning, because so much would be lost through evaporation, but she had forgotten to wring out the diapers the night before and now she had to empty the tub so she could put clean rinse water in it.

George came up with the milk as she was returning from the garden with the empty bucket. "My God! You're not watering *this* time of day?" He was almost hysterical. He acted as though he might strike her.

"I'm sorry," she said. "I know I should have emptied the tub last night. I was too worried about Dad to be able to think straight."

"Honestly, Rachel, I just don't understand why you can't keep a thing like this well on your mind *all* the time! Just what do you think we're going to do if we run out of water, anyway? Do you think I can just say abracadabra and produce an unlimited supply of water for you to waste?"

"Oh, George, you *know* I don't waste water!"

"You *are* wasting it — right now! Just deliberately wasting it! I can see with my own eyes, can't I?"

He went into the kitchen but she stayed on the porch till she got control of herself. After nine years he could still wound her by saying things they both knew weren't true. She wondered why it was that his wildest, most farfetched accusations were the ones that hurt the most. They were the ones she ought to be able to forget entirely, weren't they? She emptied the last pail of fresh water into the tub and watched while the sun flitted over its agitated surface and then settled into the trembling rings of light made by the galvanized ridges around the bottom of the tub. It was a hot light — as though the sun would drain the tub before she could come back out and rinse her clothes. Wherever she looked, she saw the greedy sun. Would the sun never be satisfied till every well in the world was dry?

❧ ❧ ❧

After breakfast George took a hoe and went out to the potato patch. As he walked along the edge of the wheat, he couldn't help noticing that the fishy odor of smut was getting stronger. "Must be the way the wind's blowing," he thought.

Lucy came too, carrying her gallon Karo pail with a cup of kerosene sloshing in its bottom. She knelt at the end of the row he was hoeing and began plucking the striped potato bugs from the leaves and dropping them into her kerosene. Some of the leaves were eaten away to the delicate lace of their skeletons; they were quite pretty, those leaf skeletons; but if there were too many of them the plants no longer breathed, and then the potatoes would be no bigger than pullets' eggs, and sacks and sacks of them together would never feed the family through the winter.

She had to watch, too, for the deposits of eggs glued to the undersides of the leaves, though there were not so many now as there had been earlier in the summer. The eggs were bright yellow, like the yolk of a hen's egg, and rather soft. Any leaves with eggs on them had to be picked off and dropped into the kerosene along with the black-and-yellow bugs. Most horrid of all were the fat squishy larvae which had not yet grown their hard beetle shells. They were made of nothing but mashy insides that popped all over her fingers.

Potatoes and potato bugs. They were about equally monotonous. After attending to ten plants she had the bottom of her pail almost covered with the bodies of bugs in both stages, a mixture of segmented larvae and striped beetles, like buttons in a drawer. They all died the moment they sank beneath the kerosene. She could scarcely bear the feel of their legs struggling against the ball of her thumb and because of that awful feeling she was not sorry that they had to die, but it did make her a little sick to have to drop them into her noxious pail. Why hadn't they gone ahead and died when her father sprayed them with the Black Leaf 40?

The heat made the fumes rise around her face till she seemed herself to be drowning along with the bugs, and she wondered, as she often did, how it felt to be a bug. Once she had sat on the porch for a long hot time after Sunday school and tried to imagine how God had started. God had made everything else, but how had *He* been made? She had decided, after thinking of all the smallest things in the world, that God must have been a bug in the empty air — a very tiny bug that made Himself grow and grow and grow until He was big enough to fill part of the sky and to start making the rest of the world. Everything started by being small and growing bigger, and that must have been the way God started, too. A tiny bug was the smallest thing there was. That had to be what He used to begin Himself with.

She had an awful feeling, when she had to kill bugs, that God had a special attachment to them. She could feel Him hovering over her shoulders, telling her through the blasting rays of the sun that she was doing an unforgivable thing.

"How many you got there?" he called.

She felt the deadly ice pierce through her and then she was embarrassed to have been overtaken and so violently surprised in her own silly feelings. She leaped obediently to her feet and made a mark in the dust with her toe, as though she could order the potato-bug commerce to stop on either side of it, and ran toward him with her pail.

George had merely meant to be companionable when he called to her. He had wanted to let her know that he knew how it was to work at a job that there was no possibility of finishing — how he understood her frustration at knowing that no matter how many bugs she found, she still would have to be aware that all the potato bugs in the patch seemed to be rushing to repossess the row behind her. He felt the same way about the weeds he was hoeing.

He had meant for her to call back something that might be friendly, or even jocular, so long as it was respectful — anything to complement the effort he had made to create in the potato patch the kind of cordial family cooperation that could refresh and inspire all those who worked together for survival. Now he felt trapped by the hopelessness of trying to be friends with her, and when she held up the pail to him, with its smell and the dead dozens of beetles circling slowly in its bottom, he tightened his lips and looked away from her raised eyes.

"Quite a fair number, I see," he said. "Now just make sure you don't miss any. One old grandma can lay a lot of eggs."

Lucy nodded her head and lowered her pail. Back on her knees at the mark she had made, she took up where she had left off, pushing each plant away from her with one forearm and letting the leaves shuffle back gradually while she watched for the yolky eggs and the black-and-yellow stripes.

Her father liked to tell her when she worked at this job that President Hoover had got paid a penny a hundred for picking potato bugs when he was a little boy. Hoover liked to talk about that in his speeches about people helping themselves. "I guess that's why he kept saying prosperity was just around the corner. I guess he had things too easy when he was a kid. He never found out how hard it really is to earn a penny!" Her father would say that and look down at her on the ground in the potato row and laugh, and she would not be able to see exactly why.

Monday, August 14

THE NEWS came from Austria that while Soviet wheat was being dumped on the world market for less than it cost to produce, millions of Russians had died of starvation during the summer. The Kremlin officially denied that anyone had starved to death in Russia, and then doubled the price of a loaf of bread.

George Custer decided that the day had come to cut his wheat, and early in the morning he went out and oiled a few spots on the reaper, installed a new roll of binder twine, hitched up the horses, and trundled the big old machine out to the near corner of the field he had planted first. He lowered the blade and let it bite its first swath of the Ceres. Despite his repairs, the ancient machine couldn't do the kind of job it should have. It flailed about like a rampaging Dutch windmill, wasting more wheat than he cared to think about. All day long the serrated blade chopped through the dry stems and the revolving wooden wings swept up the wheat and the spool of twine rotated as the bundles dropped behind him. It was an outmoded way to do things. He should have had a tractor and a combine, but he didn't. A combine handled the wheat once. With a reaper a man handled it four times: first he cut it, then he shocked the bundles, then he pitched the bundles into a hayrack to carry it to a threshing machine, then he pitched it out of the hayrack into the machine.

The smut was bad. He was out in the middle of the field now, and he rarely got a breath of air that did not smell of it. Stinking smut alone, of all the enemies of wheat, he had read in the *Sun* last night, was causing a loss of as much as eighteen million bushels per year in the United States. The stench filling his nose and mouth assured him that he would be contributing at least his share to this year's national smut losses.

Besides the initial loss in the field, he might be docked as much as ten cents a bushel by the millers who had to clean it out of the wheat. He had had the feeling all along that Adolph lied to him about the seed. Now he was sure of it, but how could he prove that Adolph deliberately swindled him?

Still, he couldn't help being excited when he began the shocking. Even if some of the heads were smutted, the stems and leaves, considering the drought, were remarkably strong and healthy. *Next* year, with properly treated seed, *then* everybody would see how right he was.

He felt sorry for people who punched a time clock all year round and never knew when one season ended and another began. And it was his pleasure in seasons that kept him from being altogether sorry that he didn't own a combine. If he had a combine he'd never see his fields in shocks. Ever since he'd been big enough to tag the men around, he'd liked wandering over the new golden stubble, through the rich marshaling of the mown treasure, between the formal ranks casting their shadows across the hundreds of acres.

It always made him proud to see shocks or bundles of wheat on the great seals and the coins of states and nations, or even to see the two heads of wheat curved around the back of a penny beneath the E PLURIBUS UNUM. Somebody a long time ago had figured out that unity and abundance went together. Now it seemed that abundance was on the verge of shattering unity. Perhaps some people whose pennies were all too abundant would be forced to think a little more, before long, about the men who grew the wheat that framed the motto.

❦ ❦ ❦

The stories about the threshers preceded them, traveling from wife to wife, from county to county, from South to North, from Texas to Manitoba. The migrant threshing crews had numbered a quarter million men when Rachel was a young girl helping her mother cook for the threshers; but now there were only a few thousand left, because combines had replaced them. Nevertheless, the straggling remnant kept alive all the traditions of the former great army. Every year somebody told Rachel the same kind of stories she remembered hearing some neighbor woman recount to her mother in the kitchen while they cooked in frantic preparation for the epic digestions that were coming to feed at their table for four or five eternal days.

Long before the threshermen got to the Custer place, Rachel had heard about the oversized Swede who ate a dozen eggs for breakfast and then demanded fried potatoes and sometimes pie besides. For the midmorning lunch he ate five sandwiches of thick-sliced homemade bread and more pie. For dinner he ate a quart of mashed potatoes, half a pound of ham, a pint of cole slaw, five or six slices of bread, and a quarter of a pie. For the midafternoon lunch he ate only three sandwiches because he did not want to spoil his appetite for supper, at which time he ate about what he had at dinner, except that he wanted cake instead of pie. Even allowing for the way Elsie Egger exaggerated things she had heard, Rachel wondered how she was ever going to manage if the whole crew ate that way. It sounded like the worst crew she had ever heard of.

There was one man who was no more than a boy, really, who could drink even the Swede under the table on a Saturday night and then go on a binge that would have finished off most of his elders. He had never been known to turn down the vilest brew, and it was only a question of time till he would get hold of something that would kill him on the spot — not that it would matter at all to him, the way he carried on. Rachel hoped he wouldn't manage to find any of it while he was around their place. It was hard to know what she should really expect because she was getting the crew before anybody else in the community. Elsie, as always, had got her stories from her sister-in-law down at Gackle.

Rachel baked two batches of bread a day for the two days before they came. She hoped she wouldn't have to feed them store bread because they always complained that there was nothing to it. She also baked a half dozen pie shells to be filled with lemon or chocolate custard just before a meal.

On the night before the threshers were due, George helped her put all the leaves in the round table, making its oval length fill the room. The oilcloth was not big enough to cover it, so she put on the good damask cloth she used for Sunday dinners, hoping she would somehow be able to get all the stains out of it again.

The next morning they were up at four. Rachel had to begin the day's cooking, and George wanted to be sure the chores were out of the way and the horses hitched and the hayrack loaded with the first bunch of sheaves by the time the separator arrived. The family sat about the table, strangely far from each other. George was nervous. Crews didn't always show up when they said they would. The wheat had been standing in shocks long enough. Every day, even though the sky remained cloudless, he feared that rain or hail or a high wind might come and knock the ripe heads out of the wheat.

Lucy, feeling remote enough from watching eyes, used her thumb against the edge of her oatmeal bowl to push the last bite of porridge into her spoon. Her father caught her, of course. "Oh, George!" her mother said. "She'll *never* eat right if you keep at her like that!"

"I just don't want her to be embarrassed! I'm trying to teach her some manners for her own good," said her father. He pushed back his chair and went down to harness up the teams.

Lucy ran up the road to wait for the threshers. There were not nearly so many grasshoppers now that the wheat was cut. If one did jump at her, he had to jump from the stubble, not the top of the wheat, and that made him land against her legs instead of her neck or her face.

The rig would be coming from the south, and she was watching in that direction when the Sinclairs' car came up behind her from town. Giles was driving it and Douglas was with him. Giles was coming to help with the threshing, but what was Douglas doing here?

He was *always* teasing her at school. Once when she was riding on the merry-go-round, the garter on her stocking broke and the end of it hung down below her dress. Douglas saw it and started laughing and pointing and yelling, "I see Germany, I see France! I see Lucy's underpants!" Everybody on the merry-go-round had laughed then, and it was almost the worst thing that had ever happened to her in two long years of school. She had to wait forever until the merry-go-round stopped and she could get off. And just before school ended last spring Douglas had chased her and gotten two pencils away from her and he had kept one of them.

"Hello there," Giles said. "Where's the thrashers?"

"I don't know," Lucy said, not looking at Douglas at all.

"Well, I'll go on down and start loading bundles, I guess." Giles started to drive away but Douglas yelled to be let out.

"Let's play hide and seek behind the shocks." He spoke in the bossy way boys always did to girls. He wasn't *asking* if she wanted to play; he was *telling* her to play.

"No," Lucy said. "I want to watch for the thrashing machine to come." Even if there had been nothing else to do, she would not have played with Douglas, but now she was especially annoyed at having him around. She had the same feelings about the threshing as she had about watching a train. She wanted to see it from the very beginning to the very end. She wanted to catch the first sight of the separator trundling slowly along the road to the waiting shocks in her father's fields, to be near it while it threshed out all the wheat, and then watch it out of sight again as it moved away toward her grandfather's farm.

"Besides," she told Douglas, "you never gave back my pencil."

"W*hat* pencil?"

She looked away from him. Wasn't it bad enough to be pestered by him at school? Did he have to come all the way out here to keep it up?

Then she saw the threshing machine. It was a spot she had had her eye on for quite a while but she hadn't wanted to say anything till she was sure. It had disappeared behind a hill and reappeared, much larger, and now there was no mistaking it — after all, it was bigger than the house she lived in. The first sounds of it began to reach them and soon she could distinguish the noise of the tractor pulling it from the sounds of its own ponderous joints.

George came up to the road to watch it travel the last half mile. He was as excited as Lucy. He'd know, now, in a few more hours, what a difference planting the Ceres had made. It was hard to judge a yield just by walking through the wheat and plucking a head of it here and there. He waved his hat, when the rig got close, and the man driving the tractor waved a speck of white.

As the noise grew louder still, it was like the finale of a resolute, yet triumphant war song. The little parade of the tractor, separator, and truck was more throat-tightening to a man like George than any city street parade of bugles, drums, or bagpipes could ever be. He was grinning and swallowing as he watched it and listened to it. The cry of the final hours of fierce and iron-hearted toil was in the chaotic music coming toward them, but there was a cry of victory, too — an incredible, prayed-for, cursed-for, watched-for victory. Just two more days without rain or hail or wind or fatal accidents or locust migrations and the war song would be unequivocally a victory song when the parade moved on again.

The tractor driver leaned down to howl over the engine, "Where do you want her?"

With one hand George pointed toward the field where he and Giles had begun to work. With the other he made a megaphone to carry his voice through the six feet of noise between his mouth and the man's ear. "Set 'er up right in the middle over there," he shouted.

The man swung as wide as the road would let him and managed to bring the threshing machine straight in behind the tractor. There was no room to spare on either side of the locomotive-like wheels as they rolled across the approach that spanned the deep ditch. He did a nice job, George was glad to see, and he seemed to take such a touchy piece of maneuvering in his stride.

George and Douglas and Lucy walked beside the rig till it stopped. The tractor driver shut off the engine and climbed down. He was the boss of the outfit and he hurried around giving orders to get the big machine ready to go. He walked past the hayrack and got a whiff of the wheat. "That sure must be damn smutty wheat!" he said. "Been a lot of smutty wheat this year, but I never smelt it any worse than I do right now. One time I got too many of them smut balls in a old separator and blew it all to hell. Damn near killed a thrasher, too."

"You got insurance on this rig?" George asked.

"Ya, but none on the men. How you going to insure a crew when they change every week on you? Looks like I'm going to have to find another man this morning if my drinkin' boy don't show up. He got hold of some stuff last night and we couldn't even find him this morning. Somebody said he went back down to Gackle."

"Has the Marquis been smutty?" George wanted to know.

"Ya, pretty bad. They figure there's some new kind of smut this year. *Everything's* smutty. You can't win. Even if you *do* get the stuff to grow, you can't sell it, can you?"

"Oh, the price is up a lot over last year," George said. He made up his mind not to wonder how much he'd get docked for the smut. In a few minutes now the crop that had required so much work and so much waiting would begin pouring out of the machine. Finally he had a little control. The crows he couldn't control had left some seed in the ground for him; the freak late frost he couldn't control had not come; the grasshoppers had not cleaned out the fields, though they tried; the black clouds had not brought tornadoes or hail.

Now at last there was a job he could do — a job to put all his strength into — a job that would quickly fill the truck, while he watched, with the results of all the work and the waiting. It was an intoxicating feeling. It made him want to slap somebody on the back and sing, even with his throat full of dust and chaff.

Despite the man-killing tempo set by the separator's roaring appetite, the field was a festive place. Once every second the engine uttered a sharp, open-mouthed sneeze — "Ka-chung! Ka-chung! Ka-chung!" It was like the engines that ran the concessions at carnivals and fairs. Down below the people whirling around in capsules called Dipsy-Doodles, and down below the people turning in the great circles of the Ferris wheels would be the same sneezing engines and the oil-smudged men with their hands on the long throbbing levers that stopped and started the machines that made the rides go round. But this field resounding with one such engine was a thousand times better than a carnival to George.

Lucy stayed at a little distance from the machine, watching them get ready. There were so many belts and pulleys to slip over wheels and tighten, hatches to batten and unbatten, spouts to extend and bolt together, levers to adjust, and cranks to crank that turned grinding parts deep inside the machine. There were steadying blocks to put beneath the separator's belly and finally there was the truck to be backed up under the grain spout and the hayrack to be drawn up beside the bundle chute.

Lucy saw her father high on top of the bundles, shoving them in by huge forkfuls. He leaned far over the chomping ravening insides of the separator. She knew that Clarence Egger had only one arm because the other one had got caught in a threshing-machine belt. And last year she heard about the thing she knew was bound to happen. She heard one thresher tell another one about a big dumb Finn who fell into a threshing machine.

"Yes sir," the thresherman said, "that Finn wanted that job so bad and he was so scared he'd get the boss mad at him. He just kept on pitching harder and harder until he went right on in with a big forkful. That was *his* last forkful. Unless the Devil give him a pitchfork when he got down to Hell. Nowadays these rigs couldn't of handled him, but that thing was one of them big steam jobs — kept two-three men busy just stoking her with wood to keep the steam up. That separator could of thrashed *ten* Finns, all at once! We hollered at the boss, 'The Finn's in the bundle chute! Stop the engine!' The boss yells back, 'He's a goner!' He was right, too. By the time we got it stopped, that Finn wasn't in the bundle chute any more. He just wasn't anywhere at all — that is, his top half wasn't anywhere at all. We hauled out his legs and laid 'em in a blanket and started up the machine again.

"When his buddy from the Old Country come back in from the

field with a load of bundles, we says, 'There's your pal down there,' but he couldn't understand the language. Somebody took him over and showed him what was wrapped up in the blanket. When he seen it was his buddy's boots you never saw such a surprised man in your life.

"Finally he pointed to himself up above his waist, and patted his hands up and down over his stomach, and felt of his head. All the time he kept yelling in his own language. We kept pointing at the thrashing machine, and when he finally come to believe it, he just up and run. You never seen a man run like that. Just took off right over the stubble and never did stop, as far as I know. Anyhow, we never seen him again. You know, there in Europe they don't have any of this machinery. Those foreigners that come over here, they just don't know what to make of it all. They're scared to death of a rig like this *here* one even, and they can't understand nothing you yell at them. It's no wonder they get theirselves killed off all the time."

He was nearly finished with his sandwich, but he wanted to spread out his rest break a little longer. Lucy had to stay and wait for his coffee cup. She remembered how he kept switching his legs as he sat on the ground, bending up the knee of the one that had been straight and laying the other one out flat.

"You know, it's hard to know just how to bury the legs of a man. Do you just build a box long enough for half of him or do you build him a full-size coffin and just pretend all of him is in it? What do you do about a man that's thrashed so you could never find a whole hair from his head? Where do you say he is, anyhow, on the grave-marker?" He gave a short laugh. "Besides, we never even knew the bastard's name! Never knew even what to call his *legs!*

"You're giving me a look like you don't believe me! Why *you* aren't even dry behind the ears yet!

"You should of been around in the days when they had them special trains full of machinery. I'll never forget the time the J. I. Case Special come into Teed's Grove, back in Iowa, when I was just a little kid — around nineteen-aught-eight — somewheres along in there. I'd never saw anything like it in my life. Right then I made up my mind to be a thrasherman. It was a whole train full of J. I. Case machinery — steam engines with ten-foot iron wheels. And thrashing machines. And on one car a crazy old son-of-a-gun, he played all day on a steam calliope.

"And then, by God, they revved up one of them new agitator thrashers — they was new at that time — and a fella got up there to show off what it could do, and you know what he did? He started feeding *two-by-six planks* into 'er! You should of seen the sawdust fly. You still think it couldn't of thrashed *one* flesh-and-blood Finn?"

Lucy herself had been totally convinced. She remembered the conversation perfectly, and even the looks of both the men — the old one and the young one.

She had always wondered what it would be like to fall into a threshing machine. Even from several yards away, the noise was almost more than she could stand. What would it be like inside?

Finally she had told the story to her mother, who had instantly said it couldn't be true. "That's just the kind of story these thrashers love to tell," she said. "Don't you ever believe a *word* they say!"

"But what if it *was* true!"

"Well . . . if it really did happen . . . he couldn't have suffered long, poor fellow. Don't you think about him. Once a person is dead he can't feel anything hurting his body, you know. It's worse for the people who are left behind. He probably never knew what happened at all. There are really worse ways to die."

Lucy could not think of anything worse than suddenly having life taken away without even knowing anything about it. She couldn't imagine everything just going on and not being there to watch it herself. She could not imagine being the legs wrapped in a blanket on the stubble while the threshing crew started up the machine again and went on with the harvest.

And yet farmers were broken in pieces every year by their own machinery. She heard people talk about it. Somehow they slipped under the cleated iron wheels of the tractors they were driving, or the tractors moved as they tinkered with the hitch of a disc or a harrow and they fell beneath the knives or the teeth and were sliced into the dirt they had cultivated all their lives. They got caught in the tines of hayloaders; they looped an ankle in the rope of a haylift and were yanked into the air and flopped back on the ground; they fell into wells and off barn roofs and windmills.

And there was the vanished arm of Mr. Egger. Her grandfather had been there when that happened. He had told her about it so she would be sure never to get too close to the threshing machine. It hadn't been so terrible, even, because it had happened so fast that nobody heard the arm come loose or noticed the blood spurt. And Mr. Egger had not even yelled. He jumped back and looked at his torn, empty shirtsleeve and said, "Why, I never even felt it. I never even felt it."

But the more dangerous the separator was, the more exciting it was, too, and Lucy couldn't have stopped watching her father up there even if she had wanted to. Even if it frightened her to see how fast her father worked and how he leaned. Not even the strongest man could keep the bundle chute full for more than fifteen or twenty minutes at a stretch. It wasn't at all hard to see how a man who had never threshed before would pitch too fast and too long until he grew dizzy there on top of the bundles and lost his balance.

The chaff blew high in the air and formed a great light cloud, and the straw blasted out and settled into the beginnings of the wide lopsided stack, and the little stream of grain poured down to make a golden cone on the rough gray boards of the truck floor. The sides of the cone slipped and trickled and the base of it inched from one row of rusty nailheads to the next. She would pick a smutted kernel to concentrate on and watch it, never blinking from the time it came out of the spout till it was buried. Then when she looked back out at the field again, she would seem to be seeing it through a solid rain of wheat.

When the cycle got going, they really missed the fellow who had gone back to Gackle on a bender. George told the boss he expected the crew to finish in two days, even if they were shorthanded. "Well, if he don't show up by noon, I'll go over town at dinnertime and get somebody else," the boss promised. "Don't worry. We'll make 'er."

They had better make it. If they began to see that they wouldn't finish in two days, George knew they'd slow down to make it another whole morning. Just paying for that extra half day could decimate the profits he was counting on.

He took a bead on the sun and went to Lucy. "You better go along in and help Mother bring out the sandwiches," he said.

Douglas tagged her into the house. He stood around in the way while Lucy helped to butter the bread. It was not quite ten o'clock and Rachel had been working as fast as she could work for more than five hours, but she was getting behind.

"If Douglas helps you," she said to Lucy, "do you think you two could take all this food out by yourselves, so I won't have to leave the baby?"

"*I* can do it by myself," Lucy said.

"I want to help," Douglas argued.

"I think it's very nice that Douglas wants to help," Rachel said. "Why don't we let him pull your wagon, and we'll load it with the food and coffee. You can pretend you're like the men with the popcorn and sandwich wagons at the fair."

"*I* want to pull it," Lucy said.

They filled the rusty red wagon with the sandwiches, a cut pie wrapped in a flour-sack dish towel, a kettle full of coffee, two gallon pails of water, and the cups. The wagon was so heavy that it took both of them to pull it, and neither of them argued as they went up the hill, walking backwards to keep an eye on the kettle of coffee.

"Let's just have one piece of pie before we take it all out to them," Douglas said.

"No!" She was amazed at the very idea. Boys were so sneaky. "Not unless there are some left over."

"Okay," he said. "Then let's have our own picnic with what's left."

"Maybe," she said.

Presently two men who had been pitching bundles climbed down from the hayrack and came toward her. One was tall, and the closer he came the bigger he looked. He was even bigger than her father and moved as though he would walk right over her. She couldn't help ducking away when he came up to her. The other man laughed.

"Don't let Swede bother you none. He loves kids, don't you Swede? He eats 'em for lunch if he don't get his pie."

The big man's face was a fiery red against the near-whiteness of his hair. He had a blank, foreign expression. He was dumb, like the Finn. His face was very long, and his lower lip swelled farther out than his upper one, giving him a very hungry look.

"Swede don't speak English, but he sure found out about apple pie in a hurry," his friend chuckled. "You better have some apple pie there."

"No, it's in the wagon, and it's cherry," Lucy said.

"Well, Swede'll take cherry this one time. Won't you, Swede? But you better bring him apple tomorrow. Huh Swede?

"We call him Swede because it's the only word he knows from the Old Country," the man told Lucy. "Pie is the only American word he knows for sure."

The giant slapped the little man on the shoulders. The little man laughed as though he liked it.

"What kind of sandwiches you got there?" he asked.

"Chicken and cheese," Lucy said.

"Swede'll have cheese," the man said. "That's what his mamma raised him on back in the Old Country, ain't it, Swede?" The little man laughed again — an insulting, high laugh.

Once Lucy had fed a colt sugar from the palm of her hand. The colt was not used to being fed that way, and when he finished the sugar, he spread his lips and nibbled at her skin, trying to get the last of the wonderful taste. The feeling of his big teeth had made her know what a big bite he could have taken out of her hand. She had the same feeling now about this great blank man. It was hard to tell what he *might* do but it was *easy* to tell what he *could* do. She held out the sandwich toward the giant, not looking at his face. The minute she saw the black-nailed fingers touch the bread, she snatched her hand away.

The men took in the food like cruising whales. They seemed to be able to swallow without ever closing their mouths. They sloshed in the water and coffee so fast it dribbled back out the sides of their mouths again. Lucy watched the debris escaping like plankton in little streams down their cheeks — bits of bread and butter, pie crust, and cherry juice, all finally mixing with the dust in their bristled chins. Sometimes men made her feel sick.

When all of them had eaten there were still a few sandwiches left. Douglas had been riding with Giles on one of the hayracks, but he came running when he saw her start back toward the house. "Let's have our picnic!" he shouted. They settled beneath one of the nearer shocks.

"You should of saved out some pie," he said.

"Phooey! The pie was for the thrashermen, not you! You didn't *earn* a piece."

"Well," he said, "when I grow up I'm going to be a thrasherman myself. Or maybe just a farmer. I'm going to get married to you, too, when I grow up." He put his bare arm around her neck and kissed her a wet cheesy kiss on the cheek. She had a swift impression of his bright blue eyes and white teeth and lips full of bread crumbs grinning an inch away from her face. He laughed and laughed as she ran away — the same way he had laughed that day on the merry-go-round. Nothing so disgusting had ever happened in her whole life. . . .

❧ ❧ ❧

After making sure that Douglas was nowhere in sight, Lucy went out to the first truckload of wheat which stood some distance from the separator, waiting to be driven to town. Though it was in the middle of a blistering field, far from the shade of so much as a fence-post, the wheat in it was cool. One of the memories she carried from year to year was that surprising coolness of the threshed wheat that had so lately been first in the hot field and then in the hotter insides of the threshing machine. Yet each year she was surprised all over again to feel it around her bare legs as she sat in its clean, shifting granules. One grain of wheat was hard, with the richness of the earth and the air crystallized into a tiny sharp gem. Yet a whole truckload of wheat was a soft and regal couch.

Once wheat was in granary bins, it was different. It was not cool, but cold, and the stillness of the granary was worrisome compared to the excitement of the threshing field. And a bin piled high with wheat was a dangerous place, for if a child worked himself too far down in the midst of the slipping grains, it was like being in quicksand. He never got out unless help was near. That had happened to a little girl her mother knew. The little girl's mother and father looked for her for days and weeks before they found her.

But she was safe out under the mounting sun. She could play until it was time to ride in to the elevator.

She made a road from the cab to the tailgate along the dark line of shadow made by the truck side across the wheat. She was starting to plow a field in her precious cool landscape when Douglas came and flopped over the side into the wheat — just as though he had never done anything terrible in his life. "Boy this is *fun!*" he said.

"I want to play by myself," she said.

"I'll tell your dad."

"All right," she said. "Take it all." She climbed out over the tailgate and jumped down.

"Aw, come on back!" he cried. "I'll do just what you want if you'll come back and play."

It was a new experience for her to have a boy beg her to do anything. This was the first time a boy had ever abdicated his birthright to be the boss.

"Okay," she said. "You can bring in the wheat and I'll be the elevator man and tell you how much I'll pay you for it and all the things that are wrong with it."

They played until dinnertime and then they followed the men in. The table was still not quite set and her father was mad. "Now Rachel," he said, "why haven't you had Lucy in here helping you with these little chores that she can do as well as you? Then you'd be all ready now."

"I let her play because she never has anybody to play with," her mother said. "I want her to have a little bit of childhood! That's why! When she has somebody to play with I'm going to let her have as much time as I can!"

Lucy and Douglas took their plates out to the porch steps to eat. They had just sat down when a young man came walking around the porch. "Well," he said. "I see I'm just in time for dinner."

Nobody except her father had talked about him much, but Lucy knew he had done something incredibly bad.

"Hello," he said. "What's the matter? Aren't you going to say hello! Cat got your tongue?"

"Hello," they both said, because you had to say that when people asked if the cat had got your tongue.

"Stuart!"

Rachel went to him but she did not touch him. He looked so much older, with all those whiskers. He was twenty now; he was a man.

The crew boss shouted from the dining room: "Stuart! Is that drinkin' bum here finally? Get in here and put some food on toppa that liquor! By God, you're gonna do a full day's work out there between now and quittin' time or I'll know the reason why!"

"Oh, *Stuart!*" Rachel said.

"Just watch to see Swede don't eat it all," Stuart yelled back. "I'll be 'long in a minute." His speech was fuzzy, like his face. His whiskers did not hide the sick greenish color of his skin. "You going to invite me in or not?" he asked her.

"Oh, Stuart!" she cried again. But still she could not touch him. The booze on his breath was revolting. "Haven't you been to see the folks yet, Stuart?"

He propped himself against the corner of the kitchen, with an elbow braced on the towel bar. He looked over her head, across the kitchen at the window, but the light seemed to hurt his eyes. He closed them. "Nope. I started over there last night but I just didn't seem to make it."

There was a frightful banging in the dining room. "Oh, get those potatoes in there," he said. "I don't know why that Swede don't learn to speak English. He just stomps on the floor when he runs out of potatoes. Liable to go right through this little house." He kept his eyes closed. Was it the light or his family he could not look at?

George came out and took a whiff of the air. "Pew!" he said.

"George!" Rachel begged.

"We need spuds in there," George said. He looked at Stuart, who would not open his eyes. "Nobody told me my wife's little brother was supposed to be the sixth man on this crew. We all sweat a little extra for you this morning!" Stuart said nothing.

George erupted. "What was it *this* time, anyhow, Junior!" "Embalming fluid? Hair tonic? Or did you get hold of some genuine rotgut moonshine? Why don't you wait till you're big enough to *shave* before you start trying to drink with the men? Maybe then you'd know what to leave alone. You better get in here and *eat* before that stuff burns out your guts!" He went back to the table.

"Just give me a plate," Stuart said to Rachel. "I'll eat with the kids."

His hand shook as though the plate was more than he could hold. "Stuart," she said. He pushed the screen door open and let it slam behind him.

It was queer, she thought, how little shocked she was. But this was so like him. When he was a little boy not yet in school and she was already in her last year of high school, he would hide for half the afternoon in the barn just so he could jump out from a manger to startle the folks when they went out to milk. "I declare," her mother would say, "what *ails* the child! Here I thought he was out with *Will* all afternoon! And Will thought he was with *me* in the chicken house. And just when we were sure he was lost and we were going to look for him, out he came, making that outlandish noise. He scared us half to death. It's the *third* time. What*ever* makes him *do* it!"

What *did* make him do it? He seemed to have a need to do shocking things, even though he was always so shy. Did he crave attention so much that the one titillating moment when he could command all the thoughts of his surprised parents was worth such a long wait lying in the manger hay? What had he thought about while he waited? What *did* a five-year-old think about?

Lucy had run away once when she was five. She had gone to sleep in a straw stack and when she woke up she came home. Rachel had never even known that the child had run away. She had just thought Lucy was exploring birds' nests or following George around. That had been the part about the running away that still haunted her. Not to know, until your child comes back — stiff, desolate, swollen-eyed — that she had run away from you because something had been so much more important to her than you had ever dreamed. Something you had said — had commanded or forbidden as you rushed through your work — had changed her whole world. If only you had not been so busy, you cried out to yourself. If only you had noticed. If only you could expunge those hours of lonely anguish from her life. Was that how it had been with Stuart? Had his mother been too busy? Rachel had hardly been at home after he started doing the things he did. On weekends her mother would only say, "What *makes* him do these things?"

And now here he was. What had made him run away? What had made him come back? Why had he come here first, sneaking in with this uncivilized crew? How could anybody find it easier to face George Custer than Will Shepard? Yet Stuart must think it easier to come here first. He must be hoping that *she* could do something. What could *she* do?

He was sitting beside Lucy now, with his plate in his lap, pretending that he and the two children were the only people there. "Do I look different?" he asked Lucy. "*You* look different."

"Yes," Lucy said carefully. "You look different."

"I'm a big man now," he said. "When I went away I was just a kid like Giles in there. Now I'm a man. When I went away you weren't even in school yet, were you? What grade are you in now?"

"Third," she said.

"No!" he said. "You're . . . let's see — you're not hardly eight yet, are you? Did you skip a grade, like your mother? Oh, I see what you mean. You'll be in the third this coming fall, right?"

"Yes," she admitted.

"That's just where you should be, isn't it? Haven't skipped any grades yet, huh? Maybe you're like *me*, instead of like your mother. What grade are *you* in?" he asked Douglas.

"Third," Douglas said forcefully.

"He's just the same as me," said Lucy.

"Is that so?" Stuart said. "Which one of you is the smartest?"

"*I* am," Douglas said.

"He is *not!*" Lucy said. "He *copies* me all the time!"

"I bet you she's right," Stuart said to Douglas. "I bet you she can beat you sixty ways to Sunday because I bet she takes after her mamma. Is that right, Lucy?"

"No, I take after Daddy," she said. "But he always got a hundred in arithmetic and sometimes I don't."

"So did your mama always get a hundred," Stuart said. "At least that's the way I always heard it from the teachers. 'Why, I can't *understand* why you aren't more like your big sister!' " he said in a silly high voice. " 'Why, I remember how she was always the smartest one in the room. Now, *Shtew*-art, I just *know* you can work harder!' " He said the last sentence with his tongue between his teeth and his lower lip, making a silly face and an even sillier sound. Lucy and Douglas thought he was very funny.

Suddenly he leapt off the porch and sprinted for the barn. After a while he came back. He looked at Lucy trying to shoo the flies off his plate.

"Much obliged," he said. "I reckon it isn't quite time for me to eat yet. You bring me something good this afternoon, huh? And tell your dad I'll be out by the rig."

He walked away up toward the field. Lucy brought the barely touched plate back into the kitchen. "He said he wasn't hungry yet."

"I *heard* him," Rachel said. She scraped the plate into the pigs' slop bucket.

She could tell when she took dessert into the men that they were more shocked than she was. They looked down at their plates as if she were a mother or a sister to them, or at least as if they thought of a woman or a family somewhere. None of *them* can go home, either, she thought, and was more shocked by all the men around her than by her brother. They can't go home and they don't know why not. It doesn't make sense. I'm thirty-two years old and I'm an old woman because I can't understand anything about the world any more.

"I *told* that kid to lay off that stuff while he's workin' for *me*," murmured the boss. "I don't want to be unwrapping his innards from the innards of that there thrashing machine. But I never hardly saw *anybody* work like him when he's cold sober."

George walked out with the rest of the crew — avoiding her as well he might after the greeting he had given to her brother.

"George!"

He came back into the kitchen.

"For heaven's sake, don't let him *kill* himself out there!" she pleaded. "And don't let him get away. We *have* to get him back to the folks! He wouldn't have come *this* far if he didn't want us to get him back."

"Now, Rachel, *I* can't order your little brother around. He's a grown man — or he *thinks* he is! Nobody could ever tell him anything. He's just as stubborn as the rest of your family. I'm not going to try and keep him here if he doesn't want to stay. But he damn well better do his job this afternoon because that's what I'm paying for! And he can pitch his share of bundles too, like anybody else!"

"Oh, George, don't let him get near the separator if he's still weaving around like that, *please!* Dad will pay you for whatever work you think you haven't gotten. *Please!*"

George simply could not understand how women's minds could work the way they did. Who the hell was she married to, anyhow? Him or her family? "Now, Rachel," he said, "just how do you expect me to figure what the work of one man of a six-man crew is worth when I pay by the job — machinery and all? I'd look pretty silly going to your father and asking him for your brother's wages, wouldn't I? I'm paying this outfit for two days of thrashing, and if it goes more than two days, we're going to be in the hole. But I'm *not* going to ask your father for Stuart's wages and I'm *not* going to try to tell a stubborn Shepard anything at all about where to stay or where to go. Talk to him yourself. He's *your* brother. If he wants to quit the crew right now, we'll go get somebody else. If he don't want to quit, he works!"

George left, hurrying to catch the crew. Lucy and Douglas were gone too. The house was so quiet now. Rachel wondered if Stuart would really be waiting at the threshing machine or if he had just kept going again.

He had begun this disappearing when he was only nine or ten. He would get up before it was light, steal out of the house, and disappear until suppertime without telling where he had been. Then one morning just before his eighteenth birthday, he had got on a freight train. Fred Wertzler saw him go. Fred was hanging the mail sack on its hook by the tracks when he glimpsed Stuart ducking behind a box car. He thought that the Shepard boy was only playing truant again.

But it was days and then agonizing weeks and finally months before the first brief letter arrived. There were a few more letters in the two and a half years of his disappearance, but none of the letters mentioned his return. It had begun to be plausible to them that this disappearance could be permanent. They were all preparing themselves to bear the pain and shame and eternal anxiety of it. Now he had reappeared and he was a man — a man who had been sleeping for the last week in fields not thirty miles from his father's farm instead of going home to his father's house. And what would such a bitter thing do to his father's heart?

Stuart was born when Rachel was twelve, and she had cherished him as if he were her own baby when he was tiny. But because he had always seemed more like her baby than her brother, she had had the instincts of a mother about him. That first time he had got drunk in high school she and her mother both felt as though he had died. He was permanently separated from them by their own incredulity. They could not believe it had happened. "Wherever did he get the taste for it?" they asked each other. "Where did he get hold of it? How can he do it? What *makes* him *do* it?"

"Males," her mother would say. "They don't care *what* they do, most of them. But how could a son of *Will's* be like this?"

How? Yes, how. And how was she to get her brother the rest of the way home? She worked feverishly in the kitchen so she could spare the time to talk to him when she took out the midafternoon lunch. She boiled the custard, filled the pies, set them to cool while she made the sandwiches, and then managed to get the meringue on them before leaving to go to the field. The baby had gone to sleep amenably for her nap. It was the first agreeable thing she had done all day and Rachel hurried out to the field so she could get back before the nap ended.

The Swede and his sidekick were again the first to come. The small laughing man stared at her body. "Swede saves his appetite now," he giggled, "but be ready for him at supper time. And he'll want a dozen fried eggs in the morning."

"I know," Rachel said shortly. She had a pretty good idea of who started the stories about the mute Swede — the stories that had got from Elsie Egger's sister-in-law down in Gackle up to her. This little man was the kind she despised most of all — the kind who got away with everything because he laughed. The kind who liked to attach himself to another man and somehow feel safe in his shadow. That was the way that fellow had been in college who had asked her to marry him. There was a basketball player he was forever talking about. She could never explain to her parents why that boy had repelled her so because she didn't really know why herself.

The small man was annoyed. No doubt he liked to think of himself as a man who could at least get a smile from any woman. When he and the Swede stood up to go back to work he ogled her again.

"You're just the type of woman Swede likes," he said as he handed back the tin cup. "Kind of nice and round. You better tell your old man to lock up your door tonight. Swede could lick him with one hand tied behind him." Swede smirked at her whenever he heard his name.

Rachel walked away from the little man — violated and despoiled by his rutting eyes. How she despised males. If George could have known what that man had said, he might have killed him. And then he probably would have taken on the Swede, too. But not for *her* sake. It would have been for his *own* honor that George would have bloodied the stubble with a filthy little stray that dared to insult *his* wife. She had never ceased to be amazed at the grossness of most men. To think of cooking for such debauched animals — of politely waiting on them for another day and a half! To think that such men had been her brother's companions for two years — to think of how they might have influenced him — how they *must* have influenced him.

Had Stuart ever stood in a harvest field eating sandwiches served by a farmer's wife, made from bread baked by the farmer's wife, and looked at her that way — as though she was nothing more than an animal who existed only for *his* animal pleasure?

He was coming for his sandwich now, moving as though his legs were melting. The field was nearly cleared and there were no shocks behind him — nothing but burning stubble, burning sky. He was a tin soldier dying in a great forge all alone — his face blank, his heart hidden. But such a fine face, even unshaven. Not like these other faces. Surely the heart of a man with such a face could be reached by somebody someday. But he must never be with this other kind of man again — never.

"Just some water first," he said, when she held up the plate of sandwiches. He took the cup in hands that still shook and drained it, then filled it and drained it again. He wiped his mouth with his dusty arm and sat down on the stubble.

He still looked very sick. She couldn't imagine how he could keep on working so hard. "Do you want a sandwich now?" she asked again.

"Wait'll I get my breath for a minute," he said. It was obviously all he could do to keep down the water.

"Stuart, you're going to go home now, aren't you?"

"I heard about the barn," he said. "Was it Dad's fault, really?"

"He blames himself," she answered. "Are you going to go home?"

"That's where I was headed for last night," Stuart said. He waited to see a hint of comprehension in her face, but there was none. She would never understand why a prodigal son might need a little alcohol to get him back through the Old Man's door. Not to mention the Old Lady's.

"You ought to try to eat," his sister said.

"A little more water will do it." He drank another cup and turned back toward the threshing machine.

"Stuart! You'll go home tonight won't you?"

"Maybe," he said.

"What shall I tell them?"

"Anything at all, just like you always did," he said.

She hurried back to the house. There wasn't time to think about what he'd said. The screen door was ajar; she supposed Douglas had left it open. The half-grown cats that had taken to sleeping under the porch in the hot weather were up on the kitchen table. Their tails stuck straight up with pleasure, as if they were still kittens drinking warm cow's milk from an old saucer. They were rapturously licking neat trails across the gleaming meringue on the pies.

Rachel seized a tail in either hand, walked out on the porch, swung her hands as far behind her as they would go, swung forward again with all the momentum the backward swing had given her, and let go of the cats. They lit running at least fifteen feet away and never stopped until they disappeared into the barn. She stood on the porch, watching them go, feeling still in her fists the narrowing vertebrae of their tails under the soft long hair and the thin warm skin, seeing still the way the tails had pointed in the air over the kitchen table as the cats ruined her pies.

I must be losing my mind, she thought. I must be losing my mind.

She went back into the kitchen and looked at the pies. Ruined utterly. What would she feed those lustful, gluttonous men? She looked at the clock. There was simply not time to make another dessert. Swede would probably stamp on the floor if he didn't get pie. It would serve him right if she just repaired these pies. What they didn't know wouldn't hurt any of them, including George. She skimmed the rest of the meringue off and tossed it in the slop pail. There were the barest traces of the busy quick tongues in the chocolate custard. The lemon showed nothing at all, being less solid. If there had been trails in it, they had all flowed together again. She hurried with the new meringue so she could get the pies back in the oven before Cathy woke up.

And all the while she broke the eggs, separated them, beat the whites, measured the sugar, poured the vanilla — all the time she worked on the meringue she felt sure that none of it had happened. She had never done a violent thing in her life — never come close to hurting an animal. And she had never lied, either, and now she was lying — covering polluted pies so nobody would ever know. But if what she was doing now was not real, then Stuart was not out there in the field, either, was he? Either this day was all true or none of it was true.

❦ ❦ ❦

Douglas and Lucy stood outside the elevator watching a long freight pulling toward Bismarck. The heat from the building pounded at their backs.

"I'm going home," said Douglas. "It's too hot out there at your place."

"Sissy."

"Sissy yourself," he said dully. He started off across the street. Then he saw Roger Beahr come out of the grocery store. "Hey Roger!" he yelled. "Got some candy?"

Roger held up a little white paper bag and began to run. Douglas went after him.

Lucy watched them run up the wooden sidewalk. She wondered what it would be like to live in town and to be a good friend of Roger Beahr, who always had pennies.

"Where's the Sinclair boy?" her father asked.

"He went home. The sissy."

"What's the matter? Didn't you act nice to him?" George said. "You can't expect to have any friends if you're not nice to people."

"I don't like him."

"Oh, now, Lucy, that's not any way to talk. You'll *never* have any friends if you talk like that. *Shame* on you!"

Lucy felt her throat start to swell and she got up on her knees to look out the window in the rear of the cab. As the truck turned she could see the two boys coming back down the sidewalk, heading for the elevator. It must be nice to have your father own an elevator. Even from a distance she could see that both of them had a cheek puffed out with a jawbreaker.

When they got back home it was nearly six o'clock. "Time for you to get at your chores," her father told her. "You haven't done a lick of work all day. Probably a good thing your boyfriend didn't come back."

"He's *not* my boyfriend! I *hate* boys!"

"Gonna be an old maid, huh?"

"No!"

It seemed to her that a man or a boy had been laughing at her all day in the wheat fields. How mean, mean, mean they were. And if you didn't want to marry one of them, they made you always be alone and called you horrible names.

She had a hopeless, forsaken feeling in her stomach as she scattered the corn for the chickens, cleaned and filled their muddy water pans, and looked in the nests for eggs that might have been laid late in the day. She wondered if Douglas would come back with Giles in the morning.

⁂

After supper the men went back to the field to smoke and then to spread their blankets on the straw and sleep. Stuart walked out of the kitchen with them.

"Stuart!" Rachel said. "Are you going to sleep in a *field* when you're half a mile away from your own bedroom?" If he did this, then she would have to give up. How could she drive over and tell her mother and father that now they could know where their son slept? They could know, but he couldn't be bothered to come home. He was answering her, speaking in a casual sensible way.

"Wouldn't be the *first* time," he was saying. "Used to do it all the time. I'd be so hot in that old upstairs I couldn't go to sleep at all, so I'd go out in the field. You'd be surprised. Twenty or thirty degrees cooler out there. Try it some time. After the thrashermen have gone, of course!" He walked away.

She had read stories about men who disappeared from their homes in crowded tenements and moved into little windowless apartments a block away and so lived out their years. She had always thought that such a pathetic insanity was proof that cities perverted the human race. People felt so hemmed in by each other that they couldn't stand even their families any longer; yet they were so timid that they could not move away from the spot where they had always lived — nor could they go home again. What could make a boy like

Stuart behave like these mole-hearted men in the slums of cities?

What did he want, anyway? Did he want his mother and father to come to him in the stubble tonight and beg him to come home, just as they had once exclaimed in the barn, "Oh, *there* he is!" She was afraid, now, to go over and tell them that he had come, for there was nothing in the world she could say or do to make him stay.

George had gone to bed long before she finished the dishes. She lay down as far away from him as she could and clung to the edge of the mattress all night. It was possible that she would do something awful if he so much as touched her. She might scream in his ear or slap him. She could still feel the cats' tails in her sweating hands. She wondered if it really was thirty degrees cooler out there where those bestial men were sleeping beside her brother.

❦ ❦ ❦

Stuart knew that he would not have to lie awake long — not after the way he had spent the last twenty-four hours. Still, it would be too long. One minute under this home sky was too long. If he were able to travel, he would not be here to see the sun come up. Well, that was the way he had done it all along. He either stayed or moved on, depending on what shape he was in when the feeling came. It was always the same feeling: He was alone among people he knew. The only relief, outside of liquor, was to hurry somewhere else, so he would only be alone among people he *didn't* know. For two years he had told himself that this feeling would go away when he was home again. It was silly to ask himself why he had not come home before, if he really believed that. It was sillier still to wonder how two years had gone so quickly. It was silliest of all to pretend, like a baby, that he didn't know how ridiculous he was — out here in the stubble.

It was funny how sky over one part of the prairie could be different from all the other skies. It was the things you could see from the corners of your eyes that *shaped* the sky you knew so well — nothing about the sky itself. It was the low blackness of hills and the lines of windbreaks. And trains sounded different in different places. Oh, he was *home* all right. Every night when he went to sleep like this in some farmer's field, he knew how silly that son in the Bible felt. Yes, almost every night he had gone to sleep wondering why he wasn't in his own bed in his father's house. Now he wondered whether he would be in that bed tomorrow night or not. He couldn't see how he was going to do it. There would be only one way to do it.

Has the cat got your tongue? What's the matter? People always used to say that to him and he always hated them for it. But he'd said it himself today, because he hadn't known what else to say. Was that why people had always said it to him, too? Did people go around all their lives saying things that didn't mean anything just because they thought they ought to be saying something? Was that all they cared for each other?

❦ ❦ ❦

Supper the second night was more rushed than the first night because they were going to move on to their next field after they had eaten and get set up to go the first thing in the morning. Before Rachel realized they were leaving, George and all the men had left the porch and gone back to the field.

It was nearly dark when George came back into the kitchen. "Well — that's that for *this* year. Boy, I think I'd rather be the thrasherman than the farmer — they sure get paid more for an hour's work than *I* do."

"Oh, George! You haven't paid them already!"

"*Rachel!* For God's sake don't *jump* at me like that! You'd startle a man half to death! Of course, I paid them. Why wouldn't I?"

"Oh, I didn't want Stuart to have any money. He won't go home now, I know he won't! Oh, dear! What can we do?"

"Rachel, it beats me the way you can carry on! We can't do *anything*, of course! He's a grown *man!* I've said to you a thousand times before — if a man wants to drink himself to death, no power on earth is going to stop him."

❦ ❦ ❦

Somewhere he found enough that night to take him the rest of the way home. Just before dawn he banged open the kitchen door. Rose scurried out, clutching her nightgown about her, afraid that the dog had been frightened by something to make him crash in the door that way.

"Is that you, Mom?" came the crucifying voice out of the darkness.

She had been preparing herself for it, but no preparation could stop in time her first horrified gasp. Nor could she stop her first words to him.

"You're *drunk!*"

"Gone for two years and that's all she has to say to me," he remarked, as though there were a third, more sympathetic person in the room.

Will lay in bed listening. He was able to get around now, but he did not go out to the kitchen. He had seemed to know exactly what was happening the instant he awoke. That was the way it was with your children. They possessed you forever, from the moment they were born. The two and a half years of his absence might never have been. It could have been the same night — the first night that Stuart came home that way. In a way it was always the same night they had been living with for three years. It was really no shock at all now to hear him speaking again in the belligerent, chaotic sentences they had heard before he left. Will's strongest feeling was one of weariness. He knew he'd never get back to sleep that night. Why couldn't the boy have waited till morning, if he was going to come in this way? When he realized what his first thought had been, he knew how sick he must be. He hoped to God that Stuart had come back to stay.

He got out of bed and stood in the hall, but he did not say anything. Stuart was still meandering on; he talked more when he was drunk than in all the rest of his waking hours put together. Rose had not lit the lamp and Will hoped she wouldn't. It would be enough to get through till rising time with the memory of his sounds; let there not be a memory of his looks to go with it. He had been waiting for two years to see his son, but not this way. There was a paradoxical, disorganized doggedness — a kind of animal forcefulness — in the boy when he was drunk that was nowhere in evidence when he was sober. One sight of him drunk established a more lasting image than many sights of him sober.

Finally Will said, "Your bed is all made up for you, Stuart. You sound tired to me. Why don't you go crawl in?"

"Why, Dad, I couldn't sleep in that bed without a bath! I'm nothing but a filthy thrasherman!"

"The sheets are washable," his mother told him. "Go on up."

In a few hours he was sober again, and as much of him as had ever been there had come back.

⸙ ⸙ ⸙

Will's Marquis yielded not quite eight bushels to the acre. He had two hundred and fifty acres in wheat, as opposed to George's hundred and sixty, but the difference in their harvest was not so great as the difference in their acreage, for George's yield was better. However, the smut in the Ceres caused George to be docked almost eight cents a bushel. It graded Number One despite his fears that the protein content was light, but the smut docking reduced it to eighty-two cents, while Will got ninety.

George sat down and worked it all out. It was the kind of thing he enjoyed doing. He could even forget, while he was doing it, that the numbers represented his survival.

Will got checks of $1800 for his wheat and George got $1296 for his. That worked out to $7.20 per acre for the Marquis and $8.10 for the Ceres. Not a significant difference. Not enough to pay for the smutty Ceres seed he had got from Adolph. He and Will paid the same freight rates. Everybody except the big fellows paid the same freight rates. And the freight rates never went down, no matter what the farmer earned or what the consumer paid. Will paid $110 and George paid $88 to ship the wheat to Minneapolis.

It cost Will about $250 to thresh and himself $180. That left George with roughly $1000, after the two major expenditures of marketing the crop were taken care of, and Will with $1440. As far as real profits were concerned, though, he had to consider so many other things. Will had used his own seed, saved when wheat was selling for twenty-six cents a bushel, which made it much cheaper seed than George's. Most of the seed money came out of George's pocket, too, after the splitting of the cash profits with James T. Vick. Vick had allowed him twenty-six cents a bushel for what he had spent on the seed. And Vick considered that the mill's price minus seed, threshing, and freight, was the net profit, a third of which was his. Vick wasn't interested in labor, food for horses all winter long, machine repair, binder twine, or other such incidentals. They were all the farmer's business. Vick just owned the land and paid the taxes on it.

Vick's cut this year, after subtracting the thirteen cents a bushel he paid for seed, would come to $340. That left George with $660. Pay Will $250 plus interest for four months — make it five months. He couldn't believe it. Scarcely $400 left from the wheat. That was quite a little more than he had made last year, the way prices were then, but he knew, without doing any more figuring, that he would have been far ahead to plant the Marquis and take the rust loss.

Still, there were reasons to hope. In the first place, the Ceres, he was sure, had not had anything like a fair trial because the seed had not been properly treated; in the second place, poor as he felt, he was so much better off than so many people below him that he really should be able to get along somehow. After all, if there were only enough other farmers below him, the things he would have to buy would have to be cheap enough, that was all there was to it.

If the USDA figures for last year's farm profits were at all accurate — figures that he had kept in his mind ever since they had been in the *Sun* a couple of months ago — then more than forty per cent of his fellow wheat farmers had gone in the hole last year and only about twenty per cent had made more than he had. Only six per cent had cleared over five hundred dollars. His father-in-law was in the six per cent, of course, and he would be there again this year. If a man could only start with enough cash, money would make money.

Look at what Vick had done with a little cash. He had taken advantage of the slump that began in 1921 and bought this half section for scarcely more than delinquent taxes in 1924, just before George moved onto it. He paid forty-three dollars a year in taxes now, while George and Rachel fretted over the state of the school, the lack of a school bus, the condition of the county road, and a score of other things that taxes ought to cover, and yet George had paid Vick as much as five or six hundred dollars a year. Some years Vick got as high as a twenty per cent return on his investment. And he was nothing but a cheap chiseling dime-store owner who had had a little spare cash at the right time. The return on his investment was a simple translation of George's sweat, good only on a farm, into the medium of exchange called cash — good anywhere in the world for anything he desired. He could buy other men's sweat with that return earned for him by George Custer's sweat, and that was the way little dime-store owners became millionaires.

George knew what he could do about it, of course. He could get out of farming and forget that he ever hoped to exercise the option rights that had been dangled in front of him for nine years. He could get out of the occupation he had been raised in and trained for, and then what could he do?

But there was the one hope left. There were still so many farmers so far below him. They were competing to undersell him, but they had to compete to buy machinery and pay rent, too. Over half the farmers in the state had to pay rent. When things got so bad that no tenant farmer could make a living, then all the tenant farmers would get together and do something about the landlords. So long as seventy-five per cent of the nation's wheat farmers made less than George did, he would either succeed because he was ahead of the majority, or else, if he fell back into that growing ruined majority, he would revolt with them.

Any time George Armstrong Custer could not make a living, one way or another, then the system had to be wrong. If a man like him tried every possible scheme and worked fourteen- and sixteen-hour days and still went broke, then the system certainly needed major repairs, didn't it?

Meanwhile, for one more winter he would figure things so closely that even the occasional pennies he gave Lucy in the store had to be considered part of his budget—and he would repay Will at an interest rate that would restore his self-respect.

When he showed his figuring to Rachel, she did not seem at all surprised that they had cleared scarcely a third of what he had predicted they would. Her lack of surprise discouraged him.

"Well, look at it this way," he said. "Next year I'll have two hundred bushels of properly treated seed. It doesn't look like cash now, but it *will* be. That will make a vast difference, can't you see that?"

"Enough to buy a tractor?" she asked.

"Well . . . sooner or later."

"How much longer can we work the way we worked this year?"

"As long as we *have* to!" he said.

Wednesday, September 27

Spanish farmers were setting torches to thousands of acres of crops. Sweden and Holland renounced the tariff truce they had signed with the United States thirty days before, and declared that they would again bar American food exports from their countries. A hundred and fifty thousand American factory workers were on strike, and a thousand farmers around Chicago were dumping milk again.

With the wheat checks all in, Will was planning to take the morning train to Bismarck to see Dr. Oliver Murdoch. His leg was in fair shape, and he and Stuart took a walk around the farm to use up the hour till it was time to go.

They went first to the far sheep pasture. A couple of half-grown ewes bleated at him as he walked among them, and followed him a few steps away from the flock. He smiled to think how they remembered those bottles.

Prince swished his tail and cantered away. He was enjoying his rest after the summer's work and he was going to make Will fight to get him into harness today. He was unaccountably mean for a gelding; but Will had never had the heart to sell him, because he knew most people who bought such a horse would beat him.

But now he thought Stuart ought not to be stuck with Prince. "For Pete's sake, sell that horse before he takes a bite out of you," Will said. "He's just about ready for the glue factory anyway.

"And we should get those truck brakes fixed. I've been putting it off for months. You might do that right away, now that we can get along without it for a day or two."

Finally, when they were coming back through the new barn still smelling of raw lumber, Will had to say it. "I hope to God, Stuart, that you'll leave that stuff alone while I'm gone! What in the world will your mother do here all by herself? She won't drive the truck and she won't ask George for help."

He went on to the other subject that must be brought up now. "We were talking last night . . . When I come back, we think you ought to go to college. You're still young — a lot younger, maybe, than you feel. I didn't feel so young myself after a couple years with a thrashing crew, but I was — now I see how young I was. . . . Your mother's calling. I never knew her not to have a fit over catching a train. Start up the truck, will you?"

Rose's face was red with heat and nervousness. "Where on earth have you been?" she said. "What do you want me to put in this suitcase?"

She was wearing her best winter dress for the trip. It was a hot day, but it was September, after all, and no decent woman would wear a summer dress to Bismarck in the last week of September. It was fine light wool plaid with a big collar and a low belt line.

Will was as hot as she was. He had on his heavy black suit, with its thick vest. She had made him wear it because she wanted to make sure he would be warm enough when he wore it home again.

She looked him over, from his hat, to the chain of his watch looped across his vest, to his freshly polished shoes. "Look at you!" she said. She snatched a whisk broom from the closet. "Come out on the porch."

She swept the bits of hay and straw from his suit. "Now take a rag and dust off your shoes. What ever made you go out in the fields after you had got all dressed up?"

"What ever made you make me put all these glad rags on at six o'clock in the morning?" he teased her.

"Because I thought it would keep you in the house! With no supper and no breakfast you oughtn't to be moving around so much!"

He had been ordered not to eat for twenty-four hours before the X-rays, which were to be made as soon as he got to the hospital.

"I wanted to take a look at the mare and remind Stuart to put her in nights now. She could drop the foal in a week or so, or even sooner. And it'll frost again any time now. We don't want to lose the colt. . . . I think Stuart's going to straighten up, Rose. . . . Just be a little easy with him. That's the ticket, don't you think?"

"I think we ought to be going," she said.

He hauled his watch out. "It's not due till eleven-fifteen. I make it only ten now."

"You're ten minutes behind the clock and I set it with the radio this morning," she said. It terrified her to think they might have depended on his watch. "It takes that old man half an hour to get far enough down the tracks to flag that fast train."

"Yes, but Stuart said he told him yesterday to be sure to stop it for us."

"Oh, you *know* he'll forget. Come on, let's go!"

Stuart swung the suitcase up into the back of the truck and Will felt, for the hundredth time since Stuart had come home, a great pride at how strong the boy had grown. Nobody in the world — not even loggers or miners — grew stronger muscles than a thresherman. Stuart had hit the work at just the right time in his life, too. A few years earlier and he would have worked too hard and perhaps stunted himself a bit, even while he grew strong — the way Will had himself. A few years later and he would have been a little overripe to do the best job of hardening. But from eighteen to twenty — those were the years to make a man out of a boy, if he had the stuff.

As for Will himself now — it was a relief not to be carrying the suitcase. It was even a relief to be able to admit, finally, that he was too miserable and too weak to walk fast or to stand up straight.

Stuart got in under the wheel, Rose sat in the middle, and Will hauled himself up with his hands braced against the door frame, like an old man. He shook like an old man from the effort of getting his weight a mere three feet off the ground. Those muscles that had served him so well all his life were burdens now. He reminded himself that he was weak from hunger, even if he did not feel hungry.

They had already had the first killing frost of the fall. This morning's baking sun was a little ironic on the blackened stalks of the hollyhocks by the house and on the slender snapped necks of the heavy-headed sunflowers he had planted along the orchard fence to shade the strawberries.

This year there had been only a few dehydrated berries, rich and sweet because they were so distilled. Next spring there would be enough for a shortcake or two. This year he had saved every one for Rachel's babies. Just the look on Cathy's baby face and the bright red berry stains all over her hands and cheeks and chin had been worth all the work he had gone to. Lucy's reactions were pure bonus. She made every berry last a good five minutes, almost eating it seed by seed like a little goldfinch.

He had covered the plants with straw and canvas just in time, only a few days before the heavy frost had come, and now they must be as hot as he was himself under this sun. Almost every year there would be as much as a month of Indian summer after the first frost, with several more frosts coming between the hot days. It was sometimes frustrating to swelter during the daylight hours long after the growing season was ended, and then have the temperature drop so far at night. Still, there was something about Indian summer that made him rejoice to shiver while he did the morning's milking and then to sweat in the field a couple of hours later.

There was something in the wild extremes that roused something in him — like the clamor in himself that responded to the clamor of the ducks and geese streaming south in their countless stately chains, or the clamor of the gold and scarlet leaves, hanging brilliantly dead in the brassy clamor of the sun itself. Let the sun make its daily withdrawal to the south, following the emerald heads of the mallards; let the sun go so far away that the green blood of plants froze black. *He* had *red* blood himself, and he would be there, ready for the sun when it came north again, waiting to hear the first mallard cries volley through the cold spring air.

He had read one of the Happy Farmer's musings on Indian summer only a day or so ago: "By gosh, I see the time is here, Again to feel the traitorous cheer, Brung by Old Sol, that Indian giver, Who laughs to see us sweat, then shiver."

The weak resignation of the poet offended him; there ought to be something better than that to say about Indian summer — something about how good it was for a man to sweat and then to shiver.

Stuart was humming a tune that sounded so familiar, yet so far removed. At last Will recognized it as a variation of a song from his own roving days — a song about some monstrous escapades of Paul Bunyan. It had the kind of words that helped a young man to get through the years of living in a womanless world. He had an impulse to start singing along with Stuart, but Rose was sitting there between them. He felt such a bond with the boy, knowing that the same words went through both their heads at the same time.

"Are they going to bring Lucy to the station?" he asked Rose. He'd never seen a prairie child who didn't love trains, but he thought Lucy must love them more than any child he'd ever known. She made him tell her, over and over, the stories of his own boxcar riding days. She even had dreams about trains.

"I think so," Rose said. "One of these days you ought to take her on the train to Jamestown. She wants to ride on one so much."

"I'll *do* that! I wonder why I never thought of that! I'll do that the first Saturday I can spare the time!" Will was elated. He'd hit upon a fine thing to look forward to.

When they got to the station, Old Man Adams was still dozing over his telegraph keys. Stuart lifted the suitcase out of the back of the truck and set it on the long platform. The sight of the mail sack already hanging on its hook threw Rose into a near panic. "For heaven's sake," she cried. "Let's get him waked up!"

Millard Adams heard their voices and straightened up in his chair, looking fully awake at once. He had spent his life as a telegraph operator, and he knew how to listen in his sleep for the things that mattered — mostly the sound of keys. He had a white moustache that fanned out over his face and made him look like a Civil War general. He did always claim that he had been a drummer boy for the Union. Otherwise, the only outstanding event in his life had been the time when, as a loyal employee of the railroad, he had gone out on one of the posses that failed to catch that notorious train robber Jesse James.

He had grown so small and thin now that his railroad watch seemed as big as an alarm clock when compared with his body. He wore a black suit and a white shirt.

He stepped out into the tobacco gloom of the depot and smiled. "Why, by golly, I clean forgot!" he said. "The railroad has got passengers today. I better get out my flag, hadn't I? How are you? Good to see you, Stuart. You been getting some free rides from my company?"

Stuart had to smile too. "I reckon," he admitted.

"How are you, Will?" Adams asked again.

"Fine, just fine," Will said, but in the shadow of the waiting room his face had the same luminous whiteness as Millard's moustache. It was because he was so hungry, Rose told herself. She nudged him, when Millard went to get the flag. "I *told* you he'd forget!"

"He's getting on," Will agreed. "I don't hardly remember when he didn't seem old to me."

"Let's go back out now," she said. She hadn't noticed his paleness so much before, she decided, because he had just gradually bleached out from being inside the house nursing his leg.

Will had finally caught Rose's nervousness. The sight of the red flag did it. His heart quickened and climbed up under his collarbone. He looked around the town. From where he stood he could see the boards across the windows of Harry's bank. A broken-down wagon hitched to the two most beautiful horses in the county stood in front of Ray Vance's garage. Otto must be in there dickering for some old scraps to patch something with.

A half-familiar man came out of Gebhardt's Pool Hall, obviously already full of beer. He seemed to float from town to town along the railroad. Just about the time one had forgotten him completely, he reappeared. He was very small; that was why one remembered him at all.

Mrs. Finley came out of Herman's store carrying a sack of groceries that was so heavy she had to balance it against her hip as she would a two-year-old child. Her head leaned to the side opposite the grocery bag to compensate for it. She had the look of an apologetic beast of burden which felt the shame of its weakness. Will couldn't stand to watch her.

"Stuart," he said, "there's lots of time yet. You take the truck and go ask Mrs. Finley if you can give her a lift home. Go on, quick! And watch the brakes or you'll smash the eggs!"

Will watched the truck move to a stop behind Mrs. Finley. It slipped and squeaked at the last minute and made her give a little jump. She looked up when Stuart leaned out of the cab toward her. They talked for a moment; she was protesting, of course. The poorer she got, the prouder she acted. But Stuart got down, took the groceries, put them in on the seat, and handed her up as though she was his best girl.

What a fine boy he really was. Whatever made a boy like him drink, anyway? He ought to be out squiring some pretty girls around once in a while — some girls as pretty as he was handsome. Will wondered if there *were* any pretty girls around. The more he thought about it, the more it seemed that the only pretty girl he'd seen in a long time was Lucy. Girls were a little like young apple trees, he thought. They could stand only so many years of drought.

"Here they come," Rose said.

Lucy was running to him, leaving the rest of the family behind. "Where is Mr. Adams's flag?" she said.

"Stuffed right in his hip pocket," Will said. He squatted down to pull her between his knees and talk to her. It was remarkable how she was growing lately — how far above his head her face was.

"How would you like to take a train ride with me?" he said. "And have Mr. Adams flag the train just for us?"

She looked at her mother. "Can I *please!*"

Rachel looked at George and George looked at Lucy. "I don't think she ought to get a treat like that unless she does something to deserve it," he said. "She doesn't even know her table of eights yet."

"I'll know them *tomorrow!* — Oh, it's coming."

Old Man Adams came out and put his ear to the tracks, kneeling down carefully, balancing on his hands and knees and toes to keep his sharp old shins from pressing against the ties. He stood up, nodded at Will, and started down the tracks with the slow shuffle of a railroad man, never stepping between the ties, never trying to take two at a time.

They could all hear the train now, and they knew how fast it would be coming, but Old Man Adams had fooled them. Like Aesop's tortoise, he had managed to get far enough down the tracks so that he looked no bigger than a blackbird, with his speck of a bright red flag.

The train flashed past the waving red speck. It was coming too fast; it would never be able to stop. The engineer's slowly waving glove passed so high above them. They were down beside the great rods pushing back and forth, up and down. It was so eccentric and yet so regular — that blinding-fast up-and-down, back-and-forth of the rods circling the centers of the wheels. One could never keep track of the motion. Everything went by too quickly — the wheels, the lunging rods, the rolling drivers, the earsplitting steam, the waving glove.

Yet each swaying car uttered lower, slower squeaks, each blurred line of windows became more nearly separate, and each whiteness behind them became more nearly a face. And all at once the faces *were* faces, and the brown man vaulted out with his little yellow step. Lucy often wondered why everybody else in the world was white except for those brown men with their yellow steps.

Stuart got there just in time. He handed the suitcase to the brown man while the conductor yelled, "Board!" in the offended voice he used at flag stops.

Her grandmother and grandfather climbed up the iron steps of the car. When they reappeared at a window they looked almost like all the other strange faces.

Lucy lost track of which car had been theirs and when she looked back from the distant train, the platform and the rails below it seemed so alone and useless — as though there would never be another train. But there would, of course — to take her to Jamestown when she learned her 8's.

"Well, it's kind of a hot day for a trip," Mr. Adams said to her father. "Awful hot for this time of year, isn't it?"

"Yes it is," her father said. "Well . . . see you later. Let me know if there's anything you need, Stuart."

"You bet," said Stuart.

They got in the car to go back to school. Lucy was in the back seat, but she could tell when her mother began to cry. The baby kept pulling at the handkerchief she held over her eyes.

"Now, Rachel," her father said, "you're probably just *borrowing* trouble for yourself. You know what a tough old buzzard he is — as tough as he is stubborn. There ain't another man his age in the county that would have come out of that fire alive. You ought to try to think reasonably about this."

Her mother never cried unless something was as bad as it could be. Lucy had tried not to notice all the other signs, but she knew for sure, now, that something bad was going to happen far away in Bismarck.

❧ ❧ ❧

Will settled back in his seat for the seventy-mile ride. "Mighty skinny bunch of cows out there," he said, looking past Rose's fine thin profile. "I wonder if they're some of Egger's."

"Probably. I don't see how those poor things will get through the winter. They look half dead now."

"Nobody anywhere in the country can get a price for feed and yet the animals have to starve to death," Will mused. There seemed nothing more to say after he'd said that.

Presently Rose asked, "Do you really think this Murdoch is the best doctor we could get? Maybe you should be going to Fargo instead. Or back to Rochester."

"Oh, he knows as much as anybody knows, I think," Will said. "Lawyers, doctors, politicians. They're all good talkers. Who knows what they know?"

He was so unlike himself, she thought. He was like an injured animal, snapping at people it had always trusted. It was because he was so hungry.

After a while she said, "My, I'm surprised it can be so hot in here."

He looked out at the telegraph wires running in liquid lines against the sharp blue sky. "Liable to get cold tonight though. I hope Stuart remembers to put the mare in."

"And I hope he remembers to turn that lock on the chicken house all the way down. The weasels are worse, now that the birds are gone."

They passed through Driscoll, Sterling, McKenzie, Menoken, slowing just enough at each station to snatch the mail sack from its post. Then they began to lose speed as they entered the outskirts of Bismarck. The train tracks crossed and multiplied into numerous sidings. They made a widening wasteland of cinders between the elevators and mills and cylindrical storage tanks. There was an air of prophetic antiquity about that cindered wasteland. The towering white columns could have been remnants of desert temples built by generations of slaves. Now the white pillars simply stood there, bursting with wheat — monuments left over from a system that had once had significance.

This very morning's *Sun* said that the domestic wheat stocks on hand came to over a hundred and fifty million bushels. That was not counting any of the grain already bought by millers, or any of the new crop en route to the mills. That was counting only the grain committed to storage — floating in ships and barges on the Great Lakes or sealed up in those tall white pillars.

" 'Whited sepulchers,' " Will thought. He didn't know exactly why the phrase had come to him, but he could not let the thought go. They *were* like tombs. Why? Perhaps it was their estrangement from the brown, billowing land. They were so white and vertical against it. They seemed more like urns filled with death than reservoirs filled with life.

A year ago the lowest prices in history had been blamed on the wheat in storage — the wheat going begging. This year prices were a little better but there was still almost as much wheat in storage. He did not believe that the drought had cut away the surplus enough to have any lasting effect on prices. The drought had scared the speculators into raising their bids a little, that was all. Soon prices might very well drop again. Except for the farmer, almost everybody who made his money from bread profited by having those white cement cylinders always filled with wheat. It made a man wonder if this government could ever change things enough to move the wheat out of the sepulchers.

❦ ❦ ❦

At the hospital he showed the woman behind the admission desk the paper Murdoch had filled out for him. "In cases like this we require an advance deposit of fifty dollars," the woman told him. He didn't like to carry cash around, and fifty dollars was more than he had with him. He wrote her a check, wondering as he did so what she meant when she said, "in cases like this." Probably nothing at all. That was the way with people who sat behind desks all their lives. He had noticed it before. They all had a few things they always said in almost any situation. She looked at the bank name and his name and said, "It'll be just a few minutes. Why don't you sit down?"

They sat on a hard leather bench that was fenced away from the desk by a high-growing potted plant. It made Will think of the plant in a Chicago hotel lobby in a movie he'd seen about bootleggers. In the foreground of the movie scene, next to the leaves of the plant, would be a closeup of the scarred jaw of one of the bootleggers. He would be hiding behind the plant, waiting for signals from the crooked desk clerk. Finally there had been a battle in the hotel lobby between the bootleggers and the prohibition agents, and the stalks of the plant had been severed by the invisible line of machine-gun bullets. It had been a ridiculous show, which the theater had run for some reason in place of the Will Rogers picture he had expected to see.

He heard his name called and he made his way around the plant back to the desk. "Now, Mr. Shepard," the woman said, "if you and Mrs. Shepard will both sign this release, you can go right on up."

The release appeared to absolve the hospital of all responsibility for exactly the sort of calamities Will had thought a hospital existed to prevent. But before he could protest, a nurse stopped beside them with a wheel chair and asked him if he wanted a ride. And before he could say no thank you, she was helping him into the chair.

She gave it a twirl, pushed him into an elevator, bumped him out again, and zoomed into a ward. Was it because he hadn't eaten that everything was double-time? Even his heart was double-time. This was all silly. There was still time to turn around and go back home — where he belonged.

"Now, then, I'll let you get yourself into bed, Mr. Shepard, if you think you can manage." She pulled the sheet curtains around the bed. "While you're busy I'll just take Mrs. Shepard back down and see if we can find a room for her. But I'll bring her back again, don't you worry."

He sat down on the white chair to take off his shoes. The sheets brushed his forehead as he bent over. It was a mighty small space they gave to a man for the amount of money they charged. He laid his black pants across the back of the chair and fitted the empty shoulders of his coat over the pants.

And there was his black suit — getting along without him much better than *he* could get along without *it*. Would he wear it home tomorrow or two weeks from now, or only for that final dressed-up occasion when it would not matter at all to *him* what he wore?

And should he not put the suit back on and go home now, before this hospital made his heart step up to triple-time and caused him to fall into a panic that would make him forget again all the things about the laws that he understood perfectly well?

Yet, while he had been contemplating his suit, he had irrationally removed his underwear. That was why the hospital employed a nurse like the one who brought him here. She hypnotized a man with her hurrying, and hurried him into bed before his good sense could reassert itself.

Suddenly her voice pounced at him from the other side of the sheet. "Mrs. Shepard is just getting herself settled. She'll be right along."

Will pulled the blankets around his neck. Without more warning the nurse drew back the sheet-curtains. "Now I want you to meet your new neighbor," she said. "This is Mr. Oblonsky. Mr. Oblonsky, this is Mr. Shepard. Mr. Oblonsky talked so much to his last neighbor that the poor man finally moved to a private room. Now I want you to let Mr. Shepard rest." She turned from one to the other of them as she talked.

The man contemplated her from under brows so long and droopy that hairs hung out over his eyes. He did not speak at all, as if to make a liar of her. "Just tell him right out when you want to be left alone," she told Will.

Rose appeared in the doorway of the ward, hardly able to bear being in the presence of so many men in bed.

"How is your room?" Will asked her.

"It'll be just fine. It's right near the maternity part. There were two babies in the nursery, but there's ten baby beds. I guess people have quit coming to have their babies in the hospital. They can't afford it any more, I suppose."

"Well, sometimes I wonder," he said, "if it's a normal birth and all, if a woman needs to go to a hospital anyhow. It's never made too much sense to me to take a new little baby away from its mother for a couple of weeks right after it's born. Why, a foal would die of fright if you did that to it. We don't do that to lambs or any other little babies except for calves, and I always hate to do it to a calf. Remember when we went to see Rachel when Cathy was born, and Cathy was all the way down the hall in the nursery, crying so hard she was purple? It just didn't seem sensible to me. Rachel was just sitting there in bed with nothing to do except listen to that woman next to her. She'd a lot rather have been with that new baby, wouldn't she?"

"You are absolutely right," came a polished voice from the next bed. "It is foolish and barbarous, but even so, it is less barbarous than a thousand other practices of this great American civilization." It was a carefully shaped sentence and delivered as though it was broadcast over the radio. There was no doubt that Mr. Oblonsky had been shaping it, and listening in, throughout the entire conversation.

Will looked at him, without being able to think of anything to say. The man's name, his coarse features, his bushy hair — nothing had prepared Will for the voice or the language. He had been steeling himself to tolerate the incomprehensible accents of a foreigner who would rattle on at a great speed, expecting him to answer as though he understood.

Dr. Murdoch came in and stuck out a freckled hand to Will. He had so many freckles on his face that they made a solid brown rim around his smiling lips. A bright green tie hung out over the lapels of his white coat and one tube of his stethoscope dangled from a big square pocket.

"Well, you're looking fine, Mr. Shepard," he said loudly.

Rose moved to leave but he said, "Oh, no, no, no, no. Just slide back an inch and let me take a little listen here." He planted the stethoscope against Will's chest for a few seconds, nonchalantly, as though he already knew exactly what Will's personal heartbeat was going to sound like.

He took the plugs out of his ears and let the stethoscope ride around his neck like a medal on a ribbon. Will thought that nobody but a doctor could look quite so sure of himself, quite so eminently and appropriately placed in the world, with the badge of his position so modestly displayed as part of his working attire. The doctor could play negligently with the end that had received the secret, desperately important sounds, as Murdoch did now, holding the little black cup in one hand and plopping it into the palm of the other. He tapped it with an irregular beat that made a man wonder if the doctor was imitating the rhythm he had just listened to.

"How's the bellyache?" he asked.

"About the same," Will said.

"Well, you're in fine shape. Wonderful physique for a man your age. We'll take your picture now, and see what we can see."

Will was awakened the next morning so he could be put back to sleep again. He was dizzily aware of being lifted from his bed to a wagon, of the wall of white-shrouded masked people around him, of Rose momentarily in their midst, of a supine levitation in an elevator, of the white people lifting him again, of the narrow cold slab, of the jolly sounds of Dr. Murdoch. He wanted to tell Murdoch just to forget it all — that he understood the laws, that he knew it was too late. But the black rubber mask came down like a vulture to clutch at the bones of his cheeks, steadying his skull with its claws in order to pluck out the delicacies of his fainting eyes. "Just breathe deeply, now," they said into his ear. "Just a few deep breaths and you'll be all right."

❦ ❦ ❦

A wind had come in the night and herded before it a multiplying flock of brilliant clouds that clambered up and up into the steep heights of the sky. Their shadows moving over the stubble seemed too thick and black to be cast by such shining white things so far away.

Lucy was walking home under the shadows, thinking of all the people who would be at her house today when she got there and how they would laugh and joke as they worked. To make the three miles seem shorter, she would fix her eyes on a distant marker — a mailbox or a big rock or an extra high fence post — and never look down at the gravel crunching so sluggishly beneath her till she reached the marker. Whenever she remembered, she would recite her 8's aloud to the empty road.

Somebody inside the kitchen had to move a chair before Lucy could get through the door. It was Mr. Egger. "Well, here's *Lucy!*" he cried. He always teased her and she never knew how to answer him. He was running the big meat press he had brought with him.

He and the grinder seemed to go together. They both had but a single arm to crank round and round. He let go of the crank and reached across his chest, across the space where his sleeve was folded back and pinned to his shoulder, and grabbed her wrist.

"Here!" he exclaimed. "Here's a hand I found. It'll give us just what we need to finish off this first pan. Umm num num! I bet it'll be the best-eating sausage of the bunch — but we'll have to watch out for the fingernails."

She stood looking down at his hand on her wrist, while the women in the kitchen laughed at what he was saying. It made her shiver to have him yanking her hand around right in the space of air where his own other arm should have been.

Her mother saved her. "You run and change into your overalls, now, Lucy, the way I told you to, and then go down and tell the men to bring up some more sausage meat." She made it sound as though it was Lucy, not Mr. Egger, who was to blame because Lucy was dallying in the messy kitchen when she ought to have been taking off her good school clothes. Lucy had begun to understand that it was always polite to blame yourself or your family instead of your company.

On her way to the barn she had to squeeze past Mr. Egger again, who was waiting for more meat to grind. He wasn't much good at most heavy butchering chores, which took two hands, so the only thing he did outside with the men was a thing which required only one finger — one very accurate and sensitive finger. He supervised while they filled the great steel barrel with water from a caldron steaming over an outdoor wood fire. When the barrel was ready for the pig, he ran his finger through the water — once, twice — if he couldn't stand to do it the third time, the water was too hot — thrice — if he could just stand it, the water was just right. But if he could do it a fourth time, the water was too cold. "Watch out, now," he would say. "She's still too hot in there — you'll set the hair on that pig! Give her a minute to cool off or else fetch me a bucket of cold water." He would motion to the man pouring the water, making him stop after a quart or so, and stir a ladle back and forth in the drum a couple of times. Then he'd test it again. Or if he could stand it to put his finger in the fourth time he'd begin to fuss and worry.

"For God's sake bring some boiling water! Shake a leg there! If those women haven't got you some boiling water up there to the house, tell 'em they can come shave this critter themselves!"

If the water couldn't be brought up to the temperature that seemed exactly right to him, and the men decided to go ahead and scald the hog anyway, he'd tuck his wet hand into his pocket and predict the troubles they were going to have. "All right, do it your own way, do it your own way! I tell you it's too cold. You're gonna set the hair on that pig."

When the water was just right, half the hair came off as they sloshed the pig up and down in it. Then the rest of the hair sloughed off easily with long strokes of the big knives. When the water was wrong, every single hair had to be cut off at its root.

It had been a perfect day for butchering — cold and dry. It was a very big pig, and they had had to use the block and tackle in order to scald it and get it up for bleeding. Against the side of the barn they had made a table of boards placed across two small barrels. The table held what amounted to nearly half of the pig — the same pig that had squealed to Lucy last night for the food he could not have. Now he was a baffling, monstrous, three-dimensional jigsaw puzzle.

The gray bristles were strewn on the ground where they had been rinsed off the table and slopped out of the scalding drum. Around the corner of the barn the stupendous innards sprawled out in swollen convolutions, seemingly ready to burst despite the pig's last hours of starvation. The veins on the organs were red, blue, even green. Lucy was always amazed at how brightly colored an animal was on the inside. The pig's blood was clotted along the several arcs which had jetted from the warm slit throat before the pressure lessened and the stream poured into the tub beneath the fat face. Even if his pieces of meat and insides *could* be put back together, what could be done about the pieces of his blood?

His narrow, flat lower jaw gaped away from the round, gristled snout, and above the snout, exactly centered between the two short rows of hoary closed eyelashes, was the rust-colored spot. Her father never missed with his rifle, no matter how an animal bucked and plunged. It was hard to shoot a pig that squarely, but it was also embarrassing to make a pig squeal. Even some of the best shooters sometimes had to shoot an animal two or three times, but her father never did. "They just lose their nerve," he would say to her mother. Lucy studied the rust-colored spot. It bothered her because it seemed to her there was something about it that she did not understand.

The pig would be dodging, taking little runs this way and that, trying to elude the men who had dragged him from his pen and stood about him in a circle. He would pause, at bay, swing his head to look toward her father, and know nothing more. He would not even hear the shot. The sudden rust-colored spot would appear in his forehead and then the men would hurry to string the wires through the tendons of the quivering hind legs and hoist the carcass up with the block and tackle. Then came the knife sticking deeply through the inches of white fat, the numberless capillaries tracing their shocked red lines in the whiteness, then the eruption from the jugular itself. But about all this the pig would know nothing.

Then, after the bleeding, the lowering into the scalding barrel, the scraping on the table, the return to the hook on the block, the long incision down the belly all the way from tail to throat, the deft slices to free the membranes of the stomach and intestines from the chops and bacon which housed them, and finally the whole severed digestive system bouncing out into an empty tub or on the ground. Thus were the parts of paramount interest to the pig dispensed with, while the parts of paramount interest to the men were subjected to a complex further division.

The men flensed away the fat, so pure white between the rim of hide and the red meat. They tossed the chunks of fat into the rendering pot and then they began cutting and sawing to separate the picnic shoulders from the spareribs and the spareribs from the ham roasts, and the ham roasts from the hams. Then they cut Boston butts, pork steaks, loin roasts, and several kinds of chops. When they had divided one half of the hog into all these pieces and more, they did the same with the other half. And the beginning of that puzzle made of all the pieces of muscle and blood and fat and bone and hair was the original riddle — the perplexing rust-colored spot. What exactly did the bullet do when it made the spot?

There was a full bucket of small pieces standing on the ground by the table. The pieces were inferior morsels to be ground by Mr. Egger into much smaller pieces.

"Is this the sausage meat?" Lucy asked. Her father nodded.

She took the pail into the kitchen and Mr. Egger said, "By golly, now I've got me a helper prit-near as good as another arm. You feed it in, Lucy, and then I won't have to quit cranking all the time. Set right over here."

She dipped her hand into the bucket and dropped some chunks into the wide mouth of the meat press, letting them fall several inches from her fingertips.

"Push 'em down there a little," Mr. Egger said. "It grabs hold better that way."

She pushed with one index finger and jerked her hand back when she felt the meat pulled from below. He laughed and laughed while he cranked and cranked. He certainly acted as though he would think it was funny to grind off her finger. If people who scared you and teased you did it because they liked you, as her mother was always saying, then it would be better if a lot of people didn't like you. Especially when *you* did not like *them.* This way a person like Mr. Egger would make you jump in a fright and then he would laugh and *you* were supposed to laugh, too, because everybody was watching. If only your family wasn't too poor, you could buy your own meat press and then perhaps Mr. Egger would not have to bring *his* and he would stay at home on your butchering day.

Rachel rushed from one job to another on butchering day, trying to make sure that each job was done to suit her. She always did the final scraping of the casings herself. They were nothing more than a flimsy, translucent pile in the bottom of an enamel pan now, but they represented a lot of work. The men did the first part of the job; they squeezed out the last of the contents and sent the casings up to her empty but still the color of what they had held. Then they had to be scraped and scraped till they were pressed absolutely clean, and then put to soak in warm water and then scraped again. She herself couldn't see a bit of difference between sausages simply fried in patties and sausages stuffed into casings. Either way they had to be canned, anyhow. But George liked them in casings, so that was the way she did them.

She gently inserted a fork handle through the center of the pile and lifted up the membranes and then let them slide off like a twisted line of writing. They were ready for the sausages.

The men brought up the brutal head, reposing on the base of its neck in the wash tub, the snout pointing defiantly up at her. The head contained a great deal of good meat which had to be salvaged. George was always after her to make head cheese, but that was where she drew the line. She used the cheeks, jowls, and tongue in the sausage and discarded the rest.

Besides the pans full of sausage there were other pans. One held the liver. Lucy hated liver, but she would have to eat what they didn't put in the sausage because it was so good for her.

In another pan lay the huge heart, letting the last of its blood into the red water around it. Considering the chicken, turkey, steer, and hog hearts she had seen, Lucy always wondered what made people think a valentine looked like a heart.

They doled out the stronger meat of the ground-up organs to the several pans, kneaded the sausage once more, inserted a finer blade in the meat press, and commenced the work of stuffing the pig's intestines with its own minced body. Lucy knew there must be some significance in such an operation — using the innards that digested the corn and slop as containers for the meat that the corn and slop had produced. She had somewhat the same feeling about this that she had about the rusty hole between the eyes in the head. There was too much to understand. What happened when a person died?

Mrs. Egger stretched the casing tightly over the spout of the meat press and held it there. Mr. Egger turned the crank again and Lucy watched while the meat forced out the tough tube of the casing into its original shape. "You got enough sausage here for the next five years," Mr. Egger told her.

Rachel got the dining room table cleared and wiped clean just as the men tramped up on the porch, walking heavily because of the weight they carried. They thumped the slabs of meat on the table and went back down for another load. The cold air that came in with them made Rachel feel how cramped and hot and loud the house was. Her mind had been in one room of the hospital in Bismarck all day. He was making a good recovery, they said. He was doing every bit as well as could be expected.

"By golly, Clarence," said Ralph Sundquist, "what a man you'd be with two arms!"

"Don't lighten the load," Clarence proclaimed. "Strengthen the back!"

And shut the mouth, Rachel nearly said. George was always wondering how Clarence put up with Elsie, but *she* wondered how even Elsie could put up with Clarence.

"That's what I've always did, too," Clarence was saying. "Any other man could never of run this here meat press all afternoon like this without changing off his hands a hundred times, but when a man hasn't got but one arm he just learns how to make it keep going.

"I come from a line of hardy men," he went on. "My old man got an arrow prit-near through the muscle of his upper right arm when he run into some renegades. He went and yanked it out backwards, barbs and all, and throwed it right back, left-handed."

"Pshaw — your old man's Indian stories. Why I bet he never left Illinois till there wasn't nothing but cigar-store Indians left loose in this country!"

"He *showed* me the *scar!*"

"Maybe he stopped a bullet with it when he was running away from the revenuers."

"You could see where the edges of the barbs was pulled out, I tell you. He was a tough old bird — but he wasn't as tough as *his* daddy, I'll tell you *that*, too."

"Fiddlesticks! Your granddaddy was the *real* booze-maker and you know it! He'd of made a *fortune* if he'd been alive the last fifteen years! *I* remember him!"

They hurried through the rest of the cutting and then they cleared off the table for supper. They could not, of course, eat any of the meat yet; it was still too warm. But they had all worked up great appetites for the beef Rachel had canned the year before, the string beans put up from this year's garden, the potatoes that had turned out fairly well despite the bugs and drought, and the two pumpkin pies she had baked.

By the time they got to the pie, heaped with sweet whipped cream, they were relaxed and triumphant. One more bit of harvest was safely put away, preserved from all future accidents. Surrounded by the bounty of the huge pig they did not feel poor. Tomorrow or the next day, depending on their feelings about how long it took for the meat to cool properly, they would all eat premium pork. George always saw to it that his meat was carefully raised and perfectly fattened. The small room was filled with a cheerful joking optimism that dimmed their anxieties the way the warm air full of sausage spices steamed the windows to hide the frosty darkness outside.

George leaned back in his chair when the meal was over, and passed the little china cup of toothpicks around to the other men. He felt expansive and proud for several reasons. In the first place, the others had been forced to admit, when they started cutting up the meat and seeing how solid it was, that his estimate of the hog's weight had been conservative if anything. Usually such a big hog would be comparatively light: his volume would be composed of such a big percentage of lard that his density would be less than that of a smaller pig. This hog had plenty of lard on him, of course, but the bacon was lean enough, and the chops and the hams were top grade.

In the second place, things in general had gone well. He had worried about the size of the barrel, but it had been just big enough to do a decent job; the water had pleased Clarence without a lot of dilly-dallying around; Ralph Sundquist had managed not to cut himself for a change — it had been, all in all, a satisfying day. But still he was not so completely satisfied that he couldn't appreciate it when Clarence said, "By golly, George, you sure called it. If that pig didn't go five hundred, I never saw one that did." Now Rachel would believe him, he thought — now that somebody else had said it — especially a ladies' man like Clarence.

"I never *saw* such a heavy pig," Ralph put in. "Anyhow I never *butchered* such a heavy pig. I guess I *saw* heavier ones — at the fair."

Ralph always made a person want to go him one better. Sometimes he seemed put on earth just to be shown up and bested.

George laughed. "*This* one was a *baby*, compared to one my dad butchered once," he said. "That hog weighed eight hundred and seventy-five pounds. My dad had to scavenge around till he found a hundred-gallon barrel to scald him in and we had to hoist him up with the hay-stacker in order to bleed him. When we got him all rendered out we had two hundred and sixty pounds of lard! *Think* of it! Two hundred and sixty pounds of lard! Why, that's enough for five hundred pie crusts! It took *two strong* men to carry that pig's head. Imagine that! How did the *pig* carry it? Two big men just to carry his head!"

"Did you have an elephant gun to shoot that one with?" Ralph asked.

"Naw! Finished him with one shot — same as I did today. He never said a word. If you aim right, it don't matter how big they are. They've all got that one spot."

The helpers filed out the door, carrying their pork in big bundles of white paper. The Custers stood in the doorway while the freezing air blew in around them, waving and calling goodby.

The voices came back to them out of the darkness: A good five hundred pounds all right . . . so glad about your father, Rachel . . . I want a taste of that new kind of ham . . . delicious pie . . . hope the sausage is all right . . . let me know how your soap turns out.

Soap. Lucy had been thinking of how her father had said *that one spot*. Now she thought of how they would render out the kettle of fat tomorrow. Her father would build a bonfire outside and when the cooking was done she would eat so many of the delicious rich cracklings that she would not want any supper at all.

Then everybody was gone and Lucy was sent to bed. George got out the kit he had ordered from Montgomery Ward. It had a stainless steel syringe for injecting the salt and sugar deep into the ham before it was smoked so the ham would cure evenly.

"My, oh my," he said gaily. "Even with the extension, I don't know if this needle is going to be long enough. What hams!"

❦ ❦ ❦

Rose was waiting when they wheeled him back. Murdoch was not with them. A strange doctor came, but he did not speak to her until he had supervised the six nurses lifting Will's body back into his bed. They behaved as though they knew the entire incision would split open if they bent his straight form so much as half an inch. When they drew the blankets up from the foot of the bed over his legs, slowly over his stomach, over his chest, Rose suddenly knew that they were going to bring the blankets on up over his head and that the strange doctor was going to turn to her and tell her that it was all over. That was why Murdoch wasn't there — that jolly man.

But then the blankets stopped at Will's chin and the strange doctor said softly to her, "He came through it very well, Mrs. Shepard. He's got the heart of a man twenty years his junior. Remarkable physique for a man his age — especially considering what he's been putting up with for God knows how long. . . . Well, Doctor Murdoch did a beautiful job. Beautiful. I sometimes ask myself why he doesn't move on to Minneapolis or Chicago — or even Rochester. Well, he's got another operation now — he'll be down to see you as soon as he can make it. Don't you worry now."

The strange doctor was following the wagon out the door before she came to herself enough to realize that he hadn't told her a blessed thing. She hurried after him. "Wait! What ailed him? Is he all right now? Is he cured?" But she didn't say even the first word. The doctor was already an inseparable and unapproachable member of the rustling pilgrimage in the hall. She could still catch the smell of the wagon, and she understood how the portentous stench of its rumpled sheets must waft through each open door, and how the people in the rooms who had had their rides, or were waiting for their rides, were looking out (even while they tried not to breathe that essence of the helpless sleep) to watch the white, masked neuter beings sweep past in their purposeful rush like the avenging Hosts flitting through the Egyptian streets behind the Lord of the Passover and sniffing for the lambs' blood on the lintels.

She understood that there was nothing at all she could do but go back and sit beside him, curtained in with the effluvium from his lungs while she listened to them labor for less tainted air.

He made no move except to breathe. Sweat began to shine on his ivory face. What if he should get a case of ether-pneumonia on top of everything else? She began to feel very hot herself, though whether it was because the ward was too hot or because she felt so nauseated from the ether, she could not tell. Nor did she have any idea of how long she waited for Murdoch to come.

He did come, finally, wearing the same tweed trousers and green tie and stethoscope that he had worn the day before. He looked fresh and hearty — not at all like the other haggard envoys descending from that mysterious bloody sanctum above her. She looked at his face and at Will's, and the difference between the faces so stopped her throat with terror and rage that she could not speak.

"I'll bet you haven't even been out to lunch yet," he chided her. "You've just been sitting here doing nothing more useful than thinking about how bad he looks, haven't you? How do you *expect* him to look after he's been carved around in for more than two hours? How do you *expect* him to look with a ten-inch cut across his belly? He's lost a lot of blood, but he'll get it back. Now don't worry about him! He's got a wonderful physique for a man of his age. Go on out and get yourself something to eat before we have to give *you* an anesthetic too!"

❦ ❦ ❦

The next morning Will showed a bit of color under the gray bristles that had grown out since his last shave. His body still produced whiskers even if he could not eat or drink and even if his mind was shuttered under sedation. When the time came for her to catch the train, she touched her lips to the bristles and left. They had agreed that they mustn't leave Stuart alone too long.

On the train she tried to read a newspaper. The J. R. Williams cartoon was entitled, "Why Mothers Get Gray." She passed over that. She tried not to wonder about whether or not Stuart would be at the depot. She would wait till she got there and either saw him or didn't see him.

The Communist riots and counter-revolutions in Cuba were getting rather monotonous. She skipped them too. The story that caught her eye was one about Herbert Hoover and his wife. They had just made a visit to the Century of Progress World's Fair in Chicago and then stopped to see how things were going on one of their farms in Missouri. She could hear the fit George would be having over that.

"What possible excuse," he would be asking, "what possible *legitimate reason* can that man have for owning farms and competing with the rest of us that *have* to make a living off a farm or starve to death! The Great Humanitarian!" George had a way of talking that made people who knew him able to *hear* him talking even when he was miles away.

But the thing about the story she couldn't get out of her mind was the Fair. Will had wanted to go to the Fair. All summer long the cars had been coming from the Fair along Highway Number 10. And Will would come back from town telling how he'd seen another car in front of Gebhardt's loaded with souvenirs and with stickers all over the windows.

Now she thought perhaps she knew why he had wanted to go to the Fair so much. She held the paper up close to her face and bent over it so no one would notice her. Why should reading about the Chicago Exposition make her lose control when she had held together through all the rest of it?

❦ ❦ ❦

The county agent had scheduled a meeting in the Town Hall for farmers of the Eureka area. He wanted to get them all to sign up for the production control campaign that was part of the Agricultural Adjustment Act. The USDA preliminary estimates of the 1933 harvest were in and formulas had been all worked out.

George had planned to boycott the whole silly affair, but Rachel begged him to go.

"*I* know what this guy is going to say, Rachel!" he argued. "I've been keeping track of all this stuff in the papers. I know this is just another scheme to get tax money out of the little fellow and into the hands of the big man—because the big man is the only man that can afford to let his ground lay idle. This damned county agent is not going to be any more good to me than the *last* man that came up here from Jimtown to talk to me! If I'd known what *that* little weasel had in his hands, I'd have torn him limb from limb and scattered him for fertilizer. No, I can't say much for the government men they send me up from the county seat!"

"Oh, George, you always complain about how the government

helps the big farmer instead of the little farmer, but what do you do to find out if you're right? Why don't you go tonight and find out exactly what the government *will* offer you?"

"I *know* what the government will offer me — a chance to retire a few acres and get paid twenty-five cents a bushel for what I could have raised on them. If I was a *big* man, and I could retire a couple thousand acres and cut down my overhead by firing two or three hired men to go on relief — why then it would pay me to go along with the government. The big men came in and *caused* the surplus in the first place, and now the government is going to pay them to cut down! I tell you, it burns me!"

"I still wish you'd go."

"I'll go, I'll *go!* But that county agent is nothing but a stooge for the rich men in the Farm Bureau. *You* know that as well as *I* do. The government has been using tax money for fifteen years to pay those extension agents to go around and wait on the big boys. *You* haven't forgotten what happened when we first came here any more than *I* have! We wanted some soil tests made — but the county agent just somehow never could get around to us, could he? But if we'd owned four or five sections of land and ten thousand dollars' worth of machinery, what then? 'Oh, yes, Mr. Custer. And just how can we be of service to you today, Mr. Custer!' They make me sick!"

"How do you know things aren't different now? Go and find out. What have you got to lose?"

"Two hours of my time and my pleasant disposition!" he said loudly.

Rachel did not reply. It was enough that he had consented to go. A little later she would suggest that he stop by and pick up Stuart. Her mother wanted Stuart to go because she thought if Stuart attended the meeting and was in at the beginning of their plans for the coming year, he might feel more like the future owner of the farm. But they didn't want to send him into town alone at night — that was a little too much like tempting the Devil.

Rachel couldn't recall trying to manipulate George for private reasons in all the years she had been married to him. She had asked him forthrightly to do things, yes, but she had never asked him to do *one* thing because she really wanted him to do *another* thing.

But she had never felt so desperate about her family, either. What would become of the farm, of her mother and father, if Stuart did not stay? What would become of Stuart if he ran away again? He had been home for six weeks now, and he had been perfectly steady for the whole time. The longer he was steady, the more reason there was, surely, to believe that he was finally ready to settle down. Yet the longer he was steady, the more reason to fear that his inscrutable tensions were bringing him nearer and nearer to another outbreak.

⁂

It didn't seem from the cars outside the Town Hall that twenty people would be there. One car in front of the hall was nearly as shiny as Clarence Egger's new six-cylinder Chrysler. Small letters under the driver's window read "United States Government County Extension Service." George had noticed how clever the government — Republican or Democratic — was at picking words to make the people think they were getting something. "Service!" he snorted to Stuart as they walked up the steps of the hall.

There was nobody whose official job it was to introduce Jim Finnegan and so he introduced himself, standing alone on the stage, looking out over his audience scattered around the floor. A covey of bare bulbs hung from the ceiling and no matter where he stood, at least one of them struck squarely into his glasses.

He smiled at them. "You all know me," he said. "Like hell," George murmured to Stuart.

"Jim Finnegan — just one of the Finnegan boys. I'm sure glad to see all you folks here tonight, but I'm sorry you didn't bring along your better halfs. . . . I have one or two things for the ladies tonight. Well, I'll just have to trust you menfolks to pass the word along, and tell them I sure hope they can make it next time. You'll do that, now, won't you?"

"Oh, you betcha," George whispered.

"The *Sun* has been pretty good about printing the releases I've passed on from Washington." There was a tinge of importance in his voice. "But I know how it is, when you're getting in a harvest."

You do, do you? thought George.

"You sometimes can't keep up with the paper when you're working sixteen hours a day [*Oh, you know all about it, don't you, down there in your little easy chair?*], and if you'll bear with me I'd like to summarize for you, as briefly as I can, some things that have happened in the last couple of months that concern you and your plans for the future. [*My plans for the future are to stay alive, damn you.*]

George thought it, but somebody else said it — "Just tell me what to pay my rent with, will you? I can't seem to plan no further ahead than that!"

Finnegan trotted out a chuckle from somewhere. "That's all right, we want it nice and informal," he said, "and if you'll just go along with me I think I can show you how you'll have a better chance to pay your rent *next* year, anyhow. The government wants to help you get a fair price for your wheat but we can't help you unless you'll do something about planning ahead. Now you know this summer at the meeting in London all the big wheat-producing countries agreed on export allotments."

"All except the Roosians," George said to Stuart.

"The allotment for this country is forty-seven million bushels for this year and ninety million for the next two years combined. Now let me remind you that in 1920, which certainly was a golden year for a lot of you men, we exported three hundred and seventy million bushels. Last year we exported forty-one million. In other words, last year we exported less than thirteen per cent of what we exported twelve years ago. For over a decade, now, wheat has been building up into more and more of a surplus problem — by far the biggest surplus problem of any farm item — or any other item, for that matter. [*Except for the item of hungry people, you jackass.*] Now it stands to reason you'll never get a decent price for wheat with more than half a year's supply in storage. It's just common sense that the millers aren't going to pay you anything for your crops so long as that extra wheat is just sitting there. And we can't sell it abroad, that's all there is to it. Nobody has any dollars over there."

[*Nobody has any dollars over in Europe because big business won't let any imports in over here, you hypocritical son-of-a-bitch.*]

"We simply have way too much acreage in wheat," Finnegan repeated. "During the war all you heard was 'Wheat Will Win the War,' and we admit it, the government did everything it could to get you to expand your operations. And you sure did. Do you realize that wheat acreage went from fifty-three million acres in 1914 to *seventy*-three million in 1919? That's almost a forty per cent increase in five years. Now the main reason that the parity years of 1910 through 1914 were such good years for farmers is that we didn't have so many acres in wheat and there was no surplus to contend with. Europe wanted everything we could produce and the prices were good. Then during the war, of course, we actually had a scarcity. Now it's true that acreage has dropped again since 1920, but not enough. The government wants to help you cut back enough so that you'll get a fair price."

"A fair price from *who?*" somebody said loudly. "Even if wheat *was* scarce again, what difference would it make? Who's got any money? You just said yourself there's no dollars over there in Europe any more."

Finnegan had no answer, of course, but that didn't stop him from talking. "Well, things are going to pick up a lot. There'll be money in circulation again. [*That's not what fourteen million men out of a job think.*] And when there's money, there'll be money for *you*, too, if we can just empty the elevators and storage bins and barges so the millers won't be able to offer whatever price they want and know that somebody will sell. And this brings me to the business for tonight." He stopped and read his notes and when he spoke again, he sounded just like another newspaper release from the mass of publications flowing from Washington desks to country mailboxes.

"This is a matter which requires the cooperation of every single one of you — and not only the cooperation, but the good faith and the solemn promises. This country was built on the words and deeds of honorable men like you, and it will endure on those same words and deeds. Now you know I've been to see some of you individually, but tonight I wanted to get you all together. I want you to look around at your neighbors and realize that you've got to work together if you want to save your own skins. I know you can say competition is what made this country great — but so did *cooperation.* And now you've got to work together or the competition between you will ruin all of you. Six million farmers are competing against each other. How are you going to get anywhere that way? I brought you together so you could look around at each other and see just who it is that's ruining you at the markets in Chicago and Minneapolis and Liverpool."

"B.S.!" A red-faced man jumped up and began to talk. It was Lester Zimmerman, and he could make quite a speech if he felt like it. "We all know damn well who's wrecking those markets. For one thing it's the Guardian Trust Company in Jimtown that's foreclosed on at least ten thousand acres in this county and plants every last one of them to wheat with great big tractors. And I'll bet you that the damned Guardian Trust Company owns *six* combines — that's what I'll bet! And *that's* the kind of outfit that's wrecking the wheat markets, mister! Don't you try and tell me it's *my* little two hundred acres that's doing it!"

"Yeah," said somebody else, "what's the government going to do about these banks and insurance companies?"

"Everything will be done on a percentage basis. There's no other fair way to do it," Finnegan argued. "*Everybody* has got to cut down. A lot of people thought the crops would be poor enough this year so as to eliminate the wheat surplus. But it just hasn't worked out that way, has it? A third of the Kansas winter wheat acreage was abandoned at harvest time last May and the rest of the acreage yielded very poorly too. Kansas this year produced only forty-seven per cent of what they produced last year, and — listen to this — only *twenty-three* per cent of what they produced in 1931 when the moisture was anywhere near normal. And you don't have to be told what happened in South Dakota this summer, because we got enough of it ourselves up here. The worst damage came from the hoppers, but what with the drought and rust and smut, South Dakota harvested *ten* per cent of what they got last year. And *still* we have a surplus that's ruining your prices. You've *got* to see that it *is* the two-hundred acre farms that have to cut back. It's *everybody*."

Another man stood up. "How *can* I plant less? What am I going to do for cash? You tell me what to use instead of cash and I'll go along with you." He sat down, then added, "Maybe it's time to get us a printing press and make our own."

"The government understands that you can't survive without a certain minimum of cash. [*Minimum!*] I'm here to try to show you how you can get your hands on that minimum and still work toward a better balance between the supply and demand in your market. The government knows that you also don't like relief. Why should you? You've lived independently all your lives and your fathers before you were independent. The government is proud that men like you keep struggling to stay independent. [*And also the government doesn't like making relief payments, does it?*] I have the contracts here with me tonight that will guarantee you a certain benefit payment next summer in addition to whatever cash you get from the acreage you leave in production. Shall we get down to business? [*"Benefit payment." They do their best to make it sound like relief!*]

"What happens if we sign and then wheat prices go way up? If the Kansas wheat crop is even worse next spring?" somebody asked. "Your measly checks ain't going to look like a heck of a lot next to what we *could* get next fall."

"Let me outline this program for you and then we'll have all your questions. How's that?" The county agent plowed ahead. "But in regard to *your* question, let me say that any man who signs an agreement to take a certain amount of acreage out of production and then reneges on his agreement is certainly being a poor neighbor, besides being dishonest. [*Do you think we'll fall for this grade-school sermon? Especially from a politician?*] Now, first of all, for sixty or seventy years the farmers have been complaining about how the middlemen get too much of the food dollar. The railroads' rates were always too high, their land grants were exorbitant —"

"Well they *were!*" somebody shouted. "They are!"

"All right, so they were. So the most important thing about this acreage-control plan is that the middleman gets soaked for it. These Triple A payments are coming out of the processing taxes the government levies on all refiners and bakers. This is so the wheat farmer can get more for his work without passing the cost on to the consumer. We all agree that the consumer cannot consume enough to keep you in business. Right?"

"Oh, George!" Lester called. "Did you bring a shovel? I clean forgot mine, and it's gettin' so thick in here! Do you realize the price of bread went up two months ago and this fella hasn't heard about it yet?"

"All right, now!" Finnegan cried. "You just let me give you some estimates here. We expect to take in at least five hundred million dollars a year from these middlemen, and it's all going to come back to *you!* Now just let me read you part of a bulletin I have in my hand here. I just got a shipment of these" — Lester stood up, made a few shoveling motions, and sat down — "and I hope you'll all pick one up when we get down to the business of filling out these contracts, but I'd like to just pick out some high points here: 'One, the total volume of wheat production in the United States must be reduced and kept within effective demand.' And . . . let's see here — 'Three, the farmers who cooperate in the program must, by reason of their cooperating, be given advantages which noncooperators would not have.' "

"*There* he's got us!" George boomed out. He couldn't see letting Lester grab the floor all the time. "Your well goes dry or your feed runs out and you either sell your stock to the government or shoot it for coyote food. So you go to your county agent, and he says, '*You* didn't buy my acreage contract; *I* don't buy your cows.' Or you tell your kindly county agent, 'I hear the government's helping us fellows to dig new wells.' 'I don't find your name here on my list,' says Mr. Agent. 'You go dig your own hole.' "

"For Christ's sake, let's hear the man out!" Stuart hissed.

So Rachel's drunkard baby brother was going to act pious and embarrassed, was he? George would have to clean his clock for him one of these days. He knew it.

Finnegan went on as though there had been no interruptions at all. He had decided to pretend their unanswerable questions did not exist. What allegiance did a man owe to a government that sent him a donkey like this?

"I'm skipping along here . . ." said the county agent. " 'Five, production control should be accomplished through acreage control. Seven, the purchasing power of the United States wheat grower's wheat must be restored to where it was in the base period, or parity period, of the prewar years of nineteen-oh-nine to nineteen-fourteen.'

"Now, there you have the outlines of the thinking and planning we've done since the new President took over. At least you'll have to admit that we've been getting some action started. I know this has all been in the newspapers, but this bulletin pulls it together for you, and you really ought to take one. It's *your* tax money that printed it. If you know a neighbor who didn't come tonight, I wish you'd take one for him.

"Now of course you will be expected to sign a three-year contract. That's partly to enable the government to plan ahead and not to exceed the production that will take care of our domestic needs and our export quota. But it's also partly to encourage *you* to do something with the acreage you take out of wheat. If you take it out for that long, perhaps you'll build it up for good pasture or hay. That will be good for you and good for the land.

"Supposing you averaged a hundred and thirty acres in wheat for the last three years. We'll take the three-year average, from 1929 to 1932 — be glad we don't include this year's bad crop — and we'll base your payments on that. Around here, the average for those three good years is ten point five bushels to the acre — last year it was only six point eight, as you know too well. So — if you withheld thirty acres, figuring at roughly ten bushels to the acre, you'd be paid for three hundred bushels that you never lifted a finger nor spent a dime to produce. We're going to soak the millers thirty cents a bushel and twenty-eight of that will come to you. Three hundred times twenty-eight cents is eighty-four dollars you'd get in a government check after I'd been out to verify your acreage for you. Eighty-four dollars is almost as much as some of you netted this year from your *entire* crop, isn't it? And twenty-eight cents a bushel is more than you *netted* this year, isn't it?"

"You know all the answers!" somebody yelled. "Tell them to my landlord!"

"We know that's a problem. We hope we can convince you to try to show your landlords that this is the best approach for all of you."

"*You're* right down there next-door neighbor to *my* landlord," George said. "*You* tell him! You send your little booklets on over to *him*."

Finnegan was trying to shout over them all. "Now that I've given you this outline and this example, are we ready to get down to a real study of the contracts? I'll pass them out to you so you can follow along with me."

As he came down the aisle, Lester started in on him again. "I want to know how much acreage the Guardian Trust Company is going to cut and why they ought to get any tax money at all for running a bunch of farmers off their land."

"Let's not worry about the Guardian Trust any more tonight," Finnegan snapped. "The Guardian Trust is not coming to the government for relief checks and free groceries, and the Guardian Trust does not have any bologna-grade cattle it might have to sell in a hurry!"

He was letting them have it now, after he had ignored George saying the same thing. This was what the little bulletin meant by "cooperating" farmers getting "advantages" not available to "non-cooperators." This was what every man who read the newspapers already knew — and they all read the newspapers. Furthermore, they all knew that County Agent Finnegan, like every other county agent in seventeen hundred other wheat counties, had his finger in up to the elbow in the administration of practically any government money. So just who was the county agent trying to kid, anyway?

"I almost forgot," said Finnegan. He had retreated to the stage after handing out his forms. "I wanted to mention some other important items. Maybe you can give me half an ear while you look over those papers. I have another bulletin here." He held it up and patted a pile on the long table beside him. "It's of interest to everybody, but particularly to the ladies. I hope you men will all take a copy home. I want to read you just a short paragraph here: 'In far too many instances the farmhouse provides only meager facilities for sheltering and feeding the family. It contributes little toward making home life pleasant. Heretofore, farm savings have largely gone back into the farm to increase production. It would be sound economy to put an increased proportion into the home. Such a course, besides raising the farm standard of living, would harmonize with the need for controlling production.' Now that's why I'm sorry not to see more ladies here tonight," he shouted over the hoots in the hall. "I'm sorry that more ladies aren't here to pick up these bulletins I have on how to brighten up your house. There are lots of little tricks here that use relatively inexpensive materials."

"Like flour sacks?" somebody called.

"And," Finnegan went on, "there are some tricks here for the men, too. I especially want to point out this little three-page booklet on an economy bathroom that you can install yourself for as little as a hundred and fifty dollars." There were more hoots.

"A hundred and fifty dollars and some labor, and you would be rid of your privy — no more of those long cold walks in your nightshirt through six feet of snow on a chilly winter's night." There was no laughter. No city man with nice inside plumbing had any right to make jokes about those walks. And besides, they weren't really so funny.

He hurried on. "And a hundred and fifty dollars and the labor put into improving your house instead of producing wheat that nobody wants would help raise the price of wheat and raise the value of your property at the same time."

"Then the taxes and rent would go up! Every time I fix up my place, the government soaks my landlord and he soaks *me!*" somebody said.

Another man observed, "By golly, I'd have to lay a new floor before I put in any of that heavy stuff. I can just see the old woman now, fixture and all, falling through into the storm-cellar."

"If I had a hundred and fifty dollars to spend on a bathroom, I'd buy a car that'd run, and get out of here," the other replied.

"Hell," the first argued, "if you had a hundred and fifty dollars to spend on a bathroom, you'd be so rich you wouldn't *want* to get out."

Finnegan had lost his audience again — this time because they were speculating on how they would use that much cash left over after simple survival. George was digging another well and installing a windmill so he could stop pumping by hand every drop of water he used. Then with the next hundred and fifty dollars he'd put in a power pump to get the water up to the house and back to the garden. Then, when he had water flowing to the house, perhaps it would be time to think about putting in a bathroom. But the water would not flow to the house unless the fine free-enterprise power company would string a line out his road. There sat Will, with his house wired for electricity ever since he'd built it almost thirty years ago. Will was still waiting, and it looked like he was going to wait a long time yet. So perhaps the second hundred and fifty dollars had just better be applied toward a tractor, after all.

"Well," Finnegan yelled, "maybe this *is* a little optimistic for this year, but it's the sort of thing the government would like you to keep in mind and plan for. It's the sort of thing you can look forward to, if only we can get this overproduction whittled down and the prices boosted up. In the meantime, there are these other bulletins here about things you *can* do. Here's one called *New Ways to Use Your Root Cellar,* and here's another — *Simple Improvements for the Farm Home,* which I know will interest your wives.

"Well, let's go over these forms, now, shall we? I have a little book here with a set of tables in it to make the figuring easier. Just hold up your hand, when you're ready, and I'll come and read them off to you."

"This isn't Russia you're in, mister," said George. "We can all read and do simple arithmetic here. And I'll tell you what little book of tables *I'd* like to see. As long as you're going to use our money to print up so many of these little books to tell us what clodhoppers we are and how we ought to go about building bathrooms — I'd like a little book to tell me how to go bankrupt and come out of it with more than I was worth to begin with, the way these bankers and big businessmen and big farmers do. All I know is what I see. I see a little guy lose his shirt and him and his family wind up on relief with every businessman in the county still trying to get something out of his hide. I see a big man go broke and I see him start up again somewheres else, making just as much as he made before. I see a Jew banker go broke right here in this town and go off scot-free with our money and make himself nice and comfortable. Now why don't you print up a book to tell us clodhoppers how to do that?"

Finnegan couldn't disregard him. There were too many approving headshakes and loud agreements.

"Well, now then, sir," he said. "I'd like to know how that's done, myself, if it is. [*Oh, it most certainly is! We all know them. We all know Harry Goodman.*] And if a little book on that subject comes out, I'll be sure to let you know. But all I have at the moment are some booklets about agriculture which I'll be more than pleased to let you have. I'm not an expert in accounting. I came here tonight to tell you about the AAA program to get farmers back on their feet, and I'll be glad to answer questions on that subject."

But nobody had any more unanswerable questions for the county agent not to answer. That was the end of the meeting. "Much obliged to you folks for coming on out tonight," Finnegan cried, "and I do hope you'll get your neighbors to come to the next one." He raised his voice another notch. "And talk about this between yourselves, and watch the *Sun* for the next meeting-time up here in Eureka, won't you?"

❦ ❦ ❦

"Well," George said to Stuart as he let him out of the car at the foot of the hill, "it was just as bad as I *thought* it would be."

"Well, I guess that's his job," Stuart said.

Somebody really must teach that boy some manners, George thought as he drove home. This was what came of spoiling them when they were little. He parked the car, kicked the blocks under the front wheels, and walked the few steps to the house. The two breaths he took and exhaled made thick gleaming clouds in the light of the rising third-quarter moon.

"How was it?" Rachel held a sock stretched over a wooden darning egg.

"I brought you something so you could get in on all the fun yourself." He handed her the pamphlet on how to install a bathroom complete with three fixtures for a hundred and fifty dollars.

"That silly little squirt!" he burst out. "I don't need him to use *my* money to print up a book to show me how to dig a hole in the ground and stick a pipe into it nor how to hook up a bathroom set from Montgomery Ward's! They send all that information with the *fixtures,* for God's sake! If you can buy the fixtures and get the damn *water,* you don't need any little book printed by the government! I just can't tolerate it, I tell you! When I think of tax money paying pipsqueaks like him to come out here and spread the rich man's propaganda for him, I get so mad I just can't see straight! It was just the way I told you it would be—only worse!"

"Well, how about the acreage-control contracts?" Rachel ventured.

"Oh pshaw! A little guy like me just can't get anywhere with them. A man like your father could retire seventy-five or eighty acres and not have a landlord to fight for the cash that was left. *I* can't do that! A man on such a narrow margin as I am has just got to gamble on making every cent of cash he can. *I* know it's not the best way to farm, but what can I do with Vick breathing down my neck?"

Then she asked what she really wanted to know. "I suppose Stuart got home all right."

"Well, why *wouldn't* he have got home all right? I let him off at his own driveway! He can't walk up his own driveway in the dark after riding around in freight cars for two years? Rachel, what *ails* you these days?"

❦ ❦ ❦

Not long after the meeting George noticed an item in the *Sun*. He read it to Rachel as she did the dishes. The Secretary of Agriculture was pleased, it said, by the response to the acreage-control program. A full eighty per cent of the nation's wheat acreage had been signed up. But only half of the nation's wheat farmers were involved in the program, which meant—said the Secretary—that it would be easier and cheaper to administer. It didn't mean any such thing to George. What the discrepancy in those percentages meant was that the big owners were going to collect tax money for doing nothing, while the fifty per cent of farmers working twenty per cent of the land were going to go right on sweating as usual.

"You know who they're calling 'farmers' in that fifty per cent that signed up, don't you?" George said. "The Guardian Trust Company. The Metropolitan Life Insurance Company. *Farmers!* Everybody who doesn't know any better is going to think that the government has gone all out to help the *farmer*. Everything is going to be just *rosy* now!"

He sat in the black leather rocking chair with his feet up on the stool in front of the stove. He'd stepped in a gopher hole this morning and turned his ankle and it had hurt him all day. Even propped up next to the heat, the damn thing wouldn't stop hurting. It made him more tired than he ought to be. He was tired and poor — as poor as ever. An inflated dollar for the farmer was an inflated dollar for everybody else, too. If he had a ten-year-old mortgage to pay off now, he might be getting a little good out of the inflation. But he'd never even got far enough to mortgage anything yet. Well, he could probably stay on the treadmill for another year. Then he'd see where he stood. He'd fight before he'd go on relief. He wasn't going to lick the boots of a Finnegan or anybody like him, nor stand in any line for any kind of government relief. There must be countless men like him — who knew their rights and would know when they had patiently taken enough.

Those other men in their lamplit houses — far-flung dots in the prairie night — a lot of *them* must be getting ready, too, just like him. Those other men, whether tenants or owners with mortgaged farms, were very much in the same boat. Owners' farms were worth a third of what they were valued at when the mortgages had been taken out, so one year of failure to meet the interest payments, and the owner was no longer an owner. In George's case, one year of failure to pay Vick would either evict him from the farm immediately or put him so hopelessly in debt to Vick that it would be madness to go on.

He could try moving to a city and going to work for the other fellow, but the government was doing its best to move surplus city people into the country. Even in a place the size of Eureka there were always displaced men sitting on the steps of the Town Hall hoping to be hired for a few hours' work. The city people were starving now on worn-out bits of abandoned ground instead of starving in bread lines. In short, the city people generally reacted like any other ignorantly transplanted thing. Still, George knew men who were going from the country to the city — faraway cities — to try their luck. It was a senseless mobility. If a man couldn't live where he *was*, how could he possibly afford to move? Yet that was what more and more millions were doing — starving and moving, starving and moving. It seemed to him more sensible to try to ride it out in a spot where he had already invested so much of himself than to join that dislodged multitude.

On the other hand, it would be intolerable to fail in a spot where you'd lived for a long time. What would be harder than taking a relief check from the hand of a man who had once sat behind you in a fifth-grade classroom? Yes, from a man you could beat in those days sixty ways to Sunday, whether you were trying to spell him down or be the first to plug a duck in the waterline at a hundred yards. Mobility at least provided anonymity for failure, and a man was compensated for the loneliness of wandering by not having to face the grudging pity of his community. Oh, he would certainly clear out before he got into any such straits as Otto Wilkes was in.

George had always thought, after it was clear that his old man would never let him off the farm to get an education, that he would at least use the education he got on the farm. He would farm this same northern prairie as two generations before him had done, and he would make good, too, as they had.

But there had been no years in his life like the early years of free land when his grandfather had homesteaded. Nor had there been any years like those when he was a boy and his father became prosperous — those years that were so good the Roosevelt administration had chosen them for the "parity years," to butter up the farmers.

The parity years — he was ten years old in 1909, fifteen years old in 1914. And those years *had* been good ones. With four boys to help him, his father was making plenty of money, expanding his farm, getting set for the killing he would make during the war. And those were good years to be a boy on the prairie, too. He had enjoyed himself. He had been old enough to be an essential part of the male brawn that it took to run a farm in those days. At twelve he had gone with his father into a blizzard he would never forget and brought back a herd of cattle that would otherwise have perished. At thirteen he had been six feet tall and could manage a ten-horse team as well as any full-grown man.

And he had been young enough not to want anything else — not to want any more schooling, not to wonder about getting married, not to worry about owning his own land some day. He had wanted only to do what he was doing — to use his strength against the strength of brutes and elements. Even when he wasn't working, he was looking for activity that would be wild enough for him. He and his brothers would each pick a steer, run up behind him, grab his tail and jump on his back. They'd twist those ornery steers' tails up into such knots that the critters would have all four feet off the ground for a quarter of a mile. They'd try to do it in sight of the house if they could. Then their mother would stand on the porch and add her bawling to the bawling of the steers.

They could ride standing barefoot on the back of a galloping horse as well as any circus rider — in fact, better, because they couldn't be bothered with well-rosined white slippers. Eventually they got a three-horse team so well trained that they could stand with a foot on each outside horse and straddle the middle horse. It wasn't nearly so hard as it looked. It was just a question of training the horses. And back at the house their mother would be screaming from the porch that they were going to kill themselves. She was as good as a circus crowd. He would never forget it.

His foot slipped off the stool and crashed to the floor. He realized that his eyes had been closed. He'd almost gone to sleep in his chair — like an old man. He was tired — even tired of his own fury. He sat staring at the hot red-black metal of the round stove till he felt as though his eyes were melting. The parity years, the parity years.

"Rachel," he called out to the kitchen, "do you suppose a man will ever be able to buy a pair of pants with a bushel of wheat again?"

❦ ❦ ❦

For three days Will lay in the nightmarish consolation of morphine hypos, curtained away from the rest of the men by the sheets pulled about his bed.

On the fourth morning the orderly bathed the limbs that were still connected to him by the various systems circulating through his bandaged middle. The nurse drew aside the sheets and he was greeted by Mr. Oblonsky. He had forgotten all about him.

"And how are you feeling this morning, Mr. Shepard?" asked Mr. Oblonsky.

Now that the sheets no longer hid the pain, it was necessary to hide it behind decent manners instead. "Much better," said Will. Once he had spoken, he lay in a sweat while the sledge hammer smashing into his belly subsided into nothing more monstrous than his monstrous pulse.

"Well, it takes a while," Mr. Oblonsky observed in a shockingly loud voice. "It takes a while. You will feel much better tomorrow. The fourth day is the dark before the dawn. I have had *three* fourth days myself now, and I know."

Appalled, Will managed two syllables in reply: "Why *three?*"

"They never tell me. Just come in and say, 'All right, let's take a little ride in the morning.' "

In spite of what it cost, Will felt that he had to set the record straight on that point. "I'll just tell them . . . to treat me . . . like the old gray mare . . . with her leg broke."

"No you won't," Oblonsky said. "And the reason you won't — that is the reason they all know."

Will was played out. "Who?" he said.

"*All* the exploiters. Doctors, bankers, mine owners, factory owners — they all know we are born with the instinct that makes us totally vulnerable. The instinct to live — to *exist,* at any cost. If we did not care whether we existed or ceased to exist, would any man in the world *choose* to go down into a mine every day of his life? That man thinks he is *alive,* Mr. Shepard, and yet he never sees the *sun!*

"These men watch their babies starve when the owners shut the mines; they see their comrades murdered — *murdered,* Mr. Shepard, by the *hundreds,* because the owners will not go to the expense of installing the simplest safety devices. Yet those owners have been able to persuade these men that they are alive. . . . You don't think that *you* can be persuaded to believe *you* are alive when your whole mind tells you that you are *not?* Wait! Wait till they come and ask you to go for another little ride. You will go!"

"No. I won't."

"Yes, you will — let me give you a hypothetical man — he is only hypothetical because he is two or three generations in one. First he is a proud, rugged, independent farmer — the backbone of the country, poor but free. Then the bank takes away his farm and he becomes a tenant — a sharecropper. If he is not too dazed by hunger to be able to think, he knows he is no longer free, but it never occurs to him to think that he is no longer alive. But then the soil is worn out and there is too much cotton, anyway. So the sharecropper must become a picker — wandering over ten states, picking whatever the exploiters want him to pick, for whatever wages the exploiters want to pay him. And he will fight other pickers for a job — for a chance to earn fifty cents a day. Isn't that a funny joke? He is not alive; yet he will kill another man in order to continue his existence. We were all born to eat each other in obedience to the commands of our disgusting digestions — I imagine you *do* find your digestion wearisome, do you not?"

"A little," Will whispered.

"But you will take as many rides as they tell you to take, Mr. Shepard, in order to keep your tortured digestion alive, because as long as you keep your *digestion* alive, you will think *you* are alive."

The last hypo was wearing off. The nurse had told him he must begin to stretch the time between them, or he would become addicted to morphine. He had thought that he had got some idea of what pain was in the past six months, but now he knew that the pain going before had been only a primer. Another day, perhaps, he could tell this man that he too knew something about these laws of living and existing.

"I think I'll have to sleep," Will said.

"I am sorry. I did not mean to get so carried away. This battle with the exploiters — it is so much more important than you know — it is my *life!* . . . I, too," he mused, "must still believe myself to be alive."

Friday, October 20

THE MUNDANE MERIDIAN that was the road rolled southward and upward, and the latitude of a fence line that began on an eastern hill invisibly crossed the road and rolled on to the west, down around the earth into the celestial meridians of sunset color brilliantly ascending the horizon. Along the mundane meridian a point that was Lucy dogtrotted almost the whole three miles between the points that were school and her father's farm. If she hurried, there would still be time to help her father with the corn picking before it got dark.

Changed into her overalls and play coat, she ran through the north grove to the edge of the cornfield where the rise of land lifted the long rows up to the sky. Her father was far enough on the other side of the rise so that she could not see him, but she could hear the sounds of the hard corn ears thumping against the high backboard he had attached to the side of the wagon. She knew he was trying to finish the field today.

She ran up the slope between the two rows of dead stalks, kicking into the rich litter of ripped husks and piles of silk. The yellowed husks were softer than they looked — much softer than fallen leaves — and the fine strands of red-brown silk compressed beneath her feet into a springy cushion over the hard ground. The cushion made her feel as though she must be bounding up into the sharp air like a jack rabbit. She had a picture of her long ears silhouetted against the skyline as she took her great leaps of alarm, scanning the hillside for the coyote she scented.

When she reached the top she saw her father just beginning another row, starting back toward her from the end of the field. He saw her, too, and waved a glove at her.

"Well, Pickle-puss," he said when they met, "what's new?"

"Don't call me Pickle-puss!"

"Why not, Snickle-frits? You like pickles, don't you?"

She decided not to answer. "Can I drive the team?"

"Just be sure you keep up with me."

She walked beside the horses and led them by their bridles. Her father twisted an ear from the stalk with an echoing crack, whisked off the husk with the help of a small hook he wore over his heavy leather glove, and then, without ever looking behind him, even while he was reaching for the next ear, he tossed the husked ear squarely against the center of his backboard. Lucy couldn't understand how his aim could be so good. He never missed once, all the way up the row.

She herself was not working hard enough, and she was getting cold for lack of exercise. If she had not been guiding the horses, she would have been running up and down the hill, ridding herself of the deadly hours of sitting at a desk and smelling chalk dust and radiators. Here was the smell for her — a blend of many smells surrounded by the cold smell of the air itself. The silk had a smell, and so did the husks, the bruised stalks, the hard ripe corn kernels, and the chaffy cobs. And there was the smell of the horses, too, and a trace of smoke from some distant outdoor wood fire — somebody perhaps was rendering lard, feasting on cracklings.

The compound fragrance meant the complex thing that excited her so much, even though she could not have said why she was excited. This fragrance signified the rush of the harvests and the sun hurrying the winter and the winter hurrying the people, and the mystifyingly close connections of so many disparate things. Here was the corn that would go to make next year's pig, like the one they had just butchered, and the corn that would be ground for her to feed to the baby turkeys next spring. This year's turkeys would be slaughtered in a few more days now. But even though this corn went to raise so many creatures for death, still the smell of the field was the smell of being alive.

She held Kate's bridle up tight under her jaw. The horse's soft nostril, lined with dewy hairs, was only a few inches from her fist and nearly as big. From where she walked beside the mare, Lucy could see only the nostril on her side, and it was so active that it almost seemed like a small separate animal. The moist breath came out of it very warm on her bare hand and wrist, and then a cold breath went back in, passing over the moisture on her hand and making it feel half frozen. Then the next breath would come out warm again, heated by all of the big body behind her. Kate's coat was already thick and brushy for winter, and it would not be sleek again until summer.

When they reached the end of a row which was still some distance from the unfinished end of the field, her father looked up at the darkening sky and decided to quit. They climbed up on the wagon wheels and swung themselves in on top of the corn. Her father untied the reins and handed them to Lucy.

"Now take it easy. This ain't hay! This is *heavy*."

He sat back on the corn, lifting up an ear here and there and working off the kernels with his thumb to see how deep and hard it was. Considering the drought, it was a good crop. The ears were pretty well filled and they were fairly heavy. Some of the corn crops he had seen this year had ears that were kerneled only a third of the way along the dried cobs. This corn was only mildly afflicted with ear rot, which meant it would store fairly well. He had switched to the Diplodia-resistant hybrid strain a couple of years ago, and the results had been nothing short of astounding. Yet now, only two years later, there were some still better hybrids on the market. His neighbors who had not switched were not getting anywhere near the harvest he was and now they were buying seed from him. Why hadn't the Ceres vindicated his judgment the way this hybrid corn had?

They stopped next to the corncrib between the barn and the house. "No time to unload now," her father said. "I'll just unhitch and leave it here till the morning. You run to the house and fetch me the milk pails." He led the horses away.

After she had taken him the pails, Lucy stopped to look up at the wagon and try to guess how many shelled bushels there might be in it. She *did* love bringing in the corn. There were no bugs and snakes in it as there were in gardens and in wheat and hay fields. She was not afraid of snakes, but it startled her to have a long fat garter snake come wriggling out at her from under a haycock or a shock of wheat. If her father saw her jump, he would laugh at her and she would know that he was thinking a boy would not have jumped. She herself knew that was not true because she herself had picked up a garter snake in the schoolyard once and scared Roger Beahr half to death with it. But with a corn harvest there were no such situations that caused a person to act afraid of something when she really was not. The snakes and bugs were all gone for the winter.

Right from the start, corn was a lovely crop. Nothing was prettier than the first bright green rows of long, slender leaves arching out against the black earth. Nothing except wild prairie roses — delicious pink Dixie cups standing up along the thin, rare briars on the barren ground, passing away too soon to have been real, but leaving the memory that they had smelled like raspberries and spice — nothing except those roses had a sweeter, more delicate fragrance than young corn. And then in the summer nothing but corn gave such high shade in its long warm rows while the slender leaves tittered and shushed each other in the wind.

Corn made such a solid, definite harvest. The kernels were big enough to be significant one at a time. The yellow stream from the spout of the sheller quickly filled bushel basket after basket while the ragged cobs spewed out to be hauled away in her red wagon for fuel or fertilizer.

The corncrib itself was a satisfying edifice — so simple, so symbolic of abundance. It was a circle of the tallest snow fence wired together to make the walls that were held up by the corn inside. The dull red slats against the gold were like treasure-house bars around real gold. When she was smaller Lucy had wondered if there might not be a little elf like Rumpelstiltskin somewhere who could be captured and coaxed to turn all the corn in the corncrib into piles of gold pieces.

For some reason she did not want to go back into the house. The night was as dark now as it would get — much darker than it would be when the harvest moon rose up a little higher. Already the clear stars swarmed over the sky and flowed into the white deluge of the Milky Way. This was like so many nights accumulated in her memory — this coming in to the little warm house from a harvest field, chilled and heroic and victorious. Those other nights before this one had already massed themselves into a nebulous yet familiar structure — a vast house of time all around her, reassuring her and enchanting her and reminding her — now that she had wandered inside without knowing what she did — that she had been here before. And the little warm house with the lamp on the dining room table called her to come and shut the door on the vast heroic house, and the regret she felt at leaving the vast house was part of the memory too.

❦ ❦ ❦

After supper that night they spread out the catalogs and began figuring out their winter order. They usually sent to Ward's, because her father had proof that Sears Roebuck was run by Jews, but once in a while if there was a great discrepancy in price or if Sears offered a brand line not available at Ward's, they made out a little order from the other catalog. It was necessary to compare the prices and offerings of both before committing oneself to the order blank on any particular item.

They usually sent no more than three orders during the year — one at Christmastime and one in the spring and the fall. For the last two years when the fall order went out, her parents had argued over whether to order high-topped shoes or oxfords for Lucy. She had worn the high ones until she went to school, but then her mother had told her father that girls didn't wear that kind of shoes to school any more and that Lucy ought not to be the only girl wearing them, especially since she lived on a farm.

"How many times do I have to say that what the other fellow does shouldn't make a particle of difference? If everybody else went *barefoot* all winter, would you let *her*, too? You're always worrying about all the colds she gets. Why not try the proper shoes for a change?"

"Oh, you always exaggerate! You *know* it's her tonsils and not her *shoes* that make her get these bad colds!"

Lucy sat at the edge of the table looking sideways across the two catalogs opened at the shoe pages. Would her mother desert her this time before the argument was won and order a pair of hideous black high-topped shoes? She stuck her thumbnail under a tiny raised piece of oilcloth peeling away from the sticky webbed backing.

"You'll just spoil her silly, that's what you'll do." He picked up the paper and said no more. Lucy had three or four bits of oilcloth off by then, and she was horrified when she realized how greatly she had enlarged the little hole that had started her in the first place. She looked at the newspaper shielding her from her father's face and quickly swept the bits into her hand. It was a good thing they were going to order a new one tonight. Maybe nobody would notice.

Her mother tore out the catalog page with the children's foot measurements marked off on it. She dusted Lucy's bare foot with powder so it would make exactly the right imprint when she stepped down on the markings.

"Just make sure you get them big enough," her father said, remaining behind his paper. "Let's try to get her through the winter on one pair this year."

"I ordered them just as big as I could last fall. Don't you remember how they were so big they slipped up and down so she had to have her heels bandaged till her feet grew? And the toes curled up and they always *were* too wide for her, even when they got too short. How can I get them any bigger than that? It isn't *my* fault her feet grow so fast. She takes after *you* and you know it!"

After the shoe ordering was done and checked and rechecked with powder on both bare feet, the wonderful noncontroversial part of ordering began. This was the year for her to get a new sleeper and a new union suit. Last year was the year to skip and by now the ankles of her underwear were nearly to the middle of her calves and her mother had had to cut the feet out of her sleepers. She took a long time to decide whether the new sleepers should be pink or blue or yellow. It was lovely to sit and imagine all that new fuzz that would soon be snuggling around her in such a friendly way.

After Lucy was taken care of, Rachel tackled the oilcloth. Only the "best" grade was shown in color and she never bought that. She always chose something from the rotogravure pictures facing the color page where the "good" quality was illustrated. She would try to imagine from studying the tiny pictures what the full-sized patterns would be like, and from reading the description what "predominantly green" might mean. They had once got a "predominantly green" that George claimed was not green at all, but blue. He despised blue. "Nobody but a Roosian could stand that color," he would say.

Rachel sighed and shut her eyes against the two gas mantles burning two feet in front of her face. She tried to visualize a new oilcloth on the table, but all she saw were the mantles thrusting like thumbs against her eyelids. Herman had some nice oilcloth in the rolls on his rack, but he was so much more expensive; even when she figured in the cost of mailing it from Chicago, she could get just as good a grade for as much as twenty-five cents less from Ward's.

There were other colors George did not like in excessive amounts. Red was all right for a kid's sweater or a pair of little girl's anklesocks, but not to look at for three meals every day. She herself found "predominantly black" not quite cheerful enough for a winter breakfast some hours before the sun came up, and two years ago she had got a "predominantly yellow" one that had turned out to be exactly the color of squash. Maybe it was just that she had been pregnant with Cathy that year, but the very thought of that oilcloth made her sick. Whatever else she got, she wouldn't choose "predominantly yellow."

The oilcloth would not have been so important if it had not been almost the only thing that ever changed in the house and if the dining room table had not been the commanding piece of furniture in the main room of the house. She finally decided on "predominantly pink," and hoped it wouldn't turn out to be either too red or too orange.

The order added up to $27.46, plus $2.97 for postage. She was just adding those two together when George cleared his throat and said from behind his paper, "How much is it going to come to, do you think?"

"A little over thirty dollars. I don't see how I can cut it down."

"Well . . . that's not so bad. Will that really do it?"

"Till Christmas it will. I don't know — we may need some things then."

"I was just thinking . . . maybe we ought to get Lucy's Christmas present early this year. She might as well get the good of it all winter. Do you want some ice-skates, Lucy? Real skates? Not these clamp-ons that are always falling off, but shoe-skates? Would you rather have them now and then not have anything much at Christmas?"

"Oh, George, can we afford anything like that?"

"She's getting big. She ought to be strengthening her ankles now, before she gets too heavy. She's got wonderful balance. She ought to be learning to skate."

"Yes, but here you worry about her growing out of her *shoes!* Shoe-skates are a *huge* investment for the amount of good she'll get out of them before they're too small."

"We'll save them for Cathy," he said. He sounded mad. Lucy could hardly breathe, she was so afraid he would change his mind. "We'll get the good out of them. If *I* say we can afford it, we can afford it." He got out of his chair and turned to the skate pages. "Here. Let's see . . . 'built-in steel arch supports . . . lined for extra warmth. . . . reinforced toes . . . hardened, tempered nickel-plated blades . . . hockey style.' That looks like what we want."

"George! That's almost the most expensive pair!"

"Now Rachel, there's no use getting a thing like this if it's going to be no good. The steel in these other blades here wouldn't hold an edge, and the shoes aren't strong enough. Why save a dollar by getting something that you're never satisfied with? This here is a reasonable price — that is, as reasonable as *any* prices are these days. If we want her to learn to skate, this is what she should have."

Lucy could hardly wait for the next morning when they could mail the letter and she could know that the order was on its way to wherever the big store was. She said over and over to herself the fine phrases describing her skates — "built-in steel supports," "nickel-plated blades, nickel-plated blades!" There might even be some ice in the slough by the time the skates got here if only the slough got some water and froze. But the main problem was the water, not the freezing.

The thing she couldn't stop thinking about, as she lay in bed, too excited to sleep, was how hard it was to understand what her father wanted. One minute he was so mad that they had to buy her just a plain pair of shoes and the next minute, out of a clear blue sky, he just got up out of his chair and came over to the table and picked out the best pair of skates in the catalog.

Friday, November 10

George planned to ship his first batch of turkeys the next day when Lucy would be there to help. Before it got too dark to see he sharpened the knives he would need, straddling the narrow board seat and working the treadle with both feet while with both hands he held a howling blade against the spinning stone. A rim of fire spat into the dusk around the side of the stone as the knife took a hot, gleaming, new edge. George was proud of the way he could operate a grindstone. He was better than most professionals even on this old thing he had assembled out of what had been nothing but junk.

His family had come to this prairie before there were any such professionals and had done very well without them. When the specialists came and built a town, they were useful, of course, but the town men, who could not live a day without the food he grew or the business he supplied, were there to serve *him,* never *he* to serve *them.* The town men lived by their specialties, he by his mastery of nearly all the things they could do individually. If he did not have enough of their medium of exchange to purchase their services, he could almost always get along without them. It would take him a little longer, using makeshift tools, but he could do it.

But that one medium of exchange — cash — undependable as it had proved to be, had become so important in the last few decades that now a man like him found himself in a paradoxical situation. The currencies his ancestors had used and he had inherited — his inventiveness, courage, strength, skill with his land and his animals — had been driven off the market by the intrinsically meaningless currency of printed paper. The currencies of his ancestors had always before added up to a sum that read "independence," a thing that no man could ever put a paper-money price tag on. Once the currencies that added up to that sum called independence had been indispensable for the kind of cosmic bargaining that required a man to fight Indians, live in a sod hut, see the grasshoppers take all of the crop that he had planted almost barehanded in virgin soil, or watch a prairie fire burning toward him across the entire round horizon.

Now his independence was the one great treasure left to him, entrusted to him by the men who founded his line in this nation and in this prairie, and he did not believe that any material reverses could ever cause him to lose a treasure that was not material. It did not matter how drastically his own inherited currencies appeared to be devalued by that worthless paper currency which was so nefariously used by Jew bankers and grain speculators. The speculators and the country had found out just how much a lot of their paper was worth, hadn't they? But *he,* G. A. Custer, still had his treasure — his independence.

Thus he would ask himself, "Can I grind this knife better than it would be ground by a city man who can do nothing else besides grind knives?" And he would answer himself, "Yes, Custer, by God you *can!*" And again he would ask himself, "Custer, is it time for you to go to work for the other fellow, and punch his time clock, go down in his cussed mines or run a cussed lathe for him?" And the answer would be, "What Custer, for the last two hundred years, has punched another man's time clock?"

A chicken that had adopted George came to grab for something beneath his banging treadle, nearly getting its head mashed. "Where did you come from?" he said. "Hasn't Lucy locked you all up yet?"

The chicken was the bizarre result of one of his minor experiments. For a while he had simply let various breeds of chickens run together and mix themselves up as their inclinations led them. After all, every once in a while a crazy mixture bred true and turned out to have some new and superior characteristics. He got a kick out of it. He had had Rhode Island Reds, Buff Orpingtons, Leghorns, and a few little black bantams. He couldn't imagine how it had happened, but although all the other chickens had turned out to be at least recognizably half and half, this one seemed to be an equal mixture of all four. It was black and red and yellow and dirty-white, and it was about three-quarters of the size of a normal chicken. It had the thick under-down of a Buff Orpington in various shades of yellow. There was Rhode Island Red on its wings and tail and Leghorn in its white neck and head and startling red eye. When it had first begun to feather out he had hardly been able to believe what he saw, and he had taken it aside from the others and fed it extra corn. He wanted to make sure it survived because he wanted to see what happened to it. Because of the corn, it began to follow him about — as though it felt more at home with him than with those whose haphazard cohabitations had produced it. It had never laid an egg as far as he knew, and he wondered if it was sterile, like a mule, or just lazy.

He would talk to it in an imitation of the desultory and witless sounds emitted by a foolish old hen who had neither chicks, unhatched eggs, a juicy food discovery, nor a laid or unlaid egg on her mind. The chicken would talk back to him and whenever he had human company he introduced the chicken and conversed with it for the visitor's amusement. It was such an improbable creature that it was like a walking parlor trick.

"You good-for-nothing freak. What are you doing here?" he asked it again. He stopped the wheel, took off his glove, and tested the knife against his bare thumb. He flicked his glove at the chicken.

It side-stepped with a mad squawk that sounded exactly like "Look *out* there!" and then came back to peck at his hand when he reached down for the glove.

"Don't you ever get enough to eat? *I* ought to eat *you!*"

He waved the knife at it. "You better make yourself scarce in the morning. I'm liable to get you in spite of myself." He went on pumping the treadle, feeling his feet begin to get heavy as the stone disk whirred against the blade.

Before he went to bed he hauled up as much water as would fill the boiler and the tub. The well was acting almost normal again, but he still felt tense when he pumped it and relieved when he had finished pumping.

As he made his trips past the turkey pen, he looked over at the dark masses of them roosting on their poles and wondered what they would bring this year. Turkeys were a lot of work. In order to have them as big as possible for the Thanksgiving market, he got the hens to set early in the year — so early that he always had to worry on a cold spring night for fear some poults would become lost from their mother and freeze to death. He would go out searching for chilled poults on those nights, and if he found any he would bring them into the house to revive them.

It was wonderful, though, to see how fast turkeys would grow, given enough food and space to scratch around in. By September the scrawny ugly adolescents had become big birds gulping down corn by the bushel, shoving and fighting each other for it, though there was plenty for all. They preened their magnificent white-tipped feathers in the Indian summer sun and strutted about so dignified one minute and so ridiculous the next. One kernel of corn down its Sunday throat would set a bird running in distracted circles, stretching out its neck and uttering frightened exclamations.

They were as brainless as a creature could be, and susceptible to all sorts of diseases. An epidemic of swellhead could not only wipe out a whole flock, but so contaminate the ground that turkeys could not be raised in the same yard again for at least three years. On the other hand, they were the last hope of the harvest year. If they were good plump birds and sold for a halfway fair price, they made up for the winter slump in the cream checks.

Saturday, November 11

As soon as breakfast was over, George took his knife and went out and scattered a little corn in the yard. He could stick a turkey the right way only about half the time. The proper procedure was to grab the first bird to fight its way to the corn, thrust the knife up through its open mouth into its tiny brain, and try to sever the right nerve there. If the right nerve was cut, all the muscles in the turkey's skin went completely limp for about ninety seconds, which was long enough for an accomplished picker to strip off the feathers while the bird was still not really dead. But after those few moments the muscles would tighten again when all life ceased and rigor mortis set in. And if the knife went too far too swiftly, then rigor mortis set in immediately, tightening around every last pin feather so that the turkey had to be scalded before it could be picked.

He missed on the first bird. He left it beating its wings against the frozen ground, circling the axis of its dead feet. He missed on the second one, too — he hadn't quite got on to it yet. He picked them both up and took them to the house.

Big as the steaming boiler was, the turkeys seemed almost too big to go into it. He lifted the first turkey almost to the ceiling and then plunged it into the boiler. With the plunge of that first turkey the smell of the little damp house was established for the long day. It was a smell of fresh heated blood, sodden feathers, filthy feet and legs, and recently functioning innards.

Until that first turkey went into the boiler, the house had smelled of the new oilcloth that had come two days before and of the top-grain leather of Lucy's new nickel-plated skates hanging on the wall, waiting for the first ice.

Lucy and Rachel held the turkeys between their knees, yanking out handfuls of hot, oily feathers and dropping them into bushel baskets. They worked fast because they knew they would probably have more any minute. As they shifted the turkeys from side to side, the long claws raked their forearms and the dangling beaks pecked against their ankles as though the turkeys were struggling to obtain revenge from the other side of death.

At noon George quit with a pretty fair record behind him. About half of his sticks had been successful, and Rachel and Lucy had only had eight birds to pick completely. He hung up his stained overall jacket on the porch and went into the kitchen. The birds were piled on the kitchen table, waiting for the finishing touches.

He looked at them with pride while he washed up. "Well, I wonder how much those swindlers'll give us *this* year," he said cheerfully. "They're certainly prime turkeys if I ever saw any. Some of those two-year-old toms will go better than thirty pounds. Perfectly fattened, too. Look at these nice yellow breasts and drumsticks."

Rachel and Lucy had spent all morning in the smell, and the yellow breasts and drumsticks did not seem appetizing.

"Look at the way their feathers have matured, too. Won't have many pinfeathers to dig out, that's a cinch."

He paused again, but no enthusiasm came to match his own. It just wasn't like the old days, when families worked happily together.

Cathy did not like being penned in by the dining room chairs and she stretched up her arms to him and cried to get out. "Oh Katy!" he said. Then he began to sing. "K-K-K-aty! Beeyootiful Katy! You're the only g-g-g-girl that I adore! When the m-m-moon shines over the cowshed, I'll be waiting at the k-k-k-kitchen door." Cathy stopped crying to listen to her name in the song.

"She wants to pick, too," he said. "She's going to make a *good* farmer. . . . Watch, Lucy, that you get that bird nice and clean. If you don't get those little fuzzy feathers out from under the wings and over the shanks there, somebody else just has to do it, you know."

He unfolded a wing of Lucy's turkey and pointed to the bluish-gray fuzz that had warmed its armpit. Lucy scraped her fingers into the hollow and got out the fuzz. "That's the way," he said. "You can get to be a fine picker if you just watch what you're doing."

By midafternoon there were twenty-five turkeys piled on the

kitchen table. Their snake-scaled legs drooped in a maze of flexed toes and spurs, making Lucy think of the tangled crisscrossings of the multiplication tables.

"If a turkey has three toes on each foot and one spur on each foot, and there are twenty-five turkeys, how many toes and spurs are there?" It was one of those tricky thought-problems where you were supposed to forget, despite the reminding "eaches," that a turkey had two feet. That was the sort of trick she never fell for, but then when she turned her paper in, it would always turn out that in all those different things to multiply she had made some silly mistakes in her tables or her addition.

When her father said her name she knew that he was going to make her get a pencil and paper and figure it all out. That was the kind of problem he liked to give her — something that had to do with the farm. But what he said instead was almost as bad. "Lucy, here's a fine kid job for you now. Mother will fix you a pan of warm water and find you a nice thick little rag and you can start washing off those feet good and clean."

He lifted a turkey from the top of the pile and laid it on the wash stand. He stretched its legs out over the pan, and showed her how the process should go. "Make sure you spread out the toes, so it's nice and clean in there between them," he said.

The ball of the gray-brown wrinkled foot was curiously soft and spongy, and her thumb pushed way into it as she steadied the toes. The toes were firm along the rim of bone on their upper side, but they too were thickly padded with skin and muscle on the walking part, and softer than a person might have expected them to be. "Make sure you wash all the way up the leg, too. Get it good and clean at the knee joint there, where it hooks onto the drumstick."

Lucy knew her 2's all too well. Forty-eight more feet to go after this one. "They sure are different from chicken feet, aren't they?" she said.

"Why sure," George said. It pleased him to have her notice things. "Look at all the weight they have to support on those feet. They have to have some padding, don't they? Just like *my* shoes are thicker than *your* shoes."

He liked leaving her with a big job like that. It was important for her to learn to work at something until she got it finished. He and

Rachel extended the dining room table, and covered it with newspapers, and began going over the birds for the last time. They dressed them New York style, with the big feathers of the wings and tails left on.

Before packing each turkey, George hooked its feet to a scale. The biggest tom weighed thirty-six-pounds — nearly three times what the young hens weighed. "Look at that! I *told* you they were going to be big, didn't I?" He read the numbers to Rachel and she wrote them down. If he got gypped on the weight, he wanted to know about it. Last year he had shipped to a local wholesaler, but the price had been so low that he decided to try this New York outfit which had quoted him a much more reasonable rate — twelve cents a pound live, and thirty cents dressed, if the birds were top quality. Of course there would be nothing he could do about it if the buyers called these birds low-grade or even unsalable. They would be fifteen hundred miles away from him and they could shyster him any way they wanted to. But they wouldn't get any more turkeys from him next fall, either. That was the only retaliatory weapon he possessed — not to do business with somebody who had cheated and exploited him. He could find somebody else to cheat him next fall.

They packed two barrels that totaled nearly four hundred pounds. Conceivably they could get a check for a hundred and fifteen dollars for this batch and another check at least as big for the batch they planned to ship next week.

George rolled the barrels back out to the porch. The birds were too warm and too well insulated to freeze, but the temperature was perfect for refrigeration. He would haul them in to the depot tonight after the chores were done and supper was over. It was already dark — time to go and milk.

After supper Lucy fell asleep in the rocking chair. Her mother came and woke her and undressed her and put on her soft, fuzzy new sleepers. It was a comforting feeling to be dressed as though she was still a baby like Cathy. Sometimes if she fell asleep in the car at night her mother would make her father carry her into the house and then she would put her to bed this way. Lucy always tried very hard to fall asleep in the car so she could have this happiness of being so drowsy, so unable to do anything for herself, of having somebody else doing everything for her. Then she would lie awake after she had been put to bed, just enjoying the feeling.

On this night it was her mother who carried her to bed, and after she was tucked in, she heard her father saying, "Rachel, what are you doing, waiting on a big kid like that and lugging her around?"

"She was so tired," her mother said. "She had to work too hard today. Those turkeys were too heavy for her to hold on her lap all day. A child her age should *play* on Saturday. Play and read."

"Phooey! She can't do *half* the work I could at her age. I tell you, this isn't the way this country was *built!* Kids her age helped make *wheat* farms out of this tough old prairie *sod.*"

Lucy lay listening to them talk about how the country was built. They both talked about it a lot, especially when they talked about what *she* should be doing. She often wondered just how a country *did* get built. After a while the song that had been in her head all day crowded out their voices.

It was a song the primary room had been learning for Thanksgiving from the green books Miss Liljeqvist passed out every Friday afternoon. *Little Songs for Little Children,* it said on the cover. The Thanksgiving song went:

There's a big fat turkey out on Grandpa's farm
And he thinks he's very gay.
He spreads his tail into a great big fan
And he struts around all day.
You can hear him gobble at the girls and boys
Cause he thinks he's singing when he makes that noise,
But he'll sing his song another way upon Thanksgiving Day.

Once more she went over all the things about the song that confused her. For one thing, she had never seen a turkey that seemed gay. And she was annoyed that the person who wrote the song thought that "farm" and "fan" rhymed, and she wondered, as she wondered about so many songs and poems and stories they had in school, why it was always *Grandpa's* farm and never *Daddy's* farm. And why did it seem to be making fun of the grandfather and why did it sound as though there was only one turkey on the farm?

And something else about the song bothered her much more than these other things — bothered her so much that she always felt a little sick to have to sing it. She didn't know why it was, but the turkey in the song seemed so different from the ones she had worked on all day. She always felt so bad about that one turkey, but never about any other turkey.

❧ ❧ ❧

Will was feeling enough better to dare to hope he would be home by Thanksgiving. The wound which had threatened to burst apart with every cough now appeared to be holding together after all. The nurse helped him get out of bed and into a chair for the first time since he had entered the hospital.

He found he had to concentrate rather desperately on relaxing some muscles that screamed for relief and tensing others that would hold him up and balance him. "Five minutes," said the nurse on her way out the door.

Oblonsky looked across the bed at him. "One becomes grateful for such small things, eh, Mr. Shepard?"

"Yes sir, you put your finger on it," Will panted, gripping the arms of the chair. It was too stiffly padded and it was a little too high from the floor for him, but still he was grateful for that chair, even though its overstuffed back felt like a bushel basket between his shoulder blades and its rounded, unyielding seat like a granite mountain-top.

"It is part of the instinct," Oblonsky said. "The only instinct that really has anything at all to do with the course of the world. The one that is such a complete handicap to most of us and such a necessary and profitable advantage to the very few of us. The instinct that makes us accept any degradation so long as we can continue to exist."

Not being a professional talker like Oblonsky, Will was always finding himself saying something that came out so different from his thoughts.

"Well, while there's life there's hope," he said.

"I suppose that is one of the most successful slogans ever used by any class of exploiters — governments, rich men, preachers, doctors —especially doctors. Yes, we are all so grateful to all these people for giving us hope to live, so that they can continue to exploit us."

Will hadn't had any idea of how weak he had become. The nurse had said five minutes. It must be twenty by now. At last she came and helped him back into bed.

Oblonsky waited till she was gone. "Ah, now, Mr. Shepard, I'll wager ten to one that you are nearly smothered in gratitude for being back in the very bed that you were so grateful to escape from a few minutes ago. Am I right? You are grateful once more to the exploiters?"

Will was too exhausted to argue; he let the words go out on a breath that was going out anyway: "You might say so."

That afternoon Murdoch came in. "Never hit a man when he's down," he said. "At least wait till he can sit up."

Will had been waiting. "Another little ride?"

"Yep. I need to do some more pretty carving."

"No you don't. I'm not going to fool with this any more. I never would have got into this if I'd had any sense."

"Yes you would. You might have held out for a few more weeks. Then you would have had no choice at all."

"There's never a time in his life when a man doesn't have a choice."

"There are *thousands* of times when a man doesn't have a choice! They would have brought you in here too weak to sit up and we would have put you to sleep and I would have operated."

"*Who* would have brought me in!"

"Your family, of course."

"Why don't you just tell my family what ails me and send me home for Thanksgiving?"

"Because I don't *know* for sure what ails you. I may know after this second look. We're going in from the other side this time. Now let me take a little listen here." A doctor with a stethoscope could always stop any argument — temporarily at least.

After he was gone, Oblonsky said softly, as though he didn't want to say it but he had to, "I *told* you that you would go for another ride any time they decided to take you. It's this disgusting instinct, isn't it? And it doesn't even have anything to do with *hope*, does it?"

"How do you know I'll go for the ride?" Will asked.

"Why do you keep on saying things you do not believe!" Oblonsky blurted angrily. He unfolded his newspaper and put it up so that Will could not see his face. Will wondered, as he did every day, how the man could read the gray blur that his shaking hands must make of the newsprint. Oblonsky was the only person Will had ever known besides George who memorized the daily paper.

It seemed to Will that today's news was scarcely the sort of thing for a sick man to be memorizing. A cloud of dust ripped up from the prairies was darkening the sky above New York State for the third day now as it passed over on its way to sink into the Atlantic. The United States Government was buying up a million bushels of wheat and thousands of bales of cotton to try to halt the falling farm prices — yes, they were falling again, the way he had had a premonition they would, looking out of the train windows at the whited sepulchers filled with wheat, that day so long ago when he came to see Dr. Murdoch. There was another farm strike in North Dakota, Illinois, Iowa, Nebraska, Wisconsin, and Minnesota. The farmers struck for higher prices while the government bought surplus farm produce that nobody else wanted or would buy at any price. Things could look mighty ridiculous from a hospital bed.

And while American politicians were making thousands of speeches to celebrate the fifteenth anniversary of the Armistice signed in Versailles, the Germans had other ways to celebrate this November eleventh. The German Reich withdrew from the League of Nations, the disarmament conference at Geneva, and the World Court.

Will had heard all this and more on the radio next to his bed. The world was as sick as he was. Why should a man fight to live in such a world? But that was the question Oblonsky was always asking. He himself was supposed to have different views. He was a grateful man. All his life he had been grateful for the world. All his life he had fought to preserve life, to nurture it. But he knew well enough that there were many things a man could do nothing about.

Every year he helplessly watched a great many things die. In every batch of incubator eggs there would be at least one that would crack as it was supposed to under the attack of the little beak inside and then look no different, for a long time, from the other cracking eggs in which little chickens worked, then rested, then worked some more. But after a while it was clear that all the other eggs which had begun to hatch at the same time as this particular egg were now broken and the new chicks were out, drying their wet fluff and looking hungry. If one listened, pressing the unhatched egg to his ear, he could hear the fragile sounds of the lonely struggle inside. It was the kind of sound that made it hard for the listener himself to breathe. And the feeling in the listener's chest made him say to himself, "Perhaps this is an unusually tough shell this poor little mite is trying to fight his way out of. Perhaps even I myself am to blame for feeding his mother too much oyster shell so that this egg she laid is too hard and thick. I'll watch this fellow, and if he is not out in a little while longer, I'll see if I can help him a bit." Then the listener would mark the shell, lay the egg down again, and go away.

When he came back he would pick up the egg and the anxiety caused by such violent motion would make the prisoner pip feebly at its prison. Thus assured that the prisoner was still alive, the benefactor would decide to free it. He would peel the shell away from the soggy thing inside, taking care not to bruise it with his big thumbnail.

The chick would lie in his hand, sometimes able to squat by bracing its little yellow breast against its tiny pink legs that would not stand up. The benefactor would feel the weakness of the stringy toes. The chick's round, damp head would droop to one side; the quarter-inch pink beak with the pinholes for nostrils would hang open a little to reveal the sliver of hard, innocent tongue. Sometimes there would be a bit of slightly bloody excrement glued beneath its tail. Sometimes there would be a smear of blood on the pink toes, but it would nearly always be impossible to find the source of the smear. Often there would be nothing at all to show why this baby was different from his stronger brothers who were already flapping their cotton wings, already bullying each other, while this one hung his head and could not keep the round white lids from drifting down over his eyes.

Not one of all the babies that Will had felt compelled to help out of their shells had ever survived. True, it took some chicks a little longer to chip out than others, just as some chicks would grow faster than others and learn quickly to boss the others around. But any chick that could not get out of its shell by itself would not live.

He looked around at the beds in the ward filled with whiskery, tired lumps of men like himself. It was very silly to compare men and baby chickens — that's what Murdoch would tell him — and he would have to admit that if there was one thing these men did not look like, it was baby chickens.

❦ ❦ ❦

It was a week after his second operation before Will got a chance to pin Murdoch down.

"I removed a second obstruction in your lower intestine," the doctor said, "and then I spliced it all back together again — as good as new, even if it doesn't feel like it right now!"

"All right, now how many more obstructions are there?"

"I'm not sure. I may have them all now. We can't tell until we X-ray again. What are you worried about? You've still got a few feet of gizzards to spare, you know, and you're in remarkable shape for a man your age."

"I'm even in remarkable shape for man with cancer, is that what you're trying to say?"

"No, I'm not. I certainly am not."

"Look, I've had enough of this. I'm just wasting money — money I've worked all my life to save for my old age and for my children. I want you to send me home — *out* of here — before it's all gone."

"Mr. Shepard, my duty is to my patient — not to his family and his heirs. There's always hope — when a man is generally in as good shape as you are."

"I'm not talking about hope. I'm talking about gambling away the last of my savings."

"It's my business not to lose hope," Murdoch said. "Of course I would never do anything that I see as hopeless. But what kind of a doctor would I be if I didn't think I *ought* to gamble, as you put it, on a hopeful proposition?"

"But I don't *want* to gamble! It's *my* money! I'm through putting up the stakes."

"But it's not *your choice*. The choice is your family's. And *they* would choose to gamble your last penny on you — you *know* that. And then they would gamble every last penny of their own and every last penny they could beg, borrow, or steal — isn't that so?"

"Yes that's so. That's why I'm simply not going to go on with this."

"This kind of decision can't be left solely in the hands of a man as sick as you are. You're depressed. It's only natural. You've been lying here in a hospital for a long time. So long, in fact, that you're obsessed by the notion that you've got to get out — one way or another. You've put yourself into my hands and now you've got to let me decide what's best for you. You're too gloomy and weary right now to have any perspective." Murdoch clapped him on the shoulder and was gone.

It was ridiculous that a man should be deprived of this choice. A haphazard clot, a small bubble of air — these things should be given more power than a man's own conscious acts and orders? Was his mind vanquished by his body simply because his mind no longer possessed the vehicle of a sound body to command? Could the condition of his body really overrule any choice his mind wished to put into action?

Tuesday, December 5

RACHEL SAT beside the dining room table churning with one hand while she held the *Sun* in the other. She rarely found time to read a newspaper at all, and when she did she found most of its contents so shocking that she wondered how anyone could stand to read a paper from the first headline to the last want ad every day the way George did. For example, the Grain Futures Administration had completed its investigation of last summer's grain market collapse and now announced that three-fourths of all the traders in wheat and corn on the Chicago Board of Trade were speculators. They were not millers or bakers or cereal manufacturers or spaghetti makers or anyone with a legitimate interest in wheat or corn. They were men who would not have been able to tell the difference between hard or soft wheat or red or white or durum wheat if sheaves of each were laid in front of them. They were men who had never laid eyes on a wheat field, but they were the only men who were making money from wheat. And they were quite obviously the only men who would *ever* make money from wheat again.

And if that wasn't bad enough, three more states had just voted in favor of the Twenty-first Amendment, which meant that the Eighteenth had been repealed. A revolting story, which she supposed was meant to be humorous, told of the lines of "parched citizens" who "gleefully celebrated the end of the fourteen-year drought" by standing in mile-long lines in a "torrential rain" in New York City, waiting to get into the department stores to spend their precious money on poison. She wondered just how much those "parched" people knew about real years of drought.

The churn was making so much noise next to her ear that she didn't know Otto Wilkes had arrived until she heard him and George on the porch. She stopped churning and listened with horrified concentration. She knew that if Otto was coming into *her* house, it meant that she was needed in *his* house. Was this the morning that he was coming to ask her to help with five little bewildered children whose mother had finally coughed away her life in the night?

She heard him chuckle as he opened the door, and she realized how her heart had begun to pound. She didn't know *why* she was so panicky lately. "Why, hello!" she said. "I *thought* I heard George talking to somebody!"

"Hello, Rachel!" Otto cried. "Congratulate me! I've got a new boy!"

Males! God save the world from males! How could that man come in here and confess that his own hideous lust had procreated *another* tragic child to grow up motherless? How had Edith ever survived another pregnancy, another delivery? He couldn't mean it. He couldn't mean that they had a new baby. She tried to count backwards and think of something to say, all at the same time. Had she really not seen Edith since it would have showed? How shameful! But it couldn't be true anyway!

"Well I *never!*" she said. "Why in the world didn't somebody tell us?"

"Well, the fact is, we thought she'd miscarry, like she did the last time. She prit-near did a couple times, too, and she never made it quite to the end, neither. But the Doc says they're both okay."

"Well, I just can't imagine why she never told me," Rachel repeated. The truth was that she had no trouble at all in imagining why. Edith was even more independent than Otto was obsequious. The longer she lived with him, the more opposite from him she became, seemingly trying to compensate for his willingness to beg. Edith hadn't been to town in over a year. She couldn't bear any more to walk into the grocery store where they always owed Herman just as much as Otto had been able to beg. Worse, even, than all the other terrible things about the Wilkes house was Edith's heartbreaking shame — the look in her eyes and the apologies in her conversation. Every cough from the lungs filled with tuberculosis was an apology. Surely now this new baby would be still another source of shame to his mother, for surely she knew what a terrible crime it was to bring another child into that house. Surely she knew that all of her children were probably contracting her disease. Surely she knew that she would almost certainly have to leave this new baby before he would be old enough even to have made his memory of her.

"Why I'll hurry over right away," Rachel said. "Just as soon as this butter comes."

"If it's just going to be a little bit, I could wait and give you a ride," Otto said.

"Oh, no. No, you get right back. I know she needs you."

"Well, then, much obliged. See you later." Otto bowed out the door George held open for him.

"How is it, I wonder," George said to Rachel, "that brassy fakes like him always get boy after boy?"

"I wouldn't know," she said, "unless it's because nothing but males could possibly be conceived from pure filth! Poor Edith! She'll never have a day of rest until she's dead and gone."

Rachel felt so ashamed of herself. No matter what you thought of people, if they were your neighbors you ought to be interested enough to know when they were expecting a baby. And besides, it wasn't that she didn't care about Edith; after all, they had gone to school together. It was just that she was so busy — and that she simply couldn't bear to go into that house unless she had to. She had a great fear of carrying the pestilence from that house back into her own. She had a superstitious conviction that she was too lucky, whenever she compared Edith's children to her own. Why was *she* entitled to have babies so much healthier than Edith's?

Despite the cod-liver oil she forced into her children and the warm clothing she managed to keep around them, would there not be a dreadful balance struck some day? Would not one of her own have to be very sick, to make up for having been well all this time, while half a mile away there were children, surely just as deserving, surely just as innocent, who had never known a really healthy day?

More rationally, she knew that though Cathy was still little enough to get most of what she needed from milk, Lucy was growing too fast and her margin of physical reserve was narrowing. Every day in school Lucy was exposed to all sorts of wintertime diseases. She did not get enough different things to eat. She got no fruit at all, and this year there were not even canned tomatoes. How long would Lucy, with her inflamed tonsils and sore throats, be able to resist the bad sicknesses that other children got?

Rachel felt so nervous that it was hard to take the time to work the butter, but there was none to leave George for his dinner and besides, she knew the Wilkeses would be out of it. Some fresh butter might tempt Edith's weak appetite. She sat down with the wooden butter dish in her lap and squeezed the pale, mushy lump with the curved paddle to get the bluish-white water out of it. Frequently she poured off the water as the lump became firmer and darker. Finally no more drops rolled down the sides of the fragrant, buttery, wet wood.

She packed half the butter and enough other food for two or three days into her big roasting pan, changed to a clean apron, buckled on her overshoes, and got Cathy ready to be left with her grandmother.

By the time Rachel had driven back from her mother's house to Otto's she was in another near panic. What if Edith had *died* while she was fussing around at home?

She picked her way through the littered yard to the house, wondering why nobody appeared on the porch to welcome her. She carried the sacks of clean towels and Cathy's outgrown baby clothes with her, but she left the food in the car till she could get a place cleaned up for it.

She knocked on the back door, but though she could hear the children inside, no one opened it. The curiously inflected voice of Irene rose above the noise, screaming at somebody to open the door. When nobody did, Irene shouted, "Come in!"

Rachel set down the sack full of towels and opened the door. "Hello, Irene."

"Hello," Irene said shyly. She was beginning to understand that her family was different, and different in a shameful way. She seemed to realize that it was ungracious of her not to have opened the door for somebody who had come to do her family a favor, and in her odd voice she made the kind of apologetic sounds her mother would have made. It was like a parody of a parody — as she herself was a parody of a younger child, so she imitated a younger child imitating its mother's ways with company.

"I didn't know it was you. I mean, I didn't know you had your hands full." She had her own hands in a pan of water, having just got to the breakfast dishes. A bubbly gray line of grease around the sides of the pan had combined with whatever soap had been in the water and neutralized it. Irene had stacked all the dishes in the skillet, which sat on the bottom of the dishpan and sent up an inexhaustible tide of leftover frying fat to settle on every layer of surfaces above it.

It seemed logical to begin with Irene and the dishes — to remove the source of the pollution she vainly struggled with and start her with new soapy water. It seemed logical until Rachel looked around. Her first look almost convinced her that there was no logical place at all to begin — and that furthermore she could never work back to wherever she did begin and recognize it as a logical place to stop.

"Won't you have a chair?" Irene said, in the parody of the parody.

"Oh, thank you, dear. I think I'll just go in and say hello to your mother if she's awake. How's the baby?"

"Oh, he's fine. He's just such a little toady. We named him after Papa, but I call him Toady." She adored the baby already, as she had adored the others when they came. Rachel remembered a girl a little like Irene who had been in her room the year she taught school. The child had never seemed to learn anything so far as her schoolwork went, but at recess she worked and clucked over all the little ones, played house with them, picked them up when they fell down — little ones who read twice as well as she did herself. Rachel had thought the child hovered over the younger ones because the older ones either ostracized her or teased her, but that was not the whole explanation. She simply loved the little ones, that was all. She probably had begun a mentally handicapped brood of her own by now.

Rachel didn't need to be shown where to go in this house that had once been so grand. She had gone back to that room for at least two other babies — the two she could hear now, fighting over some broken toy in the front room.

She walked through the butler's pantry joining the big kitchen with a hall. The hall led to a room that had been intended for a parlor or a library, with a huge bay window that sagged out into the light gray sky. In spite of all the gray light let in by the high windows, the room was still dark. Lace curtains that had disintegrated into eccentric loops hung over the panes of grimy glass like the ragged legs of insects circumambulating the sky. The wallpaper dangled in long brown strips from the wall. In places even the plaster had given way and the bare lath showed. There were dark stains on the paper, like maps of a rugged coastline showing the variations that the winds and water had traced out in the long assault of the sea upon the land.

The bedstead, its height in keeping with the height of the ceiling, was strewn with broken or twisted curlicues of tarnished brass. Two of the elegant slim posts terminated in black screws that had once held on the proud spired heads. The other two heads were still there — no longer proud, but pitted with greenish dents. A torn dishevelment of quilt lay upon the bed, scarcely more shaped by the figures under it than it would have been by its own foldings if a sleeper had crawled from under it that morning and left it.

Even the two faces in the bed matched the intricate ruin of the rest of the room.

"Hello, Edith. How are you?" Rachel spoke softly so as not to wake the sleeping baby.

"Better, I think. This one came easy. He was so little. I think I'll get my strength back real soon."

For Edith to get what she called her strength back would compare to pasting the torn strips of wallpaper back over the laths no longer covered by plaster. She would gain a bit of thickness in the skin stretching across the ribs that rose and sank over the lesions in her lungs.

Rachel tried to be light. "You certainly *surprised* us all! Why in the world didn't you tell us?"

"I thought I'd lose him. I hemorrhaged some. He's an awful thin little thing." Her voice was tender. She actually seemed happy to have brought another baby into a poverty-stricken world where he would have to be motherless. It was her second child since she had known positively that she had tuberculosis. Rachel simply couldn't understand it.

"Would you like me to give him a bath when he wakes up?" she asked.

"That would be awfully nice." Edith could sound apologetic even in a whisper. "I don't dare to trust him to Irene yet. She's so clumsy. And he's getting a little rash."

"What can I fix you for dinner?"

"Oh, I'm not finicky. Please don't go to any trouble. Anything at all will be just fine. I think there's some eggs and some Dutch cheese out there in the pantry. I made a batch just before he came. Irene can show you where things are. Now you just go ahead and help yourself before you worry about me."

"I brought over some soup," Rachel said. "There's enough for us all."

It would have been unpardonable for her to avoid eating at the Wilkeses. On the other hand, she wondered if she could get the pans and dishes clean enough so she would feel safe. She decided that she would take over the dishwashing herself and set Irene to doing something else that didn't matter so much.

She tiptoed back out of the room, took off her overall jacket and her sweater, and hung them on a hook in the pantry. Then she said to Irene, "Why don't you let me finish up these dishes, dear? Maybe you could sweep the floor and get it ready to mop. We must try to get caught up enough today so that you can go back to school tomorrow. My, you certainly are getting to be a big girl. Your mother could never get along without you, could she?"

Irene smiled with ill-founded pride. "I'd rather stay here and take care of Toady than go to school."

"Oh, but somebody your age must go to school regularly." Rachel tried to sound as though she believed Irene learned things in school. "You're a big girl, all right, but you still must go to school."

"I can't do schoolwork very good," Irene said. "I'd rather stay here. Are you going to make me go back?"

"Well, we'll see how things go," Rachel told her. Perhaps the burden of the house and children was not so bad, Rachel thought, as the burden of failure the child faced in school every day. But she was so thin she made Lucy seem almost plump. Surely, living in the same house with tuberculosis, she would have it before very long, wouldn't she?

She tossed Irene's dishwater as far as she could out into the yard. A flock of assorted fowl — chickens, ducks, and a couple of evil, hissing geese — rushed to the spot, fighting each other for whatever crumbs might have fallen with the water.

She rinsed the dishpan with some boiling water and dumped that outside also. Then she fixed some water as hot as she could stand it and started over on the dishes.

At that moment she was grateful for Irene's dullness. A brighter child of her age might have understood that this neighbor knew her family's dishes must be sterilized, but Irene was beyond noticing how differently she was doing things, let alone understanding why.

Rachel went into the pantry and saw what she had noticed before — a nearly full box of Washington apples set high on a shelf to keep the voracious little boys from eating them all in one afternoon. Even the look of the purple tissue wrappings made Rachel covet those apples. She did hope that Otto would invite her to take a few home so she could put them in Lucy's lunches for a week. Without doubt he had got them on a relief voucher. And he had got them because some Washington farmer could not sell them at all. Some Washington farmer, perhaps, who found bread a very costly thing. How ridiculous it was that when farmers wished to exchange the things they needed from each other, they had to involve themselves with such an awkward and humiliating intermediary as government relief.

When she finally had the dishes clean enough to suit her, she went out and brought in the food so the soup could be warming. Then she scrubbed the table in earnest, with the strong lye soap she had made when they butchered, and told Irene to wash the little boys and feed them. The soup was made from vegetables in her own root cellar and some canned beef. She carried a bowl of it in to Edith and supported her with one arm while she propped her up with pillows. She could feel the bones of Edith's arms and shoulders right through her nightgown.

"Oh, this smells so good," Edith said. "It just brings my appetite right back." She coughed, but not deeply. However, it was the kind of tickling cough that might bring up deeper coughs.

"I'm so glad you like it," Rachel said.

"What good bread this is! It's so fresh. I haven't baked for a week." She chewed slowly, for she had lost so many teeth.

She's not quite two years older than *I* am, Rachel thought. There were only the two of us in the Eureka Class of '17. There were no boys at all—they had all gone to war. Even Otto had gone to war. And then I went away to school. Now here we are, and she has six children and she is dying. That's how time goes, that's how life goes. Perhaps *I* will even die before *she* will. Perhaps there will be a snowstorm today and I will die trying to get home, away from this house.

"What kind of flour do you use?" Edith was asking. She might have been complimenting a friend's sandwiches at a Ladies' Aid luncheon—just as though she expected to grow old, like anybody else—old and fat, exchanging years of amenities at the Ladies' Aid.

"Dakota Maid," Rachel said.

"I'll just have Otto buy that kind next time."

After dinner, for which Otto thanked her profusely, Rachel mopped the kitchen, scrubbed the table once more, and stoked up the stove to get the oversized room as warm as possible for the baby's bath. Why hadn't they come for her before, she kept asking herself. Apparently they had had no help at all, except for the doctor, and the baby was two days old. Perhaps Otto simply hadn't been able to leave—but he could have sent one of the children. There was no understanding them. Otto was erratic enough, but Edith's pride so compounded their confusion that one could never tell why they did or did not do something. Perhaps they had not thought the baby was going to live.

As she lifted the fragile mite from the bed, she noticed how swollen Edith's breasts were. It was astonishing the way a mortally ill mother could respond to the demands of a new baby. It was either wonderful or senseless that such a woman was going to produce milk from her wasted chest.

Rachel hated to take from the baby the strength a water bath and so much handling would require of him, but she felt that she must clean him up. It looked as though he had not been changed more than once or twice since he was born, and his minute sharp hips and blue thighs were already irritated. He couldn't have weighed over five pounds at birth, and he weighed less than that now. Her own two, by the time she had come back from the hospital with them, had weighed nearly nine pounds, and she could hardly believe the difference between this one and hers. Cathy at two weeks would still turn a little blue too when the temperature changed or when she got a foot out of a bootee, but she had never been the kind of blue this baby was.

Because of his prematurity and his littleness, his genitals seemed abnormally huge and dark and mature. Any boy baby seemed overlarge to her, but this one was the worst she had ever seen. His purplish, wrinkled scrotum was bigger than his emaciated thighs. He was physically deficient in every way except one, as though that one part of him had grown first and taken all it needed before it gave anything to the rest of him — as though whatever nourishment the fetus had got for eight months reported straight to that place from the umbilical cord before daring to go anywhere else. Always and always the means of reproduction, she thought, as she made herself clean him. If he lived to grow up at all, he would be as frantic to reproduce himself as his father was. At times she found the human race almost too foolish to tolerate.

Yet she could not help pitying this baby in his helpless unconscious maleness, ruled and burdened with the desires of millions of years, bound to propagate himself whether there was room and food in the world for him or not. It was not *his* fault he was here — to grow up so miserable, to have a constant cold from the time he was two weeks old, to fight with his brothers over a mashed toy automobile. It was not his fault that he had to be here — to grow up to be so proudly and desperately male and to father, in his absurd pride, more foolish males. For males *were* foolish — there was no doubt about that. Her father was the only man she had ever known in her life who could admit he was wrong. And now even her father had proved to be too stubborn to go for help in time. She was sure of it; she spent nearly all her waking moments getting herself used to it.

But by the time she had finished bathing the little five-pound Otto and putting some of Cathy's powder on the three or four square inches of raw skin that covered his bottom, she caught herself feeling a maternal contentment at knowing that she had made a helpless baby more comfortable. She tried to tell herself that this was just the instinct in the female that corresponded to the one in the male — the one that fought and hungered to preserve life, even though the life of any sexual creature could lead only to death. But even while she tried in this way to put her feelings out of her mind, she longed to take the baby home with her, wrapped up in Cathy's clean blanket and smelling the way a baby ought to smell, of a very faint sweetness that was not the powder but a sweetness of uncorrupted human flesh — a smell of beginning humanity, innocent of the glands that one day made every baby come to smell like a man or a woman.

The little Otto was crying more earnestly than she had thought he would be able to. Everything was there for the survival of the species — not the happiness of the species, for that was totally irrelevant. Only the survival was taken care of — the outsized organs of reproduction, the bellyful of equipment for metabolizing food, and the out-of-proportion voice for demanding it. . . .

Rachel had planned to get in some Christmas sewing in the coming two weeks, but she saw that she would be spending all her spare time in this kitchen instead. There just wasn't anyone else to help. All the Wilkes relatives had sold out and gone far away and each of the other near neighbors had some reason why she could not be of much service. Ruth Johnson would be glad to come and help with the house, but she was middle-aged and childless and terrified of handling a new baby. Helen Sundquist, despite her red-faced heartiness, had all she could do to run the house for four grown men between the spells of lightheadedness when she had to sit down for a minute to get her breath and blink her eyes. Both of them would begin baking and sewing when they heard the news, but probably neither of them would be much help otherwise.

Still farther away were her own mother, who was ruled out because of a siege with pneumonia, besides having to manage the farm without Will, and the Greeders, who were afraid of getting anywhere near the disease in the Wilkes house because of Ed's own lungs, weak ever since one of his bulls had gored him. No, she was the nearest neighbor, and most of the job was up to her. It would be bad enough to give her mother the extra burden of Cathy every day, but her own baby would never come inside this house.

She stayed as long as she could. She rubbed out on the washboard enough clean clothes for the boys to wear the next day and mopped some more floors. She found two fairly clean sheets and changed the bed that Edith would share that night with the baby and Otto and his shameless lust.

Then she got Irene started peeling potatoes and making some kind of supper for them all, put on her sweater and jacket, and went out into the first skimpy flakes of snow that loosened themselves from the descending sky and flew down with the northwest wind. If they should get a big snow now, there would be even less chance of getting anybody else to help. Everybody would be snowed in for a while. . . .

How could Otto thank her forty times in one day and never offer her one of those apples to put in Lucy's lunch? All the way home she couldn't put out of her mind the longing she had to slip one of those delicious, fresh, shiny things in with Lucy's sandwiches tomorrow for a surprise treat. Rarely did she catch herself committing the sin of covetousness — but today she couldn't stop herself. Otto *should* have offered her some of those apples.

She stripped off her apron, dress, shoes, and stockings as soon as she stepped inside her kitchen. The shoes she put back out on the porch and the clothes she dropped into the boiler on the stove.

George had gone to pick up the children as soon as she returned with the car, and he came into the kitchen with them, carrying Cathy because the snow was beginning to be thick on the ground.

Her children seemed so vital and sturdy to her that she was nearly overcome by her amazed thankfulness. Cathy still clutched the gnawed spicy remnant of an oatmeal cookie. The cookie was pink with the fuzz from Cathy's warm red mitten, and Rachel wondered if the new little Otto Wilkes would ever have a pair of mittens with enough fuzz on them to come off and stick to anything else.

After the children were in bed she took a bath to make sure she got rid of as many tuberculosis germs as possible. The draft along the kitchen floor was milder than it had been a few days ago. She thought the weather must be warming up. George came out to the kitchen for a drink while she was in the tub. She hated it when he did that. *Males* . . .

In the morning she could feel the heavy predawn whiteness at the window before she got out of bed.

"Oh, dear," she said. "I wish this had held off for a few more days. I hate to send Cathy over to Mom in this mess every day, but I know I ought to be over at the Wilkeses as much as I can this week."

"Oh, Rachel, you're never satisfied," George said. "Be glad we're finally getting some moisture. What's a little snow, anyway?"

If he had really wanted to know, Rachel could have told him what a little extra snow at the Wilkeses meant — leaks in the roof, wet footprints over all the floors that she had scrubbed clean for the first time since — well, probably since she had gone to scrub when the last Wilkes boy was born.

By the time they got to the Wilkes house, the sun was rising somewhere, but it was hard to tell where. The only effect the growing light had was to extend the apparent height from which the snow was falling. Lucy's father helped her mother out of the sleigh. Her figure blurred and almost faded out by the time it reached the vague outlines of the house. Presently two small blurs emerged from the spot where the first blur had disappeared and grew into the two boys who went to school. They attacked the sleigh at the same moment and climbed up it, racing each other.

"Hey, take it easy there," her father yelled. "Don't *hang* on things that way. Where's your big sister?"

The boys crouched away in the corner. "She ain't going today," said one.

"She sick?" her father asked.

"She's gonna help."

Lucy had all she could do to make Cathy stay under the robe with her until they left her off with her grandmother. Then her father let her stand up with the boys.

They held their mittens out flat so the flakes could land in their palms and showed the shapes of the snow to each other. Sometimes an especially big crystal would land intact, cushioned by the mitten, and they could see its perfect outlines. Lucy stuck out her tongue to catch the flakes and the boys copied her, lifting their faces and shutting their eyes against the tiny, soft, cold slaps. They were the teasing hands of the frost fairies — those little soft pats — but it did no good to open your eyes, for the white little things only hid in the falling whiteness. When Lucy lowered her head and opened her eyes again, her lashes were stuck full of snow and she saw that the boys' eyebrows were thick and white like old men's.

Lucy wished that her father would put sleigh bells on the horses. She sang songs in school about the way the bells jingled when people went for sleigh rides, but she had never seen any horses or sleighs with bells. Yet in none of the songs about sleighing were bells ever absent. She hated to be missing so much. Once she had asked if they could get some bells. "Pshaw!" her father said. "Where did you get *that* idea? Why, it would drive a man crazy. Not to mention the horses. They've got enough to think about now."

Lucy could not see why the horses would mind so much. When they trotted, their harness made nice metallic jinglings, and she listened to those sounds and pretended they were bells. However, when they went as slowly as they did now, the main sounds were those of hoofs clumping into the dry light snow and runners slicing along behind the hoofs.

That afternoon they had a special singing session out of the green books. Miss Liljeqvist said, "Let's sing songs about the snow!" So they sang about the bells on the sleighs and horses. Lucy raised her hand.

"Do you have a song you want to sing, Lucy?"

"No, but I just wanted to ask . . ."

"This is singing time now, Lucy. Yes, Charley, did you have a song you wanted us to sing?"

Lucy did not sing the next song, picked out by Charley Wilkes. He always chose a song about a train — a talkative little engine that puffed and chattered about all the things it pulled behind it in the freight cars. It was a chummy engine, totally unlike the haughty and merciless engines that came through Eureka hauling a hundred box cars behind them. The song offended her and made her feel silly. So Miss Liljeqvist scolded her for not singing. "We can't always have our own way, you know, Lucy. We must sing each others' songs. How would *you* like it if *Charley* wouldn't sing 'Jingle Bells'?"

"I wouldn't *care!*" Lucy flung out.

She had to sit up in the corner by the blackboard while the rest of the singing went on. When school was out, Miss Liljeqvist stopped her as she went into the cloakroom.

"What was it that you wanted to ask, Lucy?"

Lucy looked at the floor. She was afraid Miss Liljeqvist would see how much she hated her if she looked up at her face. "I just wanted to know why the sleighs and horses have bells. My father said it was a silly idea."

"Well, because when everybody had horses instead of cars, the bells took the place of horns. I can't think of any other reason, Lucy."

"Not just because people liked them?"

"Oh . . . probably not. There had to be a reason. Is that all you wanted to ask?"

❧ ❧ ❧

As soon as she and the Wilkes boys opened the door of Herman Schlaht's store, she heard her father's voice, loud in argument, and Zack Hoefener's louder, gruffer voice interrupting her father's voice. She couldn't imagine how anyone could have the courage to interrupt her father, and it always astounded her when somebody did. She could tell they were going to wait a long time for him and she went to stand by the candy counter. James and Charley stood beside her.

Zack had once said to George, "I'd vote for a yellow dog if he was a Republican," and George had never forgiven him for that. Whenever people asked George if he was a Republican or a Democrat, he would feel more insulted than if he had been asked if he were a jackass or a billy goat. And so he always felt duty-bound to argue with Zack because Zack was so grievously wrong. And besides, Zack had a way of putting things that made George feel his entire destiny depended on the outcome of the argument.

"Men like *me,*" Zack said, "are paying taxes to keep men like *you* in business. I don't see the sense of that. If a man needs a subsidy in a business, he ought to get out and go into some other business. You don't see tax money subsidizing the *hardware* business, do you? You don't see *us* getting no subsidies, do you?"

"What do you call a *tariff!*" George roared. "If *that* ain't a subsidy to a bunch of American manufacturers and storekeepers just like you, I don't know what it is. You wreck our export markets so nobody over there has any dollars to buy *wheat* with, and then you talk about how you haven't got any *subsidy*. The *tariff* is the biggest cockeyed subsidy I ever heard of!"

"Pshaw! What good would it do *you* if other countries had a few American dollars from selling their cheap stuff over here? I tell you, in the first place, they've got their *own* farms going again, and in the second place they'll *always* be able to buy cheap wheat from somewheres. They won't need one single American dollar to buy more wheat than they can eat. Whenever a country gets a bumper crop, it's going to dump, and I don't give a damn how many agreements the brass hats sign on the dotted line. A couple years ago it was the *Roosians* and the *South Americans* that dumped. Now this year the *Australians* are gonna dump. I tell you, there's just too many of you farmers that won't admit you're licked and *quit* growing *wheat!*"

"You don't know what you're talking about! If there's too much wheat, just tell me why men are standing in line all day long for a piece of bread!"

"Because they don't want to get out and *work,* that's why! Not because there ain't enough wheat to make bread for them! This country has been having wheat surpluses ever since we got reapers and thrashing machines. Comes a little boom or a war or a drought somewheres and the prices go up and everybody and his brother starts raising wheat. Then there's so much wheat the bottom falls out of the market again. And every time the bottom falls out you think the *government* ought to buy your wheat if nobody else will. Phooey! It'd be better if you was just to take pure relief till you could get offa the farm and into some other kind of work."

"How'd *you* like it if a war come along and the government pushed a couple million men into *your* business alongside of *you*, and then when the war was over, somebody comes along and says, 'Well, Zack, there's too many of you guys in the hardware business. Why don't you just quit and go on relief?' Why I oughta bust you right in the snoot! Don't tell *me* to go on relief!"

"I tell you, you little guys are just not going to make it. When are you going to buy a tractor, George, and a combine?"

"I'll buy one! And I won't buy it from *you*, neither — not if I have to drive it all the way back from Chicago at five miles per hour!"

"Wait! I wasn't done! I'm in the machinery business and I know something about it! There's a million tractors in this country now, and there's going to be a lot more. A million tractors and six million farmers, and the million men with tractors can do as much work as the other five million men and their horses and mules all put together. And those men with tractors are going to put the rest of you guys out of business, and — no, wait! I'm not done yet!

"Here's another thing that never seems to dawn on you guys. Fifteen years ago it took millions and millions of acres just to feed all the horses and mules in this country. Now everybody's got a car. Cars, trucks, tractors, airplanes — who the hell needs *horses*? Who the hell needs oats and hay? But what do *you* guys do? You find out you got only ten per cent of the market for oats you used to have — you can only sell so many oats to the Quaker Oats Company — so you put all that extra acreage into wheat. There just ain't that many human beings to eat it up! And if *you* get a tractor, you'll do the same goddamn thing! You'll decrease your feed acreage and put it into wheat. Now just where will *that* get us?"

"I'll *tell* you where it'll get us! The wheat I'll raise will get these starving miners enough to eat for the first time in their lives and it'll get *me* some coal at a decent price. Right now those men are getting *twenty-three cents* a ton to bring coal out of a broken-down death trap, and *I'm* paying *nine* dollars for that same ton of soft coal! And right now those men are watching their little kids bleed to death because they haven't got *bread* to give them. Their kids are so hungry they go dig roots out of the ground and eat dirt and stuff that rips their insides out — they bleed right out of their guts till they finally die some night — hundreds of them — thousands of them! Don't talk to *me* about a wheat surplus! And one of these days those miners are going to figure out that there's no such thing as a wheat surplus nor a coal surplus and they're going to start fighting back. And once we all let a little blood out of you *middlemen* — then we won't hear about these *surpluses* any more!"

"Who's gonna let the first blood out of *me,* huh, George? Who?"

"Take it easy!" Herman yelled.

"Who's gonna start it, huh, George?"

"I might start it! I might start the whole damn war with one pigheaded, beer-bellied storekeeper just like you!"

"Take it easy!" Herman cried again.

"Pshaw! Get ten men like *you* together, Custer, and you'll all kill each other! Like old Jay Gould said, 'I can pay one half of the working men to go out and kill the other half.' Well, that's *you,* George. Who's gonna be left to fight this big war of yours?"

"Take it easy!"

"All right, Hoefener, if all us little men kill each other, who's gonna be left to buy your lousy overpriced nails and screwdrivers any more? Just how long are you gonna stay in business, even if nobody *does* let the moonshine out of your belly with a bowie knife?"

"Take it easy!"

"*I'll* stay in business as long as I've got my franchises! I make my money selling John Deere and International Harvester — not rivets! I still say, when are you gonna buy a tractor?"

"Maybe I'll just *take* a tractor, Zack. Maybe I'll just tear you up in little pieces right now and walk on over there and *take* one."

"Custer, aren't you ever gonna take these *kids* home?" Herman shouted.

George turned and saw them standing by the candy counter. When had *they* come, anyway?

"Well, just remember this," he told Zack. "If I get beat out of work I've put in on Vick's farm out there, watch out! If I have to get out, so will a lot of other men just like me. Just look out for us. Just look out."

"You'll kill *each other!*" Zack retorted.

George had the door open before Lucy and the boys understood that he was ready to go. Lucy had been in the store before when her father got very mad, but she had never heard him tell another man that he was going to knock him down. Her ski pants seemed to have no legs in them. She seemed to be all wool from the waist down. Her woolen legs would hardly carry her toward the door where her father stood boiling with rage.

"We're gonna hoof it tonight," he snapped. "Get a move on." He left the door in her hands and was suddenly ten feet ahead of them.

"Shake a leg, I said! It'll be pitch dark in just a jiffy now." He was twenty feet ahead.

James was Lucy's age, in the third grade, but Charley was barely six. He was afraid of the dark. He reached for his brother's hand. "He talked too long," he whispered.

"Now don't waste your breath *jawing* at one another!" he shouted back at them. "Just save it for hiking. Everybody walk in my tracks, now, and I'll tromp you a path. That's the way the Indians did it — everybody single file — braves first, women and children afterward — every person made it a little easier for the fellow behind. Come on now."

But no matter how he shortened his stride, they still fell farther and farther behind. The snow seemed to be falling harder and harder, and Charley began to whimper. He would not let go of James's hand and they were having a hard time walking single file.

"For Pete's sake," said George, "a big boy like you don't need to hang on to anybody does he? *That's* what's slowing you down. You ought to be walking straight, Indian file, like I told you."

Charley did not say anything — just sniffled wetly. James said, "He's only just in the first grade and he ain't never had to walk it in the snow. We always just stay home when it snows."

"Phooey, *I* walked it in the first grade, and I never *cried* about it either," Lucy said. She hoped her father was noticing that boys cried at least as much as girls did, and that boys were not necessarily even as strong or as brave as girls.

But her father told her, "Well it don't help any for *you* to light into him does it? Just let him be. Come along now."

Lucy kept up. She was panting and her throat burned with the cold air. Her head was sweating under her heavy cap. But she kept up, and the boys fell behind again. Charley turned into a real crybaby. All he said was, "It's too dark! It's too dark!"

"Dammit! We'll *never* get home at this rate. Come *here!*" Her father squatted in the snow in front of Charley. "Wipe your nose and then climb on my back."

Lucy thought of how her father never would carry *her*, no matter how tired *she* ever got, and she just couldn't understand it. Now her father was carrying a boy he didn't even seem to like. And he always said boys were tougher than girls. Was he carrying Charley because Charley was being a crybaby or because he was a boy or what? She felt the sissy lump get big in her throat and tears in her eyes, but she shook her head and ground her teeth and stopped it. By the time she was Charley's age she had already learned how not to be a crybaby, *that* was a cinch!

The only thing to do was to try even harder, and to hope that James would not be able to keep up even when he didn't have Charley for an excuse. That would show her father that *all* boys were not stronger than *all* girls of the same age.

She kept up so well that when her father had to stop and wait for James, she bumped into his legs. "For goodness sakes, Lucy! Watch where you're going," he told her.

She hardly heard him. She felt like the Little Match Girl. She often felt like her, because they were both in the same trouble—nobody cared what happened to either one of them. The poor Little Match Girl, all alone on the bitter-cold New Year's Eve, all the rich people hurrying past, too busy and too cold to notice the little girl or buy her matches. The little girl sitting down on the steps of a house to get in out of the wind, striking her matches to try to warm herself—and the next morning the rich man's servants finding her frozen just as hard as the marble of the steps. . . .

With the pestilential Wilkes child sniffling through blood-raw nostrils a few inches from his ear, George tramped through the snow as fast as he could go. When Rachel opened the door to them, she had a fit.

"Why, *George*, they have *circles* under their eyes! Dark circles! Just as though they'd been up all night. What *ever* possessed you? You can't expect *them* to walk as fast as you do!"

"Now then, Rachel, I *carried* this one three-quarters of the way! Do you mean to tell me that a couple of half-grown kids can't keep up with a man carrying sixty pounds through a foot of loose snow?"

"You *know* they can't! You've said yourself a sixty-pound pack shouldn't slow down a strong man in good condition. Besides, Charley can't weigh over forty."

"Not in a foot and a half of loose snow I didn't! And he *does* weigh more than forty pounds!"

"Lucy will come down with tonsillitis tomorrow!"

"Well, if she does, it'll be because *you* talked her into it! I tell you, this walk was nothing! How did people get educated twenty, thirty years ago? Did we let a little snow stop us? We never gave it a thought. I tell you, this country was not built by the kind of *panty-waists* we're raising now."

"Oh George! Why in the world didn't you go after them with the sleigh? Those boys aren't going to walk another step. You take them in the sled or else they'll have to stay here all night and you'll have to walk over and tell Edith they're all right."

"Rachel, the horses were all clear at the other end of the place, in the lee of the strawstack, and they'd never hear me whistle in the snow. Why, in the time it would have taken me to walk down there and get them and bring them back in here and harness up, I could walk in to town, so that's what I did. Why, it's not more than two miles as the crow flies. That's no distance at all!"

"It's *plenty* of distance when your legs are so short that you sink clear down to your knees with every step you take! The horses have come in now. I went down and let them in the barn a little while ago."

Oh, how stubborn she could look when she felt like it! Just like her old man. George tramped out of the kitchen to go down and harness up two horses to haul a heavy sled a quarter of a mile diagonally across his fields and another quarter of a mile back. It certainly beat the devil, the way everybody had to go out of his way for a deadbeat and his family.

Monday, December 25

On Christmas Day they ate an early lunch and then they all drove up to the hospital. The right rear window of the Ford had got cracked during the summer and George had taken it out for fear it would shatter. When it got too cold to go without something there, George fitted a piece of plywood into the window. Stuart found himself sitting next to the plywood, and by the time they had gone five of the seventy miles he was wondering how he was going to make it the rest of the way.

His mother was sitting next to him. His eight-year-old niece was on the other side of her. His sister sat in the front seat with his brother-in-law. She was holding his infant niece. His infant niece was the only one in the car with anything to say. She made sounds continually. Sometimes the sounds rose in pitch and then his sister let the baby jump on her lap and chew her finger and search through her purse. Sometimes the sounds were simply fizzy experiments the baby made with the wetness on her lips — his sister had explained that the baby drooled so much because she was teething. Sometimes the sounds had an earnest variety and inflection that was nerve-wracking — as though the baby was trying to say something that was very important to her that nobody would ever know about because she would have forgotten what it was by the time she knew the words to use.

It was these last earnest sounds that got him down. He couldn't get out of the notion that he ought to be listening and trying to figure out what she wanted to tell somebody. He'd never been around kids much; maybe that was why they got under his skin sometimes. He could never just not listen when some little three-year-old was jabbering at him; he always felt as though he had to try to make something out of it.

The dark plywood so neatly varnished by his brother-in-law was like a hand over his right eye. He wanted to shove his fist through the plywood the way he would have struck the hand away from his eye. He was getting a funny tight feeling across the top of his head, as though a line was being drawn over the center of his scalp and all the right side of his skull was going numb because of the blindness of his eye. He couldn't quit rolling and pushing that eye to try to glimpse something out of the corner of it and get over being blind.

Looking through the windshield between his sister and his brother-in-law, he saw that they were just coming into Medina. Good God! Fifty-eight more miles! The snow was deep along the highway — drifted way up behind the snow fences.

"Well, it looks like Old Man Winter is finally here, don't it?" his brother-in-law said.

If *he* started talking, Stuart knew he'd never make it. He'd open this dark door and leap out of this thirty-mile-an-hour trap and light out across the snow, even if he got a broken leg. Nobody answered his brother-in-law's question. After a while, when he moved his arm because of a cramp in his shoulder, he realized he'd been sitting there with his elbow ready on the door handle for a long time.

He'd been up to see the old man before they took the third whack at him, and he looked bad enough then. What was he going to look like now? It must be cancer. What else did they go slicing into a man three times for?

The old man was going to die, wasn't he? Soon. And yet, by God, there was the old lady praying to some God-damn God morning, noon, and night. Before every meal, praying "Thy kingdom come, Thy will be done," all the while her *husband* was up there in Bismark being a guinea pig for some small-town quacks. It was all a man could do to eat a meal after his mother got through with her praying.

When he found himself at the hospital steps, he couldn't understand how he had got there. Hadn't he thrown himself out of the car back there along the highway somewhere? *Now* where could he go? There wasn't anywhere to go now but up to look at an old, old man that had been his father — the strongest man in the world. He'd *always* been the strongest man in the world, God-damn it all. Not even the God-damn brother-in-law could do some of the things he'd seen his old man do — even when his old man was ten years older than the brother-in-law was now.

What was he supposed to *say* to the old man now, anyhow?

Rose sat down in the hard white chair by Will's bed. Rachel had gone to find a rest room where she could change Cathy and feed her.

Oblonsky said urgently, "Take *my* chair!" George looked at Stuart.

"Take it," Stuart said. "I'm sick of sitting."

Will wondered if Stuart was about to go off again. He'd stayed clear of the stuff all this time. But the tone of his voice was so dead. It was a bad sign.

George took the chair. "Much obliged," he said.

"That's a fine little girl you have there," Oblonsky observed.

"I reckon she'll do," George said.

"You do not believe in praise for children?"

"Well, you sure don't do a kid any favor by spoiling him, that's a cinch! A kid grows up and it's dog eat dog. The sooner a kid finds out how it is, the better chance he's got."

"Ah, another good capitalist. You believe in the dog eat dog system even if *you* are the dog that is eaten?"

"I don't *expect* to be eaten!"

"You expect to eat somebody else?"

"No! That ain't what I said! I just said I wasn't going to be the *underdog*, that's all!"

"But you think the *system* you call free enterprise is a good one."

"Why sure I do. It's been ruined by racketeers and rich politicians, that's all. We just need to get back to what we had when this country was first started."

"I see. When the only dogs that were eaten were the Indians who happened to be living here when your ancestors came."

George stood up and replaced the chair by Oblonsky's bed.

"We don't need any *foreigners* to come over here and reap all the benefits of living in this country and then tell us all about what's wrong with it. Much obliged for the use of the chair."

The nurse rushed in. "*Mr. Oblonsky!* You *must* not start shouting arguments! Imagine! Even on Christmas Day!"

George knew well enough that *he* was being bawled out too. If Oblonsky had been fifteen years younger and in normal health, he would have mopped the floor with him.

"Mr. Oblonsky and I have had some good conversations," Will said into the silence of the ward. . . .

The gray window behind a wreath of Minnesota evergreen was growing darker. The smells of food arriving in the hall mingled with the smell of disinfectant already there. Christmas dinner was coming earlier than regular dinners. The nurse brought in the first tray, decorated with a tiny Christmas tree in a red stand. Made in Japan, George thought.

When the nurse came to Oblonsky, she asked if he would like her to pour his cream.

"I don't need any help from *your system!*" he cried. But his hand shook terribly. Lucy was fascinated and awe-struck to see how his hand shook. She had never seen anything like it. He dumped cream all over his tray, and he swore and swore.

"Well," George said. "Time we get a bite to eat and one thing and another — those old cows'll be wondering where the heck we are — so, better say Happy New Year and be on our way, I reckon."

People always moved when George spoke. Will was grateful to see Stuart helping his mother with her coat. The boy could be so mannerly when he wanted to. There was simply no understanding him.

Lucy remembered the clever way her town friends had all yelled goodby at school before Christmas vacation started. "See you in nineteen thirty-four!" she said.

All the while they were in the room, all the while they walked down the halls, Stuart knew it would come to him. He would be able to say something so plausible that they would have to let him go — go on some plausible errand for his father, go to see an old friend, go . . . go somewhere, somewhere that would take too long so that he could not go back with them, go, *go* —

They were outside the hospital, his mother had hold of his elbow, she was slipping him a bill, she was whispering like a mad goose in his ear, "Now I want *you* to get the check," and she was flitting ahead of him in that way she had. "Now, George," she was saying, "I know a reasonable little place to go — just down the street where they wait on you right away and the food is good and clean. And I just want you to order whatever looks *good* to you, now, and let *us* take care of it. After all, *you* transported us up here and now it's *our* turn."

I can outrun them all, if it comes to that, Stuart thought. If it comes to that. But it never came to that. No plausible thing to say came either, and he was sitting with them in the Hospital Café, looking at a menu that said GREETINGS OF THE SEASON across the top. His brother-in-law ordered beef stew.

"Out of a can," his brother-in-law said when it came. He sniffed it as though it were carrion. "They just hang a piece of suet on a string over a forty-gallon-kettle at the Libby factory down in Argentina, and then they boil some dried-up old carrots and spuds in the kettle and call it — watch that *kid* there!"

His niece had almost got a fist into his mother's coffee. People were starting to look at them because of the loud rube things his brother-in-law said. When the meal was over, he could find nothing but pennies in his pockets. "Mom, have you got two bits for a tip?" he said.

"*Tipping!* That's for *Frenchmen!* It's not American," his brother-in-law said. "Over *here* we believe in paying a man what he's worth and letting it go at that. We don't believe in making a fellow toady to us to get paid for what he does."

Maybe he would fight his brother-in-law now, and then he would have a plausible reason not to ride another seventy miles in his car. "If we don't tip, the waitress just loses out, that's all," Stuart said. "She doesn't make any wages. If you want to pay what she's worth, then we ought to give her a dollar just for cleaning up after the baby."

"If *no*body tipped, then they'd have to start paying a fair wage!" George said loudly.

"Yes, but everybody *does* tip, so we have to do it the way everybody else does."

"Says *you* and how many *other* guys! I never do *anything* just because everybody else does!" His brother-in-law grabbed up the check and was gone with it.

Now the problem was not how to get away from his family, how to get out of Bismarck, how to get far away from North Dakota — it was how to escape from the Hospital Café. Even the car with the boarded-over window had not been this bad. How was it that no matter where he was, he always felt like somebody had hold of him by the hind leg? If it wasn't his mother, it was his brother-in-law. If it wasn't a damned schoolteacher, it was a doomed father. If it wasn't a car with a board for a window, it was a circle of grinning people and a mad waitress. If it wasn't a field with a fence around it, it was a field *without* a fence around it. . . .

For a long time nobody said anything in the car. The baby was asleep and everybody wanted her to stay that way.

Finally Rachel said, "My, I'm so happy that Dad has that interesting man for company. It's wonderful to have some help to keep your thoughts occupied when you're lying in a hospital day after day."

George was wounded. How could his own wife go out of her way to say something flattering about an old fool that had managed to involve him in a scene? Where was her sense of loyalty? "Rachel, are you talking about that hare-brained old Wobbly?" he exclaimed. "Why he's as crazy as a bedbug!"

A joyful flash of understanding exploded in Lucy's mind. So *that* was what ailed that shaking man! He didn't have leprosy or something dreadful and catching like that after all! He was just a Wobbly.

Monday, January 1, 1934

No matter how fast Lucy was running when she banged open the door from the icy bedroom, the cat always caught her. Every morning he waited for her. He would spring up, hook his claws into the seat of her sleepers, and skid on his hind legs — still hanging on to her — all the way across the dining room linoleum.

And every morning it made her mother laugh when she came jumping into the kitchen with Puff hanging on behind. This morning her mother laughed and then said, "Happy New Year!"

"Happy New Year!" Lucy said, wondering what a person did to make herself feel as though one piece of time was all gone and another piece was just beginning. She wondered if she would feel more different this morning if she had been allowed to stay up last night the way the town kids did — until twelve o'clock when the number changed. She wondered if seeing the clock hands on top of each other over the twelve was the way a person recognized that she was now living in a new number — in 1934. She was sure that staying up till midnight on just any old night, let alone New Year's Eve, would be exciting in some way that she couldn't imagine, but her father had made her quit begging about it. When she was *ten,* he said, then she could stay up till twelve o'clock on New Year's Eve.

Staying up late was the only thing she could think of that would make New Year's any fun. Otherwise all it meant was that school started again on the next day. She had one last day to play in the snow instead of sitting in a desk.

The snow was banked up against the south side of the house clear up to the eaves. Lucy would lie in her bed at night and think of that snow way above her on the other side of the wall. It made her feel like an Eskimo. The day after Christmas her father had dug her an Eskimo cave in the bank, leaving benches of snow around the walls and a square platform in the center for a table. The snow had been a lot deeper when he was a boy, he told her — much higher than it ever got now, not to mention a lot cleaner.

There was another bank in the yard that came nearly to the top of the clothesline post nearest the house. The clotheslines crossed the yard at a different angle from that followed by the bank down the hill so about half the lines were usable. Today was washday and she and her mother had a race every time her mother finished hanging up the batch of clothes she carried out in Cathy's oblong bathtub. Her mother sat in the tub and she rode her sled. They used the top of the buried clothesline post for a starting place and pushed off for the barn with all their might. The trouble with her mother's tub was that it wanted to go round and round, but Lucy had her own handicap, too, because her steering bar was broken. All in all, they had some fairly even races.

After the clothes were hung up, they took a dish and the tin sugar scoop and dug until they found some clean snow. They mixed it with cream, sugar, and vanilla, and set it out in a snowbank to freeze again. It was good ice cream as far as the taste went, but this year it was the grittiest it had ever been. No matter how many spots they tried, the snow always had dust in it.

For weeks there had been continual strong wind, and it had long since bared the high spots in the plowed fields. It used the burning hard snow to rub off the layers of frozen dust and then it used the particles of dust to wear away more dust and then it drove those black particles all through the snow. The wind scooped canyons that widened from shallow V's into troughs two feet deep, and every canyon was black along its floor. A thousand wavelets ribbed the sides of each narrow curving dune and along the crest of every wavelet the wind had left its black pencil line.

Lucy was sorry to see the dust come and sully the great clean world. When she lay on a dome of snow to peer into the hollow beneath its summit, or turned on her back to make a snow angel, she smelled the drought of the summer. It was the odor of heat and labor and loneliness and it was stronger than the cold, thin fragrance of the snow. . . .

The waves rolled on over the prairie, ebbing and flowing in patterns without meaning to her because she had to view them from such a little height over such a great distance. The patterns had meaning only to the wind high over them all and to the hidden stratagems of the undulating earth below. Ruled like the sea and the desert by contours of air and land, the snow was both kinds of wasteland, besides being its own kind. Sometimes it was a desert, and she hid in the grooves under the dunes while a hostile caravan passed by without ever suspecting that she was there. Sometimes the dog followed her trail into the wilderness and sniffed her out with the mad excitement of a hungry beast.

Sometimes it was the sea, and she was Jesus walking over the water to the sinking disciples. She could see them there, far away, disappearing and reappearing between the waves. She would run then, forgetting that all she had to do was say, "Peace, be still," and leap from wave to frozen wave, altering her direction without realizing it as the currents of the waves changed, so that when she stopped running she did not know where she had started from or where she had last seen the fishermen's boat or where she had left the shore behind her.

Sometimes it was a glacier and she was terrified little Gluck, slipping and clambering across the black ice while the torrents gurgled and howled beneath her and the splintered ice-people looked with their tortured faces and filled the air with screams and moans. But when she got to the top of the mountain and stood over the headwaters of the Golden River, she was cruel Hans, casting the stolen holy water into the river, feeling the icy chill shoot through her limbs, staggering, shrieking, falling into the river as it rose wildly into the night and gushed over THE BLACK STONE.

Or it was the miles-deep glacier that had once surmounted this land to press the dinosaur bones down into the ground and swallow up the long-haired mammoths. She was the solitary creature on it — misplaced there so many ages before it was her turn to live.

Monday, January 8

EIGHTEEN THOUSAND dairy farmers in the Chicago milkshed began the new year by dumping six hundred thousand quarts of milk to keep it out of the city in protest against the low prices there. The Supreme Court of the United States upheld a Minnesota law that provided for a moratorium on mortgage foreclosures.

It seemed to Will that the new year already looked very much like the old year. It wasn't just that three rides had left him knowing exactly where he stood. It was partly that he'd had time to do a lot of thinking. And he had to admit it, Oblonsky had forced him to think in some ways that he had never thought before. And all of his thoughts and all of Oblonsky's words added up to an overwhelming conviction that things were going to get worse for the small farmer, no matter how many moratoriums were proclaimed by vote-seeking governors, be they Republican, Democratic, or Progressive. The moratoriums only proved that the small farmers were now in a hopeless position. The very word simply meant *delay* — as Oblonsky said, it came from a Latin verb meaning "to delay." Oblonsky had the kind of education Will had yearned for all his life, and Will had admitted to him that he was right about that word and about what it meant for farmers. Will had conceded defeat in a number of arguments with Oblonsky, but he stuck to his guns on the only one that really mattered any more. He still believed that a man could die like a man.

He knew that he was feeling as good as he would ever feel again. He was in pain, but he had learned how to take a lot of it. He could sit up and read and he could eat enough to keep up as much energy as he needed for a while. And his mind was perfectly clear when he hadn't had any shots or pills. Now was the time to go home, and he was going.

"You know," Murdoch told him, "you never gave me half a chance."

"I took three rides."

"*One* ride taken in time might have done it. Why didn't you come in before?"

"On the other hand, why did I come in at all? Almost everything I had in the bank is gone. Let me out of here while I can still pay my bills." His mind was filled with the sight of Harry Goodman's distraught face and the sound of those words—*Lay not up for yourselves treasures upon earth. . . .* But the treasures had not been for *him*—only for his children, and their children—so the thing called life could be always a better and a nobler thing.

Murdoch held out his hand. "All right. I think I can say this to you—I think you're a man who hates waste enough . . . these rides—they aren't all for nothing. Each time we learn. And—you'll make it the rest of the way just fine. That's one thing I've had to learn how to tell about. . . . Some of us make asses of ourselves; some don't. Maybe that's all there is to it."

"Well, Mr. Shepard?" Oblonsky said. "Do you know how lucky you are to have a place to go to die? Even a dog in this world can die in private—but a *man* can't any more—unless he owns property."

Oblonsky had not stooped to pity himself in all these months. It was saddening, not to mention frightening. The man couldn't sit up much now, and his voice had lost its power, but he had found out one thing in the last week that was new enough so that he reacted with a little of the irony that had sustained him for so long.

"Don't feel too bad about the way our great country is going, Mr. Shepard. The Wilson Democrats put me in jail and took away my citizenship because I did not believe in war, but two days ago the

Roosevelt Democrats gave me back my citizenship. Now I can have a citizen's burial."

⁂

To a man who had not had his nose outside since that long-ago Indian summer day, it was a gratifying change to be riding privately in an ambulance through the walls of dirty snow thrown up along the highway. Will could leave off wrestling with the foolish hope that had kept sneaking into his mind for so long. For the moment he could just look out at the rushing walls of snow — piled so high that from his flat bed in the bottom of the canyon he could see no end to them at all. They might join the clouds from which they came, for all he could tell, and the clouds might be lying no farther away than the roof over his cot. He still could not quite manage the concept of ceasing to exist physically, and so he rode along in his white ambulance between the hovering white walls in a matching white limbo. He had no hope, nor did he have anything to take the place of hope.

He felt that something ought to come to a man to replace hope, but he couldn't think what it might be. He therefore surrendered himself to the white limbo — as though he were caught again in a blizzard like some of the ones he remembered so well, and he could be content this time not to fight his way to a fence line, but to stray with the wind until it put him to sleep.

All his life he had been as willing as the next man to take his chances with the forces he could not control, and he had been willing to fight those forces every way he could with all the strength he had. The wind and heat and hail and cold had all contended with him, and once or twice they had nearly annihilated him. He had never before confronted a force that a man could not appropriately fight. Now he had to learn a new thing — how to surrender as decently as possible.

At least he would be tortured no more by another mere man, and it *had* been torture, no matter how well-intentioned. It was not that he felt superior to any other man; it was just that he ought not to die beneath the hands of a small creature like himself when all his life he had fought the mightiest adversaries the sky and the earth could send against him.

He thought so often now of that brother who died by lightning as he was felling a tree. There beside the tree that smoked and hissed in the first drops of rain lay a strong young man who would never marry, never build his house, never beget children. Yet even while Will grieved for his brother, he had believed in the fitness of that death. A youth with a heavy, sharp axe was hewing out a place for himself to cultivate and possess — a youth whose enduring passion could not be diverted by the transitory passion of a summer storm. He had worked through other such storms and he knew how, after the sky had drenched him, it would quickly dry him again. He knew that if a man was going to make a space for himself on a hurrying planet, he could not afford to take time off to hide while the planet went about its own turbulent affairs.

And so he died in one lash of the long hot tongue — died before he heard the explosion around his ears or submitted for even an instant to the indignity of fear. The lightning came to his axe, people said. He ought to have known better. But still, thought Will, it took the sky to kill him. For a man who lived not to fight other men but to fight the accidents of the sky, that was a fitting death.

Then the seventy miles were over and Will felt his long white chariot slanting and climbing the hill to his high house. Stuart must have just cleaned off the driveway, because the tires lost traction only once before the ambulance leveled again and stopped. Will looked across the snow at the dining room window with the button-mended crack. That was the window where Rose would have been standing to watch the white car bringing him home through the blowing frozen snow. But she was out beside him now, clutching one of his old sweaters around her throat and tapping on the glass next to his face where the backwards white lettering said MERCY. And Stuart was there behind her, fitting a coat over the sweater, over the apron straps, over the shoulders that had always been too curved, as if she were old.

"Take him in through there?" the driver asked her. He shivered at the cold he had let in when he wound down the window.

He and his helper left their doors hanging open as though they wished to make it clear that this was a very brief delivery stop.

They trotted six paces along their respective sides of the ambulance, met in the back, and turned their respective door handles.

Then they were lifting him out and the wind was blasting across his face and he was trying to say hello to Rose and goodby to the wind before he passed through the portals of his house and away from the sky's last howling respects.

The covers on his bed were turned back so that a starched formal triangle of sheet cut across the embroidered spread. While the four of them were putting him to bed, he couldn't think of anything but how they were disarranging the triangle, and he wondered why in the world that should bother him so.

The men picked up the stretcher. "So long," said the driver.

"Much obliged," Will responded.

Rose pulled the covers over him. "What can I get you for dinner?" she asked.

"Almost anything liquid," he said tiredly. That had been a long ride.

Then it occurred to him that she wanted very much to do something hard and complicated for him. That was what the immaculate bedspread and the careful triangle had been telling him. All he really wanted was to have her sit beside him and talk — tell him about Rachel and the children and the neighbors. But neither of them had ever been much good at time-passing talk. They had never had the time to pass.

Now that was all he had — a little time to pass — and neither of them knew what to do about it. The limbo of the ambulance ride was over; now he must rouse himself for the last long effort.

"What kind of liquid?" she was asking.

He recited, trying not to sound too self-conscious or too apathetic. This preoccupation with his body was a repulsive monotony. "Bland," he said. "No spices, no tomatoes, no onions, no pork. Little chunks of chicken or something like that is all right. Other vegetables are all right if they're strained so there's no skin — like peas."

Rose's face took on a purposeful look and lost some of its fear. The worst fear of her life was to find herself unable to do something useful. He knew that, and he knew that his effort was rewarded. "How would it be if I opened one of those cans of stewing hens that I did up last summer when they started to molt? I could make some chicken soup in a minute."

She was eager to be doing for him — to be near him but yet to be gone from him. He knew she must have been watching for the ambulance all morning, but now that he was home, she did not know what to do. It had always been that way. The nearer he came, the more a trembling part of her urged her to flee. After he had come to understand how much she did really need him, he was no longer wounded except by his occasional sorrow that things must be this way. Once in a while he had been angry; often he had felt the pangs of his selfish lust. Now he felt his old wistfulness at seeing her ready to rush away from him and that made him realize how much he must still want to live.

Yes, he told her, he would like some chicken soup. It would be a treat to have a meal that did not come out of a hospital kitchen on a stainless steel tray.

"And will you put a little salt in it?" he added. "Salt isn't really a spice, is it? And speaking of salt — I got downright lonesome for the taste of that cussed well-water. Tell Stuart to pump me a little of it and bring me a drink next time he comes in, will you?"

"I know what you mean about that water up there in Bismarck," Rose said. She was thankful for a recent common experience to speak of. "I always notice it so when I change drinking water. It always seems to affect my bowels one way or the other —" She stopped. "Well . . . I'll go down and get that jar of chicken."

The door opening directly down on the cellar steps was right next to the bedroom door. She left it open and he felt the cold rising up into his room. He heard her fumbling in the dark to light a lantern so she could see the shelves of jars. No electricity, after thirty years of waiting. From his bed he could see two of the three outlets he had left in that room — one in the center of the ceiling for a light and the other just above the mopboard for a plug.

The dark cellar steps worried him. "Be careful, now," he called to Rose. He found that he wanted to do nothing but visualize her in whatever surroundings took her away from him. It was a way to hang on to reality, and he had been away from reality for so long.

He heard her running up the stairs and then he heard her panting at the top. "What did you say, Will?" She was more worried than ever about her hearing now.

She came into the room and he saw how relieved she was to find nothing amiss with him. "Did you change your mind about the soup after all? I could make you some good strong beef broth."

He felt so foolish he hardly knew what to say. "Why, I just said for you to be careful. I wish we had a light of some kind on those stairs. I don't know what ailed me — yelling down there at you like that. You shouldn't have run up the stairs. I couldn't have expected you to hear me way down there anyway."

There was more relief in her face. He began to see what a burden he was going to be. And every day he would be a little bigger burden.

She set up the card table beside his bed and she and Stuart ate their dinner there with him while he worked on his soup. Once more the husband and wife said the Lord's Prayer together but the son did not join them. He bent his neck enough so that he looked straight down between his knees to his damp boots and lowered his lids only as much as he had to in order to look down.

The card table had never been used for cards but it was well worn. Children had eaten holiday meals from it for many years while the older people sat at the big table, and it had provided extra space for sandwich plates and sewing at Ladies' Aid meetings. Before Will went to the hospital it had been covered with the two thousand pieces of an enormous jigsaw puzzle. The puzzle had come in a jumble of very small and very similar bits of colored cardboard in a large box, and there was no clue as to what the finished picture would look like. They had got about a third of it together before he left, with the rest of it still in its mottled pile. Nobody ever sat down and worked at it seriously; it was amusing to fit in a piece or two when one was passing by, that was all.

They had always been a family that could not ignore any game with a challenge to it, but they had never had the time to study over things very long, either. An upstairs closet was half full of dominoes, anagrams, chessmen, caroms, checkers, and playing boards, all of which got considerable use on Sunday afternoons and during blizzards. Crossword puzzles, cryptograms, acrostics, and the other teasers printed in newspapers and magazines rarely got finished unless somebody was sick in bed, but they seldom got to the used paper pile without some writing on them. Stuart especially liked them. Stuart seemed to like doing anything that required serious effort but was without serious purpose.

By the time he had finished his soup, Will wondered how he could ever have been fool enough to stay in that hospital for so long. He belonged right here, where there were some things he could still try to do — such as making one last attempt to get Stuart's energies aimed in some sensible direction.

Rose got up to take the dishes into the kitchen and Stuart got up, too, but Will stopped him. "What did you do about the production-control contract?" he asked.

"Well, we passed up the deadline, but Finnegan's been out here a couple times. He says we can still sign up. He's really been after me. But I said it was your farm and you'd be back and you ought to sign."

Will looked up at him. Stuart was in that fresh hour of manhood when a man's skin was still as fine and smooth as a little boy's. When he was closely shaven he looked almost as young as he had at twelve, with the lines of his brow and jaws just beginning to establish themselves, with the pure color of his cheeks seemingly still impervious to the weather — not one thread of vein showing yet, not one pore forced open and blown full of dust. Clean-shaven as he was now, Stuart seemed young enough so that all his worldly knowledge might easily be contained in the handful of obscenities a boy of twelve could be expected to know. But later this afternoon when the dark whiskers began to show again, then perhaps it would be easier for Will to believe that he himself was a married man when he looked like this boy.

Meanwhile, until this afternoon when his boy had aged enough to be only one generation away, how was he going to get close enough to know what the boy was saying? How was he going to know what the boy had just said when he spoke the words, "I said it was your farm and you'd be back and you ought to sign"?

Was he being optimistic? Was he saying, "I knew you'd come home"? Or was he restating his determined remoteness? Was he saying, "I am not involved or committed here. I will not make any big decision that might imply that I am"?

Handling one's children was not so different from planting a wheat crop, Will thought. A man just had to go ahead and plant, and then believe and pray that the forces he could not see or predict would be a little bit cordial, a little bit reasonable, a little bit responsive.

"All right," Will said. "I'll fill the thing out this afternoon. I'll cut the full twenty per cent the government's going to allow, because I want the cash for you, Stuart, and I don't want you tied down here. We put Rachel through college and now that you've got the gypsy out of your blood, we want to put *you* through."

"But I never finished high school!"

"Oh, you did too. You don't have a piece of paper that says so, that's all. You didn't have bad grades. It's just that they weren't perfect, like Rachel's."

"That's not what you *used* to say!"

Will felt as though Stuart had struck him. Had he really so wronged the boy?

"We didn't say that *you* should get the grades Rachel got. We *couldn't* have *ever* said that. All we ever wanted was for you to do the best you could, and it never seemed to us like you did. Did you?"

"I suppose not. I never could see the point."

"Do you see the point now? After two years of working the way you did? I'll tell you right now, *I* would have seen the point after I put in *my* time with a thrashing crew!" Dammit! that wasn't the way he had meant to put it at all! Will knew well enough that no father *ever* ought to say, "When *I* was your age . . ." Especially when the father was lying helpless in his bed looking up into the distant face of a powerful young man.

He tried to make a new start. "They have entrance examinations at Jamestown College," he said. "I know you could pass them with room to spare. *You* know it, too."

"I'd never go where Rachael went."

"All right, fine! Go to Fargo. It's cheaper anyway."

"What should I take? Agriculture? So I could be one more college boy for the farmers to laugh at? Like Jim Finnegan?"

Will reminded himself — a man had to plant — once he was committed to a farm, he had to plant. Once a man fathered a son — "Take anything you want," he said. "For heaven's sake! You're good with machinery — take engineering. Take chemistry. Take agriculture. *Farm,* if you want to, but have something else you can do too. This farm is yours, and you know it. But I don't want you to be tied to it, that's all. I don't want you to *have* to farm even if the whole blamed bottom falls out of farming."

"If the bottom falls out of farming, what good is a college education going to do me? I was just reading in the paper about how a bunch of guys in New York have got together in a no-job club. They've *all* got college educations and they figure there's ten thousand college graduates just in New York City that don't have jobs. A lot of those guys are from fancy places, too, like Harvard, and they're out on the sidewalks shining peoples' shoes. If a man with a sheepskin from Harvard can't use it for anything besides shoeshining, what chance have *I* got?"

Will had read the same papers. When Russia advertised six thousand jobs in engineering and a hundred thousand American engineers applied for the six thousand jobs, there wasn't much incentive for a son of his to go through four years of engineering study at the State College in Fargo, was there? When men with Harvard engineering degrees were waiting in line to go to Russia or to be handed a free bowl of soup?

And a man could certainly shine shoes without going to college. Will had read it often enough in the last three years so that he had to believe it — thousands and thousands of men in cities were actually trying to earn a living by shining the shoes of other men who were not so much better off than *they* were — seven thousand shoe-shiners just in the streets of New York. Not to mention Chicago, Boston, Detroit, Minneapolis, or Seattle. To a man like himself — or like Stuart — an improved, furnished, and unmortgaged square mile of even the driest land in the world looked a good deal better than a shoe-shine kit.

Was it possible that there simply was no place to go in the whole wide world? Where was there to go in America? Fourteen million people were out of work in this land. This land said to fourteen million people, "You have no place, no purpose in the world." And the cardboard Hoover Towns and Hoover Valleys in the big cities were inhabited by a goodly number of college men.

Above him stood his boy, looking out into the streaks of snow blowing between the house and the solid new barn. It would be hard to pick a worse time to be twenty years old, wouldn't it?

But it would be hard to pick a worse year, too, in which to die — to leave so many obligations unfulfilled, to abandon so many precious plantings to the drought and the wind.

If only he could start this boy back to school before he had to leave. In school Stuart would find himself. How could a man not find himself if he were busy getting the most important thing in the world — education? "All right, then," Will said. "If the bottom is out of everything, and the farmer can't get a price for anything, what else is there for you to do besides go back to school? Things'll probably be booming again four years from now, when you get out, and then you'll be ready for the boom when it comes. You'll be twenty-four years old — just old enough to have a little sense — and you'll have your pick of jobs. . . . And another thing — farming's going to take more and more capital, for machinery and enough land to make the machinery pay. And there's going to be a bigger and bigger surplus of farmers, too. We're going to be a drug on the market — just like our wheat. Get into something where you don't need so much cash and where you don't have so many other men competing for the same fat middleman's skinflint prices."

"You know," Stuart said, "a lot of other guys are sitting out this mess by going to college, too. They're all figuring it just the same way *you* are."

"They're all figuring it *right!* I'm telling you, four years from now, you won't have *half* the competition from college graduates that you will from farmers."

Stuart stretched his arms up from his shoulders. His fists clenched and worked back and forth from his wrists as though he was manacled to the wall behind him. "You want me to get a desk job?"

Will confessed to himself that it was a little hard to see a starched collar set over those shoulders or white shirtsleeves around those thresherman's wrists. It would be too bad to put such a man behind a desk or behind a window. Could a boy who had ridden in box cars for two years settle down to polite explanations of Pullman schedules to old ladies? Or could he stick out those flashing perfect teeth in a shoe salesman's smile for nine hours every day? Whether he could or not, Will would rather think of him pitching bundles. But there must be other alternatives.

"You don't have to sit at a desk just because you've got a diploma. You could build dams or look for oil or — *I* don't know what all. That's what you have to go to school to find out. If you'll just start in, I know you'll find something to suit you, and I know there'll be a job waiting for you when you get out — unless things get even worse."

"Well, they *are* getting worse, aren't they? It doesn't look to me like there's any law that says just because things have gotten bad, now they have to get better again. They can just as well get worse and worse and worse. And there won't be a damn thing I can do about it if they do."

"All right, if it turns out that one guess is as bad as another, at least you'll have an education. They can't take away what you've got in your head, but they can take away just about anything else."

"I gotta go clean out the chicken house now," Stuart said. "Looks like we might be in for it before morning. Weatherman says so."

The young man, the twelve-year-old boy, was already out of the room and into the hall. "Stuart! Don't spend your life scraping droppings out of a hen house and selling eggs for thirteen cents a dozen!" Will couldn't tell whether Stuart heard him or not. The only thing he could catch from the kitchen was the sound of dishes in the dishpan.

❧ ❧ ❧

From what meal, Stuart wondered — from what meal could his mother possibly be doing the dishes? Not from that ancient meal they ate sitting at the card table — that first meal they ate after his father came home in the Mercy Hospital ambulance — not that meal?

His mother kept her head turned away from him. She was too provoked with him even to speak to him. She was mad because he wouldn't say he'd go back to school. *She'd* been trying to get him to say it, too. He sat down with his back to her and pulled his rubber boots on over his leather ones.

He forced his feet into them, standing up before his heels were down, hobbling to the door with one rubber leg still twisted and caught on one leather heel. He closed the door, jerked his coat from its hook in the shed and pushed his arms into the cold sleeves. The cold back of it raised the tight goose pimples on his shoulders, and when he buttoned the cold across his stomach, the lump of that meal he had eaten so long ago froze under the goose pimples on his belly. And it would always be there now — this lump of the dinner he ate on the day his old, old father came home to die.

He wondered if there was any chance at all that he could get through it without some liquor. His mouth watered as though he was going to throw up, he needed a drink so much. He couldn't quit salivating even after he began scraping and shoveling out the chicken house, and after a while his throat wouldn't swallow the saliva any more, or else there wasn't any more room for it down there on top of the lump, so he had to spit it out. Back and forth he went, from the chicken house to the compost pile in the orchard, spitting and spitting into the dirty straw and the dusty snow.

⁂

Rose made the dishes last as long as she could because otherwise the tears would have outlasted the dishes, and if she finished with the dishes before she managed to finish with the tears — well, she just didn't know what she would do with herself then. She powdered her face and whitened her eyelids as well as she could and went in to Will. "Do you think we can get him to go?" she asked. "Do you think it would straighten him out?"

Will couldn't believe how tired he was. But he roused himself again. Talking made his belly hurt worse, but it was going to hurt anyway. To hell with his belly.

"We'll have to go slow with him. And I think you ought to sell the farm as soon as prices go up again. I don't want to think of him tied to it if he doesn't want to be, and I certainly don't want to think of *you* on it here alone. If George wasn't so ornery, you could figure out something — but he is, so that's out."

"I'll never sell this farm. We *built* it."

"You *must* sell it. You must *promise* me you'll sell it. You can't compete now, anyhow, unless you've got machinery. Every year these state colleges come up with new hybrids and new fertilizers — and the machinery makers come up with high-priced new gadgets to cut out manpower. But nobody anywhere comes up with any new markets. And the men that are going to make a living out of farming are the men that can buy the fancy seed and machinery and the new livestock. You can't hire five Ralph Sundquists to take the place of one of these new corn harvesters they've got. If you and I were young, and we owned this place free and clear, and the market was any good — if, if, if . . . Or if we hadn't used up so much of our cash, if *I* hadn't used up so much of our cash — you'd be in pretty good shape — you and Stuart could gamble a lot of it on a combine and a better tractor. Even then it would be a gamble. When is there ever going to be a decent price on wheat again?"

"Will, we *are* in good shape. How many farmers own their farms outright?"

"I tell you, you're not thinking right. That's the way *George* thinks. He's always talking about how he's in the top *fifty* per cent. You and I are in the top *ten* per cent, and we *still* haven't made anything for *years*. It's like — well it's practically like being in the bustle business! If you can't sell bustles, what good does it do to be in the top ten per cent?"

"People have to eat."

"There's enough wheat just in Minnesota elevators to feed everybody in this country for a year. Actually, if Mr. Wallace's figures mean anything, you and I were in the top *five* per cent last year, with a measly little net of twelve hundred dollars or so. Just ask yourself how many new tractors and combines you're going to buy with twelve hundred dollars and still have anything left over for all the other things we need. But there'll be enough for *you*, though, if you sell at the right time."

"Well — I'll have to see what Stuart wants." She said it to please him, he knew. That was all right. It would take her a while to see it.

"Can you lay your hands on that AAA contract now?" he asked. "We ought to get it taken care of."

He held the government papers on a breadboard propped against his knees while he figured on sheets of yellow scratch paper. As he filled in blanks and laid out acreages for wheat and for all the other crops, he saw the black land of his snow-covered square mile around him, and then he saw it as it had been in Indian summer. He could feel the midmorning sun soaking into the heavy suit he hadn't worn back from Bismarck after all. Then he saw it as it was in April. He could feel the air in a field just before a spring rain and he could smell the fragrance that rose from the dust as the first drops kissed it. He'd always wondered what created that wonderful smell. It was like an offering of praise and thanksgiving from the earth herself. He could see his blue field of flax blooming below the blue field of the sky. He could see all the black, brown, green, blue, and gold fields and pastures under his square mile of snow — just as he always saw them while he waited for the winter to pass. . . .

He finished the contract and signed it in writing that was beginning to show how his hand shook. He called Rose to take away the papers and help him lie down. He was straightening out his legs, slowly, so as not to use any of the muscles across his abdomen, when he heard his other child and her children coming into the kitchen.

The only thing worse than to be Stuart in these times — to be feeling the first disillusionment natural to a boy of twenty in even the best of times — was to be Rachel or George — to be losing the most productive years of life to the worst years the country had ever known. Even Will's frequent exasperation with George did not keep him from having some idea of what the man was going through.

And these children of his older child — they seemed already doomed to be sacrificed like the bright and beautiful innocents of myths. They were already marked for the monster. Or monsters. The ones who sprang from the ground that had been sown with dragon's teeth, who grew two heads for every one cut off, who leapt up stronger every time they were felled to the earth — inscrutable monsters whose existence was never quite explained by the myths. But they were there, nevertheless, to count off the procession of the hecatombs into their bone-filled caves while the country around echoed with the lamentations of their fathers and mothers. What myths, what monsters, would Lucy and Catherine have to be given to? Oblonsky had thought he knew. Oblonsky had called "free enterprise" the myth, capitalism the monster. Will could not forget how sure Oblonsky had been about these children's world — about the myths that created the monsters and the monsters that perpetuated the myths. . . .

He stretched out his hands to Lucy — his very white hands with the new green-black ink stains — and pulled her to the side of his bed with one thin arm around her waist. It was odd; he hadn't really thought about how thin he had got. Before, it was always her ribby little chest that had seemed thin to him, but when he felt how hard his arm was against her, clear through her jumper, he knew how he had fallen away from himself. He vaguely remembered the feel of the jumper. Then he realized it was made from an old tweed suit of his that had been packed away for so many years, ever since it had got too tight for him. They had thought Stuart might get some good out of it, but he was much too tall for it by the time he could have worn it.

It bothered Will to see such rough, thick material on Lucy. A little girl like her ought to be dressed in something much lighter and gayer. It seemed to him that his granddaughters ought both to wear fairy clothing of summertime things — of flower petals and corn tassels — things that would call to mind a warm wind pushing through a flax field, or the sweet, milky, infant heads of green wheat. He didn't know how their dresses ought to look, only how they ought to feel. In his weakness and fatigue, he felt a remarkable projection of his vision — a much broadened, if misty, grasp of all the things that had composed his life, from the time when he was Lucy's age through all the years up to Lucy herself, right now. It was a panorama — like the jigsaw puzzle he had gone away without finishing. All the pieces of his life were here now. None were missing, still to come. But even with all the pieces right in front of him, he still couldn't quite see what they made when they all went together.

"Say, I'll tell you what," he said to Lucy. "On Saturday you come over here and we'll work on that big puzzle all day long and finish it and find out what it's a picture of. What do you say?"

Her taut little face blazed with the smile he saw when he let her beat him at checkers or when he yielded and said yes, he'd tell a story, or when he told her she could ride standing up in the back of the truck, or when they went to feed the lambs. He tried not to think of how she would not smile because of these things any more. The important thing was the smile. Who ever saw the smile but him? Lucy's face had had a distance about it ever since she was a baby. By the time she was five, she could look as preoccupied, as unapproachable, as her grandmother had looked at eighteen when he first met her. Lucy at five — her head tilted thoughtfully downward, her hair half out of her braids, the outline of her small cheeks so pure and precise beside the straying platinum hair, the curves of her chin and mouth and nose so tiny and so separate, the gaze of her eyes under the brows and lashes so dark for her hair (for her hair would darken to match her brows, as Stuart's had) — the gaze itself so dark when she was five. Now at eight the gaze was darker. That was one of the reasons why the smile was like the sun.

He had the same desperate feeling about that smile that he once got about the problem of whether or not there could be a sound in the forest if a tree fell and no one was there to hear it. Of course there was a sound, he had insisted — whether any human being heard it or not. A certain combination of things occurred and they produced a sound, and that had to be all there was to it. But when he had first come up against that problem, he had wanted to rush to all the places in the world where a tree was falling, just to make sure that there would always be a sound. Now here was a smile that supposedly could always be smiled, but would it? Would somebody be sure to see it for him when he couldn't see it any more for himself? Above all, would somebody make sure that the smile was never lost?

She was a very beautiful child when she smiled. He wondered if everybody else knew it. He began to see that there might be so many things that he knew and that nobody else knew. He would have to try to tell everybody while he had the time.

Then the blazing smile died, the sun set. "Mamma says not to pester you to play with me," she said soberly.

"You just let *me* worry about that," he said. They were protecting him, trying to force him into more idleness. They were still trying to save him.

"Well," he went on, after waiting for somebody else to speak, "tell me the news. Has the sheriff been around to badger Wilkes any more?"

"Otto never has said," George told him. "But if I know Press, he won't be around again till summer. Mr. Press likes to stick close to home in the winter, where it's nice and warm and he can feather his nest with the pickings around town."

"How's Edith?"

"I don't see how she keeps going," Rachel said. "She's up and around now, and she doesn't seem to be any worse off than she was before. The baby seems to be all right, too."

The visit did not last long. They could all see how tired he was and they refused to stay. Lucy gave him a refreshing conspiratorial look as she left. He and she were fooling all the others once more.

He thought about how unfair he had been in his thoughts about George. All the credit for a child like Lucy could not be given to Rachel or to her side of the family. George had given Lucy some of her intensity and courage, and not a small share of her intelligence. Will was astounded to think that it had never occurred to him before to be grateful to George for Lucy and Catherine. His unfairness to George could not be excused just because George had been unfair to him, too. It came to him that rarely was a man really fair in his life. Not till a man was dying could he afford to see things as they really were. All these years he had blamed George for the hard life that Rachel was obliged to live; yet in good times George would have been a highly successful farmer. He was sensible about farming, and he worked as hard as any man Will had ever known.

There would never be the time nor the means for making amends to George, he knew. But on the other hand, he never could have seen that there were amends to be made until the time for making them was gone. He had been angry with George for insisting on repaying the loan; now he had to admit that he never could have respected a son-in-law who hadn't repaid him. He had been annoyed with George for refusing even to think about taking relief of some sort; now he had to admit that he never would have respected a son-in-law who went on relief. Now he could see . . . now that he was about to be interrupted.

He had struggled so hard with the tiredness he felt while his grandchildren were visiting that now he had a feverish second wind. His mind was leaping from one spot to another in an undisciplined way, and he had neither the strength nor the desire to try to control it. He felt as if he were in the midst of a fireworks display, with extravagant shapes and colors exploding all around him. If he tried to trace out the trajectories of one particular burst, he found himself staring at nothing but thin wiggly lines of smoke that swiftly expired in the darkness. It was better simply to float from burst to burst — fireworks were not meant to be pieced together like a jigsaw puzzle on a card table. But he would return from the fireworks and try to do something about the smile — something to bridge the coming interruption, the way his stories used to be bridges. He asked Rose to bring the breadboard and some paper back to him.

She bent over close to him while she helped him sit up, and his mind went from Lucy's smile to Rose's face — Lucy looked a little like Rose, he thought, even though she favored George's side of the family more than Rachel's.

He wondered if it was possible to love anybody without loving that person's face. People talked about loving another person's spirit, and he supposed there was something about the people he loved that could not be seen or touched, but whatever that something was, might it not easily be a thing he *constructed* for himself out of what he *could* see and touch?

What made a face, anyway? A face was made out of the same elements that were in the earth and the air and the water — the same elements that made wheat and wool — the same elements that fed man and buried him, watered him and drowned him, illuminated and burned him — the same elements that spangled the sky with the white-hot gas of stars or that circled him in the cold planets hiding in their long dark billion-mile orbits. It still excited Will to think about Pluto. Pluto's remote existence was first suggested when Rachel was so small she was barely talking. When Rachel was studying astronomy in college, Pluto was still only a highly acceptable hypothesis. But men had sought it across space until Will's granddaughter was bigger than his daughter had been when Pluto was first proposed. And four years ago a man had finally aimed a telescope in just the right spot at just the right time and caught it slipping by in its two-hundred-and-forty-eight-year circuit of the sun's nearer children.

Only God knew how long Pluto had been out there. What Will knew was that for the fifty-four years that Rose had existed, Pluto had been there, too, no matter whether *men* knew about it or not, and the same elements that made the face of Rose had also been out there whirling past them on that lifeless ball — or, more accurately — he and Rose had been whirling past Pluto.

What was to be said, then, about the face of Rose and the planet of Pluto? Were the muscles that manipulated the powdered lids of Rose's eyes and the careful shapes of her lips, that articulated the anxiety of her mind in the lines of her forehead — were these muscles simply nothing but different arrangements of the same elements that made Pluto? Could a face really be made from nothing more than a particular arrangement of molecules in space? An arrangement dense and stable enough so that a man's own eyes, being close enough, yet removed enough to encompass it, had become accustomed to it, had made of it a unique creation, and had endowed it with all the meaning it had? Could the eye of God likewise create a face from the molecular arrangement of the Milky Way or a glass of water?

He wrote on his paper, "For Lucy to read on her . . ." (She mustn't be too young or she might not understand. She mustn't be too old or she might have forgotten.) ". . . on her thirteenth birthday." He remembered Rachel at that age — so thoughtful and yet so young — Rachel, ewe, his Rachel with a lamb now, who must not forget. "A smile is one of the things that makes your face different from other faces." That wasn't exactly what he wanted to say — well . . . "I hope you will always smile, with your grown-up face, the way I have seen you smile when you were little." (She was so alive now, in her existence as an eight-year-old, that it was impossible to imagine her five years from now.) "I hope you can remember the way you always smiled at the lambs, because . . ." He wanted to say, ". . . because that smile always made me so happy," but that would not be so relevant five years from now. What would? ". . . because your face is the very prettiest that way." Once it was written, it didn't sound important enough. He crossed it out heavily back to the word "lambs" and left it at that. It was probably enough anyway. She could never forget the lambs, could she?

He folded the paper and wrote on the outside, "For Lucy." He'd have to sneak it into an envelope if he could, and seal it up and write the name and the birthday. Meanwhile he wrapped it in another piece of paper and wrote "Save" on it.

He took two pills then, and lay down for a nap before supper. "Do you want to go to sleep right now?" Rose asked. "I was just going to fix you some more soup."

"I think I'll feel a little more like eating after I've rested. I'll have the soup just before I go down for the night. It's a luxury just not to have that blamed tray coming in at five o'clock every afternoon."

He always got woozy fast on an empty stomach. The room began to go around almost before she had left it and the pills made a fast pounding in his ears. Then the faces began to go around, like the planets, and words began to go around — pealing, thundering words he had heard so often, and said so often, too, but he could not tell if it was the faces or the planets or only the pounding in his ears reciting *We give thanks to Thee for Thy great glory, O Lord God, heavenly King, God the Father Almighty* . . . He felt as though he might even be speaking the words himself — saluting the fireworks without bothering to wonder why. . . .

Friday, February 9

LUCY WAS LOOKING for faces in the catalogs. She had already cut out the best ones from the old "Spring and Summer" catalogs, and there weren't many good ones left, but in two more weeks the new "Spring and Summer" books would come and then she could cut into the "Fall and Winter" catalogs. It was after supper and her father was yelling out to her mother about things in the newspaper the way he did every night.

"Remember, Rachel, I read to you the other night how they took over all those rich landlords' property in Cuba and opened it up for the poor people? Well, it says here tonight they took over the big electric company and they shut off all the power till the Americans signed the company over to the Cubans. Served them right. American money should stay in America."

"Well, I guess that's the way they feel in Cuba," her mother answered. "I suppose they don't like to have Americans taking all the money from things like that out of the country."

"We don't like it *here,* either!" said her father. "We don't like having the money from this state all going back to Wall Street any more than the Cubans do. And one of these days, we're just going to take a lesson from those people down there."

He read another story about John Dillinger finally getting shot in Chicago. All the boys that sold newspapers ran to where he was lying with blood coming out of all the holes the bullets made. They dipped pieces of their papers in the blood and sold the pieces for a quarter each. "Imagine that! Two bits for a piece of bloody paper!"

"Oh, George! Don't read things like that aloud! They give Lucy nightmares!"

"No! I want to hear it!" Lucy cried.

"Phooey!" her father said. "She's got to find out what kind of a world she's in, doesn't she? Imagine that, Lucy! *Five* ice-cream cones! More than you get all summer long! For a piece of paper with a little blood on it!"

"George!"

"All right! . . . Here's a funnier story anyway. It was the coldest day in the history of the Weather Bureau in New York City yesterday. Now just guess how cold it was — go ahead and guess."

"A hundred below!" Lucy guessed.

"Rachel?" he asked.

"Oh, twenty-five below, or thereabouts, I suppose," she said.

"Fourteen!" her father cried. "A measly fourteen! Why, fourteen below is nothing but shirtsleeve weather! Oh, how they suffered! Says here they closed the schools and the hospitals were full of people with 'frostbite.' "

"What's frostbite?" Lucy asked.

"Why all that means is they froze their face a little, or their toes. That's all — just like *you* do all the *time* when you're out in the wind a while. Freeze their noses and go to the *hospital* to get a little cold water put on them! Why they don't know what the word 'cold' means back there! Imagine that! Temperature goes down to fourteen below and they close the schools. . . . Well, let's see here — Germany and Poland signed a ten-year agreement against war."

"Why don't they ever have *grand*fathers in the catalog?" Lucy called out to the kitchen.

"What!"

"Well, they have lots of babies and brothers and sisters and mothers and fathers, and there's a lady that could be a grandmother here, I guess, but they never have any grandfathers. I even found a dog. There's a little tiny man here, that looks like he could be a grandfather, but he's all stooped over a machine. How come they never have regular grandfathers with the coats or the underwear?"

"Well, dear, I really can't think why. I guess maybe grandfathers are just too busy to have their pictures taken. Could you cut out the one you found and just put him a little ways away from the rest of the family so it would look as though he was out working in the barn? You know how people look tiny when they're far away?"

"Yes, but I can't make any clothes for him."

"Well, I'll tell people to watch for grandfathers in magazines."

Lucy especially liked to cut her families out of the underwear pages because that was the way real paper dolls came — wearing underwear. Then when she had drawn and colored and cut out clothes for them, she could feel that they were all properly dressed. But sometimes if the best face was on a person wearing a coat or ski pants, she would take that person and just pretend he didn't already have on outside clothes underneath the clothes she made for him. Her families were always very large and usually there were no girls at all — just babies and boys. But if there was a girl, she would be sure to have a twin brother so her father would not be disappointed when she came.

When Rachel finished the dishes, she went in to start Lucy to bed. The child was sitting with her back to the window and her meticulously cut out family was lined up in front of her across the oilcloth. One or two of the family were in full color, for she hoarded the colored pages and disciplined herself not to use them all up at once. She was such a queer combination of thrift and abandon. Even the black-and-white, brown-and-white, and occasional colored scraps were neat and small, for Lucy was careful not to cut into any more space than she had to in order to get out a particular figure. Again, she was ostensibly an odd combination of coordination and lack of it. In school, Alice Liljeqvist often told Rachel, Lucy's awkwardness was always causing accidents. Rachel couldn't help wondering if the ineptness Lucy displayed in school might not be just as deliberate as this neat pile of scraps.

Rachel bent over her to look at the family. "All boys again?" she asked.

Lucy nodded, without looking up from the snowsuit she was making. Rachel shivered. The air from the window could have been coming straight from a polar ice cap.

She put her hand on Lucy's shirt and felt how cold it was. Then she pressed her wrist against the back of Lucy's neck, which still seemed so narrow and defenseless beneath the oversized oval of her skull and the great shock of hair on it. Her neck was like ice—her neck with the constant sore throats and the enlarged tonsils inside it—her thin little neck with the glands on either side that swelled into hard aching lumps every time she caught a cold. No, she was not nearly so healthy as George thought she was, and here he had sat in this room with her all evening and never noticed how cold she was getting. And of course *Lucy* would never notice. Lucy never knew when she was cold. All children were that way to some degree but Rachel was sure that Lucy was the worst she had ever seen. On a cold day she had to go outside and hunt her down every half hour or the child was liable to disappear for hours and come back wet with snow and so chilled she couldn't stop shaking. It was too bad that all her intelligence seemed to go toward making her difficult. The Custers were an exasperating lot.

"Honestly, Lucy, couldn't you feel how cold you've been getting?" she said. "George, why didn't you notice that she had got herself clear over here against the window? She's just like ice."

"Well, now, Rachel, she should certainly know how to look after herself by now. The longer you fuss around over her like this, the longer it'll be before she learns to take care of herself."

"*I'm* not cold," Lucy said. When she began to think about it, she *was* cold, but she didn't want either her father or mother to be right.

"Oh, no, *you're* not cold! It makes me cold myself to feel how cold you are. Now gather up those scraps and put them in the coal scuttle, and then get your sleepers and bring them out here and warm them up."

When Lucy opened the door to the bedroom where Cathy had already gone to sleep, the wave of frigid air struck against Rachel's legs with an impact as definite and powerful as if it had been a wave of water.

"George! It's *freezing* in that room! We *can't* put the children in there tonight!"

"Rachel, what in the world is *eating* on you tonight! You'll give us *all* the heeby-jeebies if you keep this up!"

"*You've* been sitting two feet from the stove all night and *I've* been keeping warm working. I tell you, it's terribly *cold!* Just go out and look."

George dropped his feet from his stool and took the kitchen lamp out so he could see the thermometer. The cold gust that blasted into the house was like a personal attack from the universe. He ducked back inside, shaking his head a little, looking as though he had glimpsed whatever the thing was that had been waiting on the porch behind the kitchen door.

"It's almost forty below," he said. "I can't ever remember seeing it this cold this early in the evening. What'll it be by morning, I wonder?"

Rachel felt the attack and the strange sentience of the cold. It was as though the cold was feeling *her*, as much as she was feeling *it*. There was just too much to fight. How could anybody fight it all? "What shall we do?" she cried.

"Rachel! Will you stop acting like a flea on a hot stove! Relax! Before you drive us *all* crazy!"

"All right, all right. What shall we do? I'm just asking you what we ought to do."

"There's not a heck of a lot we *can* do about a cold wave except keep ourselves warm in here, now is there?"

"They mustn't sleep in that room," Rachel said. "We'll have to move Lucy's bed out here and Cathy will have to sleep between us. It doesn't matter how many pins I use, I can't trust that baby to stay covered on a night like this."

If there was anything George hated, it was sleeping with a baby.

He was horrified by the thought that he could be wet upon and he was almost as worried by the smaller possibility of rolling on the baby in his sleep. A baby as big as Cathy would probably squirm out from under him, as a shoat or a puppy always seemed to do, no matter how big and stupid its mother. But still, if he rolled on her, she might squall in his ear like a mashed cat and finish him for the night.

"Fiddlesticks!" he said.

"Help me move the cot. Lucy must get to bed."

"You're just making a mountain out of a molehill."

Rachel's only answer was to rip up their own bed and spread a rubber sheet under the cotton sheet-blanket. Then she blocked off the light by moving the loaded clothes rack across the wide door of the alcove. She lifted the baby from the crib and managed to transfer her into the big bed without waking her.

George said no more either, as he helped her carry out the cot and fit it into the narrow space between the table and the piano bench.

"You get in bed, now," Rachel said to Lucy. "By the time you're settled, we'll be ready to turn out the light."

There were drafts on Lucy's back as she stood in the corner by the stove to put her sleepers on. She crawled in between the blankets of her cot. They were very cold and did not seem to have warmed at all since being moved to the dining room. She began to feel afraid. Her mother was right: There was something wrong.

It didn't seem as though she would ever be able to go to sleep with her head almost under the oilcloth this way. She looked in under the table. It was a landscape she knew well, since she always played with her blocks under there. There was the thick round center stem which split apart in the middle when the table was pulled out for extra leaves and there were the four broad feet, like gently spreading roots, sloping down and ending in the casters that stood in such lovely round glass dishes. She always thought it a pity that those little dishes were buried under the table where she was the only one to appreciate them. But no matter how well acquainted she was with the underside of the table, it wasn't normal to have her head under there when she was trying to go to sleep. She knew her head wasn't *really* under the table, but it *felt* as though it was under the table. And her feet began to get cold. They were too close to the window. She shuddered and turned on her side and bent her knees up tight against her stomach.

Her mother noticed. "Are you cold?"

"Kind of." She would admit it now that it wouldn't be her fault any more.

"George, we'll have to give Lucy our quilts and use the feather tick."

"You *are* hysterical!"

Her mother dragged the feather tick out of the closet and dumped it beside the stove in a wheezy rumple of sliding feathers and yellowed ticking. A stale, vault-like smell came from it. She took two quilts off the double bed and tucked them around Lucy.

"Better now?"

Lucy couldn't notice any difference, but she didn't know what else to say, so she said yes. She didn't really know whether she was cold or not, especially after listening to her mother and father telling each other that she didn't know. She stared into the deep shadows under the table. She knew that once the light was out, she would see all sorts of shapes there that *could* not be there, and she was trying to make herself believe that they *would* not be there. It was always that way when she slept in a different place. Even in the tiny room where she had slept all her life, she saw thousands of shapes that could not be there, but it was always much worse in a new place. She would have to lie there all night reminding herself that it was only the underneath parts of the table she was seeing.

There was a poem that began "Little Orphant Annie's come to *our* house to stay, and wash the cups and saucers up, and brush the crumbs away," and Lucy had heard that poem recited at least twenty times at school programs and read it at least fifty times in *The Young Folks' Treasury*. First Little Orphant Annie had to make the fire and bake the bread and earn-her-board-and-keep, but after she was finished with that, she could tell about what happened to bad children. There was a little boy whose parents sent him to bed away up stairs and when they heard him holler and they turned the covers down, he wasn't there at all. And there was a little girl that would always laugh and grin and hide and make fun of everybody and say she didn't care and all of a sudden there was two great big black Things a-standing by her side and they snatched her through the ceiling before she knowed what she was about. And Little Orphant Annie said that the black Things were Gobble-uns, and the Gobble-uns'll git *you* if you Don't Watch Out!

Lucy did not doubt that the poem applied to herself in every respect. She grinned, and she knew she wasn't supposed to. It wasn't ladylike to grin, especially when a person had such big teeth. Every time she had to have her picture taken, somebody would say, "Smile," but as soon as she smiled, they would say, "No! Don't *grin! Smile!*" It was only impolite to grin, but it was terrible to say, "I don't care!" which was a thing she often said. She sometimes kicked her heels, too, and she hid when she was mad. And she whistled just to provoke her grandmother.

She knew exactly how it would feel to get snatched through the ceiling before she knew what she was about. There were certainly enough reasons why she deserved to have the two great big black Things appear by her side at any moment. As soon as the light was out, they could hide under the table if they wanted to, the way she did herself. Tonight could be the night.

Her father emptied the coal scuttle into the two stoves and turned the dampers in the chimneys. That was almost the last thing he did every night before he put out the light. Oh, if he could only leave it on. Just for tonight.

"You all set in there, Rachel?" he said. Her mother had already gotten in bed with Cathy. If only she was a baby, too, safe in bed between a mother and a father.

"Move the clothes rack," said her mother. "We're not getting enough heat back here. I just can't get warmed up at all — even under this tick."

"Well this is *some* cold wave," her father said. "I'd like to see a few of those hothouse flowers in New York out here *tonight!*"

He turned down the gas and the hiss of it stopped. The gas left in the mantles made a few struggling sounds, the mantles became two terrible glowing blue eyes in the darkness, and then they went out.

Now there was no protection at all from any attacker — not

from black Things or white Things or hands floating around in the air above her. She wondered if a cold wave could make a glacier in one night — like the beanstalk growing to the sky in one night. Or perhaps if a cold wave was cold enough, it *was* a glacier — a wall of ice higher than the grain elevator, rumbling toward them like a thousand threshing machines. She would stay awake and listen, so if it came it wouldn't catch them the way it had caught the mammoths.

It seemed to her that she could not have slept at all — that she must have spent the whole night wondering where the glacier was, and wondering how the shapes got under the table to lurk and twitch there in the freezing light that recoiled from the marble sky and crept through the window into the warmth of the house. It seemed that she had not been asleep at all when she woke to the sound of whispers — three sets of whispers — and a vagrant flashlight beam glaring and vanishing in the kitchen.

She heard footsteps approaching her bed and she closed her eyes, for she knew that she was supposed to be asleep.

But her mother came to her in the darkness and whispered to her without ever asking if she was awake — seeming to know that she was awake.

"Daddy and I have to go, but we'll be back as soon as we can. You'll be a big girl, now, won't you? And take care of Cathy when she wakes up. Be very careful when you light the lamp. . . .

"Grampa won't suffer any more."

III

Let us now praise famous men, and our fathers
that begat us
Leaders of the people by their counsels, and by
their knowledge of learning meet for the
people.
All these were honoured in their generations, and
were the glory of their times.

And some there be, which have no memorial;
who are perished, as though they had never
been born; and their children after them.

Ecclesiasticus 44:1-9
Old Testament Apocrypha

Monday, February 12

There was a wide gate on the south side of Highway Number 10, and attached to the gate was a fence that went along the highway and then around the base of an unusually steep hill that was dotted thickly with big square stones. The gray-white lintel of the gate was scarcely distinguishable from the dusty snow on the hill behind it, but the black letters — CALVARY — stood out upon it. Near the top of the hill, several crouching men leapt to their feet and scattered across the snow, dodging or jumping the few headstones that protruded into their random flights. They dropped to their knees just as the spot near the top of the hill exploded in flying chunks of snow and black earth.

In a moment they ventured back, sniffing the burnt powder. One of them was limping, and he rubbed his leg while he studied the hole. "Thunderation," he said. "Prit-near broke my leg and it *still* ain't deep enough. I oughta get paid by the *hour* on this job."

He was a drifter they called Tiny Tim. Every once in a while he sneaked off a boxcar and over to the Town Hall to try to get hired for some piecework. He hit every town along the main line often enough to be familiar to most men who dealt out piecework.

"Don't make me laugh," said the man who had hired him. "If I was paying you by the hour, you'd of got some jack outa me and hiked in to the saloon by now."

"Sure I would," Tiny Tim agreed. "I'm too cold to work any more. What do you wanta bury a man when it's this cold for? No *need* to. *Sixty below*, two-three nights ago. I ain't been warm since — just thinking about it. All you need to do is let him freeze good and stiff and pound him in the ground."

"Haven't you got no feelings at *all!*" the boss cried. "You say anything more like that and I don't care *how* you beg me, I'll never give you no more jobs out here!"

"Ya, I got feelings! *Cold* feelings!"

"Go back down to the truck and fetch some more sticks!" the boss told him.

Tiny Tim stumped away down the hill, moving as though he didn't dare to bend his toes for fear they would snap off.

"Shake a leg! Move a little and maybe you'll get warmed up! We haven't got all day! They'll *be* here in another three hours or so. Come on, get a move on," the boss urged the men preparing the holes for the next charge. "We gotta clean it up too before they come." He looked around at the strewing of clods over the snow. "We can't let 'em see it like *this*. They shouldn't know about it. Anyway, they shouldn't *think* about it."

Once more the spot near the top of the hill erupted and finally it was deep enough. The men squared off the corners as neatly as they could. Their picks rebounded as though they were striking solid rock, but with every jolt to elbows and shoulders a few crumbs broke loose and dribbled down into the hole.

Finally they piled the frozen chunks of dirt in one big mound beside the hole. They did their best to make it look as though the grave might have been dug. They raked up the smaller dirt chunks and rocks, and they separated the larger lumps of snow from the lumps of dirt so the dirt would settle down better.

The boss untied the strings of his ear flaps and pushed his cap back to cool his forehead. "Well," he said, "I don't see how it's possible to work up a sweat on a day like this, but I done it."

He'd had this job for a long time, but he'd never got over being nervous about it. He still had nightmares about not getting the grave dug in time, or about mistaking the day and having the preacher and the whole funeral procession arrive with the casket and no hole to put the casket in.

"Let's get out of here. I need a beer. Thank God a man can go get a beer now after he digs a grave."

By the time they got back to town, the two men who had had to sit out in the truck bed could barely move their lips to speak, even though they had wrapped scarves around their faces.They trailed the boss into Gebhardt's.

Tiny Tim worked his jaw to limber up his mouth. "Let me have my money. Gotta warm up."

The boss pulled a dollar out of his back pocket. "That's more than you're worth."

"Aw — for a day like this!"

"I'll buy you a beer, but that's all the cash money you get. You know you loafed as much as you could stand to without freezing to death."

Tiny Tim drained the mug. "Much obliged for the *orderve*," he said. He headed for the back room.

"Takes a fool to drink that stuff back there," the boss said. "I ain't going to touch a drop that ain't legal. Now don't get too warmed up in here. We gotta go back out there and fill it in again."

❦ ❦ ❦

Lucy felt the tickle of tears on her cheeks, then the salt running over her lips. Then the hymn book in the rack swam away out of sight, after she had managed to keep looking at it for this whole time. She wiped her eyes with her clenched fists, wiped the fists on her coat, and then wiped her eyes again. She stopped presently, and nobody had even noticed that she cried. She was glad that she had not been able to keep from crying, even if it *was* so embarrassing. She even wished that somebody had noticed, because it was lonely not to have anybody know that she too had cried for him.

There were a great many flowers, and more people even than there were for the Christmas program. That was because they all liked her grandfather so much. But not as much as *she* did, not as much as *she* did.

They sang the hymn he liked best. It was "Abide with Me." Then the men closed the casket and carried it down the aisle. Lucy saw them lift him into the long black car. The people walked past the car to their own cars, bending their heads toward each other and holding each other by the elbows. They seemed as though they could not stand up alone — as though they had to help each other to walk against a strong wind.

The long car started down the street toward the highway and the other cars followed behind. They went very slowly because a few of the people were driving buggies.

He's not in there, Lucy said to herself. I don't believe he's even in there at all.

❧ ❧ ❧

The pallbearers, shaking with cold, lowered the casket into the grave. Reverend Brant drew from his pocket a handful of dust. It was an old trick of the trade — keeping a little unfrozen dirt in the house. While he was still speaking, the diggers got out of their truck and came in to wait by the gate.

George looked down the hill and saw that one of the diggers kept coming on up toward them and that he wasn't a digger at all. He was Stuart. George could tell, even from this distance, where Stuart had been during his father's funeral. A little man ran up and took Stuart by the arm, trying to hold him back.

"They had to dynamite it!" Stuart shouted. "He worked his whole life in the damned dirt, and then it wouldn't even let him *in!* They had to dynamite it! Took twenty sticks to make him a little hole in the ground! It wouldn't even let him in! This fella here — he *knows!* He helped 'em *do* it. He *told* me and he *knows!*"

Tiny Tim fled to the truck.

Nobody wanted to be the one to keep a son from his last sight of the box with his father's body in it — no matter what the son's condition was. Stuart forced his way through the mourners to the side of the grave. He lunged at the mound of frozen clods and straightened up with a chunk of earth the size of his head.

"Dust to dust!" he cried.

He stood with his feet wide apart like an executioner, raised the earthen missile between his hands, and hurled it down into the hole. There was a crash on metal — a gong sounding in Hell.

George was probably the only man there strong enough to handle Stuart without any help. He grabbed him from behind and jerked him from the edge of the grave. Stuart stumbled and lurched as though he could no longer keep his balance. George kept it for him all the way down the hill, scarcely feeling the effort it required. So this was the boy who pretended to be embarrassed when George had his say at the county agent's meeting, was it? But this boy didn't mind that the *whole* county would hear about *this* scene, and that of course the whole county would never forget it.

"If you're looking for a fight, you found just the right man," George told him. "But if you lift a finger to me, you'd just better kill me the first time!"

"*I* don't wanna fight *you!* I'm too *drunk* to fight. . . . I *never* feel like fightin' when I'm drunk. You know, George, *you* need a drink. Let's go on back and get a drink. I just thought you oughta know about what this fella here told me." He looked around for Tiny Tim. "Well *he* told me all about it. *He'll* have a drink with us!"

"Shut up!"

"Twenty sticks!" Stuart twisted away from George and shouted his words back up the hill.

The graveside group watched, almost as motionless as the man they had come to bury, while the man's son-in-law struck the man's son on the jaw.

The minister beckoned to the gravediggers and they moved forward with their shovels. They juggled the clods like teacups on saucer-edges and lowered them into the grave as far as they could before letting them fall. Even so, the gong sounded again and again.

Reverend Brant was accustomed to graveside hysterics of one kind or another, and Prohibition or no Prohibition, there always seemed to be about the same incidence of drunks at funerals. People just couldn't seem to really believe that the person they loved was not in the casket at all, but far away in a blessed place. He finished reading the short service and sprinkled the dust he had been holding in his hand. Then he waited for the diggers to finish and arrange the flowers over the broken earth.

George pushed Stuart behind the funeral parlor car. Here at last was somebody who needed to be hit.

"Stand up and fight, you bastard! Somebody should have straightened you out a long time ago. Dirty shiftless bastard! Roam around the country — bring the god-damned smut from Texas. *Fight*, you bastard!"

Stuart was laughing harder and harder. "That's what I call respect for the dead! They haven't even got him in the *ground* yet and you call me a *bastard!*"

George hit him again with everything he had, and Stuart stretched out on the highway without a whimper.

He'd be out for a while but he wasn't really hurt. George looked over the roof of the hearse and up the hill to see what the crowd was doing. It was scattering and heading down toward him. He grabbed the limp ankles and dragged Stuart to the delivery end of the hearse. He flung open the doors and hauled the unconscious body inside, head first. It smelled strongly in there of the bouquets that had been riding beside the coffin. That flower smell so cooped up and intensified was like the smell of death itself.

"Just *wait* till you come to!" George told the body.

The funeral parlor owner came hopping ahead of the crowd. "I *saw* that! Have you gone out of your mind? Get him out of there! Have you *killed* him?"

"*You* mewling little shrimp! You mincing little *butcher!* No, I didn't *kill* him! You haven't got another customer *yet!* Leave him be! It'll sober him right up when he wakes up in there. Just give him a ride back to town, you bloodsucking chiseler!" George was aware that he didn't really want to be shouting.

"I *said* get him out of there!" The little ghoul dressed all in black was so overwhelmed by ordinary human rage that his white face was turning to an ordinary crimson. "*Get him out!*"

"You *bugger!* You sawed-off little vampire! You've got enough of his cash so you can *afford* to give him a lift back to town. I won't *touch* him again!"

The embalmer grabbed Stuart under the arms and pulled him out the end of the hearse. Stuart opened his eyes when his feet hit the ground. He stayed on his legs long enough to stumble to the second black car and he sat down on the bumper.

It was necessary to remove him as quickly as possible. Reverend Brant had ridden in that car and he took Stuart's arm. "Can we give you a ride?" he asked.

Stuart looked around. He distinctly remembered coming out in a truck, but he couldn't see one now. "Much obliged," he said, and crawled into the car. He leaned back against the seat and looked up the hill. The bouquets made a last discordant explosion against the colorless snow and sky. It was an explosion that hurt his eyes.

"Why'd you do *that?*" Stuart said. "What makes you think he'd want all those flowers out there just to freeze? 'When It's Springtime in the Rockies' — that was his favorite song — 'Springtime in the Rockies.' How come you did that?"

"We always do it," the preacher said. "It doesn't make any difference what time of year it is, does it?"

❧ ❧ ❧

Stuart did not come home that afternoon, but Rose would not let anybody else stay with her. And since there was no one to see her cry, she cried.

She sat at the little black desk trying to get through the papers in it. They went back thirty years and more — back into the last century. Looking at so many of them all at once made her weep for his life even more than for his death.

He had been carrying much more insurance than she had thought he was. He had always been so much more generous with her than she had been with him. She knew that he had lived his life without some of the things a man ought to have with his wife. But she couldn't see how she herself could ever have been any different. For thirty-six years she had known well enough what she did. She had held him away from herself and tried to make up for it by working too hard. He had seen what she was doing — he always saw — and she had pushed him farther away because she was afraid to have him see.

I never wanted him to know what was in my mind. But I loved him. But if he knew what was in my mind, I wanted to run away. I never wanted *anybody* to know what was in my mind. But I loved him. But I loved him. But I loved him. But I hide what is in my mind even from God. Even from *God.*

Here are so many papers about the fire and the barn. What did I do? What did I do? What did I do when I came from the house just in time to see it blow up? I ran around. I remember running around like a chicken with its head chopped off but I don't remember what I did. That's how much good I was to him then. How long was it before I went in to get him? How long did he lie there with the smoke in his lungs and the cinders falling and burning him? Would he be here now if he hadn't almost died then? What did I *do?*

It was Monday we buried him and now it is Wednesday, I believe.

Yes, it must be Wednesday and I must get into this empty bed tonight or else somebody will find me asleep somewhere else and they will wonder why it is that I didn't go to bed — they will think about what could have been in my mind. This empty bed here where I held him off so often — not by anything I even said or hinted — but I held him off. But I loved him. I loved him. Did I ever say it to him? I can't remember, I can't remember — stop, God, stop trying to find out if I said it — I won't let it be in my mind and then *You* won't know and *I* won't know — nobody will ever know.

She pulled off her clothes and crept under the blankets. But it was too dark. She got out of the bed and felt on the chiffonier for matches. She lit the kerosene lamp and lay down again, but she could not close her eyes.

The useless black electrical wire stuck down at her from the very center of the ceiling. How many times had she pointed out to him what a waste of money it had been to wire the house and how much nicer the ceiling would have looked without that hole? "You just wait, now, Rosie," he would say. (Oh, the sound of his voice!) "They'll string a line out here one of these days. Then won't you be the queen? Lights, incubators, washing machine, sewing machine, water pump!"

The lamp was going dry. The oily smoke of the burning wick billowed up inside the glass chimney and coated it with an ever-thickening layer of furry soot. The lamp base was very fancy — an elegant wedding present. The painted flowers and butterflies on the milky white china were all gay and innocent of the murky storm above them. A week ago, and for all the part of her life that preceded that week, she would have run through the whole house to get to a lamp if she smelled it going dry. She could hardly believe that she was lying here watching a lamp burn dry and not even getting out of bed to blow it out; neither could she imagine why she had run through the whole house because of smoking lamps for so many years.

❦ ❦ ❦

From the Shepards' new barn George saw that the bedroom had the only light in the house. He wondered if Rose was sick. But he was certainly not going to go in to find out. He had been instructed by Rachel not even to take the milk inside the house. He was to feed some of it to the pigs and bring the rest home. Rachel had said that she couldn't imagine when her mother would ever be able to look at him again after what he had done. Then she had stopped speaking to him or looking at him herself.

George knew he had done an awful thing. What infuriated him, as he went about doing Stuart's chores, was that Stuart was not considered to be half so culpable as he was himself. He could tell by Rachel's attitude that she had already forgiven her brother. That is, she had forgiven him as much as she ever had since the night he took his first drink. A drunkard was never completely forgiven; on the other hand, a drunkard rarely got put in the kind of doghouse *he* was in, either. No matter what things made a man forget himself, alcohol was the only thing that would give him a kind of excuse with even the most bug-eyed teetotaler.

So here *he* was — the strong steady one — doing the work of the weak one while the weak one slept off a binge somewhere. The weak were cared for by the strong, covered up for and apologized for by the strong, and forgiven by the strong. But the strong never forgave each *other*, did they? In the two days he'd been plugging over here and taking care of his wife's brother's work for him, had his wife softened up one iota? Not on your life!

The weak might not be respected, but by God they got taken care of! Hell, hell, hell! he said to himself as he dumped the last pail of whole milk into the pigs' trough and closed the barn door.

The house was dark now. Should he go in and see if everything was all right? To hell with it. He struck off across the field for home, swinging his lantern and treading on the ends of the shadow legs that skipped so freely back and forth in the yellow light on the snow.

❦ ❦ ❦

Stuart had gone some place to clean up before he came home. Rose had been trying to prepare herself for the two most probable alternatives — either that he would never come back again after what George had done to him and after what he had done to himself, or that he would come home as he always had before, looking so unlike himself, filthy and unshaven. Having him come home sober and normal-looking was the one thing she was not prepared for, and perhaps that was why, in a way, she was more disturbed than if he had come the way she had been expecting him to. He spoke even less frequently than he had before, as if he wished her to understand that she would never know where he went, what he did, or why he came back.

When he did speak, it was often in such a low voice that she was sure, despite the way her ears had been behaving, that he *was* speaking in an abnormally low voice. Did his manner indicate that as soon as he could decently do so he would leave forever? Or perhaps he would leave *before* he could decently do so.

Every day there seemed to be less to talk about. They worked together to keep up with the jobs that never let up, even for death. One day she asked him if he planned to go to school in the fall. It would be necessary to start making applications.

"I'll see," was all he said.

Tuesday, March 13

It had been exactly one year and a day since the new President made the broadcast telling the people to take their money back to the banks, assuring them that everything was going to get much better very soon, and that the money situation, in particular, would be improved in a peacefully revolutionary way.

"And I told you then, didn't I, Rachel, that Roosevelt was just another rich man talking through his hat? A few more people *believe* me now, too.

"Now here he reduces the amount of gold in the dollar to sixty per cent of what they set it at in nineteen hundred. So now the dollars are '*cheaper*' and he claims the U. S. Treasury is worth three billion dollars more than it was yesterday! What nonsense! Just some more playing around with numbers on paper — that's all it is.

"Says here that Panama bounced a check for a quarter of a million dollars back to the U. S. Treasury. Can't fool *them* either. They want the rent for the Canal Zone in *gold*. Uncle Sam can't even pay his rent with his paper money any more! On the other hand, who says *gold* means anything?"

"Well, *something* has to mean something, doesn't it?"

"Yeah, but why does the *something* always have to be decided on by the guys who already have a lot of it?"

He noticed a filler of interest. "Sixty-five million Chinese made homeless last year by wars, famines, droughts, and floods. That's a lot of Chinamen. But they just keep right on breeding, don't they? I tell you, in another hundred years there isn't going to be room to turn around without stepping on somebody."

No matter how dry this prairie got, at least there was still some air to breathe and a man had a decent amount of privacy. There were a lot of things to be said in favor of living here, even in the very worst of conditions. But still the box on the front page concerned George a good deal. *Normal Moisture to date,* 1.29 inches; *Received to date this year,* .36 inches. Last year the box had given normal figures up to this time in March. Yet last year his well had almost gone out on him.

❧ ❧ ❧

Stuart had spent the afternoon in town, and after he had done the chores and eaten his supper, he stood up, pushed in his chair, and said, "I'm going to get married."

They talked so little to each other that Rose assumed this was simply another sentence of the conversation that was taking place over a period of weeks instead of minutes. She had been living in a world where time was changed, along with almost everything else. Only work was the same, and so she worked — worked so hard that the unreality of the slow-motion communication, or lack of it, between Stuart and herself was almost superseded by the reality of the accomplishments she could believe in as she fell into bed at night.

"Well, of course you'll get married," she said, getting up and starting to clear the table. They couldn't talk at all to each other unless the talk was only an ostensibly unimportant accompaniment to action. It was as though they both spoke into some neutral space between the gigantic crags of their private agonies. They let a few words go out to that space from time to time, but each let the other choose whether or not he would reach out into the space and have anything to do with the words.

"I mean I'm going to get married right *now*—you don't need to look like that. I'm the same age as Dad was when *he* got married, and I'm *older* than *you* were when *you* got married."

It was the first time since the funeral that he had sent out any words into the space which appeared to ask for reaction from her.

"You don't *know* the girl yet, do you?"

"*She* says I know her *plenty* well. I want to know if I should bring her here to the farm."

"What girl would be in such a hurry to marry you that she can't wait till your father is cold in his grave? What kind of wife would she be? Think how people would talk!"

"That's just what *she* said. 'Think how people will talk!' "

"Stuart, what's *happened?*"

"Women!" he cried.

"I asked you what happened!"

"I *told* you! Do you want me to bring her here to the farm or not? I mean, do you want me to stay here to run the farm—to help run it—or do you want me to get out? I have to support her now, one way or another."

"What do you *mean,* you have to support her!"

"Because she says *I* did it, that's why."

His words out in the neutral space were perfectly understandable. She couldn't pretend they were not there; she couldn't pretend they did not describe the sort of thing that happened every day in a doomed and filthy world. Nor did she try to pretend that the words she set beside his in the neutral space were consistent with the things she had tried all his life to teach him. The words were atrocities of contradiction; she recognized each word as an atrocity with which she would answer the world's atrocities.

"It happened after the funeral, didn't it? You *know* you aren't responsible for anything you did then. Whoever the girl is, she's a tramp, and you're not beholden to her." Rose was hardly even surprised at herself for being so calm—so clear-headed. She felt just the way she felt watching the lamp burn dry.

"I asked you a question," Stuart said. "Do you want me to stay around here or not?"

"Who is it?"

"Annie Finley."

"Stuart! Whatever you've done, you *couldn't* owe that girl a *thing!* Annie Finley! She's a *tramp*. She's from a *family* of tramps. She's nothing but scum! *No* decent girl would work in a place like Gebhardt's. You don't owe her a *thing!*"

"A decent girl might work at Gebhardt's if she made twice as much money there as she could make anywhere else. A decent girl might work there if she was watching her family *starve!* She gives everything she *earns* to her mother!"

"Yes, but *how* does she earn it!"

"She gets big tips in Gebhardt's. She's just a *kid!*"

"And what do you think *you* are?"

He didn't offer any words in answer. He only looked at her, and the look made her remember that he had been a man for a long time.

"Do whatever you want," she said. "If you bring her here, you can have the upstairs. If it doesn't work, it doesn't matter."

"I better go back in town and tell her," Stuart said. "She just told her mother and her mother's all worked up. . . . . It's terrible, Mom, how they live! And they *try!* You'll *see* how *clean* she is —"

"How CLEAN she is!"

Finally what he said was so preposterous that she understood how preposterous it was even to be wasting their breath talking about something so irreversible and so insane. She was sane again and now she could see that he was out of his mind. He even thought he cared about this girl. That was why he had said what he just said. If it pleased him to be insane, then there was nothing she could do about it, except to try to remain sane herself. Nor could she forbid him to bring his wife, any legitimate wife, to the farm that would be half his in a few more years. She could not tell Will's son to keep off the farm his father had left him.

He had turned away when she cried out at him — turned away as though he had been expecting her to make a show of sympathy for a whore. He was going out the door now, and everything that would ever need to be said had been said. He had passed his twenty-first birthday. He was free to come or go as he pleased. Every soul in this world lived by some kind of order. Each person chose how he would live. Stuart had thought he was escaping from order, if he thought anything at all, when he began to drink. But there was the tightest of all orders in apparent disorder. When a man gave himself to it, he gave himself to only one path, only one end. Why should she even be surprised at his next step down that path? After all, he had taken the first step three years ago. Now it was time for the second.

For a little while she hated him.

She even let God see that she hated her son. She went to bed before he came back from town. She didn't even wonder about what he was doing for so long. What difference did it make?

He had always surprised her. He surprised her even by being born so long after she and Will had thought that Rachel would be their only child. And he had been so different from Rachel. Boy babies were more different from girl babies than she had supposed they were. Their chests were so wide, their hips so narrow, their feet and hands and heads so big. By the time they were three or four years old, their bodies were so much harder than the bodies of little girls. She remembered how hard his little legs had felt when she pulled his stockings over them, how hard his little buttocks had been when he sat on her lap.

She remembered how she had prayed and how she had nursed him when he got blood poisoning. She remembered how he looked when he began losing his milk teeth. She remembered how he had run about the house on winter days making his lips buzz like the sound of a tractor. She remembered how he would say his own prayer before a meal, the way she and Will did. He was about three then, and the prayer was a loud, rapid "Clarence-shut-the-ice!" It had taken them a long time to figure out that there must be a little boy in his Sunday-school class who was named Clarence and who would not shut his eyes when the teacher had them pray.

Oh, God, how could a boy raised so decently do a thing like this? I know now how much I loved him — before he turned his back on me. Go ahead and see, God, how much I loved him. Nobody else will ever see. I raised him to be decent and now his decency is his downfall. Nobody but a decent boy marries a slut because she's pregnant. Was he born only to wander, God? Should we not have raised him to obey the rules that civilized people live by? Then he would not marry this girl, God. Yet what sort of a world would we have if the same rules were not supposed to apply to everybody?

And I know, God, I know that it is unthinkable for a man raised by these rules not to marry a girl of whom he has carnal knowledge — no matter *who* the girl is. I should be proud that my son finally seems to understand that he must be responsible for his acts.

I can't help it, I can't help it — I want him to run away again. Just until it all blows over. I can't help it, God. Make him run away again, God. Do this one thing for me now. Make him run away.

All through the night she couldn't make the one blasphemous thought leave her alone. The thought had a will of its own, stronger than hers: By raising her boy to be decent, she had only made him more vulnerable to the evil of the world. What chance did a boy like him have in this shameless generation?

❧ ❧ ❧

Stuart got away from Annie and her mother as soon as he could, but it was nearly ten o'clock when he went out and climbed into the truck. Mrs. Finley wanted them to have a regular marriage in her house. She wanted all his family there. He himself just couldn't quite see George there — or his mother either, for that matter.

In fact, whenever he tried to see himself doing *anything* in the future, he felt a queer numb blankness in his head. It was like having the whole empty prairie sky inside his head — and the trouble was that he himself was nowhere at all in that sky.

From the time he could remember, people had said he didn't have any ambition. He'd never been mad when they said that — only when they hinted that he was lazy along with it. There was a difference between having no ambition and being lazy. He'd never been lazy; he liked to work. He just didn't like to work in order to get a perfect score on an examination. Nobody had ever proved to him that it made any difference whether he got a perfect score or not.

Sometimes people told him he didn't have any self-respect. He'd never been able to figure out what self-respect *was*. Did it mean being willing to fight a bum who called *you* a bum? Did it mean sweating all day and worrying all night to try to get hold of some land you could call yours? Did it mean being able to see yourself somewhere in that blank sky in your head that people called the future?

If it meant doing something you said you'd do, then he at least tried to have self-respect. If there was something in the future he knew he had to do, he didn't try to imagine it; he just tried to keep himself from running away.

It was only the time at hand — the solitary present — that was unendurable. Like this time right now, when the truck kept slowing and slowing as it came nearer and nearer to Gebhardt's. He knew that if he could get past Gebhardt's for the next few days, he would find himself doing what he'd said he'd do — standing beside Annie Finley and promising Reverend Brant that he would join his whole empty future with hers. And what difference would it make? It was just the present that he couldn't get through.

❧ ❧ ❧

Rose didn't know, till she heard Stuart come downstairs in the morning and go out to milk, how much she had been wanting him to run away.

There *were* some more things she would like to say this morning. There were some questions she would have liked answers to, but they were the kind of questions she could not ask him. Had he even done what that girl apparently said he did on the day his father was buried? Did he *remember* what he had done? Was he so innocent that he didn't know that one time rarely caused a pregnancy? Did he think humans bred like cows in heat? Or had it been more than one time?

A dozen times that day she reversed herself. The girl could not come here. The girl would have to come here, or Stuart would have to leave the farm, and what would become of him then?

One could not see the girl's mother in the store or on the sidewalk and not feel pity for her. Rose understood that the Finleys belonged to a class of people that could not be said to have had any real chance in the world, and therefore the whole world was to blame for their condition and nobody in the world was blameless. On the other hand, did she and Will owe their one son to that doomed clan, to make up for the way the world had used them? How could it help the Finleys for her boy to be sacrificed to them?

When Abraham had piled the wood for the burnt offering and taken the knife in his hand, the Lord intervened for the sake of Isaac, the long-promised son of the aged Sarah — the one boy born to sow the seed of Abraham. The Lord intervened between Abraham and his obedience. But where now was the ram caught in the thicket, the substitution for the human sacrifice? Will You not find some way now, Lord, to save me and my son from our obedience?

❦ ❦ ❦

But still no way had been found when she got into the car with George and Rachel and the children to drive into town for the wedding. Every time she looked at George she could not help hating him. It was the fight that had done it. Otherwise they would have got Stuart home after the funeral.

When they passed Gebhardt's, Rose knew that either she must be insane or that the world must be insane. Otherwise, how could she be hoping that Stuart was inside Gebhardt's right now?

But he wasn't. The car he had borrowed from a friend for a trip to Bismarck was parked on the road in front of the house.

They parked behind it and walked up the path. Pearl Finley met them at the door.

"Come right in, folks!"

The day was unseasonably warm for the last of March and they sent all the children out to the yard till the ceremony was over.

Annie had not come downstairs yet. They sat in the parlor without speaking. All of them wondered how much everybody else knew. All of them knew that what anybody else didn't know he could probably guess. George tapped his feet and looked around the room. He wondered what rent Harry Goodman had charged them. They might not be paying rent to anybody at all, now that Harry was gone. The mortgage he'd taken on the place had probably been tossed out with the other worthless scraps of paper that Harry had been calling assets. From the condition of the parlor ceiling a man might suppose that there was no roof on the house at all, but George knew he had seen the facsimile of a roof from the outside.

Lucy wondered what they were doing at the house. She had never been to a wedding. She understood that something happened when people got married, so that afterwards the man had the right to boss the woman around. There were other, less forthright things about marriage which she sensed were even more significant, and though she had no idea of what they were, she felt terribly embarrassed about them.

Getting married seemed like just about the dumbest thing a person could do. As far as she could tell, people always regretted it. She couldn't understand why people went right on doing something that they ought to know they were going to be sorry for. Whenever she had to stand around in the store waiting for her father to finish a conversation, she never heard the men call their wives anything but "the old lady" or "the old woman," and they always sounded as though they hated the wives they were married to. It was the same when she listened to the women talk, when it was too cold to play outside on a Sunday afternoon and the men were all out in the barn. Women always said things like, "No matter what I do, I can't please him," or "They're all alike. They're all alike."

"Hey, let's play tag!" Audley yelled. He rushed at her, socked her on the arm, and veered away. "You're It. Lucy's It and had a fit and couldn't get over it!"

"No, I'm not! I don't want to play!"

"You *have* to play! Ma said you're *related* to me now! You're just like my sister, and you have to do what I say!"

He danced up close to her and squatted, daring her to tag him while he was at a disadvantage. "Oh, ho, ho! Lucy couldn't catch a flea!"

He began to sing, jumping from one squat to another like a frog:

My mamma saidee,
If I'd be goodee,
That she would buy me
A rubber dollee!
Now don't you tell her
I've got a feller,
Or she won't buy me
No rubber dollee!

"I haven't got a feller!" Lucy screamed.

"Oh, ho, ho! Blue and yeller, got a feller!"

"I'm *not* blue and yellow!" she screamed again.

"Oh *yes*, you are!" He was delighted at how easy it was to get her goat. All those days last summer when he was herding her father's cows she wouldn't even talk to him, she was so highfalutin. But it was all different now. They were *related!* "Your jacket's blue and your hair's light yellow," he told her.

"Hair doesn't count!"

"Lucy's It and had a fit and couldn't get over it."

"Leave me alone! I don't have to play with you if I don't want to!"

His excitement turned to fury when he saw that he might not win after all. If he didn't win now, he would look silly. He *had* to make her mad enough to chase him. Besides, he had to prove that she had to play with him. He picked up a rope lying on the ground and tied a loop in the end of it.

"Okay," he said. "If you're just going to stand there and never move, I'll lasso you. I'll show you how a Texas cowboy ropes himself a steer."

Lucy stood her ground. He tried to get the heavy rope to twirl, but he couldn't manage it.

"Ho, ho yourself. What a cowboy!"

"I'll *show* you!" he shouted. "Come here, Sandy! That's a boy!" The big mongrel collie bounded up to him and he put the lasso around its neck. The dog pulled back and the rope tightened, making his thick winter hair bulge out in a ruff.

"You're *hurting* him," Lucy cried. "You're choking his neck!"

"So what. He's *my* dog, ain't he? Come here, you!" Audley dragged him across the yard to a tree. He held the end of the rope in one hand and climbed to the first big branch and sat there, still holding the rope.

"What do you think you're going to do now?" Lucy jeered. His little sister was standing beside Lucy, looking up at him. Two females down there — to be shown something.

"Just you wait and see!" He had no idea himself of what he could do. It had to be something to make them respect him, that was all.

He jumped off the branch, landing lightly in his black tennis shoes. He saw that Lucy was looking at the big frayed holes around his ankle bones and toes. The rope dangled over the branch, and he gave a yank on it that brought the dog sliding up to him. He yanked again and the dog's front legs pawed the air and he started to cough for breath. His tongue hung out. It was turning purple.

"Let him down!" Lucy begged. "You're choking him! He'll die!"

"I don't have to do *nothing* a *girl* tells me to do! Sissy!"

He hauled on the rope once more and the dog's hind legs barely touched the ground. Thin foam lay along his black lips, and his kicks spun him around so that he kept losing his footing entirely.

"Let him down!"

"Sissy!"

The dog hung limply. His legs twitched.

"You've killed him!"

"I have *not!* I'll *show* you!" He let go of the rope and the dog fell to the ground.

Audley felt for the rope through the dog's hair and loosened it. A great gulp of air tore down the bruised throat and the dog started to pant weakly.

Lucy put her hand down to touch the matted hair of his neck, but he made a snarling sound and drew his lips even farther back from his teeth.

"See! He doesn't want *you!* Girls! Sissies!" Audley reached his own hand down to Sandy and the dog snapped his jaws shut over the hand.

"You fucker!" Audley shrieked. He jumped up and swung the toe of his tennis shoe into the dog's heaving ribs.

Lucy rushed away from him. She had never heard anyone say that word before. She didn't suppose it was ever said — only written and thought. She couldn't stop hearing it and seeing it in her head. Where could she go? Where could she escape from this boy and that word he had spoken?

Audley had won. He had won after all.

❦ ❦ ❦

George hated getting cleaned up in the middle of a workday for some damn fool reason. And nobody had told him he was going to be expected to eat food coming out of the Finley kitchen, either. He was exasperated at being blamed for this whole rotten mess, and he was damned if he'd hang around and be polite. He took a few bites of the cake and then he caught Rachel's eye and gave her the signal.

They could see the signs all over the honeymoon car as soon as they walked out on the porch. Somebody had done a quick job with white calcimine. Lucy was already down at the road reading them, and she was waiting to ask about some of them. They said, "Bismarck or Bust," "Just Married," "Whooopee!" "Watch Our Dust," and "Hot Springs Tonight!"

"What does that one mean, Mamma?" she asked.

"Why, I don't know, dear," Rachel said. "Maybe whoever painted it thought they were going to go to Hot Springs."

George looked at the sign and at Rachel and began to laugh.

Lucy said, "But it says Bismarck *too*, so whoever did it must know they're going to Bismarck."

George laughed some more and Rachel felt the blood in her face.

"Well, what *does* it mean?" Lucy asked again. "I just want to know."

"*Nothing!*" Rachel said.

George said, "Come on, hurry along here. If we don't get back home right away, there won't be enough time to bother hitching up the plow again." He stopped laughing. Stuart had a lot to learn—about the beans in the bottle and such things.

It was the final mortification as far as Rachel was concerned. Of course it was one or several of Annie's admirers who had written such a thing. A trollop from this filthy world the mother of Will Shepard's grandchild? Annie Finley the mother of Lucy's cousin? Unthinkable!

"Am I related to them now?" Lucy asked.

Rachel had never seen a child who had such a knack for startling a person who was thinking private thoughts. "Related to who?" she stalled.

"Them! Audley and all the rest of those kids."

It was preposterous. It couldn't be true. "No," Rachel said.

"Now, Rachel, what good does it do to lie about it!" George said. "Yes, Lucy, you are."

"In a very distant way that doesn't count at all," Rachel said.

Rose did not speak. They took her home and left her.

Rachel hurried to change her clothes and do the dinner dishes she had had to leave. Lucy trailed her nervously. Finally she brought it out. "He said a terrible word."

"Who? Audley?"

"Yes."

"What did he say?"

Lucy looked up at her. She would never speak that word to anybody, and especially not to her mother, because she knew that her mother would certainly never have heard of it.

"Well, what did he say?" Rachel asked again. One never knew what little boys and girls might do together. It was always a worry.

"A very terrible word."

The whole thing became steadily more preposterous. "Well," Rachel told her, "you must always be polite to him, but you don't need to play with him. After all, he's more than two years older than you. If he ever says another terrible word to you, you just walk away and tell him you weren't brought up that way."

Being related to the Finleys was beyond the power of Rachel's imagination. They were of a different world, a different species. She could never forget how Audley had come and gone so bleakly day after day when he was herding the cows. She had been repelled by his accent and by his strange ways. He represented to her everything in human existence that was rootless and meaningless, and therefore degrading. The one thing she could not bear to think of was to be rootless, to be without well-defined positions, both human and geographical. The Finleys were of that mass of human creatures in the world who were so unbelievably numerous and so unbelievably miserable that one could think of them only in statistics — hordes of Indians excreting, bathing, and worshiping in the Ganges, with a certain percentage of them dying each year from several kinds of plagues; hordes of Chinese in rice paddies along the Yellow River being swept away or made homeless by floods. Plagues, floods, earthquakes, and similar catastrophes — they always seemed to kill such people. One never even knew how they died, there were so many of them. They were simply approximate numbers in the aftermath of calamity.

The Finleys had been flooded out several times. Once his mother had whimsically remarked that Audley had almost been born in a rowboat. Rachel could not imagine the sort of people who could feel no more concern than that over the birth of a new descendant — an heir. To be connected to such a family? Unthinkable. Stuart married to a girl who had been serving beer in a saloon before she was seventeen years old? Unthinkable . . .

All afternoon Lucy marveled over hearing that word said aloud. She had seen it chalked on a culvert and inked on the gray paint of the long corridor leading from the schoolrooms out to the toilets in the shed. The corridor smelled of the toilets and the lime they put down the holes, and she connected the word with those smells, but she really knew that the word Audley said did not stand for either kind of thing that the toilets were for, because she knew those two bad words, too. Whatever did this one mean, anyway?

⁂

Rose was as polite as she could be to Annie. She did not speak much because now there was less to say than there had ever been. Part of the reason she felt so little inclination or need to talk to Annie was that most of the time she could not really believe that Annie was there.

The girl had certain habits that were distasteful. Every morning upstairs she curled her orangish hair with a curling iron she heated by suspending the handles across the top of a lamp chimney and letting the tongs hang down toward the flaming wick. Every morning a faint smell of burning hair floated down to the kitchen while Rose was cooking breakfast and Stuart was out milking. That was the only time of day when Rose deeply felt Annie's inescapable presence—perhaps because it was morning and one tended to look for some relief from the new day and there never was any.

But the girl worked very hard, and she was surprisingly clean. Rose wished, in fact, that Annie would not work so hard, because it left her with less to do herself at a time when she needed more to do. She was already planning on a much bigger garden than they had had last year. That would keep her busy all summer. And next winter there would presumably be a child to keep Annie busy. But the next month or so was going to be difficult, with Annie constantly rushing to usurp tasks that she had set out for herself. If Rose was planning to peel the potatoes at five-fifteen and went into the kitchen only to find that Annie had peeled them at five o'clock, then what was there to do at five-fifteen? However, since it still did not seem plausible that Annie could belong there permanently, the girl seemed more like a misguided helpful elf in the house than anything else. She would inexplicably disappear some night the way helpful elves eventually did.

One afternoon the Eggers stopped in for a minute. Not many people came to call these days because not many people knew how to act toward a widow whose son had married six weeks after his father died. But Clarence was his effusive self in his congratulations to Stuart, and Elsie was her presumptuous self in her speculations on what a help it was to have Annie in the house.

It was a kind of relief to see somebody like the Eggers — people who were brassy and unabashed and who could ask, "Well, how are you making out, Rose?" with so little evident awareness of the depth of her griefs that the griefs were not really touched and her self-control was not even tried.

But from the moment they arrived, Annie behaved strangely. Rose became more and more embarrassed. This was a situation she had not even thought of — how a girl from such a background would embarrass her every time there was company at the house.

When they were gone, she couldn't keep from saying, "You seem tired, Annie. Why don't you rest till suppertime? I wasn't going to have anything fancy tonight, anyway, and it won't take a minute to get it." She thought she would go out of her mind if she had to spend two hours in the kitchen with that girl.

But Annie stood there staring at her from two round eyes in a freckled face, two freckled arms akimbo, two freckled hands over round hips — looking exactly like a saloon waitress.

"*They're* good enough for you because they've got a nice new Chrysler, aren't they?" the girl said.

"Why, they brought Will home from Jamestown in that car. It was very nice of them. Of course, they're 'good enough.' We've known them all our lives."

"Oh yes! You've known them all your lives! Well how do you think they bought that car?"

"What are you getting at? They just have to cut down somewhere else so Clarence can have a car that's easy to drive, I suppose — it's hard to drive with one arm."

Why was the girl all upset? After the way that girl had been acting all afternoon, she *herself* was the one who had a right to be upset!

"All right! I'll *tell* you what I mean! Ma said not to, but she didn't *know* . . . how it was going to *be* out here! If you wasn't such *teetotalers,* you'd *know* where Stuart gets his booze. You'd *know!*"

There were tears falling down the girl's cheeks — tears! — tears on the face of the harlot whose hand had held the golden cup full of the abominations and filthiness of all the world — tears on the face of the Devil's own cupbearer, whose hands had given Hell into the hands of a ruined boy.

Rose felt the explosion in her chest, the flames coming out of her mouth.

"*You! Annie Finley! You* ask me whose hands gave it to him! Y*our* hands gave it to him! *Slut!* The mark of the Beast is on you — all of you — you and Jake Gebhardt — all of you will go down to Hell together!"

The face of the purple and scarlet whore looked down at her from the stairway and the mouth shrieked, "Then why is Clarence Egger your friend? Don't you know? Don't you know he *always* made it? He *makes* it! He makes all of it for Jake and for anybody that comes to his *door!*"

Rose sat down at the kitchen table. After a while the fire in her chest was gone, but it felt now as though her lungs might be made of cinders. She was not going to die — nothing essential to her body had exploded after all. No, she was going to have to go on for a while because her body was going to go on.

Presently she could even think again. Where *did* the Eggers get the money for the car? The Eggers lived several miles away; they and the Shepards were friendly but not intimate by any means. Certainly not intimate enough so that Rose had ever even slightly concerned herself with the way they managed their money. But where *did* he get the money? The Eggers had always had new cars, even during this last dozen years when farmers did not buy new cars.

And the liquor *did* have to come from somewhere, didn't it? She herself had asked the question a thousand times. "Where does the boy get it? Where did he *get* it that first night?" But she had never conceived of a specific answer to the question. She herself had no more idea of what liquor looked like than what the Devil looked like. They were both intangible. She saw the effects of the Devil's machinations everywhere around her but she had not seen the Devil. She saw the effects of liquor but she had never seen it. But she *had smelled* liquor; the boy *had* drunk it. Yes, liquor *was* tangible, even if the Devil was not. Yes, the liquor *did* have to come from some specific place, didn't it?

The girl must know what she was talking about. For one thing, she was certainly in a *position* to know. And Rose knew she must have been telling the truth. That strumpet with tears on her cheeks — she was telling the truth.

Thank God Will didn't know. Thank God Will wouldn't ever have to know that a man he had always thought of as a friend was manufacturing Evil and selling it to his son. Was there no limit to what people would do to each other in order to survive? Were the new cars so important to Clarence Egger's one-armed survival? Would all the little members of the human race go on betraying each other until no one was left?

The world was sunk even deeper in filth than she had believed it to be, and the filth was so much nearer and more deceptive than she had thought it was. Not an hour before, her son had sat in this house and eaten cake and drunk coffee with the man who bought new cars from the profits of his service to the Devil. Her son had politely accepted the man's congratulations on his marriage. No one even seemed surprised at how closely Evil surrounded them all.

She would have to learn how not to be so surprised, too, or else she would never be able to be in the same room with Clarence Egger again. When she was alone she would pray that some day she might be able to forgive him.

And the weeping harlot upstairs — what was surprising about *her?* She was only another child grimy with the world's dirt — no less at home in this house than in any other. Rose even had a brief impulse to go up to her. But she knew that such impulses were never followed by other impulses telling her what to say or do, so she did not go.

Monday, April 16

George was disking his south eighty acres when the northwest horizon began to go black. He had a clean white handkerchief in each hip pocket and when he had filled both handkerchiefs with dust, he headed in. He unhitched and put the team in the barn, letting them stay in harness until after he had run in the cows. By the time he was through in the barn he could not really see the house at all. He sensed its small, buffeted presence on the hill above him.

It was only when he stepped into the kitchen out of the wind that he realized how raw it had made him. He was eroding, like the land itself. The tears torn out of his eyes made rings of mud around his eyelids. His nose smarted. It seemed always full of dust, no matter how hard he blew it. Dust was the only thing he could smell.

Rachel was stuffing wet rags around the window. By now she had a special set of gray rags for catching dust. She washed out the rags after the storms and used them over and over. She held one up, wrung out enough to keep it from dripping. "Are you going out again, or shall I put this under the door now?"

"Go ahead," he said from his gritty mouth. "I'm not going out in *that* again till I *have* to. We should have kept Lucy home from school today. It's going to be quite a trip."

Rachel waited for him to begin railing against the guilty ones, especially the immigrant Russians and the absentee landlords who mismanaged the land through selfishness, stupidity, and greed, and made it behave this way. She waited for him to point out that even the government experts were advocating fall plowing up till a year ago, when they finally realized that fall plowing was a major factor causing the land to blow. She waited for him to tell her how if they would get a few men who really knew the land back there in those soft jobs instead of getting men who knew somebody's brother-in-law. . . .

But he said nothing more at all. He went into the dining room and slumped into his chair. He stared out the window into the darkness, thumping the chair arms with his fingers, making each fingertip follow the next, like soldiers marching over a cliff. He made no other movement for at least five minutes. Then he leaned forward and unlaced his shoes. His socks were black with dust and his toes were lined with it.

"Reckon I'll wash my feet," he said.

After he'd got his feet clean he went into the bedroom to get a pair of fresh socks. There was already a film of dust on the wooden drawer knobs, and the starched white dresser scarf was almost the color of the socks he had taken off.

"For God's sake, Rachel! This window in here is open at the top! What a mess! If I can round up all the stock and get them into the barn, can't you even see that the windows get closed?"

"I *did* close it! Sometimes it falls back down again. See how it slants to one side? It never *would* lock. It's the outside window. All I can do is go outside and prop it up from the bottom with a stick just the right length, and I *had* a stick but the wind blew it away."

She walked in to face him while she talked, bringing a pan full of wet rags to put around it. "*You* know it needs fixing! Why don't you ever fix it? I notice you always get around to fixing up things *outside!*" There was dust at the corners of her eyes even though she had not been out of the house since the storm began.

"And what are *you* complaining about, anyway!" she continued. "*I'm* the one who'll have to clean it all up and haul water and wash the sheets and take the quilts outside and beat the dust out of them. Just what are *you* complaining about!"

George went into the dining room, lit the gas lamp, and sat down to read the *Sun*. There were the usual kidnappings and lynchings, and a story about the big blow to the south of them which had dusted South Dakota, Minnesota, Iowa, and more states below them. The twenty-five million dollars worth of Texas dirt which blew into Nebraska a year ago was blown back into Texas again, but the Texans did not welcome it. There was a filler beneath the story that he must have read a dozen times in the last year, but still he counted the commas and the zeros to see if they always came out the same. They always did, but that didn't make them right. There was no way to prove they were right as far as he could see.

Following a violent "black storm" in the Ukraine on April 25 and 26, 1928, over seven hundred widely distributed measurements showed that a total of 15,400,000,000 tons of soil had been swept up into the air and deposited in other parts of the country as well as in Poland and Rumania.

The filler was credited to the United States Department of Agriculture. These *experts* who were so foolish as to make such unprovable statements. Of course he could not prove they were wrong, any more than they could prove they were right. He had reason to know that a lot of dirt could be moved in a mighty short time, but even so, how could anybody know whether it was billions or trillions or millions? And wasn't it ridiculous to say it was not twelve, or fourteen, or sixteen, billion, but *fifteen and a half billion?* Were they trying to scare every prairie farmer off his farm with their pigheaded assurance that there would soon be no soil left to farm?

If they were so concerned back there in Washington, with their fat rear ends in cushioned chairs and their feet on their desks, monkeying around with slide rules and statistics from the other side of the world, why did they do nothing better for him than to send out guys like Finnegan to tell him to build an inside bathroom in his house? Why didn't they get some laws with teeth in them to get rid of all the barberry bushes so there wouldn't be any host to get the damned rust spores through the winter? Why didn't they scrape up some Federal money to get rid of the grasshoppers?

No, they'd rather sit back there and play with their numbers and send out their millions of fillers and press releases, whether it was the Treasury Department, the Department of Agriculture, or any of the other departments. He opened his mouth to call out to Rachel about the hard-working statisticians the farmer had plugging for him in Washington, but he decided not to talk to her after all. She was acting so peculiar, what was the use? He scratched his head. His scalp crawled as if it was full of vermin, but there was no use washing the dust out of his hair till the storm was over.

This was the third storm they had had since plowing began. He had sat idle for three days while the tops of the acres he intended to plant in wheat blew away before he even got them planted.

Rachel kept making noises in the kitchen. What in the world could she be so busy about? What *was* there to do, with the land blowing out from under them? He went out to see what she was doing. She had the whole set of glass dishes down from the top shelf of the cupboard and she was teetering on the kitchen stool, wiping the dust from the shelf.

"What on *earth* are you doing? What good will *that* do? You'll just have to do it all over again. I wish to God you'd quit acting like the south end of a northbound horse!"

"What do *you* care what I do! What *should* I be doing? This is the second time in two weeks I've had to wash every dish in the house and all the pieces of the separator and all the sheets on the beds, besides the stove and the windows and the cupboards and the woodwork. Now just what *should* I be doing?"

"Rachel! There's no use flying off the handle at me just because I ask you a civil question! It just looks to me like you're wasting energy, that's all. Now just calm down a little and don't jump at people like that!"

"Just go and read your paper and don't provoke me then!"

He kept coming to things in the newspaper he wanted to read to her, but he knew she wouldn't talk, anyhow. He came to *one* thing he *didn't* want to read to her. They were having another so-called "wheat conference" in Rome — this world wheat conference seemed to meet in a different foreign country every month — and they had just adopted another United States motion for more curtailing of wheat production. It was nice to be told every other day that you were superfluous. It was nice to sit down and read in the paper how you were paying your taxes so a bunch of politicians could joy-ride around the world and send back statements from Rome about how superfluous you were.

And speaking of politicians, Governor Langer had got himself indicted by a Federal grand jury in Fargo for misuse of Federal relief funds. He must have thought up all his baloney just to cover up his real uses of his office. At least none of his baloney had accomplished anything — not the moratorium on foreclosure sales, not the embargo on wheat shipments (pressure from the railroads had got him on that one in less than three months), not, in short, any of his proclamations and proposals.

The *Sun* could always make a story out of the weather. His newspaper explained to George, as he sat in the noon darkness, that his worst problem was being so far behind in moisture. Last year, for instance, they had got only ten inches of precipitation, whereas sixteen was normal. This year to date they had received .89 of an inch, whereas 2.69 inches was normal. This year, the experts with the slide rules said, George's fields probably would get even less moisture than they got last year. But last year the well had almost gone dry.

George had made up his mind long ago that he was never going to plant a crop he didn't harvest. He got up and went out to the kitchen again and lifted his account books down from the cupboard. The books were black with dust and he borrowed Rachel's rag to clean them off. He tried to open the drawer where the pencils were kept, but it stuck. He squatted down and yanked at it.

"Why don't you put some soap along the bottom of this drawer?" he asked.

"I did. The soap is full of dust."

He spread out his books on the dining room table and opened the first one at random. Turkeys — thirty-five cents a pound in 1930, thirty cents in 1931, twenty-eight in 1932, nineteen for one batch last fall — the New York outfit had slickered him. But every year it cost him just as much labor and feed to raise them and get them to market. And every year the railroad charged as much or more for hauling them and every year the middleman took a little more for getting them to the consumer. The farmer was the only man who bore the shock of the dropping prices.

He looked out the window toward the barn, but all he could see was flying topsoil. Speak of unimaginable numbers — of billions of tons of dust, of galaxies a hundred thousand light-years away, of the number of atoms in the universe — just try to imagine how many particles of dust passing between him and the barn it took to blot that barn completely out of sight at a quarter of one in the afternoon. He couldn't even make out the clothesline posts a few yards from the house. There was nothing out there but screaming blackness.

It was hard for a man to shake off the feeling of being buried alive when he had to sit out a dust storm in a little trembling, groaning house, with the wet rags at the windows growing blacker and blacker, and the air ever heavier to breathe. If he blew his smarting nose, plain mud was deposited into his handkerchief. How far back into his head and how far down into his lungs could it go, anyway?

The drought was commencing its tenth year now, and the deep

root-systems were long dead. There was nothing to hold the land against the wind. Until a few years ago he and Rachel had always subscribed to the *National Geographic*, and he remembered all too clearly the articles it had run on various places in Asia and Africa — places that had once been rich in trees and grassland and now were deserts. Hundreds of years before Christ, the deforested and overgrazed hills drained by the Tigris-Euphrates river system had lost so much soil that the silt from the rivers had filled in the Persian Gulf for a hundred and eighty miles. A fellow named Woolley had been digging around way out there in the desert and discovered a buried seacoast town — a seaport one hundred and eighty miles from water. And now that whole stretch of land between the ancient and modern mouths of the rivers was mostly dunes made of sand from the ruined hinterland. What had happened there could happen here too. Maybe the professors would be excavating what was left of this house from a sand dune some day. Maybe this house would have to be excavated after this one storm, if it got much worse and lasted much longer.

He didn't need to look at the wheat records in his books — he knew by heart how the wheat disappeared into smut, rust, drought, grasshopper gizzards, middlemen's pockets, and the vast bank account of James T. Vick. He was a little better off than he was last year at this time, with all his savings suddenly gone, but he was afraid this year was going to bring him more expenses than last year had.

Rachel was probably right about Lucy's tonsils, and Lucy ought to go to the dentist this summer, too. And he had to fix up the car a little and make some machinery repairs that should have been done last year. If he had to sink another well this summer, the cost of that alone could wipe him out. Talk about the "cost-price squeeze" that was doing in the farmer! There had been plenty of talk about it all right — fifty years of talk — centuries of talk — but he noticed the squeeze got worse every year, just the same.

There was no use at all in planting wheat if he wasn't going to be able to pay to have it threshed and still have a little left over to get through the winter. There was nobody to borrow from this spring except Vick. He would have to go now and make the arrangements or he might very well find himself next fall without a roof over his head. Vick thought he was a good farmer, and if Vick had any sense at all, he would surely want to see him through this one unprecedented year in order to keep him on the property and keep on profiting from his work. Wouldn't he? And Vick ought to agree to be responsible for providing water on land he owned himself, oughtn't he?

It was time to go and fetch Lucy from school. He buttoned up his clothes as tightly as he could and Rachel tied a mask over his nose and mouth. He opened the door and stepped into a foot of dust drifted across the porch. He had never seen so much dirt moved so swiftly. He wondered if he would be able to make it to town.

In the barn he made dust masks of gunny sacks to put over the wide, unguarded nostrils of the horses. Then he led the team out to the wagon. Dust was banked high over the rims of the wagon wheels and built up in cones around the spokes. The wagon looked embedded, as though it had been sitting there from ancient times and was now being exhumed by the wind. Its wheels might have been those of an abandoned chariot belonging to a driver who had himself long since turned to dust.

George had no visibility at all, and he could feel the team wandering back and forth across the road. Once another team arose out of the blackness into sudden existence and nearly collided with his own horses. He never even saw whose team it was, he was so busy hanging on to his own. It could have been a team created from the furious dust itself, for the horses abruptly ceased to exist as his own went on trying to make some headway into the wind. Nobody drove automobiles in something like this, so he wasn't afraid of being struck by a car. Once he had been caught in the Ford when it got like this, and when he couldn't see the radiator cap any more he finally had pulled over and sat it out. But he could at least trust the horses to stay on the road.

He made it before school was out and he walked into the building to get Lucy.

"You better bring along your arithmetic book," he told her. "If this keeps up, we won't be able to bring you in tomorrow."

He put the book in his denim jacket pocket, which seemed half full of dust, and he tied a scarf over her nose and mouth. "There, now, can you breathe through that?"

She looked up at him. Her blue eyes, isolated from the childish parts of her face by the scarf, were disturbingly mature. He felt as though a strange woman was sizing him up. Then she nodded her head like any little child.

Once they were on the road leading through the open fields, they might as well have been lost in the swirling shrieking Sahara, with the wind flogging their backs, whipping the breath from their mouths, lifting at their elbows, even lifting at the wagon, tipping it, gathering strength to spill them into the blackness and blow them away. They could not have heard each other even if they had shouted into each other's ears. They lowered their heads and shut their eyes against the flaying sand and let the wind blow them to shelter or to the deaths of whatever worlds they kept inside their heads while the desert's dry convulsion annihilated the world outside.

This road that Lucy knew by heart was now the deep rumbling hole which led down to the golden palace of King Pluto, and she herself was the poor little sobbing Proserpina, swept down the tunnel in the golden chariot behind the two black horses with smoke coming out of their nostrils. And far away in the sunlight Mother Ceres was wandering over the earth, refusing to make the seeds grow because of her grief over her little stolen daughter. All the starving sheep and cattle were following Ceres, bleating and mooing and begging her to feed them. But Mother Ceres had made a rule that until Pluto gave Proserpina back, nothing would ever grow again anywhere on the earth. So the whole black earth was waiting for little Proserpina to come smiling back into the sun.

❦ ❦ ❦

Lucy stayed home the next morning because it was still gusty and dirty outside. She did two pages of arithmetic and then some more problems her mother made up for her to do, but she finished them quickly and did not know what to do next. She began bouncing a ball in the dining room. Presently it got away from her and bounced into the kitchen.

"*Must* you do that?" her mother asked.

"Can I go outside?"

"No! Of course not! If you could go outside, you could have gone to school. What's the matter with you, anyhow? Why don't you read?"

"I've read everything that's interesting. Can I go over to Gramma's?"

"Maybe Daddy can take you over this afternoon if it lets up some more."

"Well, can I bounce the ball *carefully* for a while?"

"All right. Carefully!"

She bounced it higher and higher because the game was getting more and more monotonous. She was just doing it because she'd won the argument about it and now she had to pretend it was what she wanted to do. Then the ball escaped again and she ran after it, to recapture it quickly and show that she really was in control of it. But instead she kicked it and it rose into the air as though it was possessed. It traveled in a long, unswerving arc straight for the kitchen window and slammed against it with a conclusive sound.

Her mother was peeling potatoes. She dropped her hands into the pan of water. "You've broken it!" She began to cry. Finally she sat down on the kitchen stool and covered her face with her apron and shook and shook. Lucy had never seen her cry like that. She went close enough to the window to look at the long slivers of glass and the hole in the pane. She couldn't really believe it was there; she would shut her eyes very tightly — so tightly that she saw the little designs of color in the dark — and then open them again and the window would be all right.

"Oh, how will we ever pay for another one!" her mother cried. "We'll just have to board it up the way we did the car window, and then we won't have any light at all in this awful little place!"

She raised her face from her apron and let the rumpled cloth fall back over her dress. She stood up and went back to the potatoes. She would not look at Lucy.

"You'll just have to tell Daddy yourself. *I'm* not going to do it. You'll just have to take your spanking when *he* comes in."

She put the potatoes on and swept up the glass. Then she took a heavy flour sack that she had still not ripped apart or washed out and tacked it at the four corners of the window frame to stop the dust and wind. It did make the room much darker, with the floury, dauntless Dakota Maid there, shivering and smiling in the wind.

And it made the house drafty. They would have to patch it right away.

Her father would not be in for another hour. He was out tearing the wildly rolling Russian thistles away from the barbed-wire fences. The thistles would stop the dust and then the dust would stop more thistles, and the dust bank would get so high in places that the stock could walk right up it and out of the pasture.

It was an hour that Lucy thought would never end. Yet what would she do when it ended? Her mother had never before been too mad at her even to *spank* her. She sat at the dining room table with a book open before her, too terrified to look at it, wondering why she hadn't wanted to get a book when her mother had first asked her to, because it seemed that if only she had wanted to read *then*, she would *now* be the happiest little girl in the whole world.

When her father came, black-faced and exhausted, she went to stand in the corner behind the stove. She leaned against the wall, wondering if some Gobble-uns could be good enough to snatch her through the ceiling, and wondering if her mother and father would care or if they would be glad because, like the mother and father of Hansel and Gretel, they were too poor to take care of her anyhow. She could hear nothing except the wind, but she could feel her mother waiting in the kitchen. This was the first time her mother had ever refused to stand up for her with her father. Lucy could not even guess how badly it might go with her. She watched him pulling off his shoes. At last she said, "Daddy?"

He looked up from his feet. "Well?"

"I have to tell you something."

"Shoot."

"I broke a window."

She had expected, the instant the words were out, to have him upon her as if he were the black wind itself, to feel his hand holding her arm and the razor strop falling again and again and again. She stood pressing herself harder and harder into the corner, watching him. Sometimes she dreamed that when she was trapped like this she miraculously learned to fly, and she went straight up and past his clutching hands and out the door, like Peter Pan.

He did not leap up from his chair. He only lifted his head so he could look straight at her. His eyes were all red and black. "Well, how did you do *that*, anyhow?"

"I was playing with my ball," she whispered. Now he would come — now that he knew for sure there was no excuse at all for such an accident.

He finished emptying the dirt out of his shoes and socks and whisking it out from under his toes. He put the socks and shoes back on and got to his feet. He seemed too tall for the ceiling.

"I've told you never to play ball in the house, haven't I?" he said. He always made it clear to her why she would have to be beaten.

She nodded her head once, feeling her hair brush back and forth against the wallpaper.

"Well, let's see what we can do about it. What window?"

"Kitchen."

He went and looked at the flour sack window curtained by dyed flour sacks. He took the tacks out of the flour sack and looked at the hole. "Pretty far gone for patching," he said. He got some adhesive tape from the medicine cabinet and taped the cracks running back from the break. Her mother moved about putting dinner on the table, saying nothing.

Her father cut a rounded piece of cardboard to fit the hole and taped it on the outside of the glass so the wind would help to hold it in place. He was making her wait, so she could think about what a terrible thing she had done before she got her beating for it.

When he came back into the kitchen, he said, "I have to go to Jimtown in the morning. I'll stop off at the junk yard and get a piece of glass."

Neither her mother nor her father said a word while they ate dinner. They had never acted like this before. That meant that *she* must have done a much worse thing than she had ever done before. So bad that she couldn't even understand how bad it was. So bad that it wouldn't even do any good to beat her for it. If it wouldn't do any good to beat her for it, then what *would* do any good? Nothing. The answer was very clear. Nothing she could ever do could make up for what she had already done. How much better it would have been to get a beating.

Wednesday, April 18

George stopped at the junk yard along the highway outside Jamestown. It was noon and he figured he might as well give Vick time to get back from lunch. He nearly had a fight with the junkman. The chiseler wanted almost as much for a piece of glass from a wrecked car as George would have paid for it new, cut to his own specifications. He was furious at having wasted his time with a chiseler. That was the way it was when you were poor. You frittered your time away, trying to save a nickel here, a dime there.

He hadn't been in Vick's store since the year before. He had been to Jamestown a couple of times, but he never went near *that* store for any of his buying.

He walked down the jammed aisles under the busy little funiculars flying money up to Vick. Every time he went there he thought he hated that store as much as he could possibly hate it, yet every time he went he knew he was hating it more than he had the time before. He climbed the twisted stairs and ducked under the little door.

"Well, Mr. Custer!" Vick said with his businessman benevolence — J. T. Vick and J. P. Morgan.

His heartiness was a noisome patronization. He was rubbing in his forgiveness. He was showing how he could afford to forget the way his tenant had tramped out of his office a year ago. He had just sat and waited for his tenant to come back, knowing that he would have to come back. He knew, too, that his tenant would have to shake the hand he stuck out.

"Well," Vick said, "shall we renew the lease on the same terms as last year?"

"That's what I came to see you about, Mr. Vick," George said.

"Things look kind of bad this year, don't they?" J. T. Vick was *so* sympathetic!

And Vick always took the offensive away from him before he knew what was happening. It gave him the feeling that Vick had been through the whole conversation and had all his counter-arguments already figured out.

"Too dry. Too windy," George said. "Hard to say what kind of crop I can get this year. Could be so bad it would make last year look good."

"And last year was plenty bad," Vick agreed.

It was easier to fight orneriness than this agreeableness, because the agreeableness seemed to convey not a willingness to negotiate but an intransigent decision *not* to negotiate.

"Well, I've done some figuring," said George, "and I think we're just going to have to work out something different for this year."

He plunged in before Vick could stop him. "I've got some extra expenses coming up — doctor bills and the like — and I've got to be able to count on at least three hundred dollars clear after the crop is in next fall. I just can't get through the winter and get the crop in a year from now without that much. So, I propose that for this one year we work out some sort of flexible deal that will get me through till next spring."

Vick said nothing at all; he just sat and looked sympathetic. He said nothing about what he owed George Custer, morally if not legally, for taking over that farm ten years ago and making it worth twice what it was worth when he moved on to it. Worth twice as much, anyway, if the bottom hadn't fallen out of farm real estate. Worth twice as much, surely, if it had a good dependable well.

"And there's another thing, too," George said. "The well might give out on me this summer. I don't think we'd have too much trouble finding water on the place. I know *one* spot where there *used* to be a well — I damn near lost a good mare in it! We could try around there again. But I don't have the cash to dig a well. That's one of the things I think *you* ought to be responsible for anyway. I want some assurance from you that you'll dig a well if I need one."

"Just a minute, Custer. I'm not responsible for *any well*. Your water is *your* problem. *I* lease you the *land* and *I* pay the *taxes* on it."

George hung on to himself. He *had* to hang on. "Look, Mr. Vick. None of these troubles may come up. I may not need a well; the doctor might decide the kid's tonsils can wait; the dentist might decide her teeth can wait; there's still time to get some moisture before summer comes; the grasshoppers and smut might not be so bad this year — the only thing I'm getting at is that I have to know there'll be some place I can lay my hands on a reasonable loan if I have to *get* a loan at all. I figured we could write up some kind of terms this spring that would get me through this year, and if that means you take less than your usual share this fall, we can make it up when things get better."

"What makes you think things are going to get better?" Vick asked.

"Why . . . they've just got to, that's all."

"Maybe they'll get worse."

"How could they? It just isn't in the cards. Sooner or later we've got to get some rain again."

"So we get rain. So the crops get better and prices go way down again. Looks to me like you're going to make about the same every year, whether the crops are good or bad. Good crops, no price. Bad crops, fair price. Either way, you've made about the same for the last few years, haven't you, Custer?" The way he said "Custer" made it sound as though he thought another farmer could have done better on that farm.

Still George hung on. He mustn't lose his temper again, the way he had before. This was not the time to start the big fight. He'd only end up in jail, along with the other farmers here and there around the country who'd been walking into city men's offices and blowing heads off landlords and bankers.

"Look at the prices we got before the war," George said. "The parity years, when a man could buy a pair of overalls for a bushel of wheat. When those times come back again, we'll be on our feet in a year or so."

"Custer, you know as well as I do that those 'parity years' are nothing but politicians' ballyhoo. *Those* years are *never* coming back for the farmer. They didn't have *unions* back in those days, for *one* thing. The people that worked in the mills and made the denim for your overalls — why, they got paid the price of two or three bushels of wheat for working a seventy-hour week. I *know* something about this kind of stuff. This is my *business.* Those strikers are fighting this out right now and they're going to *win,* because *Roosevelt* is on their side. And you're not ever going to buy a pair of overalls with a bushel of wheat again! And a lot of other things have changed, too. But there's *one* thing that's been the same for a long time. I was born in eighteen seventy-seven, and ever since I can remember, every so often there'd be talk about a wheat surplus.

"Back around the time *you* were born, Custer, I remember a year when they couldn't move it out of Kansas fast enough. They had a bumper crop that filled all the elevators and all the railroad cars, and finally they had to just dump it in piles alongside the tracks. *You* want me to *hope* the parity years are going to come back — the way *you* hope they will. A man doesn't do *business* on hope. There's no reason to expect wheat to be a bonanza kind of deal again. There's never going to be the kind of export market again that we had before the war. I have to look at things the way they *are*."

"All right," George said, "Look at things the way they *are*. If I can't count on three hundred dollars clear from this crop, I just can't make it, that's all."

"Go on relief."

"There are a lot of things I'll do before I'll go on relief!"

"Suit yourself. I can't guarantee you any such thing as three hundred dollars cash. That's no way to do business. Put up or get out, that's all. I can't afford to carry you without getting a decent share of the crop money."

"*Carry* me! You paid twenty-seven cents an acre taxes on that land last year. All right, I'll pay that big forty-three-dollar tax bill, how's that? It won't cost you a cent to own that land next year."

"What do you mean, it won't cost me to own that land? I have to have a return on my investment. That's the only way to do business!"

"What kind of a return do you think I'm getting on *my* investment, Mr. Vick? On *my sweat?* I've got to get a return on *my* investment, too!"

"I can find people to lease that farm on my terms."

"Yeah, and whoever you find might just put it right in the hole for you the first year they're there, too! What if the well goes dry this summer?"

"My terms don't include well-digging. Maybe I'll lease it to somebody that won't even live there. Then they won't need a well at all."

"Look, Mr. Vick, you can certainly afford to risk a return on your investment for *one* year, after the returns you've been getting."

"How do *I* know it'll be for one year? How do *I* know you won't be back here begging for the same deal next year?"

"Mr. Vick, I did not come here to beg! I'm here to offer you a deal that you ought to be able to see is to your advantage. If *I* don't farm it, *you* won't make anything at *all* from it this year."

"I don't see that you have a *thing* to offer me, Mr. Custer, besides signing a lease on our usual terms."

George managed to remind himself once again that the stakes were higher than they had ever been before. "Mr. Vick, I've put enough improvements on that farm in the last ten years to pay you two or three years' rent, and you know it!"

"That's *your* business, Custer. *I* never told you to do them, did I?"

"But the place was unlivable without them! I couldn't keep stock in a barn like that! It could have collapsed on them in a high wind. *You* know that!"

Vick shrugged again. "*You* knew it too, when you rented it. So you fixed up the place because you thought you'd be able to buy it from me. Your option is still good."

"But it's worth so much more now than it was!"

"All the more reason it seems to me you'd want to hang on to your lease, Mr. Custer."

"All the more reason it seems to *me*, Mr. Vick, that I ought to *wring your neck!* Right now!"

"Sit down, Custer! Don't make a fool of yourself again!"

"What if I just sit there on your half section and don't pay you a god-damned thing next fall? The Supreme Court says Langer's moratorium is legal, you know. No forced chattel sale to collect your god-damned rent if I don't want to pay it!"

Vick laughed. "Langer's got other things to worry about, I'd say! I reckon he's a little too busy with the Federal grand jury to worry about *you*, wouldn't you say? Besides, there are some other people a lot closer to home to worry about *me!* Dick Press would just love to have a little sale over at your place. He'd just *love* it!"

"*You* stinking storekeeper! You think you can always get a

crooked potbellied sheriff to do your dirty work for you! *You* can't bluff *me* with that big bag of wind!"

"Well, wouldn't he just love a sale at your place?" Vick held up his lease. "Sit *down,* Custer! You're making a *fool* of yourself! You *know* you're going to wind up signing this paper here, because you always do, don't you? There's no place else for you to go, is there? This is no way to do business. You're making it tough for yourself."

"There are *lots* of other places for me to go, Mr. Vick. In fact, I'd just as soon go to *Hell,* so long as I took *you* there with me!"

"Oh, cut it out, Custer! I'm not a *bit* worried by *you!* You're not crazy enough to lift a finger to me, and I *know* it. *I* know you walked out of Press's office just like a little red-haired lamb. And that's the way you're going to walk out of *this* office, too. You're going to sign this lease or I'll come up there on the first of June and throw you off the property. And you better sign it quick, too, because I'm a busy man and I'm losing my patience."

He was holding the paper up to George. "There's no place else for you to go, is there, Custer?"

George's fingertips began to act without any orders from him. They tightened on the sheets of stiff paper he had accepted from the hands of his landlord and shredded them with rending salvos that reverberated over the clackings of the little cash carriers coming home to Mr. Vick. . . .

The clacking was still inside his head — the little cash carriers were still shuttling back and forth in there, always thumping out the same message from a spot above his right eyebrow. He reached up and felt a great knot hardening on his forehead. He must have finally forgotten to duck when he went out that little low door. It must have almost knocked him out because here he was on the street without any memory of the last trip he would ever make between those disgusting counters.

❦ ❦ ❦

Rachel did not look up from the pan she was stirring over the stove. "Did you get the glass?" she asked.

"*What* glass!"

She nodded toward the round-bodied patch clinging to the kitchen window with its adhesive-tape legs.

"The United States *Treasury* hasn't got enough money to pay me to pound down another loose *shingle* nail on *this place!*"

She looked from the window to him and saw his head. "George! What happened! Were you in a fight? Oh my God! What did you do? Did you kill him?"

"No I didn't hit him! I didn't *touch* him! Because if I'd ever once started on him, there wouldn't have been anything left of him at all — just a grease-spot here and there."

"George, what did you *do!*" He had gone off to sign the lease, the way he always did in the spring. He had come back with a purple lump on his head — out of his mind. "What did you do!"

"I gave him back his lease. I gave back his jacked-up barn and his new chicken house and his new fences and his wheat fields with the rocks hauled out of them and his soil full of manure I spread on it for nine years and his granary with new bins and a new roof on it and his pasture I reseeded for him after the way it was all wore out by *sheep* when I came here and his new trees I planted in the windbreaks and *his god-damned house with a broken window in it!*"

Lucy hid in the bedroom while they talked, still hardly able to believe that she had done something so bad when she had never in this world meant to do it at all.

❦ ❦ ❦

Lucy could hardly wait to get to school. For the first time in her life, she was going to do something important. This *would* be the morning she'd be so late she barely had time to whisper to Marilyn in the cloakroom before the bell rang.

"We're going to *move!*" she said.

"Into town?" Marilyn asked.

"No! Way out West. Maybe to Alaska, even, if they'll give us a farm up there. Maybe we can even live in an igloo!"

At noon she was so excited she ran outside without her lunch bucket, but she didn't care because she wasn't hungry. For the very first time since she had started to school, the town kids were jealous of her. Polar bears, Eskimos, getting to stay up all night in the summertime because the sun never went down, rides on dog sleds, icebergs, whales, walruses. Sure, her father said, there'd be all those things in Alaska if they went. Plus a homestead in wonderful virgin soil. Well, no, he hadn't *promised* about staying up all night, but all the rest he had promised.

Nobody thought up any little jokes to play on her today, like when some of the town kids — even Marilyn — would get together and say, "Let's play hide and seek. Lucy's It!" Then they would all sneak into the building and leave her to look and look and not find anybody. But no, there wasn't anything like that *today*.

Irene Wilkes hovered around the bunch of town kids that were asking Lucy about moving. Lucy knew that if she didn't have to go home with Irene so much, the town kids would like her better — or at least they wouldn't always be making jokes about how dumb the farm kids were. It didn't matter that Lucy herself could always spell them down and read better than they could. There was her next-door neighbor they could always tease her about.

"Go and find your brothers," Lucy said to Irene.

"They didn't come today," she said in her silly voice.

Lucy got an idea — it was just like the ideas the town kids got about things to do to *her!*

"Well, then, Irene," she said, "I guess you'll just have to walk home by yourself."

Irene looked around and her bewildered face grew even more bewildered.

"What are you waiting around for?" Lucy demanded. "It's time to go home. *I'm* going to stay all overnight with Marilyn, so you'll have to walk home by yourself."

"But it's lunchtime, isn't it?" Irene took the tin lid off her lunch bucket. "Here's my lunch!"

"My goodness, but you must be hungry," Lucy said. "*You* forgot to eat your lunch!"

"Yes, Irene!" Marilyn hurried to join the game as soon as she understood it. "You must be just *starving!* How come you forgot to eat your lunch, anyway?"

It was so good that Lucy could hardly believe it. Here was Marilyn in *with her* on a trick *she* had thought up, instead of being in on a trick *against* her with the rest of the town kids. How was it that she had never gotten an idea like this before, anyway? All you had to do to keep the town kids from thinking up a trick on *you* was to think up another trick *first* to play on *another* farm kid. She really couldn't imagine why it had taken her so long to figure it out. It was such an important thing to find out that it made her stomach feel funny, the way it felt on Christmas Eve.

"Oh, you're always losing track of the time, Irene," Lucy said. "You know that's what your mother is always saying. You better hurry up now, so you can help take care of Toady. You can eat your lunch on the way home."

"Yes, but everybody's still here," Irene protested.

"That's because if you live in town, you can stay after school and play," Marilyn said. "And Lucy is going to stay with *me* tonight on account of moving."

"Go on now," Lucy said again. They had maneuvered Irene toward the gate of the schoolyard. Irene took another backward step and jarred the elbow that was looped through the bail of her gallon bucket. The lid of it fell off and rolled away, wobbling and glinting in the sun. She darted awkwardly after it and two cold, limp pancakes fell out of the pail. They had been stuck together with butter for a sandwich, and they split apart in the dirt. She picked them up and skinned off the dusty butter with her finger. She looked about in her helpless way and then wiped the grease along the inside of her skirt hem.

"Oh, you sloppy slop!" Marilyn cried. "Look at your dress! "Hurry home and change it! Your mother's going to be mad."

"Here's your top," Lucy said. "Put it on now, before you drop the rest of your lunch."

"There isn't any more," Irene said humbly.

"What's the matter? Didn't the relief give you any more apples?" Lucy demanded.

"We only got one box," Irene said.

"Aw, phooey! My father said you got a *whole* lot of boxes!"

"I can't remember," Irene admitted.

"Ya, *you* can't remember *anything*, Irene!" Marilyn said. "You can't even remember what time of day it is. It's time to go home! School is out!"

"We haven't had arithmetic yet," Irene said.

"Oh, you have too! Besides, you couldn't remember! What's eight times seven!"

"Sixty-three!"

"Oh, dumbbell! That's *nine* times seven! Dumb ox!"

"Your mother's already going to be mad because of your dress. You don't want her to be mad because you're late, too, do you?" Marilyn asked.

"No, I don't," Irene said. "Well . . . goodby."

"Goodby! Goodby!"

Irene smiled her foolish smile, showing her big buck teeth and all of her pale gums below her wet lips. "Goodby," she said again, in her high sharp voice.

She turned and walked a few steps. "Goodby!" cried Lucy and Marilyn.

"Goodby!" Irene responded, looking back and waving her skinny arm.

"Goodby!" They imitated her silly wave. She kept on walking, occasionally turning to wave and smile. They could tell how happy she was to see that they were always there to wave back at her. She had never been treated so well.

They watched until she was hardly more than two specks of light in the distance — swinging lunch bucket and golden hair under the noon sun straight overhead. Mostly by the way the light spots moved, they could tell she was still turning and waving.

Now that it was over, Lucy did not feel the way she had expected to feel. It had really only been fun while they were doing it — the way Christmas Day was the most fun only till all the packages were opened. All this time she had wanted to be in on a joke with Marilyn, and now this time she had not only been *in* on it — she had even thought it up. But now it was over.

It was over, and what if they should be caught? What if Miss Liljeqvist found out? What if her mother found out? How awful to have only two pancakes for a lunch. But now Irene did not even have *them.* They were too dirty. "I know how silly she is," Lucy could hear her mother saying, "but she likes you so much, and since you both live out in the country, I think you ought to be nice to each other. It won't hurt so much to play with her now and then, will it? After all, *you* know how it is to come from a farm *too,* and the town kids don't." Yes, her mother had said things like that a great number of times. Lucy knew she was going to have to tell her mother what she had done. She might not be able to do it tonight or tomorrow night—sometimes she saved up her terrible things for about a week and told them all at once—but sooner or later she would have to tell, because she would feel sicker every day until she did.

"Hey, we have to eat our lunch now," Marilyn said. "Come on back to the lavatory with me."

"But I don't need to go," Lucy said.

"If you don't come with me, I won't teeter with you at recess. And I won't tell you a secret, either."

"What's the secret?"

"Come with me. I'll tell you when we get to the lavatory."

"Tell me now." Lucy didn't even care much about the secret. The town kids would torment her for days over a secret they got together and thought up when she was at home. Then when they finally told her, it wouldn't turn out to be much of anything at all—that is, if they really told her the secret they'd been teasing her about.

"You know what Audley Finley told my sister?"

"No. How should *I* know?"

"Well, you *should*, because he says he's *related* to you now!"

"He is *not!*"

"Well, you don't have to get mad at *me!* You just wait and see if I teeter with you!"

"You just wait and see if I *care!*" Lucy told her. She felt a hundred times worse than she had ever felt at the end of a disappointing Christmas Day. She had thought for a little while that perhaps she really *would* get a chance to stay overnight with Marilyn, the way the town kids stayed back and forth with each other and played together every night. Now she wouldn't even have anybody to teeter with at recess. It was just the way her father always said—city people picked on farm people every chance they got. Even Audley won out over her just by living in town and telling the other town kids whatever he wanted to tell them.

And another thing her father always said was true, too. It was stupid to trust anybody. "Most people will do anything in order to get ahead," he would say. "They'll bamboozle their best friend if there's a dime in it. They'd murder their own grandmother for a few dollars."

They'd all be your friends as long as they could get you to do something they wanted you to do, or as long as they wanted to get into a game you started, or as long as they didn't have anybody else to play with.

Friday, May 25

THE SALE was going to be the next day, and the Custers all went to town to get some canned things and bacon and other provisions for their trip West. Everywhere they went there was a poster about their auction sale. Lucy saw her last name in all the windows, printed in real printing, and smiled to herself to think how much more attention their name was getting than the names of Marilyn or Audley or Douglas or even Roger Beahr had ever gotten. She could hardly wait till the town kids all came out tomorrow so they could see how much money she was going to get and so she could tell them some more about Alaska.

In the hardware store even Mr. Hoefener started talking about all the places a person could see their name.

"Well!" he said. "Looks like Custer's Last Stand around here, don't it? Especially over at the bank. Did you see how Churchill plastered them posters all over Harry's bank?"

"That's fair enough, I guess," George said. "Bank might as well be good for something. I wouldn't be selling out if that bastard hadn't stole all my money, so we might as well use his building for a few posters, I reckon."

"Well what I want to know is, where's the war? Couldn't of been six months ago you were telling me, 'Look out, Hoefener. There's gonna be *blood!* Well, here it is! Custer's Last Stand! Where's the war, George!" Zack kneaded his goiter and smirked up at George.

"And what *I* want to know, Zack, is do you want to sell me a piece for my trailer hitch, or shall I go to Jimtown for it? And if a few more men like *me* clear out, I still want to know who you're gonna *sell* anything to. I won't *have* to let any blood out of you. You're gonna sit here in this little burg till you dry right up. There won't be nothing left of you but that nanny-goat's bag around your damned useless neck."

❦ ❦ ❦

After supper, Rachel didn't have anything to do. There was not so much as a seed flat to weed and water, and since there hadn't been any of the usual spring rush of work to keep her busy outside, she didn't even have any patching or darning to catch up on. She sat down to play her piano for the last time. It was the piano her father had bought years ago when they first began giving her lessons, and it was a very good one. She had always expected to give lessons to her own children on it.

She had packed her music even though the piano was going to be sold. Perhaps at some unforeseeable time there would be another piano — not one as good as this, not one her father had given her and listened to her play — but another piano to go with the boxes of music. She played by ear now — the songs that had been popular when she was in college. She'd always liked Irving Berlin and she stayed with him for a while.

George sat listening and reading the *Sun*. Three hundred million tons of topsoil had been blown off the prairies and across the Atlantic seaboard since the first of April — or so the experts said. Drought and dust were destroying winter wheat at the rate of a million bushels every day. Textile workers, steel workers, coal miners, auto workers, longshoremen, teamsters, bakers, butchers, and candlestick makers — they all were striking by the tens of thousands, by whole areas of the country at a time. All the unions on the Pacific Coast were striking in sympathy with the longshoremen, and so it went. The Federal Government was supporting sixteen million people on relief.

The county agents and the preachers were setting aside official prayer days for people to go to church and pray for rain. Farmers were moving their stock by railroad, truck, and hoof to try to find pasture and water or to sell the animals before they became so emaciated that they would be condemned for use as human food. Minnesota, North Dakota, and Wisconsin had all banned shipment of livestock across their borders, and National Guardsmen were out patrolling state lines.

In honor of the fine state of the Union, the Century of Progress Exposition was slated to reopen tomorrow in Chicago.

Rachel had gone from "Red Sails in the Sunset" and "The Isle of Capri" to some old tunes he began to see he wasn't going to be able to take tonight. When she started on "Red River Valley," he got up and went down to the barn, but the farther he went from the house, the better he seemed to hear the piano. He stood near the smoke of this last smudge he'd built for his horses to help them through the mosquito-filled night. He rubbed Kate's nose, and she moved her big soft lips in the most delicate of nibbling kisses across his palm. He'd taught her to do that with sugar; now she did it even when she knew there wasn't any sugar.

"Hey, Kate," he said to her. "Remember when I pulled you out of the well by your tail? Remember that, Kate? If Ralph Sundquist buys you and he don't keep a decent collar on you, Kate, you kick the living daylights out of him. You hear? Kick the living daylights out of him!"

Where were the god-damned ENEMIES, anyway!

He'd been thinking all the rest of the day about what that foul-mouthed German storekeeper had said, and he'd been thinking about what he'd said himself, too. He'd blamed everything on losing a measly two hundred and fifty bucks in Harry's bank, but he'd known when he said it that he was talking through his hat.

He hadn't lost the war in that one disaster — it was millions of disasters everywhere that had caught up with him while he had been telling himself that nothing could ruin him so long as he was in the top fifty per cent of farmers. The top fifty per cent — that didn't mean any more than the moratoriums and the embargoes and the processing taxes and the prayer days.

And the damned storekeeper was right: Custer wasn't making any stand at all. Custer had been waiting and watching for the chance to strike at his destroyers, but he hadn't so much as reconnoitered the battlefield before he was down. Somebody had hit him from behind. Hundreds of men had hit him from behind. Middlemen all over the country, plus the monopolists, speculators, bankers — *they* had done him in and they didn't even have to get close enough to see the color of his hair — any more than *he* had ever got close enough to *them* to see the faces that should be smashed in.

In any last stand *he* had ever had in mind, he got at least one of his enemies before his enemies got *him.* If he could only have got his hands on *one!* He had not struck a man once during all the time he was going down to defeat — no, he *had* struck one man — a boy not dry behind the ears yet, who couldn't hold his liquor.

But God knew he'd been *fighting* all this time! Who the hell had he been fighting, if he hadn't struck one single blow at a real enemy?

What was it that silly county agent had said? Something about "I wanted to get you all together so you could look around at your neighbors and see who you're competing with. I want you to see just who it is that's ruining you at the markets in Chicago and Liverpool." Well, he was dead wrong in the second statement and dead right in the first one, wasn't he? It was Custer's own neighbors he'd been fighting, all right. They'd been climbing all over each other — *competing,* trying to get into that meaningless top fifty per cent.

And all the different kinds of big men — the ones who owned the huge farms, the ones who speculated in farm products and never set foot outside of a commodities exchange, the ones who ran the railroads and the elevator organizations and the chain stores — *they* were the ones who were ruining him in Chicago and Liverpool, and none of them had ever even noticed him so far away below them down there, entangled with the other bitter little men in the mortal struggle. All those little men could have been wrestling together in a bog of quicksand. They could have sunk from sight and perished, and none of the big men would have noticed that they were gone. Custer had never once been in a position to *compete* with the men who had ruined him.

But his *real* competitors — *they* would come tomorrow and buy his horses and his cattle and his machinery for a song, because that was the way competition worked among little men like himself. They all ought to be marching in ranks together tomorrow, not picking over each others' bones. Couldn't they *see* that everybody was in the same boat? When would little men stop slitting each others' throats? What was the difference between competing with a man and slitting his throat? George had slit throats himself, probably, while he struggled to stay in his top fifty per cent. But he hadn't ever really wanted to slit another little farmer's throat, had he? Who had put the razor in his hands and who had maneuvered it when he wasn't looking?

It was the betrayal in the ranks that kept the world from getting better. Clarence Egger getting rich on that rotgut booze, Otto turning him in to Press. What was the difference between competition and betrayal? With one arm Egger could never survive on farming alone. Otto could not survive without his Percheron stud fees. Anything that helped them survive they wrote down as competition. Was that how they thought? No — Otto didn't think about such things at all, and Egger was just a one-armed man who liked to stand on the sidelines leering and giggling over other men's fights. There must be those in the ranks who could draw a line between competition and betrayal, but where were they?

The whole world went to the defense of a deadbeat like Wilkes. The world gave Otto relief; the world took care of his runny-nosed brats and his doomed wife; yes, he himself, even Custer himself had made his only stand of the war when he broke up Otto's sale.

But the man who still had any self-respect took it on the chin alone. He couldn't understand why it always worked out that way. Tomorrow at his *own* sale the work of the prime decade of his life would be wiped out, peacefully and legally. What kind of a last stand was that?

Rachel's music had stopped. He had thought he did not want to hear it on this night, but as soon as it stopped he realized how much he must have been listening, because now it was so quiet he noticed the million needling voices of the mosquitoes following him even into the sharp smoke. He wondered listlessly how much the piano was going to bring.

Saturday, May 26

THEY GOT UP very early because they had to take things apart. They were going to sell the beds, except for the mattresses on the big bed and the cot. They did not make a fire, and Rachel heated coffee water on the little alcohol stove that left the kitchen smelling of the cool blue sweet flame in the blackened can. It was a curiously evocative smell — a smell that went with sitting in the quiet darkness and holding a tiny baby in her arms while she gave it a bottle in the middle of a hot summer night — a bottle she had warmed over canned heat because there was no fire.

Now the smell of the sweet flame meant that she was leaving the house where she had raised her babies; the smell meant that she was not going to have a place for a regular stove with a regular fire in it for a long time — not till they found a place to settle where a farmer still had a chance. What if such a place no longer existed?

George was thinking that the big Monarch was a good stove. It should bring in a little cash. He shook down the last clinkers, pulled out the drawer of ashes, and dumped it on the ash pile. He disconnected the stovepipe and took the sections of it outside to lay it beside the pipe for the heating stove which he had cleaned yesterday.

The pile accumulated rapidly in the yard — the bed frame that echoed so loudly in the house when they knocked it apart, the springs for the bed, the dining room chairs and the bare round table with its extra leaves piled on top of it, the empty bookcase and the empty dresser drawers.

Lucy put her own things all in one place. Her sled was there, with its runners nearly buried in dust, and her wagon and tricycle stood beside it.

The bigger the pile in the yard got, the less related the components of it were to each other, and the more unrelated everything was, the more everything looked like useless junk. The coal scuttle, for instance, sitting there beneath the baby's crib. It was a perfectly serviceable scuttle with a good sturdy bottom and a strong secure handle, but it looked discredited — shabby and worn next to the baby's crib. When it had stood by the stove it looked as good as new, but now it looked worthless. Rachel realized in panic that not one soul would bid on it at any price.

And the crib, solid enough against the blue calcimine of the bedroom, looked rickety and unsubstantial with its rusted link springs bare to the sun and its upended mattress propped against its side and everything slanting downhill to boot. She lifted the mattress and laid it back in the crib and beat the dust from it with her knuckles. But it still looked old and drab without any blankets in it. She couldn't believe that this was the crib in which both her babies had been so marvelously beautiful.

She picked up the coal scuttle and moved it over next to the stove pipes, both for its own sake and for the sake of the crib. That helped the crib a little, but the coal scuttle still looked like a dirty useless thing.

This yard did not look like a place in which anybody would wish to buy anything. It looked like a spot where a band of refugees had paused in flight. It looked like the pictures of trashy belongings she had seen in the paper — and the people sitting beside the belonging were flooded-out sharecroppers usually — people who looked like the Finleys. The Custers would look like the Finleys now, moved out of the house where they had thought they had roots and exposed to the pitiless sky which had finally blown them out of their shelter. Everything uprooted from the dark little house was turned into junk in the glare of the sun. Why *should* anyone buy? She suddenly knew that they were not going to make any money at all on this sale — that George had vastly overestimated, once again, the possibilities that were open to them. And *she*, once again, had allowed herself to be persuaded until the moment of sense returned to her. Always she believed too long. She must have been out of her mind to have gone along with him.

It was too late to try to save themselves. The whole world had lost its operating margin, just as they had lost theirs. In a normal May they would have got two and a half inches of rain, but in this May the newspapers had to go to two decimal places in order to report any moisture at all — .09 of an inch they had received in this parched May. And the temperatures had run very high — an average of ten degrees over normal, so that it seemed as though they had already lived through another long, hot summer.

In the five months of 1934 the prairie world had received an inch of water out of a normal five inches. It was the wildest kind of speculation to put seed into the ground under such conditions. Yet what else was there for them to do in a world where there were no margins anywhere? Was it not even worse speculation for them to give up what few roots they had? Even Pearl Finley longed to go back to the South, now that Floyd had been killed and none of them would ever get to Canada. That was the human instinct, even of people like the Finleys. It *was* an instinct — just as much of an instinct as those more obvious instincts of breeding and of fighting for food and water.

And now this instinct demanded that they hang on to the roots they had: they must go on borrowing ever farther ahead on the irreplaceable energies of their lives, but how else would they live, no matter where they went? And roots were as irreplaceable as lives, and much less expendable. It would be better to stay here and lose her life than to leave and lose her roots. Here she stood, amid the objects that had provided the civilized necessities to her family — no matter how ridiculous they might look now in this shambles of a yard. What did one do when one no longer had a bed, a stove, or a table? When those things were gone, what did one do with the few dollars that one had got in exchange for them? What did one do for an address? Without a mailing address, how did a person even know who she was? How did her children — oh God! — how would her *children* know who *they* were? And George had thought of none of these things.

She picked up the coal scuttle and walked toward the little house that was waiting to be planted with roots again. She set the scuttle by the stove. Even though the stove no longer had a pipe connecting it to the smudged hole in the chimney, the scuttle looked proper there again — useful, valuable, perhaps even *in*valuable. (After all, how would a person get along without one?)

She paused on the porch on her way to get the stovepipe and looked across the prairie to the tall yellow house she could not see because of the swelling land, but which was closer to her than any other house she would ever see anywhere. The house that had been her refuge for as long as she could remember — her refuge from the snubs of the town kids when she was in school, from advances she was too shy to accept in college, from thundering words that had resounded here in this little house — in this little house where she must re-establish her roots as speedily as possible.

The strong, gentle father was not there in the tall house now, but still his hand was everywhere — feeding the lambs, pulling the cables that opened and closed the petals of the creaking windmill above his faithful salty well; and his body was everywhere — in the fields where she had run to keep up with his affirmative stride and even in the barn, though it was another barn. Even on college weekends she had still gone out there with him to the barn while he milked, to talk and help with various small chores — to feed the calves for him, as she had done all her life.

And now a strange and garish girl had come to live in that tall house, and establish *her* roots — her "sitting room," as she called it was already installed in what had once been Rachel's own bedroom. And if Rachel did not stay here in this little house, attached forever to her own roots in that big house, then indeed she must acknowledge her total kinship to this girl and her family. Yes, she would be a Finley — she would be one of that numberless mass nobody ever counted in a census, nobody mailed letters to — that mass which might as well be called Finley as Jones or Custer. Did it make any sense at all for a rootless Finley to usurp her father's house while *she* was cast out of her own house to become rootless?

But there was still time to save themselves. George must rush off to the auctioneer. They must put up a sign at the mailbox reading AUCTION CANCELED. Then George could go down to Vick on Monday and say he had decided to go along on the same basis after all.

Then they would descend, unless things changed more radically than she could imagine, into that ineluctable bankruptcy that waited for them — recognizing that each swing of the hoe expended a part of the only currency left to them — their lives. But it would be a bankruptcy — a death — that was not so different from the deaths of all those who were committed to making great expenditures in order to live and die in dignity — as the father from the tall yellow house had died. For it was necessary to die beside one's investments, borne up by one's roots, in order to die with dignity.

She and George would stay here with their investments and die as her father had died. But if they had made this hideous mistake — if they had become wandering Finleys, then what commitments would they show to staring, disdainful people? Above all, what commitments would they give their children to live by? Lucy and Cathy would speak and think in the way Annie and Audley spoke and thought. The Custers would live out their lives in a way that would make aristocrats even of the Wilkeses in their consumptive ancestral home.

How was it that she had ever listened to George, even for a moment? She had got the stovepipe back in, for she intended to cook dinner over a regular fire. Now she was starting on the chairs, for they were never going to eat a meal that was not eaten from a table by people sitting on chairs.

George came out of the barn and saw her walking to the house with a chair in each hand. He ran up the hill to her.

"Rachel! What on earth are you doing?"

She never stopped walking toward the house — the little dark house that had always shamed her so.

He grabbed her arm. "Put those chairs *down,* for Pete's sake!" It was frightening to live with a person for a decade and find out that she was totally different from what he had ever dreamed she could be.

"We've got to *stay!*" she cried. "We can't go away. There's nothing in the world for us *anywhere,* except what's right here. We've worked too hard here. And besides there's *nothing* anywhere else. The roots are all we've got left — just roots!"

Up the hill between the two fields George had plowed and never planted, they saw a car raising a half acre of dust behind it.

"It's the auctioneer, for God's sake! Churchill is here. Put those chairs down!"

He wrenched them from her hands, twisting her wrists savagely. She swung a smarting arm at him and slapped his face hard.

He couldn't believe she had done it. Neither could she. It was not like anything else she had ever done in her life — except one thing. She had a memory of herself, flinging the cats away from the porch. She had a memory of her voice saying, I'm losing my mind.

"I'm losing my mind." She was saying it aloud now. I'm losing my mind. Only Finley men and women hit and slapped and swore at each other. She was a Finley already, and they hadn't even sold the stove and the table and the bed yet.

She walked toward the house, dazed, shaking her head, wiping the tears from her eyes with her fists like a child, streaking her cheeks with the dust of the yard. I'm losing my mind. I'm losing my mind.

She heard the men coming and she went into the bedroom. She listened to them grunting and adjusting, panting directions to each other. "A little to your left, there. Will she make it through this door?" "Sure, she will! Came *in* through this one—it's the only door there *is*." "Easy now, easy does it. Just let me get clear through here first."

A prolonged clanging of a lid lifter falling and banging against the side of the stove. Then, "Might as well leave the pyana set right here?" "Ya. No sense to move it till it's sold. They can come on in here to try it out."

She came out after their voices had gone. There was a square discolored place on the dining room linoleum where the tin pad for the four legs of the heating stove had been. A few little rolls of lint that had been snagged in it were now liberated and wandering absently about.

She felt lightheaded—no more steadied by the pull of the earth than were the rolls of lint. There was another blackened spot on the kitchen linoleum where the range had stood. Without the big stove there to be always walking around in the tiny room, to guard babies from, to stoke and shake and clean, to bake bread in and boil washings on—without that Monarch ruling her life, she felt more weightless than ever, as though now she were not standing on this blackened rectangle of floor but hanging above it.

When they took the stove away they took the coal scuttle back to sit beside it in the yard. That seemed, somehow, to settle the course of the rest of her life.

She went out to stand on the little porch where she had scrubbed diapers for two babies. The washboard and the tubs and the washstand with its wringer were already packed in the trailer—the only parts of the porch that could go with them.

It exhausted her to contemplate even the tenth part of the work she had done on that porch—the quarts of beans and peas she had snapped and shelled there, the dishpans of tomatoes she had peeled there. And when the hardest work had not been on the porch, still there was a connection between that work and the porch. The barbarous crews of threshers lined up on its narrow little floor to wash and wait to be fed. And the iron scraper by her foot — how many thousands of times had she used it to scrape the droppings of the chicken house or the balled mud of the potato patch from the blade of her hoe and the niches of her heels?

How many times had the four of them — or the three of them, before Cathy came — stood on this porch in the darkness calling goodbys to friends as they left after spending a long Sunday afternoon and evening, or after a butchering day, or after they had come to sing to her playing?

And there had been other times when they had stood together on this porch watching a cloud spurt up over the horizon, waiting to see which way it would go. Only twice had the cloud come near enough so they could see clearly the shape of the long curved funnel swirling along, feeding the insatiable appetite above it — a black appetite even blacker than the black sky. Only once had the cloud come straight toward them, and then they had gone down the steps and closed the flat cellar doors over themselves and listened for the sound of the house being sucked away into the black appetite, but the funnel had swung away again like the aimless snout of an overfed animal, leaving them to sit in their damp unlighted cave smelling of potatoes and turnips till they could finally believe that they had been spared.

There were years of investments fixed in the paintless boards of this porch. Strangers would soon see the four of them in their car, dragging behind them a ludicrous trailer made from a wagon box, and the strangers would think they were seeing only another shiftless roving family. Strangers would think they were seeing a man and a woman who would breed without responsibility for the children they produced, a man and a woman who had never been willing to make commitments, never been willing to labor and sacrifice for roots. The strangers would never be able to know about the porch.

And all the people who had been her neighbors and her father's neighbors, the friends whom she had greeted on this porch and sat with on this porch — they would pass by on the road, but they would never see the smoke of her fires again.

And she was leaving this porch and the people who cared about her and her family and allowing her husband to take them all where nobody wanted them. For no matter where they went, there would be no place for them. She could teach again someday, perhaps, when Cathy was bigger. But teachers constituted the largest group of unemployed professional people in the country. She could never get a job now. Thousands and thousands of teachers were already ahead of her on waiting lists that were four years long. School districts all over the country were bankrupt. The enormous Chicago school district owed months of back pay to every teacher in the city. No, there would be no place for them, no matter where they went.

She leaned against the side of the house, more tired than she had thought it possible to be, as though she was bearing in that one moment all the hours of the work of the porch and the fields.

She could hear Cathy's abandoned baby laughter echoing in the grove where Lucy was swinging her. Lucy had been so quiet all morning, as though she understood what a terrible thing was happening, but she had been so sweet too, keeping Cathy happy and out from underfoot. And if it was going to be bad for the mother not to have a porch or a stove, how was it going to be for the children not even to have a tree of their own again — a tree to climb into and to hang a swing from? I'm losing my mind. I'm losing my mind.

She went back into the house and desperately scrubbed her face, but the ache in her throat made such a pressure that it kept squeezing the tears out of her eyes. She couldn't understand where the tears kept coming from, but they were always there, ready to be pushed out whenever the ache got too big for the throat.

Cars were arriving now; she heard them stop and the people get out and talk to each other. The sound of a car driving into a prairie yard — Rachel had always thought that was one of the loveliest sounds in the world — until today. She looked out the window to see the people poking about in the accouterments of her life.

It felt a little like being naked before them, but it was really the opposite of being naked. Bodies were all alike without clothes, and lives, too, were all alike without their differentiating accessories. So it was more like putting out all the secrets that enclosed her nakedness. It was the uniqueness of her life that she had been obliged to lay out for all to appraise in the shadeless noon. They could all discover now what price they would put upon her uniqueness — upon the jumble of worn chattels that distinguished her from them. They would all know all her secrets now, and be so much better than she was, because she would not know all of theirs — just as millions of people could look at the pictures in their newspapers and know all about Finleys on rooftops floating over floods with all their remaining possessions piled around them, but those millions who had newspapers delivered each morning to their safe dry doors could still keep their own secrets from the Finleys.

Helen Sundquist, her face gleaming and blushing in the sun, nodded self-consciously when Rachel came out on the porch. It was hard for everybody when somebody had to sell out. People who had gone to church together, eaten Sunday dinner together, butchered together, harvested together — they found themselves unable to face each other when one had to sell out and the other had to bid. But there was no place for them to hide from each other. Everybody understood that the bidder was the survivor and that he would take the spoils that went to survivors.

Rachel began to feel that the sale would never commence. She would stand here in this naked nightmare forever, while her neighbors fingered her babies' toys, her husband's stock, her coal scuttle and her piano. The only thing that mattered to her now was release.

The auctioneer began with the household things. It was the only way to sell them at all, since most of the people had come for the stock or the machinery. A good auctioneer was hired to sell them things they hadn't come to buy, but it wasn't easy to sell people things they hadn't planned to buy — with cash as scarce as rain.

The crib and mattress went for a dollar and a half. The Monarch went for ten before Rachel had even recovered from the shock of hearing it put up for five. The coal scuttle did sell, after all, for ten cents, and the round heating stove that had preserved them through nine winters went for seven dollars. Even George gasped over the buyer. It was Otto Wilkes.

Lucy was hiding behind a tree at the edge of the grove to watch while he sold her toys. Her father had told her she could keep the money from them to buy new toys when they got settled out West or in Alaska. If they went to Alaska, she was going to buy a sled dog.

Her tricycle went for twenty-five cents. Well, she had had it for a long time and there was no more paint on it to make it look new. Still, she had supposed that any tricycle would be worth more than that. But she couldn't understand at all when her wagon was bought for another quarter. It was still not so very rusty on the metal around the outside. She was having a very hard time following what Mr. Churchill said, and she made up her mind not to worry about it, because she was sure that in all the confusion she had simply missed hearing what she was actually going to get. Then he held up the sled. He swung it up into the air in an effortless way that made it seem too light to be worth anything. It had always seemed much heavier than that when she dragged it up the hill after a race from the clothesline post with her mother.

First he shouted about ten cents being the tenth part of a dollar, which everybody already knew, and then he started saying, "Do I hear a nickel? Do I hear a nickel? The twentieth part of a dollar? Nickel, nickel, nickel, *nickel!*"

He let his hammer fall and handed her sled to a helper. Had her sled gone for a nickel? Even with a broken steering bar it must be worth more than that. So far she had fifty-five cents, if her sled had brought only a nickel. What could she buy out West for fifty-five cents?

She went over and sat down in her swing. She wished she had an ice cream cone. But she couldn't imagine how many years it would be before she even dared ask for one. Ice cream cones were very special treats for very good little girls who never had to be asked, even once, to stop bouncing a ball inside the house.

The auctioneer moved over to the bed springs and frame. "All right! Here we have a fine, solid bed. Good tight springs." He banged the coils with the flat of his hand. "*Comfort and kicks!* Who'll start at two dollars for the works? Two dollars? Two, two, two, two, two?"

Rachel couldn't believe he had meant that the way it sounded. She kept seeing "Hot Springs Tonight" painted on the car in front of the Finley house. An auctioneer wouldn't make a joke like that in front of her neighbors — men and women together —

not a joke like that about the bed of her marriage. But her face began to burn and burn and burn.

On the very day of the auction she had behaved like a Finley. On the very day of the auction she was publicly and lewdly joked about. It had never seemed possible that a person could become a Finley in one day.

People were packing away things they had bought and rounding up children. They came up to Rachel asking for pardon behind the words they actually spoke — pardon for the offenses they had felt obliged to commit. (For if a man needed a good cow, and a good cow was going cheap, well, after all, he couldn't afford *not* to buy, could he? Not and still compete with *another* fellow who was going to get *another* good cow for a third of what she was worth.)

There had been a farewell party for the Custers, but now everyone came once more to say goodby — Going to miss you folks a lot . . . Your mother's going to be lost without you, Rachel . . . Who's going to play the piano for church now, and Epworth League? . . . Good luck . . . So long now . . . Drop us a card now and then; we'd hate to lose track of you . . . Take care of yourselves . . . So long . . . Let us *know*, now, how you make out . . . Stake out a claim for *me*, if you run across anything . . . So long . . . Good luck.

Thus lightly did each parting neighbor give a little shake to the roots that had lain dying in the sun all afternoon. The last globules of drying earth, held in the last hairy root-endings, pulverized and vanished in the wind. It took but a little time, in such a sun, for uncovered roots to perish and to pass away as though they had never been.

Everyone was eager to escape. Every time somebody sold out the rest heard the hammer knocking, as impartial as death. Still, there would be a little less competition now — perhaps a little more chance for the rest. . . .

They were, indeed, eager to escape. They must get home as soon as possible and do their chores.

Everyone but Rachel and George had chores to do. For the first evening in almost ten years they had no chores to do — not so much as one old hen waiting for somebody to throw her a handful of corn.

Rachel had left the suitcase open in the dining room so she could add a last stray diaper or dish towel. She went in now and snapped the locks. The only other thing in the room — in the house, for that matter — was the piano. And the piano bench. Somebody she didn't know had bought it. They would come for it tomorrow, when she was already far away.

If I go over and touch it now — just touch the middle C above the golden lock — if I should just let myself strike that middle C again and remember the day the men brought it to the house while my father stood in the wide arch between the dining room and the parlor — smiling because he loved me and because he loved music. If I should just touch that middle C above the golden lock again, I would be turned to a pillar of salt; I would never walk out of here and get into the front seat of the car beside my husband, where the world says I belong. Even my mother says I belong there. She has changed, hasn't she, since my father died? Before, she would have said I ought to come home — that we all ought to come home — that my husband could come home or go wherever he pleased.

And now my husband and my babies and I will sleep in my home tonight and never again. And we will still have this last goodby with her tomorrow morning, though we cannot take the time to go to the grave again. How will she keep her sanity now? With my father gone and that girl in the house? How will I know about her? How she is? How she feels? How will I say goodby to her? How will I say goodbye to that only place where I was safe? How will I climb into our car and shut the door — as though we had just stopped in on our way home from town — and ride down that hill? That hill I ran down when I was little, like Lucy, to fetch the mail or to put a letter in the box or just because, at the bottom of it, where the drive joined the county road, there was a sudden small mound over the culvert that bounced me into the air?

What shall I say to my mother tomorrow, when I tell her goodby? What shall I say to my brother, who will try to make money from my father's farm, now when the whole world is dying? He is going to send me half of the profits that aren't essential to keep the farm going. (What will half of nothing be?) Will I think of something to say to his wife? That girl who is wholly related to me now. . . .

Long before sunset, the last cow — lowing to her pasture and stall companions — had been loaded and jolted out over the dusty ruts between the gray-black fields.

There were several things that had not been sold — a drag, held together by wire and not much else, some household items, some parts of things that seemed so worthless, separated from their wholes, as to be a disgrace to the earth. And Lucy's sled was still there. It hadn't been sold for a nickel after all.

Otto Wilkes prowled the yard. Like the damned yellow jackal he was, thought George, who wondered if he'd be able to talk to him without smashing his face in for him.

"You folks aim to do anything with these here things?" Otto asked deferentially.

George looked away from him, down the hill toward the empty barn, the empty pasture. It didn't seem possible that they had made so little. "Take it! Take it!" he said. "Take any of it and all of it!"

Lucy pulled at his pants leg. "Can't *we* take the sled? I thought somebody bought it for a nickel, but it's still here."

"Oh, now, don't be silly! We couldn't pack that sled in that trailer. It isn't worth it. Besides, there probably won't be enough snow to bother about, where we're going."

"But Alaska is practically *all* snow! We could get a sled dog and tie him to this sled."

"I said don't be silly! Besides, we probably won't get to Alaska at all. I've been trying to *tell* you that! We'll probably just wind up on the West Coast somewheres. You gotta be somebody's brother-in-law — you have to have some pull back in Washington to get hold of that homestead land in Alaska. They're probably saving it all to give to the railroads."

They put the last things in the trailer. George dropped some change into Lucy's hand. She counted it out. Ninety-eight cents. Her ice-skates had been sold for fifty cents. "Minus commission," he said, and he laughed. "Tie it in your handkerchief and let

Mother keep it for you. You'll have fifteen hundred miles to think about how to spend it."

The car started slowly up the hill. Lucy could feel how her mother and father both worried about the car and how they were afraid it would never haul the trailer all the way.

The mouth of the thirsty sun fastened on the dry brow of the hill beyond the road and began to drink the dust of the late sky. The black fields of James T. Vick grew pinkish as his tenant, George Armstrong Custer, drove out over them for the very last time.

Lucy got up on her knees to look out the rear window. The house was growing smaller and smaller, but she thought she could still see, in one of the three panes of fiery glass, the round dark spot of cardboard over the hole her ball had made in the kitchen window.

Author's Note

In 1933 this nation was closer to political collapse than it has ever been since the Civil War. In these present days of affluence it is hard to believe that so many of us could have been so poor less than a generation ago. The war-tainted prosperity that began in 1941 makes the preceding dozen years seem shorter and farther away than they really are. This abnormally elongated perspective with which I must deal has led me to employ some verbatim reminders. The more outrageous the scene, the more closely it may follow an unimpeachable source. For instance, most of the words of County Agent Finnegan are verbatim statements from contemporary publications of the United States Department of Agriculture.

I have moved the dates of several actual but minor events by as much as three months, but there are no other conscious deviations from historical truth in the book. If I say that the price of spring wheat went from two dollars and seventy-six cents in 1920 to twenty-six cents in 1932, that is exactly what it did. If I say that in 1925 a farmer got thirty cents a dozen for eggs and in 1933 he got thirteen, these are exactly the prices he and millions of other farmers were paid. Seven thousand American banks, most of them rural, failed between 1920 and 1930 — before the final three years of panic liquidated another seven thousand. In 1933 alone, three hundred and fifty thousand farmers lost their farms. The Great Depression began for farmers in 1921, almost a full decade before it began for the rest of the nation. And for the lower half of the farm families in the United States today, who produce only ten per cent of the nation's agricultural wealth, the Great Depression has never ended.

Nor have the other farm problems I try to deal with in this book. On the contrary, almost all of those problems have become worse, and new problems have been added to the old ones. The price supports instituted by Herbert Hoover in 1929 helped to create, one year later, a surplus that horrified his administration. Yet today our wheat surplus makes that surplus of 1930 seem small indeed. Wheat acreage has been cut by a third since those days, but the surplus has swollen until the storage costs for it run to well over a million and a half dollars a day. Now as then the wheat nobody can buy is our most troublesome surplus. And now even more than in 1933 technological advances create surpluses at the same time that they put farmers out of work.

The accuracy I have insisted upon is the minimum of respect I would pay to the people I write about. It is hard for us now to believe that these things ever happened; even while they were being annihilated, the farmers themselves could not believe what was happening. They kept on believing that things would be better soon. There was a time within their own memories when "one good year in seven" would see them through. For three times seven years they waited for that one good year with the nearly indestructible faith of the most dedicated gamblers.

If a tenant farmer included in the value of his wheat the most menial wages for the work of himself and his family, it cost him a dollar and eighteen cents to produce a bushel of wheat in 1933. But he was lucky to sell that wheat for eighty-five cents in the fall of 1933. A man who owned his farm could pay himself these wages and just break even. But for the tenant, the deficit ate into the sinking fund of his strength and faith more deeply every year. And every year more owners became tenants again, after struggling half a lifetime to become owners. When a farmer finally discovered that he was living on faith and nothing else, then faith could sustain him no longer. Too proud to admit fear even to himself, a farmer ran ahead of disaster till he lost the race, and then he went down to defeat in silence and isolation.

Each farmer believed that the combination of wars, booms, famines, crops, weather, prices, and six million other farmers would operate like a vast game — a game too complex to outguess, but too reasonable to cut him out on every single play. But it happened that the world did not function with the vigorous, harsh logic of a planetary gaming house after all; instead, it simply endured, as indifferent as that world the psalmist looked down upon from his dry hillside. . . .

> *As for man, his days are as grass: as a flower of the field, so he flourisheth. For the wind passeth over it, and it is gone; and the place thereof shall know it no more.*